The Winter Belle

Dilly Court is a No.1 *Sunday Times* bestselling author of over fifty novels. She grew up in North-East London and began her career in television, writing scripts for commercials. She is married with two grown-up children, four grandchildren and three beautiful great-grandchildren. Dilly now lives in Dorset on the Jurassic Coast with her husband.

To find out more about Dilly, please visit her website and her Facebook page:

www.dillycourt.com
/DillyCourtAuthor

Also by Dilly Court

Mermaids Singing
The Dollmaker's Daughters
Tilly True
The Best of Sisters
The Cockney Sparrow
A Mother's Courage
The Constant Heart
A Mother's Promise
The Cockney Angel
A Mother's Wish
The Ragged Heiress
A Mother's Secret
Cinderella Sister
A Mother's Trust
The Lady's Maid
The Best of Daughters
The Workhouse Girl
A Loving Family
The Beggar Maid
A Place Called Home
The Orphan's Dream
Ragged Rose
The Swan Maid
The Christmas Card
The Button Box
The Mistletoe Seller
Nettie's Secret
Rag-and-Bone Christmas
The Reluctant Heiress
A Thimble for Christmas
The Snow Angel

AS LILY BAXTER

Poppy's War
We'll Meet Again
Spitfire Girl
The Girls in Blue
The Shopkeeper's Daughter
In Love and War

THE RIVER MAID SERIES

The River Maid
The Summer Maiden
The Christmas Rose

THE VILLAGE SECRETS SERIES

The Christmas Wedding
A Village Scandal
The Country Bride

THE ROCKWOOD CHRONICLES

Fortune's Daughter
Winter Wedding
Runaway Widow
Sunday's Child
Snow Bride
Dolly's Dream
The Lucky Penny
Poppy's Choice

Dilly Court

The Winter Belle

HarperCollins*Publishers*

HarperCollins*Publishers* Ltd
1 London Bridge Street,
London SE1 9GF

www.harpercollins.co.uk

HarperCollins*Publishers*
Macken House, 39/40 Mayor Street Upper
Dublin 1, D01 C9W8, Ireland

First published by HarperCollins*Publishers* Ltd 2025
1

A catalogue record for this book is available from the British Library.

ISBN: 978-0-00-858083-4 (HB)
ISBN: 978-0-00-858084-1 (PB)

Typeset in Sabon Lt Std by HarperCollins*Publishers* India

Printed and bound in the UK using 100%
Renewable Electricity at CPI Group (UK) Ltd

For Mel, who has styled my hair
so beautifully for more than
twenty years.

Chapter One

Soho Square, London, 1862

Kitty Harte leaned forward on the window seat in the first-floor drawing room. She wiped condensation off the glass pane with her hand to get a better view of the bustling activity in Soho Square.

'Who is that rather odd-looking woman?' Kitty turned to her elder sister. 'Can you see her, Ivory? She's just arrived in a hansom cab and she's going into the Hospital for Women.'

Ivory glanced casually out of the window. 'That's the poetess, Christina Rossetti. You know, Kitty, I read her latest work to you all on Sunday evening.'

'But it can't be her. That woman is dressed like a nun,' Kitty said, frowning.

'All artistic people are a little odd.' Ivory picked

up the hoop of embroidery she was working on. 'Isn't there anything more interesting to look at? What about the Bazaar? You usually spend ages watching the comings and goings there.'

Kitty laughed. 'Yes, I do, don't I? It's just that nuns are not a common sight around here. I was actually looking for Mama. She's been gone for a long time.'

'She took Nellie with her,' Amethyst volunteered from her place on the hearth rug where she had been toasting her toes in front of the fire. 'I hope they hurry up because I'm hungry and I know there are some muffins in the larder. I really miss Cook. It's a pity she had to leave us.'

Ivory shot her a warning look. 'You know very well we have had to make sacrifices recently. Please don't repeat that in Mama's hearing.'

'I'm not a child and I'm not stupid, Ivory. Just because you are the eldest it doesn't mean you have to be so bossy.'

Kitty held up her hand. 'Stop arguing, Amy. Come here and look. There's that handsome young fellow who took your fancy the other day. He's standing in the entrance to the Bazaar. Quickly, or you'll miss him.'

Amethyst scrambled to her feet and practically threw herself onto the window seat.

'Yes, it is. He gave me a red rose, Kitty.' Clutching her hands to her flushed cheeks, Amethyst leaned her forehead on the cold glass pane.

'The flower seller had dropped it, and a carriage wheel had snapped the stem.' Ivory shook her head. 'Don't encourage her, Kitty.'

'It was still a gallant gesture,' Kitty said firmly. 'He chose Amy, not you. That's why you're miffed.'

Ivory sighed, shaking her head. 'You do know who he is, don't you, Kitty?'

'I haven't the slightest idea, although he's obviously very well off, not to say wealthy.'

'That young gentleman is the son of the notorious Lord Bracklesham.' Ivory pursed her lips. 'Mama would not approve.'

'Then it's just as well that Amy has more chance of being courted by the man in the moon,' Kitty said, smiling. 'Besides which, she is still a baby.'

'I am not a child. I'm seventeen.' Amethyst reached out to tug one of Kitty's corn-gold curls that had escaped from the chignon at the back of her neck, despite her efforts to straighten her hair into the fashionable sleek style.

'Very grown-up, I must say, Amy.' Ivory shook her head. 'I think I heard the front door. It must be Mama and Nellie. Don't let them see you were squabbling.'

'It was merely a difference of opinion,' Kitty said drily. 'I, of course, was right.'

Amethyst jumped to her feet with a cry of exasperation. 'Tell her to stop teasing me, Ivory.'

'Leave her alone, Kitty,' Ivory said automatically.

'And you should ignore her, Amy. You know she does it just to see you fly into a tantrum.'

Before Amethyst had a chance to argue, the door opened and Isabella Harte entered the room, still wearing her outdoor clothes. She went to stand by the fire, undoing the ribbons on her bonnet, which she laid neatly on a vacant chair. She glanced in the mirror above the fireplace and patted her sleek, dark hair into place.

'It's very chilly out there, girls. I wouldn't be surprised if we had some snow before the day is out.'

'Sit down, Mama,' Kitty said hastily. 'You look perished. Would you like a cup of tea?'

'Thank you, darling girl, but Nellie is making one as we speak.' Isabella shrugged off her mantle and held her hands out to the fire.

'You were gone so long, Mama.' Amethyst eyed her mother curiously. 'Where were you? I was worried.'

'Never worry about me, my love. I can take care of myself, and I had Nellie with me. She would scare off a pickpocket with one steely glance.' Isabella managed a weary smile. 'But I have something serious to discuss with you, girls. I've just come from the bank. I'm afraid it's not good news.'

'Are we in queer street, Mama?' Kitty asked anxiously.

'Not quite, dear, but we will be there very soon unless we take drastic steps to prevent bankruptcy.'

Isabella sank down on a chair by the fire, holding her hands out to the feeble flames. 'We will have to economise even more than we have already.'

'But, Mama, you let Cook go and we can't do without Nellie.' Ivory set her needlework down with a sigh. 'What else can we do?'

'Nellie refuses to take any wages until we are solvent, if that ever happens. I don't know how we would manage without her, but I've had to sack young Mary. At least I know she has a home to go to, but it means you will have to make your own beds and tidy your rooms.'

'We don't have to scrub floors, do we, Mama?' Amethyst's large blue eyes brimmed with tears. 'I'd rather die.'

'Stop being so dramatic, Amy.' Kitty gave her sister a withering glance. 'We will do whatever we have to, so don't worry about us, Mama.'

'Yes, of course,' Ivory added hastily. 'Anything to help, Mama.'

Isabella smiled. 'I'll keep the cleaning woman on to do the heavy work, but I will have to cut her hours. We will all have to do our bit or else we might lose our home.'

'Do you really think it will come to that, Mama?' Ivory asked anxiously. 'I mean, didn't Pa leave us anything in his will?'

'He invested heavily in stocks and shares, but unfortunately their value has dropped so far that Mr

Whitman told me they are worth next to nothing.' Isabella took a handkerchief from her pocket and dabbed her eyes. 'It's all right, girls. I am not crying. The smoke from the fire is making my eyes sore.'

Kitty could tell that this was a lie, but, seeing Amethyst's lip trembling, she slipped her arm around her shoulders and gave her a hug. 'We understand, Mama. We will do everything in our power to help restore our fortunes.' She glanced out of the window. 'I can find employment somewhere and contribute to the household expenses.'

'That won't do,' Isabella said firmly. 'Your papa would never forgive me if I allowed any of you girls to go out to work.'

'Papa isn't in a position to argue.' The words left Kitty's lips before she could stop herself. 'I mean he's not going to know . . .' She tailed off, looking to Ivory for help.

'You are so tactless, Kitty,' Ivory said sternly. 'But she's right, Mama. We are on our own now and we must think for ourselves.'

Isabella bowed her head. 'He loved you all. Robert would be horrified if he knew what had happened to us.'

'Don't cry, Mama,' Amethyst said tearfully. 'You're making me want to sob like a baby.' She abandoned Kitty and rushed across the room to hug her mother.

At that moment heavy footsteps on the landing

were followed by the arrival of Nellie Pickering, who had come into the Harte household when Isabella and Robert were newlyweds and was now more like a member of the family than a servant. Kitty slid off the window seat to open the door for her.

'I brought the tea, ma'am.' Nellie placed the tray on a table close to Isabella's chair. 'Shall I pour?'

Isabella nodded, wiping her eyes. 'Yes, please, Nellie. I've been telling the girls what Mr Whitman said. It's all such a worry.'

'We've been through hard times before, ma'am. We'll weather this storm, too.' Nellie folded her arms, looking from one to the other. 'You young ladies will help your mama, I'm sure.'

Kitty was suddenly serious. She fixed her mother with a straight look. 'What is the worst that can happen, Mama?'

'Don't talk about it, Kitty. I can't bear to think of such things.'

Ivory frowned. 'That's not fair, Kitty. You're just upsetting Mama even more.'

'The worst thing, Miss Kitty,' Nellie said as she picked up the teapot and began filling their teacups, 'is that you will lose your home, and we will all have to move in with your grandmama, Lady Carstairs.'

Ivory shook her head. 'Surely not.'

'I'd rather die,' Amethyst said tearfully.

'That settles it.' Kitty held out her hand to take a cup and saucer from Nellie. 'I am going to look for work. There must be something I could do. You need to think about it as well, Ivory.'

'I could do something,' Amethyst said eagerly.

'Maybe we could sell you in the Bazaar.' Kitty smiled wryly as she stirred her tea.

'What are you plotting, Miss Kitty?' Nellie demanded suspiciously. 'I know that look.'

Kitty smiled angelically. 'I know I can't fool you, Nellie, dear. But I think I might have had an idea that will help us all.'

Nellie put her head on one side. 'You think that because you look like a cherub, with your golden curls and violet-blue eyes, you can wrap me around your little finger.'

'It usually works,' Kitty said, laughing. 'Come on, Nellie, dear. You know that I am the sensible one in the family. I wouldn't do anything silly, now would I?'

'Of course not, Kitty, my love,' Isabella said hastily. 'But please don't tease Nellie. We all need to pull together if we are going to survive.'

Ivory shot a warning glance at her younger sister. 'We don't take any notice of Kitty when she's in a skittish mood, Mama. Just tell us what you would like us to do, and we will oblige.'

Isabella sighed. 'I don't know, darling girl. I wish I did.'

'Everyone thinks better on a full stomach,' Nellie said firmly. 'Give me ten minutes and I'll have luncheon laid out in the dining room. There's no need to lower our standards just because we happen to be temporarily short of funds.' She tossed her head, and her white mob cap tilted dangerously to one side. With a swift flick of her fingers she adjusted it, then marched out of the room.

'Well, that told us.' Kitty finished her tea and set the cup and saucer back on the tray. 'I have a suggestion to make. After luncheon, when you take your afternoon rest, Mama, I think it will make us all feel better if we go for a stroll in the Bazaar. Don't you agree, Ivory?' Kitty fixed her sister with a meaningful stare.

'I suppose so,' Ivory said doubtfully.

Isabella rose to her feet, tucking her hanky back in her pocket. 'We must be positive. Things will improve, but for now we'd better go downstairs to the dining room. We don't want to upset Nellie by being late for luncheon.'

Amethyst hurried after her mother as she left the room with Kitty and Ivory following more slowly.

'I know you're up to something, Kitty Harte,' Ivory said in a low voice. 'But if you make things worse, I will never forgive you.'

'As if I would.' Kitty walked on quickly. The idea forming in her head would save her family from the workhouse, she felt sure. The mere thought of a fate like that made her shiver and she quickened her pace.

* * *

After a light luncheon of vegetable broth and bread rolls, Isabella retired to her room for her customary afternoon nap. Ivory was about to return to the drawing room to take up her embroidery when Kitty stopped her.

'We're going out. Remember?'

'It's bitterly cold and it's going to rain, or even snow,' Ivory protested. 'Can't it wait until tomorrow?'

'No, it cannot.' Kitty caught her by the hand and dragged her into the entrance hall where their outdoor garments hung from a row of wall pegs. Amethyst was already putting on her fur-trimmed bonnet tied with ribbons that exactly matched the colour of her eyes.

'I would like to have a look around the Bazaar,' she said eagerly.

'What a good idea, Amy.' Kitty smiled. 'Perhaps we'll see your handsome young man.'

Ivory took her cape from the peg. 'Don't tell me you're planning to sell Amy to the highest bidder, Kitty. Is that your brilliant idea?'

'It wasn't,' Kitty said thoughtfully. 'But now you come to mention it, perhaps she is our secret weapon. Who could resist those violet-blue eyes and that glossy dark hair?'

Amethyst pouted. 'You make me sound like a lap dog.'

'That's all to the good,' Kitty said, laughing. 'Maybe someone will buy you. Come on, ladies.

Best foot forward, as Nellie would say. We're off to redeem the family fortunes. Maybe we could sell you, too, Ivory. You look so elegant and refined. Perhaps we can find you a lord or a duke. I can just see you as a duchess.'

'Stuff and nonsense,' Ivory said crossly. 'If we must brave the weather let's get it over and done with, and no silliness, please, Kitty. We have enough problems without you adding to them.'

'I can be serious when the occasion demands it.' Kitty smiled demurely.

She led the way down the narrow staircase to the ground floor of the four-storey town house. A gust of bitter wind tugged at their clothes as the three sisters stepped out onto the pavement. Holding on to their bonnets, they walked swiftly, threading their way between pedestrians, handcarts and coffee stalls, until they came to the double doors of the Soho Bazaar.

The vast building had once been a warehouse before a benefactor named John Trotter had hit upon the idea of assisting the widows of army officers and their daughters by allowing them to set up stalls selling homemade wares. Now a successful business venture, the place housed bookshops, bakeries and stands selling all manner of goods. The delicious aroma of baking bread and cakes mingled with cheap perfume and the expensive pomade used by the fashionable gentlemen for whom the Bazaar provided a seemingly endless source of entertainment, and even illicit love affairs.

Amethyst sashayed ahead of her sisters, glancing from side to side as if interested in the items for sale, but Kitty knew she was looking for young Bracklesham and, although it was tempting, she managed to refrain from teasing her younger sister. Kitty could see that Ivory was not entirely comfortable mixing with people she considered to be lower class, but there was a buzz of energy in the building that Kitty found exhilarating. The combination of voices raised to make themselves heard above the hubbub and the cries of vendors was deafening, and they were jostled in the crowd – whether deliberately or accidentally it was hard to tell. Kitty came to a halt by a stall selling jars of jam and pickles, but she shook her head when the trader offered her two for the price of one. With a murmured 'No, thank you', she walked on, stopping again before another stand. At this one there were lace shawls, embroidered handkerchiefs, tablecloths and napkins, together with a dozen or more rag dolls, all prettily dressed. Another stall was glittering with paste jewellery and shining strands of glass beads. Amethyst lingered a little too long at this one and had to be moved on by Ivory.

'I hope you are not thinking of setting up in competition, Kitty,' Ivory said in a low voice, coming to stand beside Kitty. 'I am not going into trade. Mama would have a fit if you even suggested such a thing.'

'You are always embroidering one thing or another. Why not make some money by selling the articles?' Kitty picked up a handkerchief and examined the stitching.

'Don't finger the goods unless you intend to purchase them, miss.' The woman behind the table glared at Kitty, who immediately replaced the hanky. 'Nice work, but I'll have to think about it, ma'am.' She hurried on with Ivory close behind.

'Is there a point to this, Kitty?' Ivory demanded when they had stopped for the sixth or seventh time to study the goods that were for sale.

'I'm just getting ideas.' Kitty turned to her with an eager smile. 'We could rent a stand and earn money so that we can help with the household expenses. You saw how worried Mama was when she returned from the bank.'

'I suppose so,' Ivory said doubtfully. 'Although I think she would rather we found husbands who could keep us in comfort for the rest of our lives. I hate seeing that disappointed look in her eyes whenever the topic is raised.'

'We are not débutantes, Ivory. None of us is ever likely to snag a duke, although Amy seems to be doing quite well when it comes to lower down the scale.' Kitty laughed and pointed to their sister, who was standing in front of the bakery, talking animatedly to two well-dressed young gentlemen. 'I think that is Bracklesham's son, but I've never seen the other fellow before.'

'She will soon have a reputation as an incorrigible flirt if we don't put a stop to this, and that would definitely harm our chances in the marriage stakes.' Ivory walked on purposefully, leaving Kitty little option other than to follow her.

Amethyst was still chattering, and the two gentlemen appeared to be listening intently, but they stood back when Ivory marched up to them.

'Won't you introduce me to your friends, Amethyst?' Ivory's tone was less than friendly.

Kitty realised that Amethyst was unusually at a loss for words, and she smiled, holding out her hand.

'I believe you are Laurence Carnaby. I am Kitty Harte, and this is my sister Ivory. How do you do, sir?'

Carnaby raised Kitty's hand to his lips. 'How do you do, Miss Kitty?' His green eyes sparkled with amusement as he turned to Ivory. 'How do you do, Miss Harte?'

Ivory inclined her head in silent acknowledgement, which Kitty knew was not a good sign. It was obvious that Ivory disapproved and was not in the mood to be charmed, even by someone as bold and attractive as the Honourable Laurence Carnaby.

Seemingly undeterred, Carnaby laid his hand on his friend's arm. 'May I introduce my good friend, Charles Westbrook?'

'How do you do, Miss Harte?' Westbrook bowed to Ivory and then to Kitty. 'How do you do, Miss Kitty Harte?'

'How do you do, sir?' Kitty bobbed a curtsey simply because it seemed the correct thing to do, especially as Ivory remained tight-lipped and aloof. Kitty eyed him curiously. Charles Westbrook was slightly taller than Carnaby, who was by no means short. They were both good-looking, but Carnaby had a boyish charm with dark curly hair cut stylishly. He was dressed in the height of fashion, although Kitty thought privately his style was a little too flamboyant, whereas Westbrook was clad expensively but more soberly. His fair hair was smoothed back from a high forehead and his grey eyes were fringed with thick lashes that would be the envy of any woman. Kitty tried not to be impressed, but she was beginning to have some sympathy for Amethyst.

'You will excuse us, gentlemen,' Ivory said firmly. 'But we have to leave you now.' She took Amethyst by the hand and walked away.

Kitty bobbed a curtsey. 'Good day, gentlemen.' With some reluctance she hurried after her sisters.

'You didn't have to do that, Ivory,' Amethyst said crossly. 'I was simply talking to them. There's no harm in that.'

'You were openly flirting with that young man.' Ivory headed for the door. 'I think we should return home, since you can't be trusted to behave with decorum.'

Kitty caught up with them. 'That's not fair, Ivory. Even if she was flirting just a little there is no one of importance to have seen it.'

'That's hardly the point, is it?' Ivory came to a halt. 'But I can see that I'm outnumbered. I'm going home. You two may stay here if you must, but, Kitty, don't expect me to be a part of any mad scheme to rent a stall here.'

'Do as you please, Ivory, but don't try to prevent me from doing what I think best.' Kitty faced her with a defiant toss of her head.

'I can see that nothing will change your mind,' Ivory said stiffly. 'Amethyst, come with me. I don't want to leave you here alone.'

'I'm not alone,' Amethyst protested. 'I'm with Kitty.'

'That's what I mean.' Ivory looked from one to the other, shaking her head. 'Very well, if that's how it's going to be I wash my hands of both of you.' She marched off, heading for the exit.

Amethyst turned to Kitty with an excited giggle. 'Laurence is still there and he's looking this way. You wouldn't be such a spoilsport as to stop me from talking to him.'

Kitty hesitated. 'All right. You may have a few minutes while I go in search of the matron who I believe oversees the women's stalls.'

'You're really going to rent one, Kitty?' Amethyst's

blue eyes widened in surprise. 'After what Ivory said?'

'Someone in this family must take charge. Mama seems to be helpless, and Ivory is too grand to mix with the hoi polloi. I, on the other hand, am willing to smile and take their money if it will keep a roof over our heads.'

'But what would we sell? I'll gladly help you, but I can neither sew nor make fancy goods, and I certainly can't make jam.'

'I have no idea, Amy. But I'll think of something. Meet me back here in ten minutes. I'm going to change our world for the better.' Kitty did not wait for an answer. She had noticed a door marked 'Matron' on the far side of the Bazaar. Quite how she was going to find the required amount of advance rent was something she would worry about later. First of all, she had to convince the matron that she had a foolproof business plan.

Chapter Two

Kitty smiled as she watched Amethyst hurrying to join her new friends. Ivory would not approve, but there could be no harm in a little dalliance, and Amethyst's forward behaviour was not Kitty's main concern. Now, faced with the reality of their financial situation, Kitty was suddenly nervous. It was all very well to sound bold and positive, but as she stood outside the matron's office she was assailed with doubts. She was about to back away when the door opened.

'Were you looking for me?' A stern-faced woman in her mid- to late forties stood, arms akimbo, looking Kitty up and down as if costing each garment she was wearing.

'You are in charge here, ma'am?'

'I am Matron Hume, and I am responsible for the

stands rented by ladies who wish to earn a living for themselves and their families.'

'I would like to rent one,' Kitty said firmly.

Matron Hume held the door open. 'Come inside and sit down. Let me take your particulars.'

Kitty followed her into the small, rather dark office. Most of the space was taken up by a large knee-hole desk, which was piled high with documents. Matron went to sit behind the desk, motioning Kitty to pull up a chair.

'Fill out this form, if you please, Miss er . . .?' Matron passed a sheet of paper to Kitty.

'Harte. Kitty Harte, ma'am.'

'There's an inkstand somewhere beneath these papers. I really must settle down to do some filing, but keeping an eye on what goes on out there takes most of my time.'

Kitty moved one pile of documents at a time until she came across the inkstand. She settled down to fill in her name and address, but when it came to the question of what she intended to sell, she hesitated.

'Have you a problem, Miss Harte?' Matron's expression was not sympathetic. 'Don't you know what merchandise you intend to sell?'

Kitty glanced around the office, looking desperately for inspiration. What caught her attention was a rather poor copy of *The Fighting Temeraire*, which hung on the wall behind Matron's desk.

'Is that a painting by Mr Turner, ma'am?'

Matron puffed out her chest. 'Mr Turner sold a few of his early paintings here, Miss Harte. I believe he purchased some of his artist's materials from a stall in the Bazaar. He was a great artist and his death from cholera has saddened us all.'

Kitty could see that Matron Hume was something of an art lover. 'I have seen many of his works at the National Gallery, ma'am. I am a painter myself, although not in the same class as a genius like Mr Turner, but I would like a chance to sell some of my watercolours in the Bazaar.'

'I would have to see some samples of your work before I agreed to allow you to rent a stand, Miss Harte.'

'I understand that perfectly.' Kitty handed her the completed form, which was mercifully short. 'I will bring them in later today, if that's convenient.'

'It is. I am here all day today. If I let you have a stall you will pay rent each day, but if for any reason you cannot attend you will still have to honour the agreement or get someone to take your place.'

Kitty nodded. 'Of course.' She knew who would volunteer to take her place; in fact, it would be impossible to keep Amethyst away from the Bazaar, and she might even use her youthful charm to sell some paintings. 'Thank you, Matron Hume. I will be back later.'

Kitty rose from her seat and let herself out of the office. The only problem now would be to convince

Mama that selling her artwork was a respectable trade. That was going to be the hardest task of all. Kitty walked over to where Amethyst had taken up where she had left off with her two admirers.

'I'm sorry to drag her away, gentlemen,' Kitty said, smiling, 'but we have to return home now.'

Laurence acknowledged her with a pleasant smile and a nod of his head. 'Of course. We mustn't detain you, but I hope we shall meet again very soon.'

Sir Charles bowed from the waist. 'Good day, ladies. I echo my friend's sentiments.'

Kitty felt herself drawn to him, but she was eager to return home and speak to her mother. The prospect of working in such a busy, exciting environment was exhilarating. She took Amethyst by the hand. 'Come along, Amy. I have urgent business at home.'

Amethyst opened her mouth as if to argue, but a stern look from Kitty had the desired effect. 'Goodbye, gentlemen,' she said with a pert toss of her head. 'I will no doubt see you tomorrow.' She allowed Kitty to guide her through the crowded Bazaar and out into the street.

The rain had turned to sleet so it was fortunate that their house was only a short distance away. Once indoors, Kitty took off her bonnet and cape.

'Don't say anything to Mama, Amy,' Kitty warned as she headed for the staircase. 'I have an idea that might work, but first I need to find all my sketches and paintings.'

'You're going to set up a stall and sell them?'

Kitty put her finger to her lips. 'Shhh! I don't want Mama to hear about it until I have decided if my paintings are good enough to sell. I'm not at all sure that anyone would want to buy them.' She did not wait for an answer.

On the top floor there were two decent-sized attic rooms. Nellie occupied one and Cook had had the second one to herself before she was compelled to find a position elsewhere. There was a small boxroom, just big enough for a truckle bed, where a housemaid might sleep, and at the far end of the corridor was a space that Kitty had always referred to as 'the junk room'. It was here that anything not in current use, but too good to throw out, was stored. As it was lit by only a roof window, it was difficult to make out what lurked in the deep shadows, but Kitty's easel and box of paints were fortunately within easy reach.

She pulled up a slightly rickety chair and sat down to leaf through a portfolio containing her watercolour paintings. There were a few tinted sketches of Soho Square gardens and some landscapes that she had painted when visiting their grandmother in Highgate. She had gone through a stage when all her works were detailed pencil drawings of plants and flowers, which she had then coloured with pastels. However, her best works were the sketches she had made of people, including her own sisters. Kitty closed the portfolio and took it downstairs to her bedroom, which overlooked the small yard at the back of the house. The lamplighter had already been on his rounds in Dean Street and no doubt the square would be well illuminated by the time she was ready to go out again. Kitty laid the portfolio carefully on a small table by the window and lit a candle before going to join her mother, Ivory and Amethyst in the drawing room.

Seated by the fire, her worn face pale despite the heat from the flames, Isabella looked up, frowning.

'What is this that I hear from Amethyst? You are going to take a stall in the Bazaar, even though you know what I think of that den of iniquity?'

Kitty shot a reproachful look at her younger sister. 'I asked you not to say anything, Amy.'

'No, you didn't.' Amethyst shrugged. 'Well, if you did, I obviously misheard you.'

'I'm surprised at you, Kitty.' Ivory stabbed her needle into the material stretched over the embroidery hoop. 'You will let the whole family down.'

'If I am successful, I will save us from losing our home,' Kitty said stiffly. 'Have you any better ideas, Ivory?'

'This isn't about me. I have done nothing wrong.' Ivory picked up a pair of silver scissors and snipped the thread.

'Surely there must be another way,' Isabella said desperately. 'To take a stall in that notorious place will stain your character, Kitty, and by association it will ruin all your chances of making a good match.'

'We won't meet many eligible men in the workhouse, Mama.' Kitty spoke more sharply than she had intended, and the sight of tears in her mother's eyes made her feel ashamed of her quick tongue. 'I am sorry, Mama. But someone must do something and do it very quickly.'

'Stop it, Kitty.' Ivory jumped to her feet and went to put her arm around her mother's shoulders. 'You don't know when to cease.'

'I am genuinely sorry, but none of you is facing up to the truth.' Kitty turned to Nellie, who had just walked into the room. 'What do you think, Nellie?'

'I don't know what's been said, but your mama don't look too happy. What's going on, Kitty?'

'She wants to set up a stall in the Bazaar,' Ivory said angrily. 'Neither Mama nor I agree with the idea.'

Nellie put her head on one side. 'Why not? It seems quite sensible to me.'

'But it's a place where louche gentlemen go to ogle young women,' Isabella said in a low voice. 'Kitty would be in trade.'

'Better to be in trade than in prison for debt, Mrs Harte dear.' Nellie folded her arms across her flat chest. 'As far as I can make out, the young women who run the stalls are looked after by the matron.' Nellie turned to Kitty. 'What was you intending to sell, my duck?'

'My paintings, Nellie. That's if Mrs Hume, the matron, thinks they are saleable.'

'You are a blooming good artist, Miss Kitty. Anyone would be pleased to have one of your watercolours on their wall.'

'Don't encourage her, Nellie,' Isabella said faintly.

'I will so, ma'am. And you should, too, if you've a grain of sense.' Nellie picked up the empty scuttle. 'We've just enough coal left to last the week, Mrs Harte. Maybe that will change your mind since the housekeeping money has already run out and we're only halfway through January.'

'That settles it, Mama.' Kitty faced her mother with a steady gaze. 'I am sorry you don't approve, but if Papa had known about our predicament, he would have told me to go ahead.'

Isabella brushed tears from her cheeks. 'He would not have wanted you to risk your reputation in such a way, Kitty.'

'If it's a choice between my reputation and survival, I know which one I choose, Mama.'

Kitty left the room before Ivory could side with their mother, as Kitty knew she would. Amethyst, on the other hand, would keep her opinions to herself, and Nellie would no doubt calm the situation.

Minutes later Kitty was dressed in her bonnet and cape with her portfolio tucked under her arm as she left the house and hurried to the Bazaar. She arrived outside Matron's office almost bumping into Mrs Hume as she was about to leave.

'I'm sorry, ma'am. I don't wish to detain you any longer than absolutely necessary, but I've brought my portfolio with me. Could you possibly find time to look through it for me?'

Mrs Hume glanced at the large white-faced clock on the wall above their heads. 'I am late for an appointment. Leave the folder on my desk and I'll have a good look at your work in the morning.'

Kitty stifled a sigh of frustration. 'A quick look now should be enough to say yes or no to me renting a stall.'

'You are persistent, I will acknowledge that, but I am in a hurry. Do as I say or take it home with you.' Mrs Hume held the key to her office poised ready to lock the door.

Kitty knew when it was best not to argue, and she slipped past Matron and placed the portfolio on the desk. 'There you are, Matron. I will come back tomorrow morning with the rent money in my pocket.'

'My goodness, you are sure of yourself, aren't you?' A glimmer of something like respect flickered across Mrs Hume's angular features. She turned the key in the lock. 'Very well. I'll give you my verdict in the morning.' She walked away, leaving Kitty little option other than to return home. However, she loitered amongst the stands and stalls, studying their goods for sale. The stall-holders were all women, some very young and others quite elderly. They had begun to pack up as it was nearing closing time, and nearly all of them looked pale and tired. Kitty would have liked to speak with one or two of them, but it was obvious that they were eager to finish for the day and return home. Most of the customers had already left, and the ones who remained seemed to be sheltering from the inclement weather rather than wishing to spend their hard-earned money.

Kitty stepped outside the building and found herself in the middle of a snowstorm. The gardens in the square looked beautiful as the snowflakes swirled around the streetlights, but it was not the sort of night to want to be outside for long. People were hurrying home, their faces muffled in scarves or with their collars pulled up against the falling snow. Kitty walked briskly, although the pavements were slippery and hazardous. Just as she reached her own front door, she lost her footing on the ice. She clutched at thin air and would have fallen had someone not caught her. The impact of her collision with a man much taller and stronger than herself temporarily knocked the wind from her lungs. Gasping for air, she hung on to him, while she struggled to regain a foothold on the icy paving stones.

'I've got you, miss. Take your time to catch your breath.' The stranger's voice was deep and reassuring.

'I – I'm all right, thank you, sir.' Kitty leaned against the front door. 'This is my home.'

'That's a coincidence, miss. This is the address I was given.'

The streetlamp was behind him and his top hat was tilted forward so that his face was in deep shadow. Even though he stood apart from her, Kitty was intensely aware of his presence and it was unsettling.

'Who are you, sir? What is your business with my family?'

'My name is Flinders Riley, and I have a message from your father.'

'That's a lie,' Kitty said angrily. 'My papa died abroad during an expedition to British Guiana.'

'Might we go inside, Miss Harte? Otherwise, I might be mistaken for a snowman. I'm not sure if there ever was a snow maid, but you look very picturesque.'

Kitty hesitated. She did not know whether to laugh or to tell him to be off and take his lies elsewhere, but a whisper of doubt had crept into her mind, and she turned away to unlock the door.

'You'd better come inside, Mr Riley.'

He picked up a large carpet bag from the doorstep and stepped into the entrance hall, taking off his hat. 'Despite the difference in our ages, your papa and I are good friends.'

Kitty lifted the oil lamp from the hall table and held it up so that she could read his expression.

'I don't believe you. Papa was reported missing, believed dead. We've heard nothing for the past six months. If he were alive, he would have contacted us somehow.'

'He sent me, Miss Harte.' Flinders put his bag down on the floor. 'Your papa asked me to explain the situation to his family, and that's why I am here.'

Kitty gave him a searching look. He seemed to be sincere and there was no shadow of deception or cynicism in his eyes, which were a startling blue against his deeply tanned face. Kitty found herself assessing Flinders Riley as a man rather than someone who purported to be a messenger sent by her deceased father. She had to admit that he was personable, if not exactly handsome, and there was something about his rugged features that made him appear to be trustworthy. She took a deep breath.

'Can you prove what you say, Mr Riley?'

He nodded. 'I have a letter for your mother. May I give it to her in person? It was your father's request.'

'You haven't told me why my father couldn't come home.'

'The truth is that he was badly injured in a rock fall. He is being cared for by nuns in a convent near Georgetown.'

Kitty clutched the banisters for support. 'How bad are his injuries?'

'I believe he broke his back. It's quite possible he may not be able to walk again. I'm so sorry, Miss

Harte. This is not the news I wanted to bring, but at least he is alive.'

'I can't imagine Papa living life as a cripple. I think he would rather have died.' Kitty broke off on a sob but regained her composure quickly. 'Please don't tell my mother that. It would be too much for her to bear.'

'I will be very tactful.'

'The news has come as a shock to me, so I can only imagine what it will do to Mama. I think it might be best if I break it to her gently. Will you wait here until I call you?'

He nodded. 'Of course.'

Kitty shrugged off her cape and hung it back on its peg together with her bonnet. It seemed inhospitable to leave Mr Riley in the entrance hall, but Kitty's main concern was for her mother. She was tempted to take the stairs two at a time, but she managed to ascend more sedately. She entered the drawing room and found her mother dozing by the fire with Ivory, as usual, working at her embroidery and Amethyst poring over an old fashion magazine.

Kitty went to stand beside her mother, gently tapping her on the shoulder. 'Mama, there's someone to see you.'

Isabella opened her eyes. 'I wasn't asleep, Kitty. I was just resting my eyes.'

'What's the matter with you, Kitty?' Ivory asked wearily. 'You're not going to involve us in another of your dramas, are you?'

'You're white as a sheet,' Amethyst observed casually.

Isabella raised herself to a more upright position. 'You are rather pale, Kitty. Are you all right?'

'Who is the visitor?' Ivory demanded suspiciously.

Kitty cleared her throat nervously. 'He is a friend of Papa's. His name is Flinders Riley, and he's come all the way from British Guiana with a letter for you, Mama.'

'A letter from your father?' Isabella's lips trembled. 'Show him up, Kitty. What are you thinking of, allowing him to wait downstairs?'

'It's not just a letter, Mama.' Kitty tried vainly to think of an easy way to break the bitter-sweet news and failed. 'Mr Riley says that Papa was hurt in a rock fall. He was badly injured and is being cared for by nuns.'

Isabella fell back against the cushions, fanning herself with her hands. 'He's alive?'

'Papa is alive?' Amethyst echoed.

Ivory let out a yelp of pain as she pricked her finger on the embroidery needle. 'If you are teasing us, Kitty . . .'

'As if I would. At least not on such a delicate matter.' Kitty backed towards the door. 'I'll go and fetch him.' She hurried from the room and leaned over the banister rail. 'Mr Riley, would you come upstairs, please?'

* * *

Flinders Riley joined her at the top of the stairs. 'I hope you don't mind, but I hung my coat up in the hall.'

'Of course not. I should have offered to take it from you, but your arrival took me by surprise.'

'I understand.' Flinders gave her a searching look. 'How did your mother take the news?'

'I don't think it's really sunk in properly. If you can give her more details about Papa's condition, that will help more than the letter.'

'I hope so. Your papa is naturally very concerned for all of you and especially your mother.'

Kitty crossed the landing and opened the drawing-room door. 'Mama, this is Mr Flinders Riley. He has come all the way from Georgetown to give you the letter.' She ushered Flinders into the room.

Ivory and Amethyst stared at him, their faces expressionless, while Isabella attempted to rise from her chair.

Flinders held up his hand. 'Please don't get up for me, Mrs Harte.'

'Won't you take a seat, Mr Flinders?' Kitty pulled up a chair, but he declined the offer with a smile.

'I only came to deliver this letter. I won't impose on your hospitality.' Flinders put his hand in his pocket and took out a dog-eared envelope, which he handed to Isabella. 'I must apologise for the state of the paper, ma'am. I'm afraid it's suffered from the long sea voyage.'

'You poor man. Please don't leave yet. I have so

many questions to put to you.' Isabella clasped the letter to her bosom. 'You must stay for dinner, and we can have a proper talk.'

'Thank you, ma'am. Only if you are sure. I realise this is a difficult time for you and your daughters.'

'Amethyst, dear, will you go downstairs and find Nellie?' Isabella said firmly. 'Tell her we are one more for dinner.'

'Yes, Mama.' For once Amethyst did not argue, which amused Kitty. She could see that her sister was dying to pass on the news that Pa had survived, despite his serious injuries.

Ivory, on the other hand, seemed unconvinced. She perched on the edge of the sofa, embroidery put aside.

'So how do you know our father, Mr Riley?'

Flinders remained standing with his back to the fire. 'We are fellow geologists, Miss Harte. Your papa is, of course, the senior member of the expedition.'

'Shall I open the letter for you, Mama?' Kitty could see that her mother's hands were trembling as she tried to break the seal.

Isabella handed the document to her. 'Thank you, Kitty. I'm all fingers and thumbs. It's come as such a shock to know that your father is alive, but you say he is badly injured, Mr Riley. Is he likely to be in hospital for long?'

'That I can't say, Mrs Harte. I'm truly sorry but the doctor who is treating him could not give me any more information. Perhaps it would be better if I left now, rather than accept your invitation to dinner? This is a family matter, and anyway, I came straight from the railway station. I need to find a hotel or a guest house for tonight.'

'We have a spare room, Mama,' Kitty said hastily. 'It's not the sort of night to be wandering around London, looking for accommodation.' She handed the letter back to her mother, the seal neatly broken in half.

Isabella opened it and her hands shook. She rose to her feet. 'I need to read this in private. But of course, you must stay with us, Mr Riley. I know that's what Robert would want.' She hurried from the room with the letter clutched to her bosom.

'What is the prognosis, Mr Riley?' Ivory asked nervously. 'If Papa is still in hospital that doesn't sound very promising.'

'I believe his injuries are serious.' Flinders subsided onto a chair, holding his hands out to the fire. 'I really cannot tell you more.'

Kitty realised that he was not telling everything he knew, but she decided to refrain from saying any more. Amethyst in particular was devoted to Pa, and although Ivory said little, Kitty knew that her sister's feelings ran deep. There was an awkward silence until Isabella returned minutes later.

'It is a very good letter, but not in my husband's handwriting. How do I know this is genuine, Mr Riley?' Isabella passed the letter to Ivory. 'This isn't your papa's hand, is it, Ivory?'

Ivory took one look and shook her head. 'No, Mama. It is far too bold a script.'

'I can explain that,' Flinders said firmly. 'Mr Harte dictated it, and I wrote it down for him. His injuries are grave, Mrs Harte – I won't pretend otherwise – but his spirit is still as strong as ever.'

Isabella managed a weak smile as she sank down onto her chair. 'My husband will never give way to circumstances, Mr Riley. The fact that he is alive is enough for me.' She turned to Kitty. 'I think a glass of sherry wine to celebrate that is called for. Will you do the honours, Kitty, dear?'

Kitty glanced at the empty decanters on the side table. 'We seem to have run out of sherry, Mama.'

'Oh dear. Never mind, we will save the celebrations for when your papa returns to us.' Isabella turned to Flinders with a wide smile. 'How soon do you think that might be, Mr Riley?'

Kitty could see that Riley was momentarily at a loss, but with perfect timing Nellie entered the room to announce that dinner was served.

The dinner table was set with care as always, even though the meal was simple. However, Nellie could make a delicious broth with a couple of butcher's bones and some root vegetables, served with freshly baked bread. The dessert of creamy rice pudding was another success and Flinders won Nellie's heart with his praise.

'I haven't had food like this since I last left

England, Miss Pickering,' Flinders said earnestly. 'It was absolutely delicious.'

Nellie blushed rosily. 'Get on with you, sir. It was nothing out of the ordinary.'

'Now that is where you are wrong.' Flinders shook his head. 'Thank you again.'

Kitty watched in amusement as Nellie, clearly flustered, flapped her apron at him and hurried from the dining room, giggling like a schoolgirl.

'I think it's time we adjourned to the drawing room for coffee.' Isabella rose from her seat at the head of the table. 'You will join us, won't you, Mr Riley?'

Flinders stood up. 'If you'll excuse me, ma'am, I have notes to write up and an appointment at the Geological Society in Burlington House first thing in the morning. If I may I will go to my room.'

'Of course,' Isabella said, smiling. 'It's a pleasure having you to stay. I feel so much closer to Robert now.'

'I'll show you to your room.' Kitty went to the door and picked up a chamber candlestick. 'If you would follow me.' She led the way without waiting for an answer. 'Nellie has made up the bed for you.'

'I hate putting you to all this trouble, Miss Harte.'

Kitty stopped on the landing outside the spare bedroom. 'It's no trouble,' she said.

She opened the door and ushered him inside. 'I'm afraid it's a bit chilly in here. We haven't had a delivery of coal this week.' Kitty stood by the door while Flinders laid his carpet bag on a stool beneath the window.

He turned to her with a serious expression. 'I don't wish to offend you, Miss Harte, but it's obvious that you and your family are in dire straits. I will pay my board and lodging while I am in London.' He held up his hand as she opened her mouth to refuse. 'Believe me, I quite understand. I've suffered from lack of funds in the past. I know what it feels like.'

'Thank you,' Kitty said confidently. 'We are a little hard up at present, but all that is going to change very soon.' She crossed her fingers behind her back. 'I am going to restore the family fortunes and bring Papa home. Good night, Mr Riley.' She left the room hastily and closed the door, but then her smile faded, and she uncrossed her fingers before going downstairs to join her mother and sisters in the drawing room. Now she would have to prove that her words were not an idle boast, if only to herself. She doubted if Flinders Riley cared one way or another.

Chapter Three

Next morning Kitty had just finished her bowl of porridge when Flinders entered the dining room. He smiled when he saw her.

'I thought I might be a little early for breakfast, Miss Harte.'

'No, not at all. I usually come down at this time, and today I want to be the first person in the Bazaar when it opens. Do help yourself.' Kitty lifted the lid off the tureen and passed him the ladle. 'I hope you like porridge.'

'As a matter of fact, I do.' Flinders pulled up a chair and sat down. He filled a bowl and began to eat. 'Why do you want to be first in the Bazaar? I wouldn't have thought it to be the sort of place you might frequent.'

'Possibly not, but I am hoping to rent a stand.

Mrs Hume, the matron, was going to look through my portfolio of watercolour paintings and decide whether or not they are good enough to sell.'

'You're an artist?'

Kitty laughed. 'I wouldn't be so bold as to call myself that. I do enjoy painting and, to tell you the truth, I have nothing else to sell.' Her smile faded. 'You mustn't tell Pa about this when you return to British Guiana. I assume that is the plan?'

'Yes, indeed. Although I don't know when exactly. I have several reports to complete for the Geological Society, who partly funded our expedition. I also need to find fresh backers.'

'It seems that we are both short of funds,' Kitty said with a wry smile.

'I will pay for my keep, Miss Harte. Or I could move into a hotel.'

Kitty shook her head. 'No, don't do that. I think having you here will be good for all of us, particularly Mama. You will be able to tell us about your exploits and give us a picture of what life is like on an expedition.'

'Doesn't your father give you all those details when he comes home?'

'No, not really. He is always so pleased to be home that he never speaks about what he does when he's away. Then it seems it's time for him to go off on his travels again. We rarely saw him when we were growing up.'

'That is hard indeed. I wouldn't want my children to think of me as a casual visitor.'

'You are married?' Kitty stared at him in surprise. Somehow, she had not envisaged him as a family man.

'No, and not likely to be either. That is the trouble with my profession. We are never in one place long enough to form any sort of relationship. I'm just saying that, if I should ever be lucky enough to find someone who could put up with me, I would not wish to leave them at home for months or even years at a time.'

There was a genuine note of sincerity in his voice, which made Kitty drop her gaze. She glanced at the brass clock on the mantelshelf and rose hastily to her feet. 'I'm sorry, Mr Riley. I have to go now. Perhaps we can continue this conversation later.'

He stood up politely. 'Of course. Good luck, Miss Harte.'

It was warm in the Bazaar, in complete contrast to the square, where snow lay thickly underfoot. People were just setting up their stalls and the aroma of baking bread filled the air, along with the sweet, cloying smell of hot sugar. There was a low buzz of conversation as stall-holders acknowledged each other and passed the time of day, but Kitty found herself ignored as she made her way to Matron's office. She realised that this was a tight-knit community, mainly of women, who thanks to Mr Trotter were now able to earn money without being forced to go on the streets as a last resort. Mrs Hume was already at her desk, and she barely looked up when Kitty knocked and opened the door.

'Good morning, ma'am.' Kitty stood in front of the desk, hands clasped behind her as if facing the headmistress of the private school she and her sisters had attended. It was there, at the Academy for Young Ladies, that Kitty had discovered a talent for art. Unfortunately, Papa's money had run out and all three sisters had had to leave and finish their studies at home.

Mrs Hume looked up. 'It's a busy morning for me, Miss Harte. I have glanced through your portfolio. I wouldn't say you are a great artist, but your pictures are very pretty and might have some street value.'

'Does that mean you will grant me a stand, Mrs Hume?'

'You may have a trial period of three months. After that we will know whether or not you are going to earn enough to pay the rent for the stand, and we will speak again.' Mrs Hume heaved herself to her feet. 'My bunions are giving me hell. I don't know why I put myself through this every day. Not that I get much thanks for the job I do, mostly complaints.' She shot a wary look at Kitty. 'You are not a complainer, I hope?'

'No, indeed, ma'am. I am very easy-going.'

'I'm glad to hear it.' Mrs Hume thrust the portfolio into Kitty's outstretched hands and limped out of the office. Grumbling and groaning, she threaded her way between the stalls, stopping by an empty stand. She turned to a middle-aged woman who was setting up a display of knitted goods.

'What happened to Miss Clancy and her pottery, Aggie?'

'Her new man didn't appreciate her earning more than him, dear. He busted up her pots and threw out the wheel. I don't think she'll be back.' Aggie shook her head and went back to arranging a rather ugly knitted doll with one eye embroidered askew.

'There you are then,' Mrs Hume said, sighing. 'It happens like that. You haven't got a man who's going to tear up your pictures, have you, Miss Harte?'

Kitty shook her head. 'No, ma'am. Certainly not.'

'You may have this stand then. Rent a week in advance. Pay Miss Pollitt, the cashier. Aggie will point you in the right direction. I've got to go and sit down before I fall down. Now me back has started to play up. I'm a martyr to pain, Miss Harte. A real-life martyr.' Mrs Hume limped off in the direction of the office.

'Is she always like this?' Kitty asked in a low voice.

Aggie grinned. 'No, dear. Sometimes she is much worse. Good luck with whatever you're selling. You'll need it.'

Kitty stood back and stared at the space allotted to her, which consisted of a trestle table covered in unbleached cotton duck. She experienced a moment of sheer panic as she wondered how she was going to display her paintings to their best advantage. As she gazed around at the other women who were busy setting up their stalls, she could see how much thought and effort had gone into making them attractive and appealing to would-be purchasers. Kitty tucked her portfolio under her arm and headed for home.

She burst into the dining room just as her sisters were finishing their meal.

'I need your help, Ivory. You, too, Amethyst. I've rented a stand, but I don't know how to show off my paintings to their best advantage.'

Ivory and Amethyst exchanged surprised glances.

'You are asking us for help?' Ivory folded her table napkin and set it down beside her empty plate.

'That's the first time ever,' Amethyst added seriously. 'This must be important.'

'Of course it is.' Kitty made an effort to speak slowly and calmly. 'We are in desperate need of funds. Flinders is going to pay for his keep, but even so, Nellie has to buy extra food, coal and candles.'

Amethyst jumped to her feet. 'You know I will do everything I can to help. I am sure I could sell all your paintings in one morning, given half a chance.'

'You would spend all your time flirting with the gentlemen who frequent the Bazaar for one purpose only.' Ivory rose from the table. 'What exactly do you need, Kitty?'

'I don't know how to display my work,' Kitty said humbly. 'The other stalls look so professional and all I have is a flat table and a pile of papers.'

'We need to take a look at it first.' Ivory pushed back her chair. 'I don't hold with going into trade, but as you say, Kitty, needs must.'

There was a slightly undignified scramble for their capes and bonnets, with Amethyst forgetting her manners and shoving Kitty out of the way in an attempt to get out of the house first. However, they arrived at the Bazaar just as the doors were opened. They were the only people entering, but the lack of customers could be attributed to the weather. Snow had started to fall in earnest again. Ever the optimist, Kitty took this to be a good thing, giving them time to set up her stand in the most appropriate manner.

Aggie had finished putting out her handiwork and she stood back, arms folded, eyeing their efforts and dropping the odd remark, which she obviously thought was helpful. Kitty was too polite to tell her to be quiet. Ivory walked around the stall, looking serious.

'What are you doing?' Kitty demanded impatiently. 'It's the same all the way round.'

Ivory gave her a condescending smile. 'That is where you are wrong, Kitty. You see I have the true artistic talent, and I know it all depends upon the light.' She selected a watercolour painting of sweet peas in a glass vase. 'If I place this just so, it looks a little dull.' She held up her hand as Kitty was about to argue. 'But if I place it this way, in order to catch the light from above, you can see the difference.'

Kitty nodded. 'I see what you mean, and it looks better when you hold it up. I need something to pin the paintings to.'

'Better still, get them framed.' Ivory laid the picture down. 'But that would cost money we do not have.'

'You got to catch the punters' eyes, love,' Aggie said suddenly. 'We're all after the same thing in here.'

'Yes, thank you, Aggie. I see that.' Kitty turned back to the table and began to lay out her work. 'This is hopeless, Ivory. It was a mad idea in the first place.'

Amethyst had been watching the entrance rather than paying attention to Kitty's problem, but she seemed to sense Kitty's genuine distress. 'You're not going to give up so soon, are you, Kitty?'

'What do you suggest, Amy? You've been very quiet.'

Ivory rolled her eyes. 'You know why that is, Kitty. She's been watching the doorway waiting for that roué Laurence Carnaby to stroll in and start ogling the young girls.'

'Carnaby is my friend,' Amethyst said crossly. 'He does no harm, and he enjoys the atmosphere.'

'That doesn't help with my problem,' Kitty said, sighing. 'I really am at a loss.'

'Just set up your paint box and easel and start painting something – anything – and you'll draw a crowd eager to watch.' Amethyst puffed out her chest. 'I can sometimes be quite brilliant.'

'Kitty isn't a sideshow,' Ivory said icily. 'You'll have her dancing with a bear next.'

'That would bring in the crowds.' Kitty's smile faded. 'But it's not a bad idea, Amy. Not dancing with a bear, but me sitting here painting. You're right, it would make people curious.'

'You'd be making a spectacle of yourself,' Ivory said sharply. 'What would Mama say?'

'She wouldn't know because normally it's beneath her to set foot in such a place.' Kitty thrust her portfolio into Amethyst's hands. 'Hold on to these while I go home and fetch my paints and easel. I'll give it a try.'

Despite Ivory's protests Kitty walked back to the house and collected everything she would need to start work. She parted with Ivory at the front door.

'I know you disapprove, but please don't tell Mama. Just give me a chance to at least pay the rent on the stall. If it's a total failure, I'll give up and try something else.'

'It really isn't a terribly respectable place. You do know why gentlemen frequent the Bazaar, don't you?'

'I do, but don't worry, I'll keep an eye on Amy. She may chat to Carnaby and his elegant friend, but I won't allow it to go any further. Trust me, Ivory.'

'I trust you, Kitty, but I do not trust them. If Amethyst gets out of hand, I will have to tell Mama and she will put a stop to Amy's visits to the Bazaar and yours, too, I do not doubt.' Ivory closed the door, leaving Kitty to trudge through the snow carrying her easel, paint box and pad of paper.

Amethyst was waiting for her at the stand, but she was not alone. Laurence Carnaby and Charles Westbrook were leafing through Kitty's portfolio.

'That belongs to me,' Kitty said, placing the easel on the floor with a meaningful thud. 'Those are my paintings.'

'And quite delightful,' Carnaby said with a beaming smile. 'You are very talented, Miss Kitty.'

'Yes, indeed,' Westbrook agreed, nodding. 'I am particularly taken with this one of the Square.'

'Thank you,' Kitty said stiffly. 'Now if you don't mind, I am here to earn money, not for idle chitchat.'

Carnaby held up his hands with a bold grin. 'Forgive us both, Miss Kitty.'

Amethyst shook her finger at him. 'Don't tease her, Laurence. You had better go away and flirt with someone else. I am done with you for today.'

Carnaby clutched his hands to his heart. 'Oh, no! I am a broken man.'

'Come along, Laurence. We're in the way here.' Westbrook took him by the arm and hustled him away. 'I'll be back later, Miss Kitty. If that painting has not sold, I will buy it myself.'

Amethyst started laying out the paintings. 'You see, Kitty. They are not the louche idlers that Mama and Ivory would have us believe.'

'I'm not entering into a discussion about those gentlemen,' Kitty said firmly. 'I am going to take your advice and set up my easel. It's what I love doing anyway so it will pass the time while I have to sit here in the hope of earning a few coppers.'

'What subject will you paint today?' Amethyst put her head on one side. 'I wonder what would attract the most interest.'

Kitty gazed at her younger sister as if seeing her for the first time. With her dark hair and her blue eyes there could be no denying that Amethyst was the beauty of the family.

'Borrow a stool and sit there at the end of the stand. I'm going to paint you, Amy. Let's see what happens.'

Amethyst needed no second bidding. She took off her bonnet and perched on the stool, posing like a professional artist's model. Kitty found a stick of charcoal at the bottom of her box and began sketching. She was so absorbed in her work that she did not notice that a small crowd of curious onlookers had gathered, and Amethyst was in her element as the centre of attention. Kitty broke off only to fetch a jug of water in which to wash her brushes and dampen the little pans of colour that she was about to use.

'That's lovely, ducks.' Aggie had been there from

the start and had managed to get a good view of Kitty's efforts. 'I'd like a picture of my little granddaughter.'

'Of course,' Kitty said, nodding. 'But I'd have to charge for it, Aggie.'

'I know that, dear. I've got a little saved.'

A murmur of expectation rippled around the spectators.

'How much, love?'

Kitty found herself inundated with requests for sketches of loved ones even though she quoted the price of a shilling for a plain charcoal sketch and one and sixpence for a colour wash.

'But, of course,' Kitty said firmly. 'I will charge more for clients who do not work here, so please don't tell anyone what I asked of any of you.'

A ripple of appreciation ran around the group, but the sudden appearance of Matron made everyone disperse. She stared at Kitty's work, frowning.

'Is this what you intend to do, miss?'

'Well, yes, perhaps,' Kitty said evasively.

'It's good.' Matron stood back to get a different perspective. 'Very good, miss. I approve.' Seeming to forget her previous aches and pains, she strolled off to inspect the other stands.

Kitty breathed a sigh of relief. 'I never thought of myself as a portrait painter.'

'It's not bad,' Amethyst said, stretching her neck to get a better view. 'But my nose is prettier than that, and my eyelashes are definitely longer.'

'I think it's perfectly charming. I much prefer a pretty face to a bunch of flowers.' Laurence Carnaby had come up behind them, together with Charles Westbrook, who nodded in agreement.

'You could purchase it and have a lasting memory of me,' Amethyst said coquettishly.

Carnaby put his hand in his pocket and took out a silver half-crown. 'I'll be your first customer, Miss Kitty Harte.'

Amethyst snatched it from him. 'I am Kitty's bookkeeper and cashier, Carnaby. You may collect my portrait when the paint is dry. I wouldn't want it to smudge.' Amethyst turned to Westbrook. 'Perhaps you would like your portrait painted, sir?'

He smiled and shook his head. 'I would not put Miss Harte to that trouble, but I have a younger sister. I think a likeness of her would be a nice present for Mama's birthday.'

'There you are!' Carnaby said triumphantly. 'You see, we are not the idlers and time wasters that you once thought we were, Miss Kitty.'

Kitty washed her brushes and shook them dry. 'I never said anything of the sort, sir.'

'Ah, but you thought it. I know that your mama was of that opinion, which, I might add, is totally misguided.'

'Come along, Laurence,' Westbrook said, taking him by the arm. 'Allow Miss Harte to do her work. Anyway, we have a luncheon appointment at Rules.'

'So we have.' Carnaby took Amethyst's hand and raised it to his lips. '*Au revoir*, my dear. No doubt I will see you tomorrow when I will collect my painting.'

'I might be here in person,' Amethyst said casually. 'If not, you will have the portrait to remind you of me.'

Kitty watched Carnaby and Westbrook as they walked away. 'He will not tolerate your impudence for long, Amy. I hope you are not serious about Laurence Carnaby.'

'Who, me?' Amethyst slipped off the stool and stretched. 'I could not care less for him. It amuses me to tease Carnaby.' She turned to a well-dressed couple who were gazing at Kitty's paintings. 'May I help you? These are all original Kitty Hartes. I'm sure you must have heard of her. She's an up-and-coming young artist.'

'They are very pretty pictures.' The silver-haired lady picked one of the flower paintings that Kitty had done last summer. 'This would look lovely with a nice frame, don't you think, Donald?'

The distinguished-looking gentleman with her smiled indulgently. 'If you like it, I will buy it for you, my dear.'

'I do like it, very much.' The lady held it at arm's length. 'It would look nice in the front parlour.'

'And a bargain at two shillings, sir.' Amethyst bore down on them with one of her most charming smiles. 'You won't find another like this.'

'May I have it, Donald?'

He nodded and took a leather purse from his pocket. 'A florin, young lady. That's what you said.'

Amethyst's hand shot out and grabbed the coin before he had a chance to think twice. 'Thank you, sir.' She slipped the money into her pocket before rolling the watercolour and tying it with a scrap of ribbon. The couple went off smiling happily.

'There, you see. I can be very useful,' Amethyst said proudly.

'That's my second sale today. We've got four shillings and sixpence towards the housekeeping. That is incredible, but I might not sell another painting for days. We can't be complacent.'

'You are too pessimistic,' Amethyst said, laughing. 'Come on, Kitty. You may paint me again. It will attract attention, even if no one wants to buy a portrait of me. I can't expect Carnaby to purchase a second one, even though he clearly loves me.'

'I wouldn't count on that, Amy. You know his reputation with women. Be careful, that's all I can say.'

Amethyst tossed her head. 'I can handle Laurence Carnaby, Kitty. You do what you do best, as will I.' She settled down on the stool and struck another pose.

Kitty finished the portrait, but although there was a great deal of interest there were no buyers. Amethyst had grown tired of posing by mid-afternoon and Kitty did not want to waste expensive paper by continuing to paint. The customers were gradually disappearing into the early darkness and there was no sign of Carnaby or his friend. Amethyst was beginning to sulk and so Kitty sent her home. There was a buzz of conversation as the other women began packing away their stock and there was a queue to pay their daily rent at Miss Pollitt's desk. Kitty had already paid her dues, and she was just wondering how she was going to get her easel, paint box and portfolio home on her own when Flinders strode into the Bazaar. Shaking snowflakes off his top hat, he spotted Kitty and waved.

She beckoned to him with a feeling of relief. Flinders Riley seemed to have an uncanny knack of turning up when he was most needed.

'I'm glad to see you, Mr Riley,' Kitty said, smiling.

'Flinders, please. Now that we are living in the same house, I don't think there's any need for such formality.' He glanced over his shoulder at the sharp intake of breath from the woman at the next stall, who was boxing up her stock of lace shawls, mittens and fans.

'Now you've set the cat among the pigeons,' Kitty said, laughing. 'It will be all round the hall that we are living together.'

He shrugged. 'Well, we are, to all intents and purposes. Or would you like me to climb up on this table and make an announcement to the fact that I am merely a lodger in your family home?'

'Don't you dare.' Kitty caught hold of his sleeve as he made as if to carry out his threat.

'All right. I won't do anything to embarrass you further, Kitty. But I did call in to help you with your equipment. Your sister told me she had abandoned you.'

'Amethyst gets bored very quickly, but with her help I sold a portrait and a watercolour, so today has been quite successful.'

'Do you think you will continue to work here?'

Kitty met his candid gaze with a nod. 'Yes, for the time being, at least. As I said before, we are in a bit of a fix financially.'

'Yes, your father told me that he relies on the lecture tours he undertakes to provide for his family. It doesn't seem to be a very satisfactory arrangement, considering that he will be incapacitated for some time to come.'

Kitty folded her easel and passed it to him. 'It has done well enough in the past. I'm just glad he's alive. I don't mind doing my bit to help; in fact I've quite enjoyed today.'

'We've only just met but it seems to me that this is just the sort of opportunity you have been waiting for.'

'Why would you say that?' Kitty shot him a wary glance.

'I don't know exactly, but I get the feeling you are not the sort of young lady who is satisfied with sitting at home and waiting for some gentleman to come along with an honourable proposal.' Flinders eyed her curiously. 'Or perhaps I am wrong.'

Kitty shook her head. 'No, not really. I try to be more like Ivory, who is a perfect lady, and Amethyst is actively hunting for a wealthy and preferably titled husband. She admits it freely.'

'It seems to me that you have an adventurous spirit, however hard you try to hide it.'

'Just don't mention it at home, Flinders. I don't want Mama having a fit of the vapours if she thinks I might do something out of the ordinary.' Kitty put the last drawing back in her portfolio. 'Please forget that we had this conversation. Mama has enough to worry about at present. I'm supposed to be helping, not making things worse.'

'Forgotten already.' Flinders tucked the easel under one arm and picked up the paint box. 'I expect you'd prefer to carry your portfolio, just in case I happen to drop it in the snow.'

'I can manage it very well, and I do appreciate your help.'

'Let's go home then, shall we?'

Kitty smiled. 'I think I'm beginning to like you, Flinders.'

'The feeling is mutual, Kitty.'

Chapter Four

Nellie smiled with pleasure when Kitty handed her a greater part of the money she had taken that day. This was unusual because Nellie was not normally given to bouts of hilarity or demonstrations of emotion. Kitty thought for a moment that Nellie might tell her it was too much, and she was to keep some of the money, but her worn fingers closed over the coins with the precision of a gin trap.

'I knew you could do it, Miss Kitty. Miss Ivory is not entirely of this world and Miss Amethyst is flighty, but you are going to be the one who saves this family. What with this and Mr Riley's contribution, we will eat well this week and still have enough left for a sack of coal and some candles. I'm a happy woman.' She marched off towards the basement kitchen with her head held high.

Kitty was momentarily at a loss for words. Such high praise from Nellie was unheard of and it made her realise just how precarious their situation had become. Any doubts she may have had as to the necessity to earn money by selling her paintings in the Bazaar were banished by Nellie's words. Kitty had kept back enough to pay the rent for her stall for the next few days, but she could not afford to be complacent, and she would have to work even harder to attract customers. It had come as a total surprise, but what had started out as little more than a game had proved to be a way in which she could help to support her family.

'A penny for them.'

Kitty looked around to see Flinders at the foot of the stairs. She smiled. 'I was in a state of shock, having received praise from Nellie, who is usually my most vocal critic.'

'I find that hard to believe. What could you do that she might consider wrong?'

'Any number of things. You'll find out when you've been with us for a while. I am the scapegrace of the family. Ivory is an angel, above reproach, and Amethyst is an incorrigible flirt but the one of us most likely to marry well, unless of course she runs off to join the circus or some such thing.'

'You are very hard on yourself, Kitty,' Flinders said with a wry smile.

'It's hard being the middle sister, and twice as difficult

to assert oneself. The eldest is the perfect one, who is the role model, and the youngest is the spoiled darling.'

Flinders laughed. 'It seems to me that you are the one who gets things done, Kitty. I admire you for that. Let the others bask in their glory. I think your time is yet to come.'

'One can only hope,' Kitty said, smiling. 'By the way, is your room all right? We didn't have time to air it properly.'

'It is perfectly fine, although I was wondering if I could have a fire lit. I have spent so much time in hot countries that I feel the cold very much.'

'Yes, of course. I'll see to it myself.'

'Surely you have a maid to do such menial tasks?'

'We used to have several servants, but Mama had to let them all go. I can't expect Nellie to do everything. She's cooking the dinner now.'

'Then tell me where to find the coal and kindling, please. I'll see to it myself.'

'I can't allow you to do that. You're a guest.'

'One thing I am very good at is building a fire. When living in camp it is necessary to do such things.'

'The coal cellar is in the basement. If you go downstairs to the kitchen Nellie will show you where to go. But I'd prefer to do it myself.'

'And risk damaging those talented hands? I think not. You are an artist, Kitty. You must take care of yourself if you are to continue selling your paintings. I am more than happy to fend for myself.' Flinders headed off towards the back stairs, leaving Kitty with little alternative than to let him have his own way.

At dinner that evening Nellie proudly served lamb collops, parsnips and roast potatoes with her own special gravy and mint sauce, followed by suet pudding with a generous helping of treacle.

'Is it Christmas all over again?' Amethyst asked as she spooned the sweet sticky dessert into her mouth.

Isabella frowned. 'Nellie is an excellent cook.'

'Yes, of course, Mama,' Amethyst said, rolling her eye. 'All I meant to say was that we haven't eaten like this for months.'

'My daughter exaggerates, Mr Riley.' Isabella sent a warning glance in Amethyst's direction. 'We have had to be rather frugal occasionally, but hopefully that is all at an end now that you have brought us the wonderful news that my husband is still alive.'

'I understand, ma'am,' Flinders said quietly. 'These past few months must have been very difficult for you.'

'Have you any idea when Papa will be fit enough to make the journey home?' Ivory asked, placing her spoon and fork neatly on her empty plate.

Kitty leaned forward, fixing Flinders with an eager look. 'Do you think the Geological Society would help to finance his return to us?'

'That's one line of questioning I am putting to them, Kitty. I can't anticipate their response, but I am hopeful. I won't rest until I see him safely back with his loving family.'

Isabella raised her water glass in a toast. 'Well said, Mr Riley. Will you join us in the drawing room for a cup of coffee?' She rose from her seat, waiting for his response.

Flinders stood up hastily. 'Thank you, ma'am, but if you'll excuse me, I have notes to write up that I must present at the Geological Society tomorrow afternoon.'

Amethyst eyed the remains of the pudding with its glistening crown of treacle. 'I could manage another slice, Mama.'

Ivory shook her head. 'You will get fat and then no one will want to marry you, Amy.'

'I think Nellie might be hoping there is some left,' Kitty said hastily. 'You wouldn't want to disappoint her, would you?'

Amethyst pushed her chair back and sprang to her feet. 'You are all so mean. Of course I wouldn't want to deprive Nellie of her dinner, and I'm not fat, Ivory.'

'That's not what I said.' Ivory sighed and shook her head.

Isabella ignored them and left the dining room with Ivory following close behind her. Kitty glanced at Flinders, who was standing back.

'Have you got any brothers and sisters, Flinders?'

'Sadly, I was the only child. My father died some

time ago, but my mother and grandmother live in the wilds of Essex.'

'You must miss them.' Kitty linked her hand through the crook of his arm. 'My sisters drive me insane at times, but I wouldn't be without them. Are you sure you haven't time for a cup of coffee with us?'

He smiled as they walked side by side into the hallway. 'Thank you, but I will be literally burning the midnight oil in order to get my report finished.'

Kitty released his arm. 'Then I will bring a cup of coffee to your room.'

'I can't ask you to do that.'

'Believe me, Flinders, my sisters and I have grown used to doing the work of chambermaid, housemaid and even kitchen maid since our fortunes diminished. Go to your room, which I hope is nice and warm now. I will bring your coffee.'

'That's an offer I can't refuse. Thank you, Kitty.' Flinders leaned over to brush her cheek with a kiss. 'I am most grateful to you and your family for making me feel welcome. It means a lot to me.' He walked away, leaving Kitty to hurry downstairs to the kitchen to fetch coffee for everyone.

She returned to the drawing room with a tray of coffee, which she placed on a small table close to her mother's chair.

Isabella picked up the silver coffee pot and filled three cups. She did not replace the pot immediately but held it up, gazing into the polished surface with a sigh.

'I thought we were going to have to pawn this piece of the family silver. Thank goodness it didn't come to that.'

'Yes, we know, Mama,' Amethyst said, adding cream to her cup. 'It's part of the set given to you and Papa as a wedding present by Grandmama Carstairs.'

'It's a family heirloom.' Ivory took her cup and saucer, adding a small lump of sugar, before resuming her seat.

Isabella paused as she was about to raise the cup to her lips. 'Whatever you do, girls, please don't tell Grandmama Carstairs about Kitty's venture into the world of commerce. You know how much importance she places on propriety, especially in difficult times.'

'It would be worth telling her what I'm doing just to see the expression on her face,' Kitty said, laughing. 'But of course none of us would go that far,' she added hastily.

'I hate to think what your papa will say when he finds out that you are going out to work like a common shop girl.' Isabella sipped her coffee. 'I'm not happy about you spending your days in that place, Kitty. Perhaps we should try to manage with Mr Riley's contribution to the housekeeping budget.'

'He might only be here for a few weeks, Mama.' Kitty reached for the sugar bowl and then changed her mind. Sugar was expensive and she did not really have a sweet tooth. 'It would be difficult to find an alternative source of income.'

'Kitty's right, Mama,' Ivory said, nodding. 'If Mr Riley returns to British Guiana we might have to take in another lodger, and who knows what sort of person we might get?'

'That would be awful.' Isabella's hands shook, spilling her coffee into the saucer.

Kitty reached out to take it from her. 'Don't distress yourself, Mama. That won't happen. I promise to work hard and do my best to supplement what little income we have.'

'I will marry a rich man,' Amethyst declared solemnly. 'Then all our money worries will be over.'

'I'm not sure that the gentlemen who frequent the Bazaar have marriage in mind,' Kitty said drily.

'Don't say any more, Kitty.' Isabella rose from her chair. 'I know I ought to forbid you to work in that den of iniquity, but one must be practical. However, I think you should accompany your sisters, Ivory. You should act as chaperone.'

'Really, Mama? Every day?'

'Yes, my love. I want you to stay with Kitty and watch over her and keep an eye on Amethyst.'

'I have behaved perfectly, Mama,' Amethyst protested. 'Haven't I, Kitty?'

'I can't fault your behaviour, Amy. And you are an excellent model.'

'Nevertheless, I insist that Ivory accompanies you

from tomorrow onwards.' Isabella swept from the room, putting an end to any objections that might have been raised.

Kitty and Ivory exchanged rueful glances.

'I'm sorry, Ivory,' Kitty said earnestly. 'I know it's not the sort of place you would enjoy frequenting, but it's not so bad really.'

Ivory held up her hand. 'Don't say any more, Kitty. I've seen what it's like and I know I will feel very uncomfortable, but I have no choice. I will do as Mama wishes.'

Next day when she entered the Bazaar Kitty felt almost as if she really belonged in the busy commercial world. She was beginning to recognise some of the female stall-holders and she took time to speak to them whenever there was an opportunity, although these were very few in the busy life of the Bazaar. There was Aggie, of course, and the stand next to hers was run by Mrs Tucker and her daughter, Bella. The array of shiny jewellery, glass beads, stick pins and silver rings would have been a jackdaw's idea of heaven. Moll Tucker was always ready to purchase unwanted items from the other women for as little as possible, which she then sold on, making a substantial profit. Bella, however, was much more generous and was sympathetic to those who were less well off. There were several others whose names Kitty had not yet grasped but who smiled and nodded when she walked past their stands. She was just setting up her easel when Aggie sidled up to her.

'What's she doing here?' Aggie jerked her head in Ivory's direction. 'She looks like there's a nasty smell beneath her stuck-up nose.'

Kitty frowned. 'That's my sister. Our mother insisted that she should chaperone Amethyst and me. Poor Ivory feels very uncomfortable so please don't make things worse for her.'

'Well, far be it from me to make anyone feel unwelcome.' Aggie surged forward, holding out her hand to Ivory. 'Good morning, miss. My name is Aggie Brown and that there is my stall. If you ever feel like a chat, I am your woman. I know virtually everyone here, so I can answer any questions you may have.'

Ivory's pale cheeks flushed prettily. 'Thank you, Mrs Brown. That's very kind. I will remember your offer.'

Kitty winked at Aggie, who had the grace to look embarrassed as she shuffled back to her stall.

'You see, Ivory. They are quite a nice lot here, really.' Kitty gave her sister a hug. 'Why don't you model for me today? I haven't painted your portrait for ages.'

Ivory held her hands to her ears. 'It's so noisy in here, Kitty. I don't know how you stand it. Everyone seems to be talking at once and some are even shouting. It hurts my head.'

'Just sit on the stool and look pretty.' Kitty

finished setting up her easel. 'Where is Amethyst? She'll show you how to pose.' She glanced around and saw Carnaby, on his own this time, strolling towards them.

He came to a halt, gazing at Ivory with a puzzled frown. 'I see you have a new model today, Kitty.'

'This is my sister Ivory,' Kitty said hastily. She had just caught sight of Amethyst, who was in the bakery, no doubt purchasing something sweet and sticky with the penny that Mrs Tucker had just given her for a string of blue glass beads.

'Of course I remember her. Who could forget such beauty?' Carnaby took Ivory's hand and raised it to his lips. 'Good morning, Miss Harte. We met not long ago, but in case you have forgotten, I am Laurence Carnaby.'

'If you are looking for my younger sister, she was here a few moments ago.' Ivory eyed him warily. 'I am here to chaperone her as well as Kitty, and I warn you, sir, I am very strict.'

Carnaby threw back his head and laughed. 'The face of an angel and the soul of a governess.'

'I don't know what you mean, sir.' Ivory turned her head to send a desperate look in Kitty's direction.

'Now, now, Carnaby,' Kitty said firmly. 'Please don't upset my sister. I need to sell a couple of paintings today at least, so perhaps you would be good enough to take yourself off to another stall.'

'I won't say another word.' Carnaby clutched his

hands to his heart. 'I am hurt by your rejection, Miss Kitty. By the way,' he added. 'I was supposed to collect the painting of Miss Amy.'

'I have it here.' Kitty passed him the package.

'I have decided to make a present of it to my good friend Charles, as he is such a lover of art.' Carnaby bowed to Ivory and turned away, but then he spotted Amethyst as she emerged from the bakery, and he waved. 'Ah, now there is a young lady who truly appreciates me.' He threaded his way between the stands, doffing his top hat to all the pretty young women and their mothers.

'Don't take any notice of Laurence Carnaby, Ivory,' Kitty said as she opened her paint box. 'He's harmless enough, especially if his friend Charles Westbrook is with him. Westbrook keeps him in check.'

'He is very good-looking,' Ivory said thoughtfully. 'I can see why Amethyst is so taken with him.'

Kitty laughed. 'Ivory Harte, don't tell me that you have fallen for Carnaby's charms?'

'Of course not, silly. I am here to keep an eye on Amy and on you, too. Although you are perfectly capable of looking after yourself . . . in my opinion, anyway.'

'Quite right. I am too practical a person to allow myself to be flattered by a mere man, especially a louche individual like Laurence Carnaby. I believe he's broken a few hearts in this bazaar alone.'

'All the more reason for Mama to worry.' Ivory

pursed her lips. 'I wish there was another way to earn money, Kitty.'

'This will have to do for the time being. Now please sit still. I am going to make a sketch of you first and then, when I am satisfied with the likeness, I will start painting.'

At that moment Amethyst sashayed over to join them. She held a large sticky bun in her hand, or rather what was left of it, and she licked sugar crystals from her lips.

'I couldn't resist this bun. I was going to save some for both of you but I'm afraid there's not much left.' She glanced over Kitty's shoulder. 'There's Carnaby. Why is he talking to that ugly girl on the book stall? Did you send him away, Ivory?'

'No, I did not. He seems quite pleasant, but you need to be careful, Amy. Gentlemen can take flirtatious behaviour to mean something else.' Ivory shifted uncomfortably on the wooden stool. 'How long do I have to sit here, Kitty?'

'For as long as it takes,' Kitty said, sighing. 'And it will take longer if you keep fidgeting.'

Amethyst stood on tiptoe. 'Poor Carnaby. I think I'd better go and rescue him from that bluestocking, and there's Charles, too.' Amethyst waved frantically.

'Don't do that,' Ivory said in a low voice. 'You're making a show of yourself, Amy.'

'All my eye and Betty Martin.' Amethyst rolled her eyes as if to emphasise her words.

'Don't be vulgar, Amy.' Ivory glanced around anxiously. 'Anyone could hear you.'

'You are turning into Grandmama Carstairs,' Amethyst said crossly. 'At least Carnaby and Charles treat me like a grown woman.' She tossed her head and melted into the crowd before either Kitty or Ivory had a chance to stop her.

'Well done, Ivory.' Kitty wiped the charcoal from her hands on a rag. 'You know she does exactly the opposite when she's warned not to do something.'

Ivory sighed. 'I am not the best person to act as chaperone. I can't even handle my youngest sister.'

'She'll come back when she feels like it. In the meantime, I am going to start painting, so you can relax, but not too much. I still need to check that I haven't given you two noses.'

Ivory's hand flew to her face. 'No, you haven't done that, have you?'

'Of course not. It was a figure of speech.' Kitty laughed as she opened her wooden paint box. She was satisfied with the initial sketch and now she was determined to do justice to Ivory's delicate colouring. Her light brown hair had golden highlights, and her large brown eyes shone with the glow of warm honey. Kitty had always secretly envied her sister's classical beauty, knowing that her own fair hair and blue eyes, together with a *retroussé* nose, might be considered pretty, but nothing out of the ordinary. At least that was her honest opinion, based on the knowledge that both her sisters were remarkable for their loveliness.

Kitty began painting and was immediately lost in the process. She was not aware of anything or anyone other than committing her sister's image to posterity.

'That is a truly amazing likeness.'

Kitty turned with a start to see Charles Westbrook studying her work.

'It isn't finished yet, sir.'

'I can see that, but it's going to be quite remarkable. You are very talented, Miss Kitty.'

'Perhaps you would like to purchase the painting, Charles.' Amethyst had followed him, accompanied by Carnaby. 'What do you think, Laurence?'

Carnaby studied the portrait with surprising intensity. 'It is quite brilliant. You have captured your sister's soul on paper, Miss Kitty.'

'You buy it then, Laurence,' Amethyst said irritably. 'Since you are such an art critic you ought to start a collection. You could hang it next to mine.'

Carnaby looked away. 'Actually, Charles now has the painting of you, Amethyst. He is the collector of fine art, aren't you, old boy?'

'I'm taking it to be framed,' Westbrook said apologetically. 'I thought it too good to be kept in a folder.' He glanced at Kitty as she dipped the brush in water and then applied it to one of the small pans of colour. 'I would like to purchase this painting as well, if you would entrust it to me?'

Kitty met his earnest gaze with a smile. 'You are flattering me, sir.'

Westbrook shook his head. 'No, on my honour, it's true what Laurence said. I really am a keen collector of art, and I like to encourage new talent.'

'He is what he says, and very boring it is when you get him on the subject.' Carnaby laughed, but his attention wandered, and he grasped Westbrook's arm. 'Look over there, Charles. Isn't that Sebastian Marriner with the little piece he picked up in Covent Garden?'

'That's enough, Laurence. It's not a fit topic to speak about in front of ladies,' Westbrook said hastily.

'I'm sure the young ladies have heard worse,' Carnaby said casually. 'If not, please excuse me, Misses Harte. However, I must leave you now as I have business to discuss with Marriner. I believe there's a party at Marriner House tonight, Charles. Are you coming?'

Westbrook shook his head. 'I might or I might not, depending on the circumstances. Marriner is not my favourite person.'

'Maybe not, but he throws a dashed good party.' Carnaby turned to Ivory, who was sitting stiffly and staring straight ahead. 'Perhaps you would like to accompany me, Miss Harte? I would be proud to walk into a society party with a lady like you on my arm. A few glasses of champagne will melt that frosty attitude.'

A sharp intake of breath from Amethyst broke the stunned silence.

'Why are you asking her, Carnaby? I am your favourite. You told me so.'

Kitty had put up with Carnaby's veiled remarks until now, but she had had enough. She pointed her brush at him. 'Such remarks are beneath you, sir. I would be grateful if you would take yourself and your friend elsewhere. I don't care how wealthy you are, or how important, I am simply asking you not to bother us again.'

'I agree with my sister.' Ivory took a deep breath and slid off the stool, facing Westbrook with a defiant toss of her head. 'I do not wish you to purchase my likeness, sir. You should go away, too.' She spoke with such pent-up anger that both Westbrook and Carnaby eyed her warily as they backed away.

'I beg your pardon, Miss Harte,' Westbrook said humbly. 'I can assure you that no insult was intended.'

Ivory turned her back on him.

'No, really, I was joking, of course.' Carnaby looked to Kitty for support, but she glowered at him, saying nothing. He shrugged. 'Very well, then. We'll do as you say, Miss Harte. Come, Charles.' Carnaby grabbed his friend by the sleeve and virtually dragged him away, heading towards the couple who had just entered the building.

Amethyst stamped her foot, tears standing out in the tips of her thick eyelashes. 'How could you both? Carnaby meant me, of course. He isn't interested in you, Ivory. Now you've sent him away and I'll never get another chance to attend a ball at Marriner House. I've read about the parties that Lord Marriner gives. All society will be there.'

'And a great many people with whom Mama would never allow you to associate,' Kitty said tersely. 'Keep away from Laurence Carnaby, Amy. He is a libertine.'

'That's right, dear.' Aggie had come up behind them without anyone noticing. 'That fellow has ruined the reputations of several young women who work here. I've seen it happen too many times not to warn you about him.'

Ivory shook her head. 'Surely that doesn't apply to Sir Charles. He seems too much of a gentleman.'

'Beware of all them toffs, Miss Harte.' Aggie tapped the side of her nose. 'That's all I can say. If you young ladies want to earn money here, you need to be very careful who you associate with. If things get too rowdy, you'll have Matron to deal with.'

Kitty felt a shiver run down her spine as she gazed around the crowded Bazaar. The loud voices and laughing faces seemed to merge into one entity that spelled danger. She and her sisters had led sheltered lives until now, but if they were going to survive in a commercial market they would have to learn quickly or face disaster.

Chapter Five

By mid-afternoon the portrait was finished, and the crowds has largely dispersed, due it seemed to the sudden hailstorm that battered the roof and hurled in tiny pellets of ice every time the double doors were opened. Kitty took the opportunity to suggest that Ivory, who had been clearly upset by the altercation with Carnaby, and Amethyst went home, leaving her to pack up her things and follow on when ready. There had been no sales so far, although there had been a lot of interest in Kitty's watercolour paintings of flowers. Carnaby and his louche friends had drifted off at midday and had not returned, which was a relief, and many of the stall-holders had already packed up and gone home.

Ivory did not put up an argument, and Amethyst was sulking because Carnaby had gone without speaking to her. They left, carrying the easel between them, and Kitty put her work back in the portfolio. The portrait of Ivory was the last to go in as it was not completely dry. Kitty held it up, examining it with a critical eye. She was reasonably satisfied with her efforts, although there was, she thought, still room for improvement. She was about to pack it away when a smartly dressed young woman walked up to her stand, accompanied by her maidservant.

'Are you Miss Kitty Harte?'

Kitty stared at her in surprise. There was something oddly familiar about her although Kitty had never met her before. 'I am Kitty Harte. I don't think I know you.'

A smile lit the young woman's face, and her grey eyes sparkled. 'We have never met until this moment.' She peeled her fur glove off her right hand and held it out to Kitty. 'I am Frances Westbrook. I believe you know my brother, Charles.'

Kitty shook her hand. 'Yes, I am acquainted with him, but briefly.'

'Even so, Charles admires your work, Miss Harte. He sent me here specifically to purchase the portrait that you hold in your hand. It is your sister, is it not?'

'Yes, my elder sister, Ivory. Might I ask why he sent you here, especially in such wild weather? Surely it could have waited until tomorrow?'

Frances sighed. 'I gather that Laurence Carnaby caused a commotion this morning. That man is always upsetting people, and then he claims that he has no idea why they have parted company with him, but Charles isn't like that.'

'If that's true, why does he keep company with Carnaby?' Kitty eyed her suspiciously. Frances Westbrook was obviously a lady, and her candid gaze was slightly unsettling.

'Charles is very loyal, and Carnaby likes to shock, but he is not altogether bad.' Frances blushed prettily. 'He can be very amusing when he wants to be. Anyway, that is not why I am here. Charles still wishes to purchase the painting and has given me the wherewithal to pay for it.'

Kitty was inclined to refuse as the scene that morning was still fresh in her mind. However, she could not afford to be proud. 'A crown,' she said boldly. 'Five shillings, please.' It was more than Carnaby had paid for Amethyst's portrait, but Kitty was banking on the fact that Charles Westbrook must really wish to own this particular painting.

'That is what he thought.' Frances opened her reticule and took out a silk purse. She selected a silver crown piece and handed it to Kitty. 'Thank you, Miss Harte. He will be delighted to own such a pretty picture. Your sister is very beautiful.'

Kitty pocketed the money. 'Thank you, Miss Westbrook.'

'If you could wrap the painting, Clara will take it to the carriage.'

Kitty had brought a few sheets of brown paper

specifically for this purpose. She handed the wrapped picture to the maid.

'Before we go,' Frances said casually, 'Charles wondered if you would paint my portrait, Miss Harte. Just a watercolour sketch, similar to the ones you have executed of your sisters.'

'Yes, of course. I would be very pleased to do so.'

'The only thing is that I wouldn't wish to sit here in the Bazaar, if you can understand. It would have to be done at our London home in Duke Street.'

'I don't see why not,' Kitty said thoughtfully. 'Although I would have to ask one of my sisters to mind the stall.'

'That's settled then.'

Frances reached out to shake Kitty's hand. 'Thank you. Charles will be delighted. Now I'm afraid I will have to face the elements, but the carriage is close by. Good day, Miss Harte.' Frances swept out of the building with Clara dutifully following behind her.

An hour later Kitty sat in front of the drawing-room fire with a crumpet impaled on a long brass toasting fork. Ivory had opted for a slice of Nellie's Madeira cake, while Amethyst had already eaten her crumpet and was ready for another.

'Do hurry up, Kitty. I'm starving.' Amethyst held a fresh crumpet between her forefinger and thumb. 'You'll burn yourself if you're not careful.'

Kitty inspected her crumpet. 'Don't be in such a

hurry. Mine is done enough now anyway.' She eased it off onto a plate and passed the fork to Amethyst. 'Where is Mama? Is she resting in her room?'

Ivory shook her head. 'She took a cab to the Geological Society in Piccadilly. Flinders promised to meet her there and introduce her to the person who is responsible for organising the expeditions.'

'What did she think she could do?' Kitty buttered her crumpet. 'I thought Papa was too badly injured to travel, so they can hardly bring him home.' She took a bite and licked her lips. 'This is delicious.'

Amethyst turned the crumpet on the fork and held it back over the flames. 'It's a waste of a cab fare, if you ask me.'

'We didn't ask you,' Ivory said dismissively. 'I quite understand that Mama feels she has to do something, even if it's unlikely to make any difference to our situation.'

'You just agreed with me, but you don't want to admit it.' Amethyst wafted the fork around to put out the flames as the crumpet caught fire. 'Oh dear, and this is the last one. See what you made me do, Ivory.'

Ivory sighed. 'Don't be so childish, Amy.'

Kitty wiped her buttery fingers on a linen napkin. 'Stop arguing. It won't solve anything. I have some good news, which might cheer you up a little.'

'It's a bit burned, but it will have to do.' Amethyst laid the singed crumpet on her plate and buttered it generously.

'What good news, Kitty?' Ivory asked eagerly. 'We can't go on working in that frightful place.'

'It's not so bad,' Kitty said vaguely. 'Anyway, that's not what I was going to say. After you two had gone I had a visit from a very pretty and elegant lady, who introduced herself as Frances Westbrook.'

'Charles is married?' Ivory stared at Kitty in amazement.

'She is his sister, and she purchased the portrait of you that he wanted to buy, but you refused to allow him to have, Ivory.'

Amethyst swallowed a mouthful of over-crisp crumpet. 'You see, he does like you, Ivory. What did I tell you?'

'That's not all,' Kitty said triumphantly. 'She gave me five shillings for the painting and, what's more, Charles has commissioned me to paint his sister's portrait as well.'

'That's good, I think.' Ivory frowned. 'I mean the money will be very useful, but why is he encouraging you so enthusiastically, Kitty? Heaven knows, you are talented, but you aren't a professional artist.'

'That's not fair,' Amethyst protested. 'Kitty is only doing all this to save us from the workhouse. Isn't that so, Kitty?'

'It really doesn't matter why I have started painting again,' Kitty said patiently. 'I don't consider myself to be the next Gainsborough, but if my sketches can earn enough to keep us in coal, candles and food, then I'm happy.'

Amethyst rose to her feet and went to the window. 'I thought I heard a cab stop outside. It's Mama, and Flinders, too. Maybe they will have some good news.'

Minutes later they were joined by their mother, followed by Nellie, who was fussing around her.

'You should take off those wet shoes, ma'am. You'll catch your death of cold and then where will your girls be?' Nellie grabbed the teapot. 'A nice cup of tea will warm you up. I'll be very quick.' She shot a wary glance at Isabella. 'Maybe a mustard foot bath would be a good idea.'

Isabella smiled tiredly. 'Thank you, Nellie. I don't need a foot bath, but a cup of tea would be lovely, and a slice of cake, too.'

'Sit down, ma'am. I'll be two shakes of a lamb's tail.' Nellie whisked out of the room, taking the teapot with her.

'Well, Mama?' Kitty said eagerly. 'Did you have any luck with the Geological Society?'

'The gentleman I spoke to was very kind and sympathetic.' Isabella sank down on a chair by the fire. 'But until the doctor says that your papa is fit to travel, there is nothing they can do to help us.'

'I don't suppose there was any money forthcoming?' Ivory cut a slice of cake and put it on a plate, which she handed to her mother. 'I really don't want to spend the rest of my life as a chaperone in that madhouse they call the Bazaar.'

'But, of course, we will do everything we can to bring home enough money to run the house, Mama,' Kitty added hastily. 'I did well today. I sold a painting for five shillings, and I have a commission to paint a fashionable young lady whose family have a house in Duke Street.'

Isabella smiled. 'That's nice, dear. I'm very proud of you all, and when I tell your papa how you've all rallied round to keep us from abject poverty, he will be very touched.'

Kitty glanced around the comfortably furnished room. Somehow her mother's idea of poverty did not compare with the wretched people she saw if she ventured out of the relatively affluent area of Soho Square. But Mama had been brought up to be a lady in a country house run by a sizeable staff. She had been protected from the realities of the outside world, which made it doubly difficult for her to accept her change in circumstances.

'What did the gentleman say exactly, Mama?' Kitty asked gently. 'Will they bring Pa home when he is fit to travel or will he have to remain abroad until the expedition is completed?'

'I think they will pay his fare when he is deemed fit to travel, and Mr Riley has promised to accompany your father. Flinders really is a nice man. However, he is a geologist, like your papa, and I would not advise any of you to have romantic thoughts about him. You know how we have had to struggle on our own.'

'You don't have to worry about me, Mama,' Amethyst said brightly. 'I am going to marry a rich man, and I promise to be very generous to my poor sisters.'

'You are a dreamer, Amy.' Ivory shot her a warning glance. 'Take no notice of her, Mama. Amy is still a child, but both Kitty and I will do everything we can to help you. I will return to the Bazaar, if that's what is needed.'

The sound of approaching footsteps made Kitty jump to her feet and open the door. Nellie marched in, bearing a tray with the teapot and a plate of freshly made crumpets.

'Here's a pot of tea, ma'am.' Nellie sniffed. 'Perhaps one of you young ladies would like to take a cup and a couple of crumpets upstairs to Mr Riley's room? My lumbago is playing up something chronic in this cold weather.'

Kitty took the tray from her and put it on a side table. 'I'll see to it, Nellie. We need to look after our paying guest. I think we need him more than he needs us.'

'What is the world coming to?' Nellie rolled her eyes and hobbled out of the room, leaving Kitty to fill a cup of tea for her mother and one for Flinders. She put two crumpets on a plate and handed the rest to Amethyst. 'Maybe you could toast one for Mama?'

Amethyst pulled a face, but she did not refuse,

and Kitty left the room to carry the tea and crumpets upstairs to the top floor.

She found Flinders seated in a chair by the fire, taking off his shoes. He struggled to his feet, hopping with one shoe clutched in his hand.

Kitty laughed. 'Please don't get up on my account. Nellie sent this for you, which proves that she's taken one of her rare likings to you, Flinders.'

'Crumpets,' he said, smiling. 'It's a very long time since I last had a toasted crumpet.'

Kitty put the tray down on the table by the window. 'I just realised you haven't got a toasting fork.'

Flinders reached for a large carpet bag that he had brought with him and opened it. He took out a canvas pack and produced a fork, which he tied to the poker. 'We learn how to make use of the few things we take with us on our expeditions. It comes in handy sometimes.' He impaled a crumpet on the tines of the fork and held it to the fire.

'I am very impressed,' Kitty said, smiling. 'I wanted to thank you for assisting our mother today. I doubt if she would have plucked up the courage to visit the Geological Society if you had not gone with her.'

'I think you underestimate her, Kitty. Your mama is much more resilient than you seem to think. I went with her, but she did all the talking and she handled the interview very well. I did nothing.'

'You say that, but I think you gave her the courage to speak up for herself, and at least we know that the society will pay Papa's expenses when it comes to his return fare. That will be an enormous help.'

'From what I've seen of you and your family, you deserve all the assistance it's in my power to give.' Flinders examined the crumpet, turned it over and held it back to the fire. 'You have all made me feel very welcome and that is really important to me.'

Kitty eyed him warily but when she met his earnest gaze, she was certain that he was sincere. 'It was a good day for all of us when you decided to come here, Flinders. You seem to have brought us luck.'

'I don't think I've ever done that before.' A mischievous twinkle lit Flinders' blue eyes. 'What happened today?'

'I sold the portrait of Ivory, and I have a commission to paint Charles Westbrook's sister, Frances. I have to visit their house for her first sitting next week.'

'I happen to have some free time. Perhaps I could accompany you and carry your easel and paints?'

'Would you do that? I mean, I will have to leave my sisters to look after the stall, so it would be a kind gesture on your part.'

Flinders laughed. 'I don't know about being kind. I am simply being nosy. I would like to see how these people live in their smart London houses. And I feel a little protective of you and your sisters. Your father has talked fondly about all of you, so I felt I knew you even before we met.'

'You are full of surprises.' Kitty could see that

he was in earnest, and she found it oddly touching. 'I'll leave you to enjoy your tea and I'll see you at dinner.' She left the room hurriedly. The thought of their father so far away and helpless made tears well up in her eyes. She blinked them away as she went downstairs, but instead of rejoining her mother and sisters she went to her room and lit the oil lamp on her desk. She sat down and began working on a sketch that she intended to wash with watercolour and add to her portfolio. The girls needed something to sell other than the work that had already been seen.

The house in Duke Street was a typical London town house with the servants' quarters in the basement and on the top floor. The weather had improved and a thaw had set in. Kitty had to lift her skirts above her ankles as she crossed the slushy pavement and climbed the steps to knock on the front door. Flinders was close behind, carrying her easel and portfolio.

The door was opened by a liveried footman, who ushered them inside and asked them to wait in the entrance hall while he went to find Miss Westbrook. The hall was oak panelled with an imposing staircase. Kitty immediately noticed the gilt-framed oil paintings displayed on the walls. However, there was little time to study them as the footman reappeared and led Kitty and Flinders upstairs to the drawing room, where Frances was seated by one of the three tall windows that overlooked the street below. She rose to her feet and came towards them, smiling a welcome, although her expression hardened when she saw Flinders.

'Might I introduce Mr Flinders Riley?' Kitty said hastily. 'He is a geologist who was on the same expedition as my papa . . .'

'Flinders,' Frances said, smiling, 'I almost didn't recognise you with that beard and moustache, but there cannot be too many men with your name.' She extended her hand and Flinders raised it to his lips.

'Frances, it's been a long time since we last met.'

'You know each other?' Kitty was so surprised she could hardly speak.

'I'm sorry, Kitty. I should have told you before,' Flinders said apologetically. 'But Frances is my cousin, although we haven't seen each other for a very long time.'

'So that is why you were so eager to accompany me here today.' Kitty looked from one to the other.

'Not entirely,' Flinders said hastily. 'I wanted to make sure you got here safely.'

'We will have to get together and have a chat, Flinders. But Kitty is here to do a sketch of me. It's unfair to take up her time by going over family matters.' Frances turned to Kitty with an apologetic smile. 'As in many families, there was a quarrel some years ago that was never fully resolved, leaving bad feelings on both sides. Although I'm glad to say that Flinders and I were not directly involved.'

'It's an amazing coincidence that Flinders happened to be staying with us when your brother requested a portrait of you.'

'Charles is quite old-fashioned,' Frances said dismissively. 'He wants to add me to the family gallery. Perhaps you could put his likeness on canvas next.'

Kitty smiled. 'I don't think I am up to doing a huge oil painting like the ones you have displayed on the staircase and in the entrance hall.'

'You won't know unless you try.' Frances glanced down at her turquoise silk morning gown. 'I thought this was a good colour, but if you think I ought to wear something different, please say so, Kitty, and I will go upstairs and change.'

'That gown is perfect. The colour reflects in your eyes.' Kitty nodded to Flinders. 'If you would kindly set up my easel I will make a start. If I can get a satisfactory likeness today, I will be able to add the colour wash later, Miss Westbrook.'

'Kitty, I would feel more comfortable if you would use my first name. Call me Frances and tell me all about yourself while you work – if that's possible, of course. But first of all, where would you like me to sit?'

Kitty walked around the room, assessing which area would give the best light. 'Flinders, would you mind bringing that chair over here?' She pointed to a spindly gilt chair with a tapestry seat.

'Of course.' Flinders obliged, but when Frances sat down her face was in shadow. It took a while, moving the chair to different parts of the large drawing room with Frances sitting and posing until Kitty was satisfied that the light and position were exactly right. She selected a piece of charcoal and began sketching with small deft strokes. However, despite Frances's request for her to talk, Kitty found it difficult to make a running commentary while she worked.

Flinders seemed to understand, and he pulled up a chair. 'Perhaps it would be easier if I told you both about the expedition to British Guiana and the difficulties we encountered.'

'Why not?' Frances said, shrugging. 'Although to be honest I do not find geological exploration a very interesting subject, but I seem to remember that you like to have things your way, Flinders.'

He laughed. 'You were a very stubborn little girl, Frances. Perhaps it is a family trait. If my travels are of no interest perhaps you would like to tell me how you have been faring these past few years. Do you spend much time at Westbrook House?'

'You've been away too long, Flinders, or you would know that we always go to the country at the end of the Season, which cannot come quickly enough for me. I find the endless parties, soirées and balls rather boring these days. I am no longer a débutante, so there is little excitement in being paraded on the marriage market. Soon I will be on the shelf and must suffer being referred to as an old maid.'

'That's utter nonsense,' Flinders said, frowning. 'You can't be more than twenty-one or twenty-two. Any man would be fortunate to find favour with you.'

Kitty looked up. 'You are beautiful, Miss Westbrook – I mean, Frances. I agree with Flinders.'

'I am sure you are both flattering me.' Frances pulled a face. 'Perhaps Charles wants the portrait so that he can show it to his wealthy acquaintances and sell me off to the highest bidder.'

'Shame on you for even saying such a thing in jest,' Flinders said severely. 'I'll have words with Cousin Charles.'

'Please don't, Flinders. You'll alienate the only members of the family who are still willing to talk to anyone from your side.' Frances tossed her head. 'I'm sorry to keep chattering, Kitty. How are you getting on?'

Kitty stood back to study the rough sketch she had made. 'I think I will make two or even three studies, Frances. Then perhaps you and your brother would like to choose which one you would like me to complete.'

Frances sighed. 'Yes, I suppose you are right, Kitty. After all Charles is paying for the portrait, although to be honest I really dislike sitting still for so long.'

'I will work as fast as I can,' Kitty said firmly. 'Now, perhaps you could turn your head to the right, just a little. That's splendid.' She could tell that Frances was getting tired and she worked quickly. It was at times like these that Kitty realised what a good sitter she had in Amethyst, who clearly adored the attention and would sit for hours without moving. Frances, on the other hand, was a restless spirit and obviously found it difficult to keep still.

Flinders lapsed into silence, as did Frances, enabling Kitty to finish well within the allotted time. She put her dwindling stick of charcoal back in its box. 'There, that is enough for today. I will work on these sketches at home, Frances.'

Frances rose from the chair, shaking out her full skirts. 'Thank you. I'll ring for James; he'll see you out.'

Flinders packed up the easel, leaving Kitty to put away her sketches.

They were ready to go when the door opened, and Charles Westbrook strolled into the room. He came to a sudden halt when he saw Flinders.

'What the hell are you doing here, Riley?'

Chapter Six

Frances jumped to her feet. 'Don't make a scene, Charles.'

'I've every right to be angry when I come home to find Riley here. You are not welcome in my home, sir.' Charles faced Flinders with a menacing scowl marring his good looks.

Flinders held up his hands. 'I didn't come to cause trouble, Charles. In fact, I came to accompany Miss Harte.'

'I think we had better leave now Flinders.' Kitty gathered up her sketches and was about to put them in her portfolio when Charles crossed the floor, ignoring Flinders.

'I'm sorry, Miss Harte. You ought not to be involved in our family arguments. May I see what you have done so far?'

'Of course.' Kitty shot a warning look to Flinders, who picked up her easel and moved towards the door. 'Which of these would you like me to work on?'

Charles examined each sketch before selecting one, which he handed to Kitty. 'I think this version shows the most promise.' He glanced over her shoulder. 'Do you agree, Frances?'

She shrugged. 'If you say so, Charles. You are paying for the portrait, after all.'

Kitty slipped the drawing into her portfolio and Flinders opened the door. 'I'm sorry things turned out this way, Kitty. I wish I could have spared you the embarrassment of a family feud.' He turned to give Charles a stern look. 'Which could have been avoided with a little consideration for the feelings of others.'

'I don't need you to teach me manners, Riley.' Charles frowned ominously. 'And I don't know how you managed to ingratiate yourself with Miss Harte's family, but I assume your stay in London will be brief.'

'I have little control over that, as you very well know, Charles. I am not going to apologise for something that happened when I was barely out of petticoats, but I suggest that you revise your opinion of me. I personally have done nothing to harm you or your sister. Think about that, if you will.' Flinders ushered Kitty into the hall and closed the door before Charles had a chance to respond.

'I apologise for my cousin's rudeness, Kitty.'

He led the way, walking briskly as if he could not wait to escape from his cousins' home. He hailed a passing cab and helped Kitty inside before passing her the easel and paint box.

When they were heading back to the Bazaar, Kitty could contain her curiosity no longer. 'I'm sorry, Flinders, and I don't want to appear nosy, but what did happen in your family to cause such a rift?'

Flinders stared straight ahead as if unable to look her in the eye. 'As I said, it happened more than twenty years ago. I am not certain what caused the argument between Charles Westbrook's father and my father, but it was something so serious that my parents left London and moved to a small village on the East Coast. To my knowledge my father and Charles's never spoke again.'

'Are your family still there?'

'My father was fatally injured in a riding accident, but my mother and grandmother still live in Little Foxbury.'

'And the Westbrook family have nothing to do with them?'

Flinders turned his head to give her a faint smile. 'I don't think that bothers either my mother or my grandmother. They are very independent women.'

'Do you see them often?'

'Not as often as I should. I'm afraid my job takes me away too frequently to allow me to spend much time at home.'

'That must be hard on your mother and grandmother.' Kitty patted his hand as it rested on the low door of the hansom cab. 'And difficult for you, too.'

He smiled ruefully. 'It is. I understand a little of what your papa must feel being separated from his family.'

Kitty leaned back against the stale-smelling leather squabs. 'It's a shame that you two cannot put the past behind you and become friends.'

'You sound like my mother. She is the most forgiving person I have ever met, but Grandmama is not so generous. She's a wonderful woman but it's best not to get on the wrong side of her.'

'I would love to meet them,' Kitty said, laughing. 'They sound like an indomitable pair.'

'They are indeed.' Flinders leaned forward to undo the doors as the cab drew to a halt outside the Bazaar in Soho Square. 'I'll take the easel first and then I'll help you down, Kitty.'

She tossed her head. 'Thank you, Flinders, but I am quite capable of alighting from a cab unaided. I'll pass you my paint box and portfolio.'

The warm air inside the Bazaar made Kitty gasp as she entered. The snow might have almost melted away, but it was still bitterly cold. It seemed as if the crowd had come into the Bazaar to get warm as the babble of voices reached deafening proportions and the smell of unwashed bodies mingled with that of cheap scent and the more appetising aromas from the bakery. Kitty made her way to her stall and found Ivory seated in a chair, looking bored. There was no sign of Amethyst.

'Thank goodness you've come to relieve me,' Ivory said, yawning. 'It's been a long morning, and no one has bought anything.'

'Where is Amy? I can't see her anywhere.' Kitty looked around anxiously.

'I don't know,' Ivory said crossly. 'She was flirting with Carnaby not so long ago, but I lost sight of them.'

Kitty looked to Flinders as he placed her portfolio and paint box on the stand. 'Did you notice Carnaby and my sister as we came in?'

'No, I can't say I did.' Flinders set the easel down. 'Shall I set this up for you, Kitty?'

She shook her head. 'No, thank you. I'm worried about Amy. Surely, she would not be silly enough to go anywhere with Carnaby?' Kitty stared at Ivory, who had paled alarmingly. 'Is something wrong?'

'I saw them talking to that man Sebastian Marriner. You remember, Kitty? He came in the other day with a girl who looked as though she ought not to be in polite society, if you know what I mean.'

'Lord Marriner has quite a reputation,' Flinders said thoughtfully. 'I don't think he is the sort of person your parents would approve of, although I've been told that he is very wealthy.'

Kitty looked around in desperation, but there was no sign of Amethyst or of Carnaby and his friend. 'I can't believe that she would have been so stupid as to leave the Bazaar with either of them.'

Ivory rose to her feet. 'This is Amy we're talking about. You know very well she is capable of anything, Kitty.'

'What will we tell, Mama?' Kitty turned to Flinders. 'Have you any idea where they might have gone?'

'No, I'm sorry. London is a big place. If she is with Carnaby he could have taken her anywhere. The only thing you can do is to wait here and hope they return quickly.' Flinders took off his top hat and mopped his brow with a handkerchief. 'I'm sorry, Kitty. I don't know who to ask. I've been away from London for too long.'

'It's our problem, anyway,' Kitty said firmly. 'But I think you are right. We have no idea where to start looking for her so the best thing to do is to wait here.'

'But what if she doesn't come back before it's time to go home?' Ivory's voice broke on a sob. 'I was supposed to look after her. I've let Mama down and I've let Amy down, too.'

'There's one person who might know where Carnaby could have taken her,' Flinders said slowly.

Kitty knew instantly what he was thinking. 'Surely you aren't going to face your cousin again, Flinders?'

'I'll wait for an hour or so, and if your sister has not returned, I will go back to Duke Street and demand to see Charles. It's time we had a man-to-man talk anyway. You were right, Kitty. The old family feud should have been put to rest years ago.'

Kitty laid her hand on his sleeve. 'Thank you, Flinders. I know that can't have been an easy decision. I just hope Amethyst turns up before it becomes necessary for you to do anything at all.'

'What are you two talking about?' Ivory demanded crossly. 'What happened this morning and how does Flinders fit in with the Westbrooks?'

Flinders backed away. 'I'll go to the bakery and get us something to eat while you explain, Kitty.' He turned on his heel and made his way through the crowd to the baker's shop.

'Well?' Ivory said impatiently. 'I'm waiting, Kitty. Will you tell me what's been going on?'

'We went to Duke Street, as planned, and then the most surprising thing happened.'

'Don't keep me in suspense,' Ivory said impatiently.

'Flinders and Frances Westbrook recognised each other. They are cousins, kept apart by a family feud that has never been resolved.'

'But Flinders must have recognised the name Westbrook, so why didn't he tell you before you arrived at the house?'

'I don't know, but he's coming back from the bakery. I think this would be a good time to find out.' Kitty waited until Flinders joined them. He held a piece of brown paper in his hands on which rested three sugar-crusted buns. 'I'm afraid this was all they had left. It's rather late in the day for luncheon.'

'They look delicious.' Kitty took one and bit into it. 'Just what I needed.'

'Kitty has told me what happened this morning,' Ivory said calmly. 'However, it seems odd that you didn't tell us that you are related to the Westbrooks.'

'I couldn't be certain, that is, until I saw Frances and then, of course, I recognised her even though it's many years since we last met.' Flinders offered the buns to Ivory. 'There was no deception intended.'

Ivory shook her head. 'No, thank you. I ate earlier. However, I do think you might have warned Kitty before you went to Duke Street. She could have been very embarrassed.'

'I apologise for not saying anything,' Flinders said meekly. 'It was rather stupid of me.'

'It really doesn't matter.' Kitty concentrated on eating the delicious, sugar-coated bun, but Flinders set his aside, his appetite apparently gone.

'I need to speak sensibly to Charles.' Flinders frowned. 'This is a ridiculous situation and he knows where Carnaby lives. I'll go now and see if I can have a word with him.'

'Are you sure? He didn't seem to be very friendly,' Kitty said worriedly.

'He's not likely to resort to fisticuffs.' Flinders

grinned. 'And if the worst comes to the worst, I can handle myself in a fight, if I have to.' He picked up his top hat and put it on at a jaunty angle. 'Wish me luck, ladies.' He strolled off before either Kitty or Ivory had a chance to speak.

They exchanged wary glances and Kitty shook her head.

'It all started out so well with Frances and her portrait. Then there's the money from other sales to keep us for another week or two, but Amethyst could be in trouble, and we have no idea where she might have gone.' Kitty ate the last of her bun and eyed the one Flinders had left, but she knew that to eat his share would be pure greed. She sighed. 'What are we going to do, Ivory?'

'Well, I have been here for hours. I've sold nothing and, to be honest, I have had enough. I am going home to sit by the fire. Amethyst has got herself into this bother and she can get herself out of it.'

'But Mama will be distraught. You mustn't tell her we've lost Amy.' Kitty clutched her sister's sleeve. 'We are in this together.'

Ivory shook off Kitty's restraining hand. 'I didn't ask for any of this, Kitty. It was Mama who made me come to this awful place, and now Amy has made it look as if I failed in my duty to keep her safe.'

Kitty could see that, despite her angry words, Ivory was genuinely upset by Amethyst's disappearance. She patted her on the shoulder.

'Go home and relax. I will stay here until either Amy or Flinders returns. Don't say a word to Mama until it's absolutely necessary. We don't want to add to her troubles.'

'You're right. I'll tell her that I've left you in charge, which is true, after all. I don't want to lie to Mama.' Ivory tied her bonnet strings and slipped her mantle over her shoulders. 'If Amy turns up before the Bazaar closes, please send her home. I will have a few choice words to say to my little sister.' Ivory marched off towards the tall double doors, leaving Kitty alone with two sugared buns staring teasingly at her.

With little to do other than to set up her easel and open her paint box, Kitty selected a sheet of paper and began sketching. She found herself making a drawing of the interior of the cavernous warehouse that had been turned into the Soho Bazaar. She chose a particularly busy corner and made quick drawings of both customers and stall-holders. She was so immersed in her work that she did not notice the passing of time, nor did she see who had approached her until she heard Amethyst's cheerful voice.

'Kitty, that's a lovely picture. You are so clever. Come and look at this, Sebastian.'

Kitty looked up and saw her younger sister hanging on the arm of a tall, handsome gentleman. His looks and bearing, together with impeccably tailored garments, proclaimed his status, but his knowing smile was disconcerting.

'You are very talented, Miss Harte. Amethyst has told me all about you and your family.'

'Amethyst?' Kitty said sternly.

'Where are my manners?' Amethyst giggled and shot a flirtatious glance at the gentleman. 'Kitty, my dear, may I introduce you to Sebastian Marriner, Lord Marriner? Sebastian, my sister Kitty, the artist.'

'How do you do, sir?' Kitty said icily. She turned to Amethyst, frowning. 'Where have you been? We were all frantic with worry.'

Amethyst shrugged. 'You didn't look frantic when we walked up to you. In fact, you were so immersed in your sketch you didn't even notice me until I spoke.'

'Don't turn things round so that I am at fault,' Kitty said in a low voice. 'You know you should not go off like that, particularly with a gentleman you have only just met.'

'You must forgive me, Miss Harte,' Marriner said smoothly. 'It was my fault. I was under the impression that your elder sister had given Amethyst permission to accompany me to luncheon at Rules.'

'You went out for a meal on your own?' Kitty stared at Amethyst in horror. 'What will Mama say?'

'We weren't on our own, as you put it.' Amethyst tossed her head. 'Carnaby was there. Then Charles Westbrook joined us. We were a very merry party, weren't we, Sebastian?'

'Merry indeed, my dear.' Marriner slipped his

arm around Amethyst's waist, which was too much for Kitty.

'That is totally inappropriate, sir. Kindly leave my sister alone. You are making a spectacle of her. That is not the behaviour of a true gentleman.'

Marriner leaned towards Kitty, his dark eyes narrowed. 'But your sister does not behave like a lady, Miss Harte. If you do not wish her to mix with society then perhaps you ought to keep her locked up in a cupboard.'

'Oh, Sebastian, no,' Amethyst said, laughing loudly. 'You are incorrigible. Now you've embarrassed my dear Kitty.'

Kitty threw her charcoal back in the paint box and slammed it shut. 'We are going home, Amy. You will be in a great deal of bother when Mama finds out what you have been doing.'

'You wouldn't tell her?' Amethyst's blue eyes opened wide in horror. 'But we were only having fun, Kitty.'

'There are different ways in which to have fun, and making a show of yourself in public is not one of them.' Kitty turned on Marriner, her lip curled. 'I suggest you take yourself off, sir. My sister is coming home with me. Do not try to contact her again.'

Marriner's smile froze, masking his good looks with a menacing expression that sent a shiver down Kitty's spine.

'I have influence in a great many places. You

would be very sorry if I used it to your disadvantage,' he said in a low voice.

'You don't frighten me, Lord Marriner, or whatever your name is. You are a nobody in my estimation and my sister will not be seeing you again.'

'Oh, Kitty, don't say things like that.' Amethyst's eyes filled with tears. 'Don't pay any attention to her, Sebastian. She is just jealous because she does not have a beau, and I do.'

Marriner's bland expression returned. 'I can soon find a gentleman who will be only too happy to tame her. All she needs is a man with a strong character.'

Kitty faced him angrily. 'Leave my sister alone, sir. Come, Amy. We're going home. You may carry my paint box. I will take the easel and my portfolio.' Kitty thrust the paint box into Amethyst's hands. 'Don't try to stop us, my lord. And in future keep away from my sister.'

'I rather think that decision is up to Amethyst herself, my little jewel.' Marriner clicked his heels together with a mock bow before sauntering off in the direction of the exit.

Amethyst eyed Kitty warily, her lips pursed in a petulant pout. 'If you spoil this for me, I will never speak to you again, Kitty.'

'Have you any idea how this looks, Amy?' Kitty faced her angrily. 'That man is a notorious libertine. I don't mix in society, but I've read about his exploits and the scandals surrounding his name.

Your reputation will be ruined simply by associating with him.'

Amethyst tossed her head. 'You won't say that when I am a titled lady. Sebastian told me that he had been searching for someone like me all his life. You will change your tune when I have a title and I live in a grand mansion.'

'If you believe that, you are more of a fool than I thought.' Kitty picked up her easel. 'We're going home.'

Amethyst followed her. 'You won't tell Mama, will you? I mean, you don't need to upset her unnecessarily, do you, Kitty?'

'You should have thought about that before you acted so rashly, Amy.' Kitty walked on and she did not stop until they were outside on the pavement. The snow might have melted, but it was still bitterly cold and the icy air took her breath away. 'I won't say anything this time, but if you insist on seeing that fellow again, I will have no alternative but to tell her. You need to sort matters out with Ivory. She was furious so you will have to be very tactful.'

'You are both jealous of me because I am the pretty one,' Amethyst said sulkily. 'I can't help it if gentlemen enjoy my company.'

Kitty walked on ahead, not trusting herself to speak. She could only hope that Ivory had not told their mother about Amethyst's behaviour. She quickened her steps, eager to get home and speak to Ivory in the hope of diverting a family argument that might escalate, especially if Mama became aware of the full extent of Amethyst's involvement with a man like Sebastian Marriner.

Amethyst caught up with her as she was about to enter the house.

'I'll give you the coral necklace that Papa brought back from one of his expeditions, Kitty. I know you've always liked it.'

'I don't want it, Amy. All I want is for you to behave yourself and think about others before you do the next stupid thing.'

'But are you going to tell Mama?' Amethyst put her head on one side, fixing Kitty with an appealing gaze. 'You really don't want to upset her, do you?'

'It's not me who'll be causing the upset,' Kitty said crossly. 'Go and find Ivory and apologise for causing her so much worry. If you're lucky, Mama will still be resting on her bed. If not, you had better hope that Ivory has not mentioned your disappearance.'

A look of genuine concern wiped away the rebellious expression on Amethyst's pretty face. She set Kitty's paint box down on the hall table before taking off her bonnet and mantle, which she allowed to fall to the floor. She picked up her skirts and raced upstairs, leaving Kitty to tidy up after her.

Kitty was about to make her way to the drawing

room when she heard the rattle of teacups on their saucers and Nellie trudged towards her from the direction of the back stairs.

'I hope you've found your sister, Miss Kitty. Your poor mama has been in a terrible state since Miss Ivory came home and told her what had happened.'

Kitty nodded. 'Yes, I brought Amy home, Nellie. I just hope that Ivory hasn't told Mama everything that occurred.'

'Miss Amethyst has been a trial since the day she was born,' Nellie said, sniffing. 'I hope she'll apologise for upsetting everyone.'

'Let me have the tray, Nellie.' Kitty held out her hands. 'I'll take it upstairs to the drawing room.'

'Let me know if I need to make a tisane to soothe your mama's nerves.' Nellie passed the tray to Kitty. 'I need something more than that to calm me down. I think a nip of cooking sherry might be called for.' She ambled off, still muttering beneath her breath.

Kitty mounted the stairs and as she drew nearer to the landing, she could hear someone sobbing. It did not bode well.

The drawing-room door was ajar, and Kitty only had to give it a gentle nudge to open it wide enough to enter, carrying the tray. She realised with something of a shock that it was Ivory who was sobbing loudly. Their mother was crying softly while Amethyst was attempting to squeeze out a few tears. Kitty placed the tray on the small tea table. She was at a loss as to whom to comfort first but she decided to put her arm around her mother's shoulders.

'It's not so bad, Mama. I'm sure Amethyst is truly sorry.'

'We're all sorry,' Ivory said in between gulping sobs. 'It couldn't have come at a worse time.'

'Ivory is right.' Isabella mopped her eyes with a tiny handkerchief. 'After everything we've been through, and then this happens.'

'What did you tell them?' Kitty turned to Amethyst, frowning. 'What has been said?'

'Nothing. I said nothing.' Amethyst shrugged. 'They were both weeping when I came into the room. I can't get any sense out of either of them. It's not my fault, Kitty.'

'Well, if it isn't about you, Amy, what has happened in the meantime?' Kitty filled four cups with tea, added milk and sugar and handed one to her mother. 'Sip that, Mama. It will make you feel better.'

'Nothing will help now. We are ruined, Kitty.' Isabella's hand shook so that the tea slopped into the saucer.

'Amy is very sorry, Mama. She won't do it again, will you, Amy?' Kitty sent a warning look to Amethyst, who stared at her blankly.

'Yes . . . I mean no.' Amethyst threw up her hands. 'I don't know what I'm promising I won't do.'

Ivory raised her finger to her lips. 'It's not that,

Amy. I didn't say a word. It was the letter that has so upset Mama.' She dashed her tears away with the back of her hand. 'Pass me a cup of tea, please, Kitty.'

Kitty handed her a cup and saucer. 'What letter? What has happened? It's not Papa, is it? He hasn't succumbed to his injuries?'

'Don't say things like that.' Isabella's voice broke on a fresh sob. 'I can't speak about it. I am so upset. Show her the letter, Ivory.'

'It's there on the sofa, beside Mama.' Ivory sipped her tea. 'As if things couldn't get any worse.'

Kitty snatched up the letter and studied it. She read it again before looking up to meet her mother's anguished gaze.

'Why would our landlord do this, Mama? We've always paid the rent on time.'

'We have until the end of the week to pack our things and move out,' Ivory said dully. 'On top of everything else, we have to find somewhere else to live.'

'But we've been here for years.' Kitty stared at the copperplate handwriting until it began to move, forming serpentine swirls on the paper. 'Why would this be, Mama?'

'Perhaps I have been a little remiss with the rent money,' Isabella said wearily. 'There are always so many bills to settle. I might have forgotten that it was the end of the quarter. It was your papa who made the financial arrangement with the landlord.'

'And now we are going to be homeless.' Kitty looked from one to the other. 'Has anyone a suggestion that might help? Presumably the money has been spent elsewhere, Mama?'

'I'm afraid so. It has been so difficult since your papa stopped sending money home. The bank will no longer allow me any credit.' Isabella clasped her hands together. 'I am so sorry, girls. The fault is mine. I should have been more careful.'

'I don't suppose it would do any good if we went to plead with the landlord,' Kitty said thoughtfully. 'Perhaps he will be more sympathetic if we tell him that Papa will come home when the doctors allow him to travel.'

'I've tried. I went to see him a couple of weeks ago because I realised things would get complicated.' Isabella rose to her feet, wringing her hands. 'I thought I might persuade him to be lenient, and he did promise to think about it. Then today I received this letter.'

Kitty placed her arm around her mother's shoulders. 'We will think of something, Mama. Please don't upset yourself. There must be a way out of this without losing our home.'

Chapter Seven

Kitty was in the kitchen helping Nellie to prepare dinner when Flinders walked into the room. He came to a halt, looking from one to the other.

'I couldn't find Carnaby or Charles. Did you find Amethyst?'

'She returned on the arm of Sebastian Marriner.' Kitty chopped an onion in half with unnecessary force and her eyes began to sting. She wiped them on the back of her hand. 'It's no wonder you couldn't find the others – they had all been enjoying luncheon at Rules.'

Flinders frowned. 'I'm sorry, Kitty. Mrs Harte must be very upset.'

'You would be, too, sir,' Nellie said abruptly, 'if you was given less than a week's notice to move out of the home you've lived in for years.'

'I was talking about Amethyst's behaviour. Have I missed something, Kitty?' Flinders turned to her with a questioning look.

'Mama received a letter from our landlord.' Kitty forced herself to remain calm even though she was close to tears of anger and frustration. 'Apparently Mama has been a little absent-minded when it came to paying the rent. She didn't tell anyone and now it's too late. The landlord is evicting us unless we can pay the three months' overdue money and a deposit for the next quarter.'

'That's appalling. But perhaps you could speak to the landlord personally, Kitty. The man might listen if you explained the situation to him.'

She shook her head. 'It would only make matters worse, Flinders. We don't know when Papa will return or even if he will be able to work again. I can't earn enough money with my paintings to pay the rent as well as everything else.'

'I can help financially. I'm not rich, but I might be able to get my hands on a proportion of the money your family owes.'

'You'd be throwing your money away, sir.' Nellie wiped her floury hands on a cloth. 'If the master can't work for months the same thing will happen again and you'll be gone abroad by that time.'

'Nellie is right,' Kitty said sadly. 'It's very kind of you, Flinders, and much appreciated, but it wouldn't be fair on you. I don't know what the answer is.'

'Does Mrs Harte know about Amethyst's involvement with Marriner?'

'Not exactly. In fact, it's worse than we feared.' Kitty turned away to stir a pot bubbling on the range. 'Amy had luncheon at Rules with Marriner, Carnaby, Charles Westbrook and goodness knows how many other gentlemen. Her reputation is already ruined.'

'Good grief!' Flinders laid a sympathetic hand on Kitty's shoulder. 'I am so sorry.'

'We've kept the worst of Amy's lapse from Mama so far.' Kitty's voice broke as she struggled to contain her emotions. 'That would be too much for her to bear at the moment.'

'Why don't you go to the drawing room, Miss Kitty?' Nellie said gently. 'You've had enough for today. I'll serve dinner in half an hour. Everything looks better with a full stomach.' She nodded to Flinders. 'Take her upstairs, sir. I can manage better without interruptions. At least I have my own kitchen to work in for the time being. Heaven knows where we'll all be this time next week.'

'That is not what I need to hear, thank you, Nellie,' Kitty said with a wry smile. 'I know you're just as upset as the rest of us, but whatever happens we will need you to look after us, as you've always done. You are an important part of our family.'

Nellie wiped her eyes on her apron. 'Get away with you, Miss Kitty. You'll have me bawling me eyes out next.'

'Come on, Kitty,' Flinders said, taking her by the hand. 'I think Nellie needs a moment to herself.'

'Yes, you're right. Will you come with me, Flinders? You always seem to know exactly what to say to Mama. I imagine she is still very distraught.'

'Of course. I'll do anything I can to help you and your family.' Flinders opened the door. 'Let's hope that Amethyst hasn't decided to add a complete confession to your mama's other problems.'

The warmth of Flinders' fingers wrapped around her cold hand was a source of unexpected comfort as Kitty went with him to the drawing room. However, as he ushered her into the room she could tell by the expressions on her mother and sisters' faces that the truth about Amethyst's escapade had been made known.

'What were you thinking of, you silly girl?' Isabella demanded tearfully. 'I don't mix much with society, but I've heard the gossip about Lord Marriner. He's the last person with whom I would want you to associate.'

'It was just luncheon at Rules, Mama. We were not alone.' Amethyst's lips trembled and tears glistened on the tips of her thick eyelashes.

Kitty held her breath, torn between the desire to silence her younger sister forcibly, which was an impossibility, or to try to make a joke of the whole abysmal tale.

'You are a nincompoop, Amy,' Ivory said bitterly.

'And you are totally selfish. You only ever think of yourself.'

'That's not true,' Amethyst protested angrily. 'You can't say things like that to me. After all, you were supposed to be keeping an eye on me. A fine chaperone you turned out to be.'

'That's enough, both of you.' Kitty stepped in between them. 'Mama is upset enough already without you squabbling like alley cats.'

'I resent that.' Ivory rose to her feet. 'I'm sorry, Mama, but Amy is a spoilt brat. I am tired of being put in charge of her. She needs someone to take her in hand.'

A delighted smile wiped away Amethyst's tears. 'That's exactly what Sebastian said. I think he is in love with me, Mama. If I married him, I would be Lady Marriner.'

Ivory curled her lip. 'Don't be silly. He has no intention of marrying a commoner. Marriner is toying with you, Amy. All those gentlemen at luncheon will have very different ideas other than marriage.'

Isabella buried her face in her hands and wept, but Kitty faced her sisters with a determined lift of her chin.

'Stop it, Ivory. You, too, Amy. This is getting us nowhere and upsetting Mama into the bargain. You know what the answer to our problems will be, don't you?'

Ivory sank back onto the sofa and Amethyst clasped her hands to her cheeks.

'Yes, that's right,' Kitty said firmly. 'We will all be packed off to Bridlebank to stay indefinitely with Grandmama Carstairs, and you know what that means.' She paused for effect, looking from one to the other. 'We will have days, weeks or even months of endless sermonising and lessons in etiquette, deportment and all the things that Grandmama holds dear. There will be afternoon teas with her boring lady friends and dreadful meals because she is too mean to pay for decent food and a good cook.'

Isabella raised her head, mopping her eyes with her hanky. 'That's not fair and it's not true. Mama does what she believes is right. It's sometimes difficult to live up to her standards, but she means it for the best. Anyway, as I see it, we have little or no alternative.'

'There is one thing you might consider, Mama,' Kitty said slowly. 'I know it would be very hard for you, but we could pawn the family silver.'

'Or sell it and be done with all that polishing and cleaning,' Amethyst added triumphantly. 'That would give me time to reel Sebastian in.'

Kitty pulled a face. 'You make him sound like a fish.'

'Lord Marriner has no intention of marrying you, Amy,' Ivory said coldly. 'He is entertaining himself at your expense, and your reputation is already in tatters.'

Isabella held up both hands. 'Girls, please. My head is spinning. I can't think if you argue all the time.'

Kitty went to sit beside her mother, placing her arm around her shoulders. 'Amy has a point about the silver, Mama. It must be worth enough to pay the rent with some to spare.'

'I came to that conclusion myself,' Isabella said between sobs. 'Nellie packed it up and I took it all to the pawnbroker this morning. He paid us a substantial sum, but not enough to cover the extra three months' deposit.'

'But if you have enough to repay the debt maybe the landlord will allow us more time.' Kitty clasped her mother's hand. 'I know what it must have cost you to part with the items that meant so much to you.'

Flinders cleared his throat. 'I can tell by your expression that there is more, Mrs Harte. Where is the money now?'

'The pawnbroker told me that he knew how to double the money he had given me in exchange for the silverware.' Isabella sighed. 'His son is a bookmaker.'

Flinders gazed at her in horror. 'Tell me you didn't put the money on a horse, Mrs Harte?'

'But it's a sure winner, Flinders. All our troubles will be over if what Mr Dagg said is true.'

'When is the race, Mama?' Kitty demanded anxiously. 'What is the name of the bookmaker? Maybe we can get the money back before it's too late.'

'Just tell me, Mrs Harte,' Flinders said urgently. 'I'll go to the racetrack first thing in the morning.'

'I think the race was this afternoon, Flinders.' Isabella's lips trembled and her eyes brimmed with fresh tears. 'Mr Dagg promised to send word if our horse won, but I'm still waiting.'

Kitty clasped her hands to her breast, hardly daring to breathe. A sudden silence engulfed the room as each of them grasped the full meaning of Isabella's words.

Ivory was the first to speak. 'You mean the money is lost, Mama?'

'No . . . yes. I don't know. It can't be, because Mr Dagg swore that it was impossible for this horse to lose. I'm sure he will contact me soon.'

'I'm afraid you might have been swindled out of your money, Mrs Harte,' Flinders said gently. 'Where will I find this man Dagg? I'll go there now and have it out with him.'

'His shop is in Brewery Yard, but no one goes there after dark, Flinders.' Isabella clutched his hand. 'I'm sure he'll send word. He promised that the animal would come first.'

Flinders patted her hand. 'Don't worry, Mrs Harte. I'll get some sense out of this man, Dagg. If the horse didn't win, I might be able to persuade him to recompense you in some way. I'll go now and catch him before he shuts up shop.'

'I'm coming with you, Flinders,' Kitty said eagerly.

He shook his head. 'It would be best if you stayed here and looked after your mother.'

'Do you know where Brewery Yard is, Flinders?' Kitty faced him with an obstinate toss of her head.

'No, but I can ask for directions.'

'And get yourself set upon by thieves who are simply looking for someone like you?'

'I am used to taking care of myself, Kitty.'

'Nevertheless, it would be quicker if I accompanied you. Ivory will take care of Mama.' Kitty rose to her feet. 'I am coming with you.'

The smell of boiling hops hung over Brewery Yard in a noxious cloud, mingling with the fog that had enveloped the city. Kitty had often had to visit old Dagg the pawnbroker and she knew exactly where to find his one-room shop where he lived and worked. The stench of urine and unwashed flesh wafted out as soon as she opened the door. Phineas Dagg was eating his supper from a chipped enamel bowl as he perched on the counter, cross-legged and hunched over his food.

'Ain't you never heard of knocking before you barge in on a man trying to enjoy a meal?' he demanded crossly.

'The light was on, mister,' Flinders said evenly. 'You need to lock the door if you're not open for business.'

Dagg uncrossed his legs and slid to the floor, placing his bowl carefully on top of a ledger. 'I'm always open for business, especially after dark, which is when most people like to slink in unseen. What have you got to pawn, or are you redeeming an item? Speak up, me soup is getting cold.'

'I think you know why I'm here, Dagg,' Flinders said calmly. 'You cheated a trusting woman out of her money by allegedly placing a bet on a horse.'

'Oh, that. Yes, such a shame: the horse is in the knacker's yard as we speak. It fell at the first fence. Sadly, the lady lost her money.'

Flinders stepped forward and grabbed Dagg by the lapels. 'You didn't place the bet, did you? Return the money or I'll send for a constable, and you can explain your actions to the magistrate.'

Kitty held her breath. Dagg was thin but wiry, and for a moment she thought he was going to put up a fight, but suddenly he relaxed and his lined faced creased into a grin.

'Now then, guv, no need to get shirty. The lady knew the odds. I warned her that she might lose but she was desperate for the money.'

'I'm not a violent man,' Flinders said through gritted teeth, 'but if you don't pay up, I will make sure this place is closed down and all your assets seized. You will no doubt spend the next few years breaking up stones in the nearest prison yard.'

'Now, now, don't get nasty.' Dagg held up his hands, cowering beneath Flinders' icy gaze. 'I've had a bad day, too. Look in me till. Take what's there and be damned to you and her.'

Flinders nodded to Kitty. 'Take a look and see if he's telling the truth.'

Kitty moved behind the counter, wrinkling her nose as she stepped on a pile of filthy blankets and an equally dirty pillow. She unlocked the metal cash box. 'It's empty, Flinders.'

'You see. I was telling the truth. I'm a poor man, guv. I didn't cheat no one.'

Flinders released Dagg and stepped away. 'You are a disgusting person who dupes the innocent and steals from those who cannot afford to lose money. I will report you to the authorities, Dagg.' Flinders opened the door. 'We're leaving, Kitty.'

She emerged from behind the counter, catching the soup bowl with the tips of her fingers. 'Oops, clumsy me,' she said as she tipped what remained of the soup onto the floor.

'That was me supper,' Dagg wailed.

'You'll get used to being hungry when you're in Newgate.' Flinders held the door for Kitty, slamming it after her.

'I'm so sorry,' he said as they started off in the direction of Soho Square. 'I will report that man to the authorities, but he's probably been in that kind of trouble before and somehow wormed his way out of it.'

'I don't know what we can say to Mama.' Kitty quickened her pace to keep up with him. 'It looks as if we'll have to go to Grandmama Carstairs after all. If she finds out that Mama pawned the silver and then lost the money, she will never allow any of us to forget it.'

'Dagg has virtually stolen the silver from your mother, Kitty. After dinner I will go to the police station and put in a report. We might even get some of the items back if I can convince the law that Mrs Harte was cheated out of her belongings. I don't suppose she is the first person to fall for Dagg's tricks.'

Despite the stew that Nellie put on the dining table, the only person who seemed to have an appetite was Amethyst.

'I thought you'd had luncheon at Rules,' Ivory said, rolling her eyes as Amethyst finished her second helping.

'There was barely time to eat,' Amethyst said airily. 'The conversation was so witty and charming that I completely forgot to sample all the delicacies.'

Isabella rose to her feet. 'I'm sorry, I can't manage even a mouthful. I can't believe that I allowed myself to be tricked so easily. You'll excuse me if I go to my room.'

'I'll come with you, Mama,' Ivory said hastily. 'If I remain at table I will say something I regret to my foolish sister.'

'I didn't put the money from the silver on an old nag,' Amethyst protested.

Kitty silenced her with a frown. 'Good night,

Mama. Flinders is going to report Dagg to the police. Maybe they can retrieve some of the silver.'

Isabella hurried from the room with Ivory following her. Nellie passed them in the doorway. She shot a questioning look in Kitty's direction.

'What now?'

'Mama is worn out with worry,' Kitty said quietly. 'She's going to bed, although I doubt if she will sleep.'

Nellie busied herself clearing the table. 'I'll make her a camomile tisane, which will help her to relax a little. I've made a rice pudding for dessert, but I don't suppose there are any takers.'

'Don't I count?' Amethyst replaced her knife and fork on her empty plate. 'I would like some, please, Nellie.'

'The day you lose your appetite, Miss Amy, hell will freeze over.' Nellie picked up a pile of crockery and marched out of the room.

'Sebastian said he likes to see a woman with a good appetite,' Amethyst said smugly. 'He thinks I am perfect.'

Kitty pushed her chair back and stood up. 'You will have to finish your meal on your own, Miss Perfect. I'm going to the police station with Flinders.'

He stared at her, frowning. 'I don't think that's a good idea, Kitty. You would do better to stay here with your family.'

'Flinders, I am more afraid of spending the rest of my life at Bridlebank with Grandmama Carstairs than I am of any dangers on the streets of Soho. Besides which, I can describe the silver items that Dagg has virtually stolen.'

'Very well. I can see that your mind is made up, but you must stick close by my side. The streets are particularly dangerous after dark.' Flinders stood up. 'You'll excuse us, Amethyst. But if there's any rice pudding left after you've had your fill, please save some for me. I might have found my appetite after a brisk walk to the police station.'

Nothing untoward happened on the way to the police station in Tottenham Court Road. The sergeant who took their details was young, and despite his professional detachment he could barely disguise his admiration for Kitty. He introduced himself as Sergeant Barton, focusing his attention on Kitty as he spoke. She found herself blushing when he questioned her directly. His dark brown eyes were fringed with lashes that would make any woman jealous, and his clean-cut features, firm chin and wide brow gave him the look of a poetic hero. Kitty found it hard to concentrate and she stammered a little when she had to describe the silver items that had been pawned.

'Thank you, Miss Harte. I think that's sufficient.' Barton completed the paperwork and turned to Flinders.

'That's all I can do for now, sir. But I would advise

you to be very careful on the way back to Soho Square. There have been several cases of garrotting recently.'

'Thank you, Sergeant Barton. I will take care to keep to the main roads.' Flinders held his hand out to Kitty. 'We'd best head for home.'

Kitty turned to the sergeant, smiling. 'Thank you for taking our complaint seriously. My mother is very upset and embarrassed at being caught out by Mr Dagg. I hope you can prevent him from cheating some other innocent person of their desperately needed funds.'

'You may rest assured that we will treat this case as seriously as any other, Miss Harte. I will probably need to call at your home tomorrow to speak to Mrs Harte in person. What time would be most convenient?'

'My mother will be at home all day, and my sisters too, I would imagine. I will be at the Soho Bazaar where I have a stand.'

Flinders cleared his throat. 'I can arrange to be at home in the morning, if that would help, Sergeant Barton.'

'That won't be necessary, sir. I have all the details you gave me. We will be questioning Mr Dagg, too. Have no worries about that.'

'Thank you, Sergeant.' Flinders shook his hand. 'You've been most helpful. Come now, Kitty. Let's go home. I've worked up quite an appetite for that rice pudding. I hope Amethyst has left some for me.'

Kitty flashed a smile at the good-looking sergeant as Flinders ushered her out of the building. 'That went much better than I thought it might, Flinders.'

'I have a feeling that you were largely the reason for that, Kitty. I think Sergeant Barton was quite smitten with you.' Flinders linked her hand through the crook of his arm.

'He was just being polite,' Kitty said, turning her head away as she felt herself blushing. 'Let's walk a bit quicker, Flinders. I don't fancy being garrotted on my way home. That really would be the last straw.'

'Don't worry, you're safe with me. I've been on expeditions to the wildest places imaginable.'

'Let's walk faster anyway. I need to get home to tell Mama that the police will deal with Mr Dagg. I'm afraid it is all too much for her, especially with all of us facing eviction.'

'I understand that your mama is very upset, but it seems to me you all need to sit down and discuss the next step. I know you talk about your reluctance to go to live with your grandmother, but it looks as if that is your only option, unless the police can get the money back from Dagg.'

'Even then, I don't think there will be enough to make the landlord change his mind, Flinders. I'm afraid we will have to face the inevitable and just pray that Pa gets better very quickly and is able to come home.'

'He would be devastated if he knew what was happening to his family. Your father talks so fondly of you all that I felt I knew you even before I arrived in Soho Square.'

Kitty clutched his arm a little tighter as a sharp east wind whipped at her bonnet and mantle. 'It's always a sad day when Papa goes away on an expedition, but that is his life and his work. We all appreciate that.'

'He's very fortunate to have such a loving family to come home to.'

Kitty was quick to note the wistful tone in Flinders' voice. 'You will have that one day, too. But you do have a family in Essex, so you told me.'

Flinders laughed. 'I love my mother and grandmother, but they are not exactly a normal family.'

'In what way, Flinders?' Kitty shot him a sideways glance.

'Maybe one day I will take you to meet them . . . but now we're almost home. Would you like me to be with you when you tell your mama that the police are going to investigate Dagg?'

'No, I can do that. You've done enough for us today.'

'Your father always treated me like a son. The least I can do is to help his family in a time of need. I just wish I could do more.'

'You've helped us enormously, and I will tell Pa so when I next see him.' Kitty withdrew her hand as they reached the front door. 'My most difficult task now will be to persuade Mama and my sisters that we must make a very difficult decision. It looks very much as if we will have to rely on Grandmama Carstairs, at least for the time being.'

'I'm afraid you are right.' Flinders followed her into the entrance hall. 'Are you sure there's nothing more I can do tonight?'

'Quite sure, thank you, Flinders. At least the police have taken our complaint seriously and something is being done, although I don't hold out much hope of having either the money or the silver returned.' Kitty took off her bonnet and mantle and hung them on their peg.

'You know you can rely on me, Kitty,' Flinders said earnestly. 'If there is anything I can do, anything at all, just let me know.'

'Thank you. It's a comfort to know that you are on our side.' Kitty did not wait for his response. It was obvious that Flinders liked her – perhaps a little too much in the circumstances – and she did not want to take unfair advantage of his innate sense of chivalry or his obvious devotion to her father. Besides which, her own emotions were heightened by the dramatic circumstances that threatened her family, and she realised that this made her vulnerable. She did not look back as she ascended the stairs and made her way to the drawing room.

'Has Mama gone to bed?' Kitty looked to Ivory for an answer, Amethyst seeming to be in a world of her own.

Ivory nodded. 'Yes, I helped Mama to undress, and Nellie brought her a camomile tisane, so hopefully it will help her to sleep. What happened at the police station?'

'We gave all the details to a very nice officer, who will call tomorrow to speak to Mama. The police are going to question Dagg and his son, although I don't hold out much hope of getting anything back.'

'We can't just give up, Kitty. There is too much at stake. I cannot face the prospect of spending weeks or even months with Grandmama Carstairs.'

Kitty glanced at Amethyst. 'It's obvious where Amy's thoughts are.'

'She's been like that ever since you and Flinders left. I think she's planning her grand wedding to Lord Marriner.' Ivory rolled her eyes. 'Amy lives in a world of her own.'

'Maybe she's the lucky one,' Kitty said with a wry smile. 'I don't want to sound too pessimistic, but I can't see any way out of this other than to move to Bridlebank, for the time being at least.'

'If I was religious, I would pray for a miracle,' Ivory sighed, shaking her head.

'After a few months with Grandmama Carstairs I think all of us will be ready to enter a nunnery.' Kitty tried to make light of the situation, but she realised they would have to face reality, organise putting the furniture into storage and make the dreaded move.

Chapter Eight

Kitty was hardly surprised next morning when Amethyst insisted on accompanying her to the Bazaar, despite Ivory's attempts to persuade her otherwise. Amethyst insisted that she wanted to help Kitty sell her paintings, but Kitty suspected that her younger sister's real objective was to meet Sebastian Marriner again. Kitty could have sided with Ivory, but she knew only too well that once Amethyst made up her mind absolutely nothing would stop her from doing exactly as she pleased. However, there were more pressing things to worry about than Amethyst's reputation. Their mother had remained in bed with one of her sick headaches, and if Sergeant Barton called later that morning it would fall to Ivory and Nellie to give him any further information he might need.

Kitty's heart was not really in her task as she set up her easel and opened her paint box. Amethyst stood by her side, looking around expectantly. She was dressed in an emerald-green afternoon gown with a matching bonnet, trimmed with a pink silk rose. Her outfit was far too smart for someone working on a stall, especially as the other women were following Matron's rules and dressed soberly. However, Kitty was in no mood to argue with her wayward sister. She left Amethyst to lay out the remaining paintings from the portfolio, while she studied the sketches of Frances Westbrook and decided which was the best and most appealing.

Although it was early, the level of sound in the former warehouse was growing louder by the minute. Women were bustling around, either finishing off setting up their stalls or walking about, inspecting what other people had to sell. The aroma of warm yeast and baking bread from the bakery was mouth-watering, but it would soon be replaced by the mixed smells of sweating humanity, cheap perfume and gentlemen's pomade. Aggie, on the adjacent stall, was talkative as usual, and she warned Kitty that Matron Hume was on the rampage, going from stand to stand, inspecting the goods on sale and checking that all rents were paid up to date. As the noise level rose and more people crowded into the Bazaar, Kitty tried to work, while Amethyst hovered expectantly, obviously waiting for Marriner to arrive. However, the next person to approach Kitty's stand was Sergeant Barton himself.

He doffed his top hat. 'Good morning, Miss Harte.'

Kitty could see Amethyst edging closer and closer. 'Good morning, Sergeant Barton.'

'I've just come from your house. I spoke to your sister, and she confirmed what you and Mr Riley told me last evening.'

Amethyst squeezed between them. 'I am Miss Amethyst Harte, Sergeant. Perhaps you would like to interview me?'

Barton eyed her coolly. 'Thank you, Miss Harte, but I think I have all the information I need – for now, at least.' He turned back to Kitty with a genuine smile. 'I just wanted to let you know that my men apprehended Mr Dagg and his son. They are both being questioned at the station. We made some enquiries and discovered that there were no races yesterday afternoon. Dagg lied about putting your money on a horse.'

'Do you think we will get our silver back, or the money?' Kitty asked anxiously. 'We only have until the end of the week to pay the arrears in rent.'

'I wish I could be more positive, but people like the Daggs are very crafty and quite clever when it comes to covering their tracks. I will let you know if we succeed in getting anything useful out of them, but Dagg himself is an old lag and unlikely to give anything away.'

'I understand.' Kitty tried hard to hide her disappointment. 'Thank you anyway, Sergeant Barton.'

Amethyst cleared her throat. 'I don't want to worry you, Kitty, but old Mother Hume is limping this way. I don't think she likes having a copper chatting to her ladies.'

'Don't let Mama hear you using such common language,' Kitty said automatically. She could see Matron advancing on them with a set look and a fierce frown. 'I'm sorry, Sergeant, but would you mind moving on? I can't afford to lose my stall.'

Barton grinned, looking almost boyish. 'Leave this to me, Miss Harte.' He tucked his hat under his arm and walked slowly towards Matron Hume, who came to a sudden halt.

'Good morning, ma'am,' Barton said in a clear voice, obviously intending to be heard. 'There is no need to look alarmed. I merely came here to bring news to Miss Harte regarding a matter that occurred outside these walls.'

Matron Hume eyed him coldly. 'Well, it isn't good for business to have a johndarm invading the premises.'

'Your French is excellent, ma'am,' Barton said, smiling. 'However, there is some truth in what you say, and my business here is concluded. Good day to you.' He placed his hat back on his head and walked towards the exit with a measured tread, giving Kitty a wink and a smile as he passed her stall.

Amethyst sniggered, covering her mouth with her hand. 'That put her in her place, the old hag.'

'Shhh! Amy, she'll hear you and then we'll be thrown out.' Kitty turned her attention back to her work and pretended she had not heard her sister's comment. She could not afford to offend Matron Hume. Their position was precarious enough without adding to their problems, and to lose her only source of income would be catastrophic. She had barely done a few brush strokes when Amethyst uttered a cry of delight.

'There he is, Kitty.' Amethyst jumped up and down and waved as Marriner sauntered into the Bazaar accompanied by Carnaby.

'Stop that,' Kitty said crossly. 'You're behaving like a common street girl.'

'Don't be such a prude, Kitty,' Amethyst said crossly. 'You were happy to flirt with the police sergeant, so why shouldn't I have some fun with Marriner? At least he's rich and well connected.'

Kitty stared at her in disbelief. 'I did not flirt with Sergeant Barton. I was simply being polite.'

'So you say, but I know what I saw.' Amethyst did a twirl. 'I wish I had something more fashionable to wear. Sebastian is so elegant.'

'For goodness' sake, Amy, stop waving at him. You're making a show of yourself.' Kitty sighed. 'I sound like Ivory, but now I know how she feels.'

Marriner beckoned to Amethyst, and she grabbed her mantle. 'He wants me to go with him, Kitty.'

'Don't do it, Amy. Nothing good can come of this.'

'You are just jealous because the only beau you can get is a dull policeman.' Amethyst tossed her head. 'When I am Lady Marriner, I will find you a rich husband, and Ivory, too.'

She waltzed off before Kitty could stop her, although it would have taken physical force to prevent Amethyst from joining her gentlemen friends. Kitty was aware that Marriner was laughing at Amethyst's antics, but she chose to ignore him. There was only one good thing about the inevitable move to Bridlebank and living in Grandmama Carstairs' strict household, as far as Kitty was concerned. It would mean that Amy's wings would be well and truly clipped and Marriner would be sent packing. Amethyst linked arms with Marriner, pausing to wave to Kitty as they left the building, followed by Carnaby.

There was nothing Kitty could do about it so she bent her head over her work, intent on finishing the portrait of Frances Westbrook. She was so immersed in her task that she did not notice time passing until Ivory joined her, bringing a packet of sandwiches wrapped in newspaper.

'You must eat,' Ivory said firmly. 'Nellie made these especially for you. She knows you like cheese, and anyway that's all she had.'

Kitty smiled as she unwrapped the paper. 'I love cheese. I'll thank her when I get home.'

Ivory glanced at the portrait. 'That's very good, Kitty. I don't know Frances Westbrook, but this makes her look very pretty so I'm sure she'll love it.'

'I hope so.' Kitty took a bite of the cheese sandwich. 'I didn't realise I was hungry until now. This is so tasty.'

'We'll be on the equivalent of bread and water at Grandmama Carstairs' house. She is such a skinflint when it comes to food,' Ivory said grimly. 'By the way, where is Amy? I brought her some sandwiches as well.'

'She went off with Marriner and Carnaby. I couldn't stop her, Ivory.'

'Don't tell Mama. She has enough to worry about, especially after a visit from your handsome police sergeant.'

Kitty almost choked on her sandwich. 'I didn't say he was handsome.'

'You didn't have to, Kitty. I could tell from the way you spoke about Sergeant Barton that he was rather good-looking and quite charming – for a policeman, that is – and I have to say I agree with you.'

'At least he has done something about our case,' Kitty said firmly. 'I doubt that we'll get anything back, but Dagg and his son will probably go to court.'

'Whatever happens it will be too late. It's Wednesday and we have to pay the landlord by

Friday. It's simply impossible, as we all know, even Mama, although she won't admit it. She is praying for a miracle, but Nellie has started packing up the best china.'

Kitty glanced around the crowded Bazaar with a genuine feeling of regret. 'I will miss this place. It might be noisy and vulgar, but the people here are decent and hard working. I admire the women and girls who spend all their days here, eking out a living. Our misfortunes are temporary, and our situation will improve when Papa is well again, but they have to face whole lives of hard work and penury.'

'That may be so, but I don't think much of the society people who come here to see how the poor live, or the louche lotharios who prey on innocent young women like Amy.' Ivory's voice shook with emotion. 'Amy is easily led, but we cannot allow Marriner to treat her as his plaything.'

'I agree, but there are more pressing matters on hand, and I see two of them have just walked into the warehouse.' Kitty glanced over her sister's shoulder. 'Frances and Charles have come for the painting. Let's hope they like it enough to pay me.' She crumpled up the newspaper sandwich wrapping and thrust it out of sight.

Ivory turned her head to look. 'Maybe Charles can help. He's friendly with Marriner. Perhaps a word from him might encourage his lordship to find another girl to take Amy's place.'

Kitty eyed her doubtfully. 'It might be best to keep that to yourself for the moment. At least until Charles settles up. Here they come.' She managed a bright smile. 'I've just finished your portrait, Frances. I hope you both approve.' She stood aside so that they could view the picture on the easel.

'I think it's excellent,' Ivory said firmly. 'We haven't been introduced, Miss Westbrook, but I feel I already know you simply from this portrait.'

Charles smiled apologetically. 'I'm sorry, Ivory. I should have done the honours.'

'I'm delighted to meet you, Ivory,' Frances said earnestly. 'And I agree with you entirely. The painting is excellent, Kitty. You've flattered me, I think.'

'No, not at all,' Kitty said hastily. 'I paint what I see.'

Charles stood back, studying the painting with a serious expression. 'It is very good, Kitty. You have a definite talent.'

'Thank you.' Kitty could not hide her relief. 'I'm glad you like it.'

'I do. May we take it now?' Charles took a leather pouch from his pocket and selected some coins, which he placed on the counter beside Kitty. 'There you are, paid in full.'

Kitty scooped the money into her reticule. 'Thank you. The painting is still a little damp and might smudge. Perhaps I could bring it to your house when it is completely dry.'

Frances smiled. 'Of course. Why don't you and Ivory come to tea tomorrow afternoon, although I'd prefer it if Flinders did not accompany you.'

'Is the rift so deep that you cannot reconcile yourself to your cousin?' Kitty had to ask the question, even at the risk of alienating a client.

Charles frowned. 'It is a family matter, Kitty.' He proffered his arm to Frances. 'We have business to conduct elsewhere. Good day to you both.'

Frances smiled apologetically. 'I'll see you at four o'clock tomorrow afternoon, with my lovely portrait.' She allowed her brother to lead her away.

'What was that all about?' Ivory asked in a low voice. 'What has Flinders done to upset Charles Westbrook?'

Kitty shook her head. 'I have no idea, although he did say it was an ongoing family feud.'

'I suppose every family has its own problems,' Ivory said. 'Ours are just beginning. Do you really want to go to tea in Duke Street tomorrow?'

'Frances could be useful. She must have many well-off friends who might like their portraits executed in watercolours. I still intend to earn my own living, Ivory, even if we have to reside with Grandmama Carstairs until Papa comes home. I will go quietly insane unless I have something useful to do while we are incarcerated in Bridlebank.'

'Which brings us back to Amy.' Ivory glanced at

the open doors leading into the street. 'Where do you think they've gone?'

'I have no idea,' Kitty said wearily. 'I suppose I should have asked Charles, but he didn't seem very friendly today. I really don't know how to take him. Sometimes he is quite charming and at others he is withdrawn and almost rude, whereas Frances has been so open and friendly.'

Ivory shrugged. 'I have no time for people like that. Charles Westbrook obviously thinks that a title, wealth and a handsome face put him above the rest of us.'

'I thought you rather liked him, Ivory.'

'I may have been taken in at first, but now I know better. Anyway, I don't know about you, Kitty, but I am going home to start packing my things, and I need to persuade Mama to order a carrier to take our furniture to storage, otherwise we are likely to lose everything, especially if the landlord sends the bailiffs in.'

Kitty nodded. 'Yes, you're right. Even if the police get our money back, or the silver, there is not enough to settle with the landlord. I will finish early here, and if Mama won't order the removal van, I will. The money I earned from this portrait will go towards the cost of that. At least we will salvage something from this disaster.'

'I agree, but I won't tell Mama about Amethyst and Sebastian Marriner until it's absolutely necessary.'

'Just another thing,' Kitty said as Ivory was about to leave. 'Do you know if Mama has actually asked Grandmama if she will take us in?'

'I'll question her when I get home. This is all such a terrible mess, Kitty.'

'We'll survive,' Kitty said hopefully. 'I'll follow you as soon as I've cleared up here and settled today's rent for the stall with Miss Pollitt. I'd better give my notice in for Friday, too. It's becoming all too real, Ivory. I must admit, I'm a little scared.'

'What do we do if Mama hasn't contacted Grandmama?' Ivory asked urgently. 'I don't fancy going to see her on my own.'

'If that's the case we'll go together, but we need to do it quickly as it's quite a long carriage ride to Bridlebank.'

'I'll go home now and speak to Mama. She must be made aware of the seriousness of our situation.'

Kitty nodded. 'I'll finish up here and join you. If Mama won't take charge, then it's up to us.'

Kitty returned home an hour later, having given her notice to Matron Hume with some regret, although she knew she would not miss the daily inspections and the long hours. When she walked into the entrance hall, she found Flinders and Ivory in earnest conversation.

'Ah, Kitty, you're just in time.' Ivory managed a tired smile. 'Flinders has been helping me to convince

Mama that we have no choice other than to move in with Grandmama Carstairs.'

Flinders took the easel from Kitty's hands and propped it against the wall. 'Your mama was convinced that something would happen to save you from losing the house, but in the end she understood. I've booked the carter to collect all your goods on Friday morning and store them until you can have them returned. Nellie is doing a splendid job of packing.'

'And I persuaded Mama to write a note to Grandmama, which I sent with a messenger. We're waiting for her response. It's not too far to Highgate, so it should not take too long.' Ivory laid her hand on Flinders' sleeve. 'I don't know how I would have managed without Flinders' help.'

'It's the least I can do. And now I must find alternative accommodation. If I had the money, I would rent this house and you could all stay in your home, but unfortunately my income does not stretch to such luxuries.'

'Where will you go?' Kitty took off her bonnet and hung it on a peg, followed by her mantle.

'It's high time I visited my mother and grandmother in Little Foxbury. I'll stay there while I work on my report for the Geological Society and then I hope to return to British Guiana. I'm anxious to get back to the convent hospital to find out how your father's condition is progressing.' Flinders smiled sadly. 'But I hate to leave you like this.'

'You've done more than enough,' Kitty said hastily. 'We wouldn't have managed this far if you had not arrived on our doorstep. I know we'll all miss you, Flinders.'

'We have a couple more days . . .' Flinders hesitated as someone hammered on the front door. 'Would you like me to answer that?'

'Please do,' Ivory said nervously. 'It might be the Daggs, released from the cells and come to threaten us.'

'I doubt it. Not even they would be so stupid.' Kitty followed Flinders as he went to the door.

A liveried footman tipped his hat. 'Is this the residence of Mrs Robert Harte?'

'It is.' Flinders opened the door wider.

Kitty glanced over his shoulder. It was dusk and the streetlamps had just been lit. In the flickering golden light, she could see a familiar carriage with a lozenge on the door bearing the family crest.

'Oh, my goodness,' Kitty exclaimed, covering her mouth with her hand. 'Ivory, it's Grandmama Carstairs. She's come in person. Fetch Mama.'

The footman went to open the carriage door and put down the steps. He handed the small lady to the pavement. Dressed in black from head to foot, Honoria Carstairs leaned on an ebony cane as she crossed the wet pavement.

'Come inside, Grandmama.' Kitty extended her hand, but it was brushed away.

Lady Carstairs stepped inside. She raised a lorgnette and looked Flinders up and down. 'Who is this?'

'May I introduce Flinders Riley, Grandmama?' Kitty said hurriedly. 'He is a geologist who works with Papa in British Guiana.'

Flinders bowed over Lady Carstairs' hand. 'How do you do, ma'am?'

'I don't know why you are here, young man,' Lady Carstairs said bluntly. 'Has Robert returned from abroad at long last?'

'I regret to say that Mr Harte met with an accident, ma'am. He is currently in a convent hospital in Georgetown,' Flinders said calmly.

'Not dead then? If that is the case, why are you all being turned out of your home?' Lady Carstairs turned to Ivory. 'You, girl. You are usually the most sensible of the three silly sisters. What have you to say?'

'It's true, Grandmama. We have to leave the house because the rent is overdue and has not been paid for several months.' Ivory sent an anguished look to Kitty. 'We have no choice in the matter.'

'Your mother was always a fool when it came to men and money. I warned her against marrying a man who could not keep her in the style to which she was raised, but she was in love and didn't heed my advice. Now you can see what has come of her headstrong behaviour. Where is she?' Lady Carstairs looked up the staircase. 'Isabella, come down here at once, or do I have to come up to you?'

Isabella peered over the banisters. 'Is that you, Mama?'

'Of course it is. Who else would travel all the way from Highgate to find out what is going on?'

'How did you know we needed you, Mama?' Isabella asked nervously.

'Someone went to the expense of sending a messenger to my home, which was foolish in the extreme considering your present financial status. What else was I to do?'

Isabella appeared at the top of the stairs. She was still wearing a wrapper over her flannel nightgown and her feet were bare. She descended slowly, eyeing her mother warily.

'I suppose one of the girls must have sent the note, Mama. I didn't want to bother you.'

'You didn't want to admit that your feckless husband had let you down yet again, that's the truth of the matter.' Lady Carstairs turned to Ivory. 'I am not going to walk up those steep stairs. Have you a room on the ground floor where I might rest a while before I return to Bridlebank? And a cup of tea would be nice. What happened to hospitality?'

'I'm sorry, Grandmama,' Kitty said hastily. 'Please go into the morning room. Ivory will show you the way and I'll ask Nellie to make a pot of tea.'

'Earl Grey tea, of course,' Lady Carstairs said imperiously. 'I never drink anything else.'

'Yes, Grandmama.'

Kitty beckoned to Flinders, who followed her downstairs to the kitchen. 'We only drink Darjeeling.' She put her hand in her pocket and took out some coins. 'Will you go to the shop and get some Earl Grey tea, please, Flinders? I don't want to give her even more reason to complain.'

'What's that?' Nellie demanded angrily. 'She hasn't come here in person, has she? Not the old harridan from Highgate?'

Flinders grinned as he took the money. 'I wouldn't have missed this for the world. Don't worry, I'll be double quick. I want to see the rest of the performance.'

'It's not funny, Flinders,' Kitty said, suppressing a giggle. 'You don't have to live with Grandmama. We will have to bear the brunt of her criticism and her constant carping.'

Nellie shooed Flinders out of the kitchen, thrusting a jug in his hands. 'Fetch some milk, too. We've run out again. I hope to goodness that we've plenty of sugar. We need something to sweeten the old witch's temper.'

'Just put the kettle on, please, Nellie. I'm going to the morning room.' Kitty did not wait for an answer. She followed Flinders upstairs to the ground floor. 'Please hurry. Grandmama doesn't like to be kept waiting.'

'I'll run all the way.' Flinders left the house without bothering to put on his coat and hat, leaving Kitty to brave her grandmother in the morning room.

Lady Carstairs was seated by the fire with her fur-lined cloak wrapped around her as if she was sitting in an icehouse, while Isabella and Ivory perched on the edge of the sofa, their faces pale and strained.

'Well, Kitty, this is a pretty to-do, isn't it?' Lady Carstairs tapped the floor with her cane to emphasise her words.

'Robert will sort everything out when he comes home, Mama,' Isabella said faintly.

'It seems to me that he should have foreseen such an emergency.' Lady Carstairs curled her lip. 'He thinks of nothing but his stupid rocks and minerals. He should look after his family better, and now I am supposed to step in and put a roof over your heads.'

'It will just be a temporary measure, Mama.' Isabella trembled visibly.

'Where is the other child?' Lady Carstairs looked around the room as if expecting to see Amethyst hiding behind a chair.

'Amethyst is dining with friends,' Kitty said hastily. 'She should be home very soon.'

'Friends? I suppose you mean the flighty piece has gone off with a couple of roués. I know exactly what is going on with you all. I have my spies everywhere, and I know that you, Kitty, have been working like a shop girl in that disreputable place they call a bazaar.'

Isabella sent a pleading look to Kitty, but she was not going to give her grandmother the satisfaction of catching her out in a lie.

'Yes, Grandmama, I have been selling my paintings in the Bazaar and I've done a couple of portraits for which I was paid. I'm not ashamed of helping my family to survive in hard times.' Kitty met her grandmother's steely gaze with a defiant toss of her head.

'You don't seem to have disciplined your daughters properly, Isabella,' Lady Carstairs said angrily. 'I suppose you want me to take them in and do your job for you.'

'We just need somewhere to stay for a while, Mama.' Isabella's dark eyes filled with tears.

'Very well. Never let it be said that I did not do my duty by my family. I will take you, Isabella, and you, Ivory, but Kitty thinks she knows better than I, so she must find other accommodation. As to the flighty one, she can stay with Kitty. I do not wish to be associated with a shop worker and a girl of questionable morals. That is my last word.'

Chapter Nine

'I don't understand,' Isabella said dazedly. 'What are you saying, Mama?'

Lady Carstairs looked down her patrician nose and sighed. 'I thought I had made myself plain, Isabella. You and Ivory are welcome to come to Bridlebank and stay with me until Robert decides to return, but Kitty and the other one must find alternative accommodation.'

'I don't think that is fair, Grandmama.' Ivory rose slowly to her feet. 'Where are Kitty and Amethyst supposed to go, if not to Bridlebank with us?'

Kitty laid her hand on Ivory's arm. 'It's all right, Ivory. I can stand up for myself.' Kitty turned to her grandmother, controlling her anger with difficulty. 'I can fend for myself, Grandmama, but Amethyst needs to be with Mama and Ivory.'

'You cannot expect me to abandon two of my children, Mama,' Isabella said tearfully.

'You should have thought about that before you squandered the rent money on fripperies, Isabella, and you should have exerted more control over your youngest daughter. No doubt she is off somewhere behaving outrageously, as she did when she came to stay at Bridlebank a year ago. She spent all her time flirting with one of the under-gardeners.'

'Better a gardener than Marriner,' Kitty said in a whisper meant for Ivory's ear only.

'I heard that, Kitty.' Lady Carstairs glared at her. 'I may be old, but I am not deaf nor am I stupid. You are the clever one in the family. I leave it to you to find a solution.' She thumped her cane on the floor. 'Where is that tea? Must I travel back to Highgate without so much as a sip of Earl Grey?'

The momentary silence was broken by Nellie, who opened the door with the toe of her booted foot and marched in to lay the tea tray on a low table.

'Tea, your ladyship? Earl Grey, of course.' Nellie eyed Lady Carstairs defiantly.

'It's too late. I don't want it now,' Lady Carstairs rose to her feet. 'And you're not wanted at Bridlebank either. You had better find yourself another position, Miss Pickering.' Lady Carstairs marched out of the morning room, brushing past Flinders in the doorway. She gave him a cursory glance. 'And if you have designs on any of these young ladies, just remember that I hold the purse strings, and if they marry beneath them, they will not inherit a penny from me. Kindly summon my coachman. I'm leaving.'

'Yes, ma'am.' Flinders cast a sympathetic look around the room before hurrying off to do as she asked.

Isabella burst into tears and Ivory went to sit by her side and comfort her.

'Do something, Kitty,' Ivory said urgently. 'I don't want to go to Bridlebank without you.'

'You know Grandmama won't change her mind,' Kitty said angrily.

'Please try.' Ivory sent her a pleading look, which was impossible to ignore.

'All right, but don't get your hopes up.' Kitty followed her grandmother into the entrance hall. 'Grandmama, please reconsider.'

Lady Carstairs came to a halt as Flinders opened the door and stepped outside to summon the carriage.

'Go back to your mama, Kitty,' Lady Carstairs said dismissively. 'My mind is made up.'

'This isn't about me, Grandmama. I'm not looking for anything for myself, but I beg you to reconsider your decision with regard to Amethyst. She needs her mother and the protection of her elders. She's wayward, but she's a good girl at heart. And Nellie is part of the family. She's an excellent cook and I'm sure she would be of great assistance to you.'

'And you wonder why I don't want to take you into my home?' Lady Carstairs pointed her cane at

Kitty. 'You have too much to say for yourself, young lady. You need to go out into the world and find out what it is like on your own. You have an untamed spirit in you that needs curbing, and harsh experience will soon cure that.'

Flinders returned and stood by the door. 'Excuse me, ma'am, but your carriage awaits.'

'You should return to British Guiana, young man. Tell my son-in-law that his neglect is largely responsible for this situation.' Lady Carstairs swept out of the house.

Flinders closed the door. 'That went well,' he said drily. 'I didn't hear all of it, but I gather you and Amethyst are supposed to find somewhere else to live.'

'Nellie, too.' Kitty shook her head. 'I suppose I should have seen that coming, Flinders. My grandmother has never liked me – or Amethyst, come to that. Ivory is everything that Grandmama thinks a young lady should be, but Amy and I are the misfits.'

'Perhaps she will change her mind when she has had time to think about the situation. Surely, she cannot really intend you both to be left homeless?'

'She might decide to take Amy into her home so that she can save her soul, but I am obviously past redemption.'

'What did you do to earn such censure, Kitty?' Flinders' lips twitched, and his eyes twinkled irrepressibly. 'I cannot imagine you as a rebel.'

Kitty shrugged. 'Everyone in the family kowtows

to her. I've never openly disobeyed her but maybe I'm not very good at hiding my true feelings.'

Flinders opened his mouth as if to reply but was interrupted by a knock on the front door.

'Perhaps she's changed her mind, Kitty.' He opened the door and Amethyst breezed in on a gust of cold air.

'Was that Grandmama's carriage I saw tooling away at a fast rate?'

'Yes, it was,' Kitty said shortly. 'Where have you been, Amy?'

'You know where I went.' Amethyst shrugged off her cape and untied her bonnet. 'I was with Sebastian and Laurence. We went to Verrey's for luncheon and then on to the Zoological Gardens, but it was too chilly to stay long, so Sebastian brought me home.' Amethyst looked from one to the other. 'Why? What's wrong?'

'Amy, you know you should not go anywhere without a chaperone, especially with two gentlemen who are notorious rakes.' Kitty hesitated. She knew she should tell Amethyst what had just occurred, but her sister was so radiantly happy that it would be like plucking the wings from a beautiful butterfly.

'You worry too much,' Amethyst said gaily. 'Where is Ivory? I want to tell her about the fashionable ladies I saw at Verrey's. Their gowns and hats must have cost a fortune, let alone their gloves and reticules, all matching. How I wish I could dress like that.'

'Ivory is in the morning room with Mama.' Kitty caught Amethyst by the hand as she was about to walk past. 'I should warn you that there's been a bit of an upset since this morning.'

Amethyst laughed. 'It can't be all that bad. I'll go and cheer them up.' She danced off in the direction of the morning room.

'What can anyone do with her?' Kitty said, sighing. 'I could probably find a room to rent in a boarding house and pay for it from my paintings, but I can't support Amy and her grand ideas.'

Flinders frowned. 'I won't hear of that, Kitty. Your pa would never forgive me if I allowed that to happen.'

Kitty stared at him in surprise. 'It's not your problem, Flinders. You'll return to British Guiana soon. We have to keep going until Papa is fit and well again.'

'It is my concern, if you put it that way. I, too, am suddenly homeless – in theory, anyway – but I can go to Little Foxbury.' Flinders paused, frowning thoughtfully. 'You could come with me, and Amy, too.'

'I don't think your mama and grandmama would be very pleased to have two strangers foisted on them, Flinders. It's a kind thought but not very practical.'

'I meant it, Kitty.' Flinders moved closer, taking her hand in his. 'My mother is the most generous person I know, and she would love you. My grandmother is always busy, but she will be equally welcoming. Amy and Nellie could accompany you if they so wished.'

'I don't know, Flinders. It's tempting but it would be asking too much of your mama and grandmama.'

'I told you that my family were not like other families, Kitty. But both Mama and Grandmama are hospitable people and would never allow someone like you to be without a roof over your head. Besides which, Mill House is large enough to house everyone comfortably.'

Despite her reservations, Kitty was intrigued. 'Mill House? What sort of mill, Flinders?'

'It's a windmill. Grandmama is a miller. She took over the work when Grandpa died four years ago.'

'She works the mill?' Kitty stared at him in disbelief. 'I mean, she must be getting on in years and I imagine it must be very hard work physically.'

Flinders laughed. 'Don't let my grandmother hear you say things like that. She might not be in the first flush of youth, but she is quite remarkable. She runs the mill as if she was born to it.'

'Even so, to foist three strangers onto your family is a huge imposition, Flinders. Not only that, but I imagine Amethyst will have something to say about being sent to the country to live.'

'There's only one way to find out, Kitty. I'll be in my room, packing, if you need me.' Flinders headed for the stairs. 'You would have all the time in the world to paint beautiful rural scenes or seascapes at Foxbury Mill.'

* * *

Kitty had little alternative other than to return to the morning room and face her mother and sisters. Amethyst was in the middle of describing some of the fashionable and no doubt very expensive outfits she had seen that day. Ivory seemed to have lost the power of speech and their mother was staring into space, occasionally mopping her eyes with her handkerchief.

'So, you haven't yet told Amethyst.' Kitty looked from one to the other.

Ivory shook her head. 'She's done nothing but chatter on about stupid fashions. I can't get a word in edgeways.'

Amethyst came to a halt. 'What's the matter? Why are you all so glum?'

Isabella rose to her feet, clutching her hands to her breast. 'I'm going to my room. Kitty, you'd better tell your sister what happened. I don't trust myself to speak.' She hurried from the room, closing the door behind her.

'Well, that's a surprise. I thought I was going to suffer a lecture. Did you tell Mama that I've been seeing Sebastian?' Amethyst giggled excitedly. 'Perhaps she's waiting for me to announce our engagement.'

'Grandmama was right in one thing,' Kitty said drily. 'You are a silly girl, Amy. You think only of yourself.'

Amethyst pouted as she flounced down on the nearest chair. 'I might have known it would be left to you to scold me, Kitty.'

'I'd better make sure that Mama is all right.' Ivory stood up and walked quickly to the door. 'You can tell her what's happened, Kitty. That is, if she can be quiet for long enough to listen.'

'Why is it always left to me?' Kitty said as the door closed on Ivory. She turned to Amethyst with an exasperated sigh. 'Sit down, be quiet and listen to what I have to tell you.'

Amethyst's smile froze. 'What has happened? Why are you looking so serious?'

'You do remember that we are losing the house, don't you?'

'Yes, of course. I'm not stupid, Kitty. I suppose we will have to stay with Grandmama at Bridlebank, unless of course Sebastian proposes before then.'

Kitty stifled the desire to shake some sense into her sister. She took a deep breath.

'Grandmama doesn't want you or me, Amy. That's the plain truth. She's asked Mama and Ivory to stay with her, but we have to find somewhere else.'

Amethyst smiled delightedly. 'But that's wonderful news. I can stay with Sebastian. He has a huge house in town as well as a mansion in the country. I expect he could find room for you, too.'

'You know that is not going to happen, Amy. It's just your vivid imagination.'

'Sebastian will take care of me,' Amethyst said firmly. 'Perhaps he will rent rooms for me in one of the smart squares, but if that happens I'm afraid you will have to find someone else to take you in.'

Kitty sighed. 'You really are a selfish, spoilt brat, Amethyst Harte. You only ever think about yourself.'

'That's not true. If Sebastian looks after me then you do not have to worry. I'm sure we could find someone who would take care of you.' Amethyst wagged her finger at Kitty. 'What about the handsome police sergeant? He took a liking to you, Kitty. You would only have to appeal to his better nature, and I'll wager he would produce an engagement ring out of his top hat.'

Kitty summoned up all her patience. 'Listen to me, Amy. On Friday you and I and possibly Nellie too, are going to travel by train to a village in rural Essex where Flinders' mother and grandmother live in Little Foxbury, at Mill House. If we are lucky, they will invite us to stay until Pa is well enough to return home.'

'What? A mill house? Have you lost your mind, Kitty? I would die rather than live in the country.'

'I'm sorry, but that's the way it is, Amy. But please don't die. We can't afford a funeral, and they would have to bury you in a pauper's grave.' Kitty left Amethyst to mull this over while she went downstairs to the kitchen to speak to Nellie.

'What now?' Nellie demanded, folding her arms across her thin chest. 'Has the old witch gone?'

'I need to talk to you, Nellie,' Kitty said seriously.

'Grandmama has agreed to have Mama and Ivory to stay at Bridlebank, but we have to find somewhere else to live.'

'I never expected her to welcome me into her house, but what about you and Miss Amethyst? Surely her ladyship would not see you two cast out onto the streets?'

'I don't think she cares,' Kitty said wearily. 'I tried to persuade her to have Amy to stay with her, but she would have none of it.'

'I imagine Miss Amethyst would have little difficulty in finding a gentleman to offer her protection, but that must be avoided at all costs.'

'My thoughts exactly. In fact, Flinders has invited us to stay with his mother and grandmother in Essex, and that includes you, Nellie.' Kitty looked at her hopefully. 'You will consider it, won't you?'

'Are you going to accept his offer?' Nellie gave her a searching look.

'I don't see that there is any alternative. Flinders is certain that we will be welcome, but it will only be temporary. We need you, Nellie. I don't think I can handle Amy without you.' Kitty eyed her speculatively. The latter was not strictly true, but she knew it would influence Nellie when she made her decision.

'I'd have to think about it, Miss Kitty.'

'Of course. I understand. But we only have tomorrow. We must be ready to leave on Friday.' Kitty knew better than to labour the point and she returned to the morning room, leaving Nellie to think about Flinders' offer.

Amethyst was seated primly on an upright chair, her hands folded demurely in her lap. Kitty knew this was not a good sign.

'I'm not coming with you,' Amethyst said bluntly.

'You have very little choice, Amy.' Kitty sank down on the sofa. She was already feeling as if she had been on a battlefield and was close to exhaustion.

'Sebastian will take care of me. I'll see him tomorrow morning and I know what he will say.'

'You are underage, Amy. You cannot do anything unless Mama agrees.'

'She seems to be happy to abandon me,' Amethyst said sulkily. 'She is obviously happy to go and live at Bridlebank without you and me.'

'I don't think that's true. She was very upset, but you know what Grandmama Carstairs is like when she gets a bee in her bonnet.'

Amethyst pulled a face. 'I'm glad that the old horror doesn't want me. I think I would prefer rural Essex to the misery of living with Grandmama.' She stood up with a purposeful twitch of her shoulders. 'I am going to write a note to Sebastian and send it by messenger to Grosvenor Square. He will know what to do.'

'I suggest you sleep on it, Amy. Do you really want to plead with a man to make an honest woman of you? Or do you want to live like one of those fallen women who put themselves at the mercy of a man who could throw them out when they became tired of them?'

'That sounds horrible. Sebastian isn't like that.'

'There's only one way to find out,' Kitty said sharply. 'And then it will be too late.'

Amethyst's eyes filled with tears and her lips trembled. 'You're being mean to me, Kitty.'

'No, I am being honest, Amy. If you want to risk everything for a mere dalliance then I can't stop you.'

'Sebastian loves me; he says so constantly.'

'I wonder how many other young ladies he has said that to. He is a lothario, and he seeks out naïve young women like you in the Bazaar, as do Carnaby and other bored gentlemen of leisure. It appeals to their hunting instincts, and girls like you are the trophy.' Kitty looked around at the sound of the door opening and met Flinders' concerned gaze.

'Sergeant Barton wants to see you, Kitty. Is this a bad time?'

'No, I think I've said everything I can to persuade Amy to come with us on Friday. Perhaps you will have more luck.'

He smiled. 'I'll try.'

Kitty laid her hand on Amethyst's shoulder. 'Listen to Flinders, Amy. I'll see what the sergeant wants and then I'll be back.' Kitty hurried from the room to where Barton was waiting in the hall.

He met her with a smile. 'Good afternoon, Miss Harte. I hope I haven't come at a bad time.'

'I would ask you into the morning room, but my sister is a little upset. We have to move out on Friday, unless of course you have persuaded Mr Dagg to return our money or the silver.'

Barton clutched his top hat in his hands, his smile fading. 'I'm sorry. I wish I had better tidings for you, but the Daggs refuse to cooperate, and the magistrate committed them both to prison for another crime. This isn't the first time they have deceived members of the public.'

'I thought it was too much to hope for. Thank you for taking the trouble to come here in person, Sergeant.'

'Where will you go? I mean, should your property turn up I need to be able to contact you.' Barton took a notebook and pencil from his uniform pocket.

'Yes, of course. My mother and elder sister will be living temporarily with Lady Carstairs at Bridlebank, Highgate.'

'You are not going with them?' Barton stared at her with a look of genuine concern.

'My younger sister and I have been invited to stay with the family of our father's colleague in Little Foxbury.'

'I know the village. It's close to my family home near Manningtree.' Barton noted it down on his pad. 'May I have the address, just in case I cannot contact Mrs Harte?'

'It's Mill House, Little Foxbury.' Flinders emerged

from the morning room and came to stand beside Kitty. 'My grandmother, Adeline Saunders, is the local miller.'

Barton looked up, pencil poised. 'Your grandmother is the miller?'

'She took over when my grandfather passed away,' Flinders said calmly. 'She is a very capable woman.'

Barton scribbled something on his notepad. 'Thank you. I doubt if it will be necessary to contact you, Miss Harte, but it's best to be prepared for anything, as I have learned during my time in the Force.'

'Perhaps if you do get news, it would be best if you did get in touch with me, Sergeant,' Kitty said after a moment's thought. 'My mother is very delicate and easily upset, so I am the obvious one you should notify.'

'Of course, Miss Harte.' Barton tucked his pad and pencil back in his pocket. 'You never know, some of your silver might turn up in an auction room or one of the street markets. I'm sorry I cannot do more.' He hesitated, as if reluctant to leave.

'I'm truly grateful for your efforts on our behalf,' Kitty said, smiling.

'It's my job, Miss Harte. Anyway, I won't take up any more of your time. Good day to you both.' Barton let himself out of the house, closing the door behind him.

'I'm sorry, Kitty,' Flinders said softly. 'But it was

a slim hope that you might get anything back from Dagg.'

She nodded. 'I wasn't expecting a miracle, but at least I have some money now I've finished Frances Westbrook's portrait.'

Flinders smiled. 'You have a real talent, Kitty.'

'I can catch a likeness, but I don't purport to be an artist, Flinders. I haven't had any training and am never likely to do so.'

'I don't think that matters too much. People love what you do. Isn't that enough?'

'It is when they pay for my work,' Kitty said with a wry smile. 'That is very satisfying. Perhaps I can still sell some paintings in Little Foxbury, or maybe I could work in the mill with your grandmother. If a lady of advanced years can be a miller, then so can I.'

'I admire your spirit, Kitty. I always have, but never more so than now.' Flinders leaned over and kissed her gently on the cheek. 'And I think I have managed to convince Amy to accompany us to Essex on Friday.'

Kitty felt the blood rush to her cheeks. The embrace had been passionless and yet intensely personal, a seemingly casual gesture that took friendship to a more intimate level.

'Thank you, Flinders. Now perhaps you would like to exercise your persuasive powers on Nellie. She is very independent, not to say proud.'

'I'll tell her that I will fade away without her

cooking skills. My mother is a wonderful woman, but she is a culinary disaster and Mrs Potter, our cook-housekeeper, is getting on in years. I think we need Nellie more than she needs us.'

Kitty laughed, all traces of embarrassment gone. 'If you explain all that to her, she can't refuse your offer.'

'Don't worry, Kitty. All this seems dreadful now, but it will probably work out for the best. At least I know that you will be well looked after when I have to return to British Guiana, and hopefully when I do there will be some better news about your papa.'

'We want him to come home, of course, but I can't help worrying about the future, Flinders. What will I and my family do if Papa is too crippled to work again?'

'You mustn't think like that,' Flinders said gently. 'But if that should be the case, I'm sure that your father could find employment as a teacher of his chosen subject, or maybe he could write a book about all the expeditions in which he's taken part.' He took Kitty's hands in his and held them in a firm grasp. 'You've kept your family going all this time. Don't give up now.'

'I'm not usually a defeatist. I think it's the thought of my family being split up that is so upsetting. But you're right. I won't give up until we're back together and we have a home again.'

Chapter Ten

Isabella accepted Kitty's decision to stay with Flinders' family in Essex for the foreseeable future, and although she protested that rural life would be quite unsuitable for Amethyst, there was nothing she could do other than to accept the fact. Amethyst herself was convinced that Sebastian would save her from such an ignominious fate, and next morning she insisted on going to the Bazaar to wait for him. It did not seem to occur to her that these meetings were clandestine or that a man with honourable intentions would never stoop to compromise her reputation. Kitty knew that to Amethyst all the secrecy surrounding her relationship with Sebastian Marriner made it even more romantic. However, there was no time to be lost, and Kitty, Ivory and Nellie set about packing everything that they would either take with them or would put into storage. Isabella made a feeble attempt to sort out her own belongings but in the end it fell to Nellie to make certain that her mistress had everything she might need for a sojourn at Bridlebank.

By mid-afternoon they had all done as much as they could and Kitty changed into a blue linsey-woolsey afternoon gown with a white lace collar, which she deemed suitable for a visit to Duke Street. Frances Westbrook was always so smartly dressed that it would be an insult to turn up for afternoon tea in the same clothes that Kitty had been wearing that morning. Ivory opted to accompany her, and she also changed, choosing a chestnut-brown woollen gown that flattered her peaches-and-cream complexion and made her brown eyes appear even more lustrous. Kitty suspected that this amount of preparation was more for Charles Westbrook's benefit than his sister's, but she said nothing. Ivory was already upset at the prospect of weeks, or even months, staying at Bridlebank, and Kitty did not wish to make things worse.

When they arrived at the town house in Duke Street they were admitted by a stern-faced butler. Kitty and Ivory took off their gloves and mantles and gave them to a maid before following another parlour maid upstairs to the first-floor drawing room.

Frances rose to her feet as they entered and came towards them, smiling and her arms outstretched.

'How kind of you both to come. I can't wait to see my portrait again.'

Kitty handed her the painting wrapped in brown paper. 'I hope you are happy with it, Frances.'

'Of course. There is no doubt about that. Do take a seat and I'll ring for tea.' Frances moved to the fireplace and tugged at an embroidered bellpull, before unwrapping the portrait. She gazed at it, smiling. 'It is very good, Kitty. You should set yourself up as a portrait artist.'

'We have to leave town for a while, Frances.' Kitty took a seat in a velvet upholstered armchair. 'I don't imagine I will be doing a great deal of painting.'

'What a shame.' Frances glanced at Ivory, who chose the sofa, where she arranged her skirts neatly around her. 'Are you going away, too, Ivory?'

'It's a little complicated,' Ivory said carefully. 'Mama and I are going to live with Grandmama Carstairs for the time being.'

'And your wayward little sister?' Frances's grey eyes sparkled with curiosity. 'I hear that Amethyst has fallen into the clutches of Sebastian Marriner.'

'He has convinced her that his intentions are honourable.' Kitty could see no point in prevaricating. It must be well known in society that Marriner had claimed another innocent victim.

'I am sorry,' Frances said earnestly. 'Sebastian has no conscience. All he thinks about is having a good time and doing exactly as he pleases.' She looked up as the door opened and her brother strode into the room followed by two parlour maids carrying laden trays, which they placed on a tea table on the far side of the room.

'Good afternoon, ladies,' Charles said, bowing to Ivory and then to Kitty. 'I've come to view the portrait properly, Kitty.' Charles took the painting from Frances and studied it. 'Yes, it's excellent. Thank you, Kitty.'

'The girls are going away, Charles,' Frances said casually. 'They are leaving town.'

Charles turned to Ivory. 'Really? This is rather sudden. I trust that your father's health has not deteriorated further?'

'No, sir. It's a matter of necessity. Our family finances have suffered due to Papa's incapacity. Mama and I will be residing at Bridlebank.'

Charles raised his eyebrows in surprise. 'But what about you, Kitty? Are you staying on at the Bazaar?'

'No, sir. Amy and I have been invited to stay with Mr Riley's family in Little Foxbury.'

'Little Foxbury?' Frances leaned forward, her brow creased. 'Isn't that close to Westbrook Park, Charles? I seem to remember riding through that village.'

'Yes, I believe so.' Charles nodded. 'That's a coincidence. Who knows, we might even see you there when we go to our country estate at the end of the Season, or sooner if I have my way.'

'Charles is not one for balls and soirées in London,' Frances said, with a wry smile. 'Whereas I am the exact opposite. I love being in London and enjoying everything that society has to offer. I find the countryside quite dull, and I have no interest in hunting or other tedious country pursuits. Anyway, enough of that. You came to have tea. Would you like to sit at the table?' Frances rose to her feet without waiting for an answer. 'Are you going to join us, Charles?'

An hour later Kitty and Ivory were seated in a hansom cab on the way home to Soho Square.

'I think he likes you, Ivory,' Kitty said seriously. 'Charles Westbrook is not the sort of man who enjoys taking tea with ladies, of that I'm certain, but he sat with us the whole time.'

'He was just being sociable.' Ivory turned her head away. 'He's never shown much interest in me before.'

'Maybe he realises that he's lost his chance with you as we're leaving town.'

'Don't be silly, Kitty. He probably had nothing else to do and he was just whiling away the time. He paid you for the painting, didn't he?'

'Yes, he did. I think he wanted to make a good impression on you. He's a handsome man and very wealthy. You ought to cultivate him, Ivory.'

'Stop it. You sound like Mama. Charles might have been in a good mood today, but I've seen him when he can hardly be bothered to be polite. I don't believe that he is interested in me at all.'

'But how do you feel? You can't keep anything from me, Ivory. I know you too well.'

'It really doesn't matter how I feel because I'm going to be incarcerated in Bridlebank for the next goodness knows how long. By the time I am free he will have found some other female, probably an heiress who rides to hounds and loves dogs, who will be far more suitable than I'll ever be.'

'You love horses and dogs,' Kitty said hotly. 'And he's so rich he doesn't need someone to bring more money into the Westbrook family.'

'I don't want to talk about it, and anyway we're home. Please forget about the Westbrooks. I doubt if I'll ever set eyes on either of them again.'

Kitty took the money from her reticule and handed it to the cabby as she alighted outside the house. Flinders was standing in the doorway, and he greeted them both with a wide smile.

'How did it go in Duke Street?'

'Very well,' Kitty said, smiling. 'Charles actually sat down to tea with us, didn't he, Ivory?'

'Yes, he did, but please don't keep on about it, Kitty. I expect he was just hungry. Anyway, I'm going to check on Mama.' Ivory brushed past them both and entered the house.

'Has someone said something to upset her?' Flinders asked, frowning.

'No, she's just concerned about the move, as we all are, Flinders.' Kitty eyed him curiously. 'Why were you waiting on the doorstep?'

'I'd only just arrived myself. I've ordered a carter to take all our belongings to Mill House tomorrow morning. He'll be here before the Pickford's van comes to take the main part of the furniture and goods for storage.' Flinders followed her into the entrance hall. 'I'm so sorry you're having to suffer all this, Kitty. Your pa will be very distressed when he learns about it.'

'I don't think you ought to tell him,' Kitty said seriously. 'At least keep the details from him until he's back on his feet. There's nothing he can do, and we are managing. We will be all right, and when he comes home, we can start again.'

'You're very plucky. He will be proud of you all, but particularly you, Kitty.'

Kitty laughed. 'Why me? We're all doing our bit.' She smiled and pulled a face. 'Well, maybe not Amy, but that's to be expected. I hope we'll be able to cure her of her obsession with Marriner when we're away from London.'

'We'll do our best. By the way,' Flinders added as Kitty started to walk towards the stairs. 'I think I've persuaded Nellie to come with us to Little Foxbury.'

Kitty stopped with her hand on the banister rail. 'How did you manage that? I couldn't get anything definite out of her last evening.'

'I told her that I would fade away if I had to eat Mrs Potter's food for however long I have at home. I said that perhaps she could show Mrs P how things should be done. She seemed quite keen on the idea.'

'Nellie loves to be in charge. That would definitely appeal to her. You are very clever, Flinders.'

'Not really, but I have had to stand up to two powerful ladies in my early years. My mother and grandmother would make the Iron Duke tremble if they got together against him.'

'I can't wait to meet them. But now I must finish packing the things I want to take with me tomorrow. What time did you say the carter was coming?'

'At eight o'clock, but I'll be up long before that. I need to make sure I pack all my books and papers so that I can work at home.'

Kitty acknowledged him with a nod before ascending the stairs to her room. There was really very little to be done as she had carefully selected and packed what she might need, although she had to think ahead for the changing seasons. Spring would be upon them in a few weeks, and she would need to add lighter garments. The things that were most important to her were her art materials, easel and paint box. Perhaps she might get a chance to do some sketching out of doors. The village, according to Flinders, was on the coast. It would be wonderful to be near the sea and breathe the clean, salt-laden air. In an odd way Kitty realised that she was looking forward to the change in surroundings and meeting different people. Her main problem from now on was Amethyst and how she would react to their change in circumstances.

Kitty finished her packing and laid out her travelling costume ready for an early start next morning. There was nothing more she could accomplish for herself, and she went to Ivory's room to see if there was anything she could do to help her sister. However, Ivory, with her usual calm and efficiency, had everything in hand.

'I'm going to finish sorting out Mama's belongings,' Ivory said solemnly. 'I've done most of it with Nellie's help, but there are bound to be things we've missed.'

'I'll check Amy's room. I went over what she should and should not take to Little Foxbury, but I doubt if she paid much attention.' Kitty stepped out onto the landing. 'Oh, no! That sounds like Amy crying her eyes out.' She exchanged worried glances with Ivory. 'You know what that means.'

Ivory sighed. 'Marriner did not come up to scratch. Not that I ever thought he would. I'd better have a word with her.'

Kitty laid a restraining hand on Ivory's arm. 'No, you look after Mama. I'll sort Amy out. After all, I'll have to put up with her tantrums while we're in Essex, so I'd better start now.'

'I wish you well with that.' Ivory headed off in the

direction of Isabella's room, leaving Kitty to knock on Amethyst's door.

When there was no answer apart from an even louder burst of sobbing, Kitty opened the door. She found her sister lying on her bed, her face buried in the pillows.

'What's the matter, Amy?' Kitty went to sit on the edge of the bed. 'Come on, it can't be as bad as all that.'

'It's worse.' Amethyst raised herself on her elbow, her face streaked with tears. 'He doesn't care about me, Kitty.'

Kitty reached over and brushed her sister's tumbled dark curls back from her forehead. 'What happened today?'

'We met as usual and Carnaby was there, too. We went out to luncheon and then Sebastian wanted to go to Tattersalls to purchase a horse. I didn't want to go to a boring auction, and I thought he would change his mind.' Amethyst sniffed and reached under her pillow for a rather damp handkerchief. She blew her nose.

'What did you do then?' Kitty could imagine the scene but she did not want to pre-empt Amethyst's dramatic narrative.

'He said I could find my own way home then, but we were in Hyde Park, and I didn't have any money in my reticule. It's a long walk to Soho Square.'

'He could have put you in a cab and paid your fare.'

'But he didn't, Kitty.' Fresh tears spilled from

Amethyst's eyes. 'Carnaby thought it hilarious and then I told Sebastian that I was going away, and he would be sorry.'

Kitty sighed. 'Of course you did. I don't suppose that went down too well.'

'He laughed and I told him I never want to see him again.' Amethyst buried her face in her hands. 'I walked home and my feet are sore.' Tears seeped out from between her fingers.

'He's not worth it, Amy.' Kitty wrapped her arms around her sister and held her while she sobbed. 'He will get a shock when he discovers that you really have gone away. You're not a rich man's plaything, Amy. You deserve better.'

Amy gulped and swallowed, moving away from Kitty with an attempt at a smile. 'You're right. I do deserve much more. I will come with you to the wilds of Essex tomorrow. I promise I won't complain.'

Kitty laughed. 'I won't hold you to that, Amy. You always grumble at everything, but I will be patient.'

'You are not always patient,' Amethyst said, mopping her eyes. 'We will do well together. I hope Flinders' family have a lovely big country house by the sea. That would be perfect.'

Kitty had a sudden vision of a windmill and a modest mill house. She decided that this was not the right time to tell Amy the truth.

* * *

The parting from Ivory and their mother next day was painful. Kitty was not normally overemotional, but it was the first time their small family had been split up so brutally, and even she shed a few tears as Grandmama Carstairs' carriage drove off, followed by a smaller vehicle carrying two trunks and an assortment of carpet bags and valises, plus a pile of hat boxes. Even Nellie had little to say, having organised everything that the carter had collected earlier, and made sure that everyone had eaten a good breakfast, including the carter. Eventually he had set off for the Essex coast, his cart packed with their cases and a small chest containing all Kitty's art materials.

Kitty, Amethyst and Flinders had to wait in Soho Square until the Pickford's van had collected the furniture and tea chests filled with all the things they used in their day-to-day lives. Kitty wondered how long it would be before they found a new and more permanent home and had all their belongings restored to them. The future looked very uncertain, but she had to maintain a brave face, if only to keep Amethyst from breaking down in tears yet again. Flinders had business at the Geological Society headquarters earlier that morning, but he returned just as the Pickford's van drew up outside the house in Soho Square. After that it was just a matter of time before everything was safely stowed away and finally driven off to the storage unit. Then the journey to Essex began with a cab ride to Bishopsgate station.

They caught the train to Colchester, where they changed to a different line, arriving at Manningtree station mid-afternoon. Amethyst slept for the last part of the journey, and she awakened bleary-eyed and complaining, which Kitty took as a good sign. It was only when Amy was quiet and submissive that there was any need to worry about her. Nellie had also fallen asleep with her chin on her chest, snoring loudly, but she awakened as the train came to a halt.

Flinders had been the ideal companion for Kitty during the long train journey. This, he said, was his part of the country and he regaled Kitty with an interesting commentary, including the history of the area as they passed through the rural towns and villages. He also seemed to know the staff when they arrived at Little Foxbury railway station and, having surrendered their tickets, they left the main concourse, stepping out into pale wintry sunshine. They were met by a tall, handsome woman, whose likeness to Flinders was so strong that Kitty knew instantly this must be his mother. Edith Riley wore a bowler hat with her light brown hair confined to a bun, and her statuesque figure was emphasised by a tight-fitting black riding jacket over a skirt that barely came to the ankles of her riding boots. She climbed down from the driving seat of a horse-drawn shooting brake, handing the reins to a porter, who hurried to assist her.

'Ma, you received my note.' Flinders went to greet her, holding out his hand, which his mother ignored.

'The train was late, Flinders. I've been waiting for nearly an hour,' she said abruptly, waving away his attempt to touch her. 'So, these are the two young ladies you mentioned, and their maid?'

'I'm their housekeeper, ma'am,' Nellie said crossly. 'I ain't no maid. My name is Nellie Pickering.'

'Very well, Pickering. We have room enough for you, but I will expect you to earn your keep.' Edith met Nellie's belligerent look with a straight gaze that seem to rob Nellie of the power of speech.

Kitty held her breath, hoping that this was not the start of a difficult relationship, but then she realised that she was next in line for Edith Riley's piercing gaze.

'Aren't you going to introduce us, Flinders?' Edith said sharply. 'Where are your manners?'

Flinders turned to Kitty with a smile. 'Mother, may I introduce Miss Kitty Harte and her sister, Miss Amethyst Harte?'

'Yes, well. How do you do, young ladies? Now, if you please, hurry up and climb into the brake. I have work to do at home.' Edith turned away and walked briskly to the brake where she climbed nimbly onto the driver's seat and took the reins from the porter with a nod of thanks.

Flinders helped Kitty onto the vehicle and then Amethyst, throwing their hand baggage in after them. Nellie declined his assistance and somehow managed to heave herself onto the brake, while Flinders joined his mother on the driver's seat. Edith seized the carriage whip and cracked it over the animal's head. The old horse moved forward with a start as if it had been snoozing quietly in the pale sunshine. Kitty clung to the side of the brake as it jerked into motion, bumping over the cobblestones as they left the station and turned onto the main road. There was very little traffic, just a couple of farm carts and a few pedestrians, all of whom tipped their caps to Mrs Riley and she acknowledged them with a gracious inclination of her head. As they drove through the narrow country lanes Kitty was able to enjoy the fresh, clean air, smelling pleasantly of damp earth with the tang of salt from the tidal reaches of the River Stour. There seemed to be acres of sky above the flat landscape, and the fields behind the neat hedgerows were ploughed in rigid lines, waiting for the green shoots to show their heads. Brave clumps of primroses made sunny patches on the side of the road, the harbingers of spring. Kitty was quite enchanted with everything, but one look at Amethyst and she knew her sister was not so thrilled by her new surroundings.

Edith drove with the confidence and dexterity of someone used to handling the reins. Eventually they reached the village, where the horizon was dominated by a white painted windmill with four sails catching the wind from the North Sea. A scattering of houses and cottages had been built around a Norman church and a village green complete with duck pond.

On the far side, near to the mill but without danger of taking its wind, was Mill House and it was here that Edith drew the old horse to a halt. She leaped down to the ground and held the reins.

'Get them into the house, Flinders. I'll take Button to the stables and then I'll join you.' Edith dismissed him with a peremptory wave of her gloved hand.

Flinders climbed down to open the door at the back of the brake, and he proffered his hand to Nellie, who accepted this time. He swung Amethyst to the ground before lifting Kitty and holding her a little longer than was necessary so that her feet dangled above the gravel.

'Thank you, Flinders,' she said breathlessly. 'I can stand on my own now.'

He pulled a face. 'Sorry. I was rather enjoying holding you, Kitty.'

She eyed him warily. 'I'm perfectly capable of taking care of myself, Flinders, but thank you, anyway.' She shook out her skirts. 'So, this is Mill House. It's not as close to the mill as I imagined.'

'It was all built this way for a reason. I don't pretend to be an expert but I dare say Grandmama will be able to explain.'

Amethyst shuffled her feet. 'Are we going to stand outside, or might we go indoors? I'm cold and tired and I would love a cup of tea.'

'I hope the cook here knows how to make a brew,' Nellie said darkly. 'It don't look like a very grand house. We've come down in the world, in my opinion.'

Kitty sent her a warning look. 'Don't let Mrs Riley hear you say things like that. We should be grateful to her for taking us in. She's coming now, so remember what I said.'

Edith walked towards them with a measured tread. 'Why are you still standing outside? Follow me, if you please.'

Nellie tossed her head, but she followed Kitty, Amethyst and Edith Riley into the house without saying another word.

The entrance hall was long and narrow with a staircase on the right. As Kitty followed their hostess, she was confused by the number of rooms opening off the main corridor, which led to a large, old-fashioned kitchen. The heat from the range enveloped them as they entered, but the acrid smell of burning caught Kitty in the back of her throat, making her cough.

A short, plump woman was stamping out the flames on a kitchen cloth, covering the flagstones with ash.

'What have you done this time, Potter?' Edith demanded angrily. 'How many times have I told you not to hang cloths on the brass rail when you're cooking?'

'Too many, ma'am. I forget.' Mrs Potter bent down to pick up what remained of the charred material.

Nellie bustled forward. ‘Let me help, dear. You’ll burn your fingers if you’re not careful.’

‘Who are you?’ Mrs Potter demanded anxiously. ‘I hope you haven’t hired a replacement for me, Mrs Riley. I will try to do better.’

‘This person is a visitor,’ Edith said tersely. ‘But you’ve had plenty of warnings, Mrs Potter. Our paying guests have been complaining about the food. I only keep you on because my late husband was fond of you. However, I am not so sentimental. Take heed of the fact.’ She turned to Kitty. ‘You seem to be the most sensible person here, Miss Harte. Flinders will take your luggage to your rooms. I have put you next to your sister on the second floor, front rooms. Your servant will find space on the top floor. Gertie will show her where to go and sort out some bedding for her.’ Without pausing for breath Edith turned back to Mrs Potter. ‘Where is that dratted girl? If she’s in the stable flirting with Jem Jobson I will personally strangle her.’

‘They’re handfasted, ma’am,’ Mrs Potter said nervously.

‘Handfasted!’ Edith curled her lip. ‘Paganism has no place in my world. They can stop that nonsense, or I will sack the pair of them.’

Flinders walked into the room. ‘Don’t be hard on Gertie, Mother. She’s worked for you since she was a child of ten and has always been a good help.’

‘Much you know about it, Flinders. You’ve been away collecting samples of ore and minerals for months on end. You don't know how difficult it is to run a guest house for commercial travellers.'

'Of course not, but you are the most capable woman I have ever met.' Flinders crossed the floor to give her a hug, from which she wriggled free.

'None of your soft soap, my son. Take the young ladies up to the second floor. I've had the two best rooms made ready for them. I keep the gentlemen guests to the first floor only. We don't want them wandering around the house at night and going into the wrong room.'

Amethyst had been silently clinging to Kitty's hand, but she tightened her grip. 'Oh, no! That won't happen, will it, Mrs Riley?'

'Of course not, you silly girl. It was just a figure of speech. Now go upstairs with Flinders. My gentlemen dine at six, and we have our meal later. There are only two in tonight, as well as old Mr Beadle, but he doesn't count. Anyway, it won't take long to settle them.'

Flinders frowned. 'I hate to see you working so hard, Mother. One day I hope to earn enough to allow you to live a quiet life, which you so richly deserve.'

'Nonsense, my boy. I enjoy meeting people and keeping busy. I was not born to be a lady of leisure, so don't worry about me. Now, do as I ask, please, Flinders. Look after the young ladies.'

'Yes, Mother.' Flinders beckoned to Kitty and Amethyst. 'Follow me.'

Chapter Eleven

Mill House, as Kitty soon discovered, must have been designed for a large family, although they would have needed a good map in order to find their way around. The narrow passageways seemed to lead off in all directions, some of them dead ends. There appeared to be dozens of rooms, although this, Kitty decided, was an illusion. It was just the rather haphazard design of the building, or rather the lack of it. Perhaps the builder had made up the layout as he went along, or maybe the architect had been bored and had doodled the plans at random. Whatever the answer, she and Amethyst definitely had two of the best bedchambers in the house. They were not large, but the many-paned windows let in the light, and from Kitty's room she had a good view of the windmill and the village at the bottom of the hill.

Amethyst barged in and flopped down on the bed. 'This is such a strange place, Kitty. I don't know if I like Mrs Riley. She's very forthright.'

'It's probably just her way,' Kitty said hopefully. 'We need to be very tactful so that we don't offend her or outstay our welcome because we have nowhere else to go.'

'What will we do for the next few months? Or at least what shall I do? You can get your paints out and make pretty pictures. I will have nothing to occupy me.'

'I'm sure we will find something for you to do. For one thing, we could get Flinders to take us to the mill and introduce us to his grandmother.'

Amethyst pulled a face. 'If she is anything like her daughter, I will be very afraid.'

'Yes, I grant you that Mrs Riley is rather outspoken, but she is used to being in business and I dare say she has had to deal with difficult people.' Kitty eyed Amethyst with some trepidation. She had to agree with her, but she did not want to dash all her sister's hopes before they had even spent one night at the Mill House. 'Flinders' grandmother must be a very resourceful lady if she runs the mill on her own. I am looking forward to meeting her,' she added hastily.

Amethyst sighed. 'I wonder what Sebastian is doing now. Do you think he might come looking for me, Kitty?'

'I couldn't say,' Kitty said evasively, although

she was quite sure that Sebastian would have set his sights on some other pretty young woman by now. 'But you never know, Amy. You will just have to wait and see.'

Amethyst stood up and walked over to the window. 'It's getting dark already. There are no streetlights, Kitty. It must be quite frightening here in the dead of night.'

'Maybe there will be a full moon and lots of stars. It's all going to be very strange at first because we are townspeople. We've never lived in the country before, but I am sure we will get used to it.'

'You might, but I don't think I ever will. I miss the square and the gardens and most of all the Bazaar, and we've only been away for half a day.'

'It's only until Papa recovers enough to travel home. Then we can return to London and find somewhere else to live. We will have to enjoy a summer by the sea and the delights of the countryside. It can't all be bad, Amy.'

'I would unpack, but the carter hasn't arrived with our things. What will we do if they have been stolen or perhaps damaged in some way?'

Kitty glanced out of the window. The sky was darkening but she could see the bobbing light of two carriage lamps and a white blaze on the head of a hefty cart horse as it pulled a large wagon up the hill. 'There's a vehicle approaching. I dare say it's our luggage collected from the station.'

'That's good. I was beginning to think it would never come,' Amethyst jumped to her feet and went to peer out of the window.

'It will give us time to unpack before dinner,' Kitty said with a sigh of relief. It was the first time that Amethyst had shown anything like enthusiasm for days. 'You'll feel better with some of your own things around you, Amy.'

'Maybe,' Amethyst said doubtfully.

'I'm going downstairs to see if I can help unload the wagon. Are you coming?'

Kitty left the room without waiting to see if Amethyst was going to follow her. Doing something constructive was one way to take the edge off the inevitable feelings of homesickness and the nagging ache of missing their mother and Ivory.

Flinders was already helping the driver to lift the cases and boxes from the cart with the help of Jem, the stable boy. Nellie was supervising and there was little Kitty or Amethyst could do other than stand back and watch. When everything had been unloaded, Flinders tipped the driver and, between them, he and Jem carried the heavier bags and valises into the house, leaving the lighter items to Kitty and Amethyst.

'I'm sure you can manage those things yourselves,' Nellie said casually as she claimed her own luggage. 'I'll see you both at supper or dinner – whatever they call it in these parts.' She disappeared upstairs as if afraid that someone might purloin her treasured possessions.

Amethyst grabbed a small valise and headed for the stairs. Kitty was about to follow her when Gertie came hurrying from the direction of the kitchen, clutching an oil lamp in her hand. She spotted the easel as she came to a halt and her eyes lit up.

'Are you an artist, miss? We had a gentleman to stay a few months ago and he was a painter. He did some lovely sketches of Mill House and the mill.'

'I wouldn't call myself an artist,' Kitty said modestly. 'But I do like to dabble in art.' She looked closely at Gertie. In the glow of the lamplight her snub-nosed face, thick sandy eyelashes and the few copper curls that had escaped from her mob cap, made her look almost angelic. She would make an excellent model, with her youthful freshness and innocent smile.

'I like paintings,' Gertie added enthusiastically. 'I seen lots in the big house where Ma scrubs the floors every morning. Sometimes I goes with her to help out if she has a fit of the miseries in her bones. They have walls covered in big gold frames filled with pictures of the countryside and likenesses of people long dead.'

'Gertie, where are you?' Edith's stentorian voice echoed off the walls. 'The gentlemen are waiting for their dinner.'

Gertie clapped her hand to her mouth. 'I'm for

it now. I was supposed to ask you to come to the kitchen.' She turned and fled towards the back of the house, leaving Kitty staring after her and wondering if she was supposed to help with the service or wait on table. Maybe she and Amethyst would be expected to work to pay for their keep. Somewhat reluctantly, she abandoned her things, picked up the candlestick left on the hall table and followed Gertie to the kitchen. The aroma of cooking was not unpleasant, although there was still the acrid hint of burned dishcloth hanging in a pall above the range. Mrs Potter was red in the face as she ladled stew into large bowls while Edith sliced bread and tossed it into a small wicker basket. She looked up, frowning.

'Miss Harte, I thought this a good opportunity to introduce you to my gentlemen. It will give you an idea what to expect during your sojourn here.'

'You mentioned a Mr Beadle. Is he a commercial traveller, too?'

'Mr Beadle was the miller here until seven years ago, when fate brought us to the mill and Mill House. He is an old man with no family to care for him. At first, he stayed on to teach my parents to operate the mill, but now he has become a fixture. You will meet him in a minute or so when you help me to carry the plates into the dining room.' Edith indicated the bowls filled with mutton stew. 'Gertie, take the bread. Miss Harte and I will bring the rest. I don't trust you to carry the hot stew because you will either spill it or burn yourself.' She picked up two bowls, leaving Kitty to bring the third. 'Follow me, Kitty.'

Kitty did as she was told and joined the procession to the dining room, which was situated at the far end of a side corridor, dimly lit by candles in wall sconces.

The gentlemen were already seated at the head of a large oak table. The elderly man, whom Kitty took to be Mr Beadle, sat at the far end with a white linen napkin tucked into his collar. With his bald pate surrounded by a fluff of white hair and his pale blue eyes peering around short-sightedly, he looked like a lost child and Kitty was instantly sympathetic.

'Good evening, gentlemen.' Edith set a bowl on a table mat in front of the two at the head, leaving Kitty to take the last dish to Mr Beadle. 'This young lady is a guest in my home with her sister and their housekeeper. I'm just letting you know because you will see one or all of them at breakfast in the morning.'

Gertie trotted around the table, laying slices of bread on side plates, then scuttled out of the room.

'Good evening,' Kitty said politely.

'We won't bother with introductions as Mr Ayres and Mr Wheatley are only here for tonight,' Edith said loudly. 'Except, of course, for Mr Beadle.'

'How do you do, sir?' Kitty placed the bowl in front of him and, seeing how he felt around for the spoon, she guided his hand. After a few unsuccessful attempts he managed to shovel a portion of the stew into his mouth. He barely chewed it and swallowed, repeating the process as if he had not eaten for a very long time. His only response to her question was a sideways glance and a nod.

'Enjoy your meal, gentlemen,' Edith added, raising her voice even higher. 'Pudding will follow directly. Come with me, Miss Harte.'

Kitty hesitated, unwilling to abandon Mr Beadle, who was still struggling to feed himself and spilling most of the gravy on the napkin around his neck. It was obvious that his sight was poor, but no one seemed to bother about him, the other two gentlemen plainly only interested in their own food. It was painful to see the old man having such difficulty eating, and she would have liked to stay and help him, but Edith was already out of the door. Reluctantly, Kitty followed her hostess to the kitchen.

'Mr Beadle seems to have difficulty eating,' Kitty said anxiously.

'His sight is poor, but he manages well enough.' Edith gave her a challenging look. 'I keep the old man here out of charity. He's well fed and has a warm bed to sleep in. Otherwise, he could end up in the workhouse.'

'And yet he once owned the mill and presumably this house, too.' Kitty was not about to stand down when she saw someone being treated unfairly.

'Don't feel too sorry for Beadle. He rented the house and the mill, which my parents purchased at the going rate from the previous owner. It's true that Beadle made a good living from his work, but he had a weakness for ale, and that is where his money went. He is fortunate that I am a generous woman.'

'Yes, indeed.' Kitty was not about to argue. She could see that Mrs Potter was wrestling with a heavy saucepan in which a large pudding had been steaming, no doubt for several hours. Kitty hurried to her side and helped her to lift the pan off the flames. She grasped the handle while Mrs Potter lifted the pudding basin onto the table and untied the wet cloth. The smell of hot jam made Kitty's mouth water, but when the pudding was turned out onto a dish it looked grey and soggy.

Edith rolled her eyes. 'Another disaster, Potter. Cover it with jam and custard. They won't notice the difference.'

Mrs Potter backed away, trembling visibly. 'The custard burned, ma'am. I only turned my back for a moment.'

'No custard then. Add more jam and I'll take it out of your wages.' Edith shrugged. 'Kitty, you may serve the pudding. I'm going to my sitting room for a rest. We'll eat when the gentlemen have gone to their rooms.' She walked to the door, pausing to look over her shoulder. 'Does your servant cook? I fancy some decent custard with my pudding, otherwise it will be inedible.'

Kitty nodded. 'I'll see what I can do, Mrs Riley.' She waited until Edith had left the kitchen before turning to Mrs Potter, who was clearly upset.

'Don't worry, ma'am. Nellie will help out, but she isn't interested in taking your job from you.'

Mrs Potter wiped her eyes on her apron. 'I never seem to get it quite right.' She picked up a spoon and began serving the pudding. 'Gertie, come here. Your help is needed in the dining room.'

Gertie sidled in from the scullery. 'What shall I say if the gents complain, Mrs P?'

'Tell them to take it up with the missis. That will scare them into silence.' Mrs Potter spread jam liberally over the soggy mess.

'If you two can serve the pudding I'll go upstairs and fetch Nellie,' Kitty said hastily. 'I know she can make custard, and she might be able to save what's left of the suet pudding.'

Mrs Potter sighed. 'Ta, miss. At least that will keep Mrs Riley happy this evening.'

Kitty found Nellie in a room on the top floor. She had a broom clutched in her hands and was sweeping under the iron bedstead. She picked up the fluff with a cloth and straightened up, frowning.

'I don't know when this room was last cleaned, but it was some time ago. I'll need to take the rug out in the garden tomorrow and give it a good beating. Whoever was the last occupant must have been a lazy cow.'

'I'm sorry, Nellie. That's not a good start, but this is only temporary,' Kitty said hastily. 'Actually, I need your help, or rather the poor old cook needs you. She's a bit of a disaster in the kitchen, as far as I can see, but if she loses her job, she'll be homeless and we all know how that feels.'

Nellie sniffed and pursed her lips. 'That's her problem, Kitty. She shouldn't be a cook if she doesn't know what she's doing.'

'Not everyone is as talented and adaptable as you. After all, you weren't taken on as a cook in our household, but you stepped in when Mama couldn't afford Cook's wages. You have a talent for the work and Mrs Potter's steamed suet pudding is a disaster. She burned the custard, and Mrs Riley is not happy.'

Nellie propped the broom against the wall. 'All right. I'll help out tonight but I'm not promising anything more.'

'Of course not. I wouldn't expect you to do Mrs Potter's job, but I have to say I'm starving, and the others must be very hungry. We haven't eaten for hours, so maybe you could work some of your magic on the mutton stew. I served it to the gentlemen in the dining room and it didn't look too appetising.'

'That sounds like a challenge.' Nellie shooed Kitty out of the room. 'I will show Mrs Riley what can be done with a few herbs, a pinch of common sense, and a little expertise.'

Kitty was awakened early next morning by the sound of cartwheels on the gravel drive. She rose from her bed, and when she looked out of the window she saw the two gentlemen boarders placing their luggage in the wagoner's vehicle by lamplight before climbing in and taking their seats. A flick of the whip and the sturdy shire horse started off in the direction of the village. Today, Kitty realised, was the real start of their stay in Little Foxbury, and it would set the tone for the rest of their time in the country. It was Amethyst who would have the most difficulty in settling down, and therefore it was important to find something that would interest her and take her mind off her separation from Sebastian Marriner. Convincing Amethyst that he was a philanderer was going to be difficult, but it would have to be faced sooner or later.

Kitty washed in cold water, dressed and put her hair up before going downstairs to the kitchen with a vague idea of helping Mrs Potter to make breakfast. To her surprise it was Edith who was in the kitchen, kneading bread dough.

'You're up early, Miss Harte.'

'Good morning, Mrs Riley. Yes, I heard the wagon arrive and I saw your gentlemen leave.'

Edith nodded. 'They wanted an early start as it's

Saturday and they will be travelling home to spend Sunday with their families. I don't usually take gentlemen in on a Saturday. I like to have a couple of days' rest before I start all over again.' She thumped the dough into a bowl and covered it with a damp cloth. 'That will be ready for the oven in twenty minutes or so. I suppose you would like your breakfast now?'

'Please don't go to any trouble on my account. I can wait for the others.'

Edith wiped her floury hands on her apron. 'I dare say you're wondering why I am here in the kitchen making bread when I have a cook to do such work.'

Kitty smiled. 'Not really, ma'am. I've tried my hand at bread making under Nellie's instruction and I rather enjoyed it, especially when it came to tasting the results.'

'I may seem hard on Potter, but she was not trained to be a cook. Her late husband worked at the mill and died tragically in an accident. She was left destitute, and I took her in. She does her best and I'm afraid I am not always patient with her, but she is not very talented in the culinary arts.'

'I see.' Kitty eyed Edith with new respect. 'It is very difficult for widows to survive, or even families whose breadwinner is absent for no fault of his own.'

'Is that the reason for your need to stay here, Kitty? I may call you that, mayn't I?' Edith spooned tea into a Brown Betty pot and added water from a steaming kettle. 'Would you like a cup of tea?'

'Yes, please. I would prefer it if you called me Kitty, and I know Amethyst would feel the same.'

'Your sister is not happy to be here. I gathered that last evening.'

'She isn't used to the countryside. We were both born and raised in London, so it is a big change in circumstances, and we had to leave our mother and elder sister with our grandmother.'

Edith poured the tea, passing a cup to Kitty. 'How so?'

'Grandmama Carstairs has no time for me because I speak my mind, and I don't always conform to her idea of how a young lady should behave. She doesn't approve of Amy because she is high spirited and a little wayward.' Kitty sipped the tea.

'That must have been hard for all of you,' Edith said thoughtfully. 'Especially your mother. Might I ask what happened to your father? Flinders gave me very little information other than the fact that Mr Harte is still in British Guiana.'

'Papa had an accident. Flinders is the best person to give you the details. He's told us very little, probably for fear of upsetting us more, but Papa is still abroad and being cared for by nuns. We're hoping he will soon be well enough to travel home.'

'I see,' Edith said slowly. 'Well, Kitty, you are welcome to stay here for as long as need be. But I will expect a little help from you and your sister in return.'

'Of course.'

'There is very little clearing up to do after my last two gentlemen. They were tidy souls, and Gertie can do their rooms. I will expect you to undertake some light duties next week when my new gentlemen arrive, but until then I think it best if you settle in.'

'I will do whatever I can to help.'

'Then that's settled. However, if it suits you and your sister, I will take you to the mill later this morning. You will meet my mother and see how a flour mill operates, if you're interested.'

'That sounds very exciting. We would love that,' Kitty said eagerly. 'Your mama must be a remarkable lady to take on such a mammoth task.'

'You mean in her advancing years?' Edith laughed and her whole persona changed. 'Please don't say anything like that to her. She insists that age is irrelevant and doing difficult things is just a matter of concentration and determination.'

'I look forward to meeting your mother. She must be a redoubtable lady.'

'She is indeed.' Edith put her cup down. 'That sounds like Gertie's footsteps outside. That girl is as flat-footed as a duck, but she usually arrives on time, although she is five minutes late this morning. Mrs Potter will be down shortly, and I believe Flinders went for a walk earlier. I saw that his hat and jacket had gone from its peg.'

'He was always up early in London, but I'm surprised he does the same at home.' Kitty drank her tea to the last drops. She swirled the cup around, smiling. 'Nellie is very good at reading the tea leaves. Perhaps I ought to ask her when Papa will be coming home.'

Edith tossed her head. 'I don't believe in all that nonsense.'

'It's just a little light amusement.' Kitty took her cup and saucer to the sink in the scullery just as Gertie burst into the room.

'Oh, you made me jump, miss. I wasn't expecting anyone to be in here.' Flushed and breathless, no doubt from hurrying, Gertie took off her bonnet and shawl. 'Is Madam up yet? I'm a bit late.'

'Yes, I am up, and I'll forgive you this time, Gertie.' Edith's voice rang out loud and clear from the kitchen. 'I was just telling Miss Harte that you are normally very punctual.'

'I'm sorry, missis. I had to take Ned to the doctor's house. He fell out of a tree and hurt his arm. I think he might have broke it.'

Edith emerged from the kitchen. 'Well, let's hope not. You'd best get your pinny on and start work. See to the fire in the sitting room first, and then you can do the gentlemen's rooms. They've both left now.'

'Yes, missis.'

Kitty could see that she was in the way, and she headed for the door. 'Perhaps I'll go for a walk. I might come across Flinders along the way.'

'He loves the sea,' Edith said vaguely. 'You will

probably find him on the beach.' She lifted the cloth off the bread dough. 'It will be ready in time for breakfast at eight o'clock, Kitty.'

'I understand.' Kitty left the kitchen and went into the entrance hall to take her bonnet and cape from the row of pegs. She glanced at the clock and saw that it was only half past seven, giving her plenty of time for a walk before she had to wake Amethyst in time for breakfast at eight. Kitty had already gathered that Edith ran her household strictly to time, and that must be observed if they were not to upset their hostess.

Outside it was cold and fresh, with a chilly wind from the sea. The sun was peeping up over the horizon and already the sails on the windmill were turning around at a steady rate. It was an impressive sight, and the white painted weatherboards gleamed pink and peach coloured in the early rays of the sun. Kitty quickened her pace and made her way through a thicket of gorse bushes and brambles to a narrow path leading down to the beach. The briny sea air filled her lungs, and the wind tugged at her cape and skirts as she walked. She had not gone far when she spotted a familiar figure walking towards her. She waved and Flinders responded. Kitty waited until he drew closer.

'You are out early,' she said, smiling.

'I love the early morning,' Flinders said. 'It's the best part of the day.'

'I agree, but Amy would argue with you. She

loves evenings and would dance all night if she had the opportunity.'

Flinders took Kitty's hand and tucked it in the crook of his arm. 'Did my mother send you to find me? She's very particular about punctuality, particularly at mealtimes.'

'So, I gathered,' Kitty said, laughing. 'She was in the kitchen when I went downstairs, but we had a good chat, and I think we understand each other a little better. She's going to take Amy and me to meet your grandmother at the mill later this morning.'

'As I said before, Grandmama is someone to be reckoned with. She is an amazing woman and very forthright. You will know instantly if she takes to you or not.'

'I'm scared already.' Kitty tightened her grip on his arm. 'But I'm looking forward to meeting her.'

'She'll like you so don't worry. I think you two are kindred spirits.'

'You can tell that already? We've only known each other a short time, Flinders.'

'But I've seen you in adversity, Kitty. I know how you dealt with earning money at the Bazaar to help feed your family. You lost your home and are parted from your mother and Ivory, but you never complain. I think Grandmama will like you very much, as do I.'

Chapter Twelve

Flinders left shortly after breakfast, saying he had to visit his tailor in Manningtree, but he would be back later. His mother immediately produced a list of articles that she wanted him to purchase for her, which he accepted with a wry smile.

Kitty left them discussing the items while she went to the dining room to make sure that Mr Beadle had managed to eat his breakfast. As far as she could gather, the food was always put in front of him, but no one had the time to check that he was able to see well enough to know when his plate was empty. Kitty sat with him for a while, waiting until he had drunk the last drop of tea and eaten the last crumb.

'You're very kind, miss.' Beadle clutched her hand. 'What is your name, dear?'

'I'm Kitty, Mr Beadle. I was christened Katherine, but everyone calls me Kitty.'

'I like Katherine better.' Beadle sat back in his chair and closed his eyes. 'Thank you, Katherine.'

Kitty could see that there was nothing more she could do for him at present, and she cleared the table, leaving him to nod off in his seat. She took the dirty crockery to the scullery and left it with Gertie, who was up to her elbows in hot water and baking soda with a squeeze of lemon juice as she washed the dishes.

'Are you going to the mill today, miss?' Gertie gave Kitty a sideways look.

'Yes, Mrs Riley said she would take me and my sister. I can't wait to see inside the windmill.'

'Jem's cousin works there, miss. He's very good-looking and he's got muscles like the strong man at the fair.'

Kitty laughed. 'I'll be sure to look out for him, Gertie.' She walked back through the kitchen where Nellie had started preparing the meat and vegetables for luncheon.

'Are you making one of your amazing pies, Nellie?' Kitty could see that Nellie was not entirely happy. 'Whatever it is, I'm sure it will be delicious.'

'You needn't soft-soap me, Miss Kitty. I'll do my bit.'

'As will we all,' Kitty added hastily. 'I know it's not easy, but it's only temporary. I'm sure that Papa will come home very soon and then everything will get back to normal.'

'We can but hope.' Nellie set about chopping an onion with such vigour that Kitty was afraid she might slice off one of her fingers.

'I'll leave you to it then.' Kitty could see that Nellie was not in the mood to chat and she went in search of Amethyst.

Although Kitty was excited at the prospect of visiting a windmill, it took some time to convince Amethyst that the interior of a working flour mill would be interesting. In the end Amethyst agreed to accompany them, but she dawdled behind Kitty and Edith during the short walk. When they reached the bottom of the steps leading up to the mill Edith glanced over her shoulder.

'You can take that look off your face, young lady. My mother is very astute, and she doesn't suffer fools gladly. If you get on the wrong side of her, she will lose no time in putting you in your place.'

Amethyst stared at her, open mouthed. 'I – I didn't say anything, ma'am.'

'I was a governess to a wealthy family with five daughters before I married Mr Riley. I have dealt with more tantrums and fits of the vapours than you can imagine, so do not think you can get away with sulks and bad behaviour for the sake of it.'

'I'm sure that Amy didn't mean any disrespect, ma'am,' Kitty said hastily.

'Your sister has been warned.' Edith sent Amethyst a warning look. 'I'll say no more on the subject.' She climbed the steps, opened the door and stepped inside. 'I'm here, Ma. Where are you?'

Kitty followed Edith into the mill with Amethyst close behind her. The grinding noise of the mill wheel and giant cogs that drove it, together with the whirring of the sails, was almost deafening. Even more startling was the sight of a small woman covered from head to foot in a fine dusting of flour that made her look for all the world like a ghost.

'Edith, who have you brought with you? They don't look like farm workers.'

Edith laughed. 'No, indeed, Ma. These two young ladies are going to be staying with me for a while. Flinders works with their papa, who suffered an unfortunate accident and is unable to leave British Guiana until he has fully recovered.'

'Unlucky indeed.' Adeline Saunders looked Kitty up and down before turning to Amethyst, who managed a nod and a half-smile. 'I can see that you two have been brought up to be young ladies. Well, my dears, you can forget all about that if you are to stay at Mill House. My daughter will expect you to earn your keep, as would I.'

'Don't worry, Ma,' Edith said sharply. 'I have had that conversation with Kitty. She knows what to expect. I brought them here to show them how a mill works, but if you're too busy we can leave now.'

Adeline held up a floury hand. 'You will have to take them round, Edith. I need to get on with this order.'

'Don't you ever rest, Ma?' Edith demanded, smiling fondly.

'There'll be plenty of time for that when I'm dead. For now, I need to keep Farmer Hughes happy. He pays up promptly, which is more than I can say for some of our neighbours.' Adeline disappeared up a winding staircase leaving footprints on the floury steps.

Kitty glanced with interest at the machinery overhead, but Amethyst covered her ears with her hands.

'I don't want to see any more, Kitty,' she said in a loud whisper. 'It scares me.'

'The mill isn't for everybody.' Edith shrugged. 'Go outside if it's too much for you, Amethyst. Take a walk on the beach if you like.'

'Yes, Amy. There's no need for you to see the rest of the mill, but I would love to.' Kitty turned to Edith, smiling. 'It's the most impressive thing I've ever seen.'

Amethyst backed away, shaking her head. 'It's not for me. I can't stand the noise.' She hurried out of the mill, leaving the door to close behind her.

It was difficult to hear Edith's commentary as Kitty followed her up to the next floor, but she grasped the basics of how the wind turned the sails, which in turn worked the various giant cog wheels that operated the millstones. The noise and dust and the reverberation made Kitty feel quite dizzy. By the time they had negotiated all the working floors she was in total awe of Adeline Saunders.

'I can't believe that your mother runs this mill single handed,' Kitty said as they returned to the ground floor.

'She has a young man from the village who comes in daily. He does the heavy lifting and tasks that are beyond my mother. In fact, he should be here now.' Edith went to the door and opened it. She sighed. 'I might have guessed.'

'What is it?' Kitty looked over her shoulder to see Amethyst in animated conversation with a tall, young man with a shock of chestnut-brown hair, partially concealed by a flat cap. He was leaning forward as if captivated by whatever it was that Amethyst had to say. 'I'm sorry, Edith,' Kitty added apologetically. 'My sister has a way with gentlemen. They find her irresistible.'

Edith hitched up her skirts and began to descend the steps. 'Turner, you're supposed to be working.'

Turner backed away from Amethyst, who was smiling coquettishly.

'Adieu, Jacob.' Amethyst blew him a kiss.

'Sorry, ma'am,' Jacob said hurriedly. 'I had an errand to do for Mrs Saunders.'

'And you were waylaid, by the look of things,'

Edith said tartly. 'Best get inside before my mother realises you were wasting time out here.'

Jacob tipped his cap and took the steps two at a time, brushing past Kitty, who was still standing in the doorway. 'Sorry, miss.' He disappeared into the mill before she had a chance to speak.

Kitty joined Amethyst and Edith on the grassy slope outside the mill.

'I'm sorry,' Amethyst said crossly. 'I didn't know he was supposed to be working.'

'Well, you know now.' Edith shrugged and turned away. 'Jacob is paid to help my mother in the mill, so please let him get on with his work, Amethyst. You'll have to find something else to amuse yourself.'

Amethyst tossed her head. 'I don't flirt with common miller's boys. My gentleman friend has a title and a country estate.'

'Does he now? So where is this rich gentleman in your time of need?' Edith folded her arms. 'I don't see him knocking on my door asking for you.'

Kitty shuddered. Of course, what Edith said was true, but it was brutally honest and Amethyst was visibly upset.

'That's not fair, Mrs Riley. He doesn't know where I am.' Amethyst sniffed and searched for a handkerchief.

Kitty took her own hanky from her pocket and handed it to her sister. 'I'm sure he will ask around, Amy. I wouldn't be surprised if he does turn up on our doorstep one day.'

'Do you really think so?' Amethyst blew her nose and passed the hanky back to Kitty, who tucked it in her pocket.

'Yes, I do.' Kitty turned to Edith, smiling. 'Thank you for taking me round the mill. It was fascinating. I might bring my easel and paints down here after luncheon so that I can make some sketches.'

'That sounds like a good idea, but now I have things to do. I suggest you both take a walk on the beach. The exercise will give you an appetite for luncheon, but if I find a wealthy young gentleman waiting outside my door, I will tell him to come and find you.' Edith tempered her words with a smile before heading off towards her house.

Amethyst waited until they were out of earshot. 'Why is she so mean to me, Kitty? I haven't done anything to her.'

'It's just her way, Amy. Don't take it personally. But if I were you, I wouldn't mention Lord Marriner again, and it's probably best not to flirt with every good-looking man you meet.'

'I don't flirt. That's not fair, Kitty. I can't help it if I am pretty and charming, and gentlemen seem to like me.'

'No, you can't, but just try to be a little less amenable. That's all I'm saying. Now, let's go for a walk on the beach. We could pick up some shells and maybe you could amuse yourself by decorating a box or something.'

'I am not eight years old, Kitty. I don't do things like that. You can amuse yourself with your paints and charcoal, but I will have to find something else to occupy my time in this dreary place.' Amethyst held on to her bonnet as a strong sea breeze almost ripped it off her glossy dark curls.

Kitty linked arms with her sister. 'We'll think of something, Amy. Perhaps we can persuade Flinders to take us on a tour of the local places of interest tomorrow. We should take advantage of having him here because his leave must be up soon and then he'll have to return to South America.'

'Maybe we could go with him,' Amethyst said hopefully. 'We could help the nuns to make Pa better and then we could bring him home.'

'It's a nice thought, but I don't think that will happen.' Kitty sighed. 'It would be wonderful to have a magic carpet so that we could fly there and bring Papa home in comfort, but that is as impossible as the idea of you and me accompanying Flinders to Georgetown. For one thing, we have very little money and for another, it's simply out of the question.'

'Maybe if we wish hard enough, we could find the magic carpet.' Amethyst slipped her hand free and bent down to pick up a shell. 'This is pretty. If I could find a lot of these, they would make a nice necklace.'

Relieved to have a change of subject, Kitty followed her gaze. 'That's a good idea. If you made a few you could sell them on Aggie's stall in the Bazaar when we get back to London.' She bent down and scooped up a handful of sand, shells and pebbles.

They were both so engrossed in finding the small pearly shells that Kitty lost all sense of time. She came to a halt as the distant chiming of the clock in the church tower struck twelve, and like Cinderella at the ball she realised that it was time to return to Mill House for luncheon.

'It's midday, Amy. We must get back to the house.' Kitty called, raising her voice to make herself heard over the sound of the waves shifting sand and stones as they ebbed and flowed on the shore.

Amethyst stopped reluctantly. She held her skirt in a bundle filled with shells. 'Really? I was just beginning to enjoy myself.'

'I think you have plenty to get on with. I have enough to make several necklaces and bracelets. You just have to find a way to pierce them so that they can be strung together.'

Amethyst came running towards her. 'I hadn't thought of that. Maybe I could ask Jacob to do it for me.'

Kitty had no answer for that. She turned and set off for the path that led eventually to Mill House. No doubt Amethyst would find a man to do her bidding, as always. But hopefully she could do it without offending either Mrs Saunders or Edith Riley. Perhaps Flinders could help, although Amethyst would not find that so exciting. She and Flinders had developed a friendly brother-and-sister-style relationship with not a hint of romantic attachment. Kitty quickened her pace as she reached the top of the slope. In the distance she could see a horseman riding towards Mill House, and unless she was very much mistaken it looked as though he was wearing police uniform. She broke into a run with the shells rattling together in her bunched-up skirt.

'Why are you hurrying?' Amethyst called out breathlessly. 'What's wrong, Kitty?'

Kitty was running too fast to answer and she arrived at the house, panting for breath, but still holding on to the shells. With her free hand she shielded her eyes against the sun as the horseman slowed down and drew his steed to a halt in front of her. He dismounted and came towards her, taking off his top hat. He ran his hand through his thick dark hair, smoothing it in place.

'Good afternoon, Miss Harte. I hope I haven't called at an inconvenient time.' His lips twitched as he glanced at her bunched-up skirts, which revealed the hem of Kitty's red flannel petticoat.

Kitty felt her cheeks flame with embarrassment. Nellie had always insisted that young ladies must wear red flannel in winter, replacing it with cotton and lace at the beginning of summer. She let her skirt drop and tiny pink shells showered onto the gravel. 'Sergeant Barton! I wasn't expecting to see you today.'

'Good heavens. It's the police.' Amethyst reached them, breathless and red in the face with exertion. 'Have you come to bring us good news, Sergeant, or are you going to arrest Kitty?'

Barton laughed. 'I'm not here to make an arrest, Miss Harte. I have some good news. Part of your family silver has been recovered and I have it here in my saddle bag. I just need you to identify it. Then I must take it back to the station to be held until after the trial.'

Kitty found her voice at last. 'But I thought the Daggs had already been convicted and sent to prison.'

'Yes, for another crime, but we did not have enough evidence to charge Phineas Dagg and his son with theft of your silver. This will be enough to make sure that they are both put away for a very long time.'

'You obviously know that we are staying here,' Kitty said cautiously. 'I don't think that Mrs Riley will mind if I ask you in.'

Barton smiled. 'I am on official duty. She can hardly refuse, but I will do my best not to put her out in any way.'

'If you wait here, I'll go and speak to her.' Kitty hurried to the kitchen, where she found Edith supervising Nellie as she prepared to serve the meal.

'What is it, Kitty? You look flushed.' Edith shot her a sideways glance as she moved away from the table when Nellie took the pie from the oven.

'I've been running, ma'am. I saw someone approaching on horseback and it turned out to be the police sergeant who dealt with our case in London. He thinks they have retrieved some of our family silver, but he needs me to identify it.'

'Well, ask him in.' Edith turned to Nellie. 'I'll cut up the pie if you drain the potatoes and cabbage.'

'Yes'm,' Nellie muttered as she lifted a heavy pan from the hob and took it to the scullery.

'Don't just stand there, Kitty,' Edith said irritably. 'Go and ask your policeman if he would like to stay for luncheon. It's only polite as he has come all this way. Where is your sister?'

'She was not far behind me when I arrived at the house. She's probably in the hall talking to Sergeant Barton.'

Edith raised an eyebrow. 'Was that wise? I mean leaving her alone with a gentleman. She seems to regard them all as fair game.'

'I wouldn't put it like that exactly, but yes, you have a point. I'll go and rescue Sergeant Barton and ask him if he would like to join us for luncheon.' Kitty went out into the hall and sure enough Amethyst was busy exerting her charm on Barton, who seemed to be more amused than anything.

'Mrs Riley wonders if you would like to join us for luncheon, Sergeant.' Kitty sent a warning glance to Amethyst, who walked off towards the kitchen, still clutching her bunched-up skirts and bundle of shells.

'That's very kind of her. Yes, that would be fine. I left London at a ridiculously early hour this morning in order to get here by noon. I came by train and hired a horse at the station.'

'And will you return to London this afternoon?'

He nodded. 'Yes, I'm afraid so. Although it is so pleasant here it seems a shame to have to leave so soon.'

'Then stay for a while, Sergeant.' Amethyst appeared from the direction of the kitchen, this time without her collection of shells. 'We've only been here for a short while, but I miss London.'

Barton shook his head. 'Alas, duty calls, Miss Harte. But you should think yourself very fortunate to be staying in such an interesting and beautiful part of the country. My family home is not very far from here, but I don't manage to visit them as often as I would like.'

'That is a shame,' Kitty said, smiling. 'I've never been to this part of Essex until now, but I think it's quite charming.'

Amy cleared her throat impatiently. 'I am supposed to tell you that luncheon is being served. Kitty, you are needed in the kitchen. I will show Sergeant Barton where to sit.' Amethyst took him by the arm and propelled him towards the dining room, leaving Kitty little alternative but to go to the kitchen and help with serving the food and carrying the dishes to the table.

When everyone was settled and had begun

eating, Kitty found it almost impossible to make herself heard. Edith and Amethyst's attempts to gain Barton's attention were like a verbal game of lawn tennis, with Barton the centre of attraction and Kitty very much on the sidelines. She spent most of her time assisting Mr Beadle, who was so deaf that he could not make out who was talking or what they were saying. Kitty managed to make him understand that the meal was meat and vegetable pie, boiled potatoes and cabbage, which he dutifully ate when prompted. However, the moment Kitty turned her back, Beadle seemed to forget what he was doing and nodded off.

When everyone had finished eating, Kitty helped to clear the table. It was only when she reached the kitchen that she realised that Cook was absent.

'Where is Mrs Potter?' Kitty asked, frowning. 'Have you locked her in a cupboard, Nellie?'

Nellie curled her lip. 'Very droll, I'm sure. No, the good lady has relations in Sudbury, wherever that is. Mrs Riley suggested that she take a few days off to visit them.'

'When did she leave? I haven't seen her today.'

'First thing this morning, miss.' Gertie popped out of the scullery as if on a spring. 'She took umbrage at having someone else in her kitchen. Said she wasn't good enough so she'd leave, but the missis persuaded her she needed a rest and would feel better by the time she came back.'

'Oh dear, we do seem to have caused some upset in the household,' Kitty said ruefully. 'I hope she does return when she feels better. We won't be here forever.'

'Nellie is a better cook than Mrs Potter,' Gertie said, grinning. 'You can all stay, as far as I'm concerned.'

'Get away with you, you cheeky urchin.' Nellie put on a stern face, but Kitty could see that she was secretly pleased.

'Is that treacle tart, Nellie?' Kitty changed the subject. 'And custard, too. Sergeant Barton won't want to leave when you serve this.'

'He should hurry back to London and set about finding the rest of the silver,' Nellie said grimly. 'If we had sold it properly, at a respectable auction house, we might have had enough money to rent another property in Soho Square or thereabouts. I can't say I'm too fond of being out here in the wilds.'

Kitty picked up a pile of clean dessert plates. 'I haven't seen the pieces he's brought with him, so I don't know for certain they're ours, but as soon as we've finished luncheon, I'll get him to show them to me.'

Barton unwrapped a Georgian helmet-shaped cream jug, which he set on the dining table, followed by a set of six rat-tail dessert spoons.

'Are these some of the silverware that was pawned with Dagg, Miss Harte?'

Kitty picked up the cream jug and examined it carefully. 'Yes, this one is most certainly, as are the silver spoons. Where did you find them?'

'They were discovered in an auction house that has a slightly tarnished reputation, to put it mildly. We always check the usual sources and very often it pays off.'

'Mama would be so happy to see these pieces again. Do you really have to take them away with you?' Kitty fingered the cold, reflective surface of the jug. Its elegant lines and superb craftsmanship always gave her pleasure.

'I'm sorry, but the answer is yes. As I said before, these are evidence, and now you have identified them that will help to keep Dagg and his son in prison for longer.' Barton packed the spoons away and held out his hand for the jug. 'I can see how much this means to you, but you will get them back after the court hearing.'

Reluctantly, Kitty handed him the jug. 'I'm glad I've seen these pieces. At least I know we will get them returned eventually. The money that Dagg gave Mama for the silver was only a fraction of its value.'

Barton placed the jug in a leather bag together with the spoons. 'Mrs Harte was cheated twice by the Daggs and I'm going to make sure that they pay for it. I doubt if she was the first to fall for their persuasive talk, but at least we can protect other innocent people from falling prey to their swindles.'

Kitty eyed him curiously. 'You really believe in what you're doing, don't you, Sergeant?'

'Yes, I do. We are not generally popular, at least with the people who have something to hide, but I believe that most ordinary folk understand that the police have a job to do in keeping the public safe.'

'That sounds like a sermon, Sergeant.' Flinders stood in the doorway, glaring at Barton. 'Do you usually come all this way from London merely to have a stolen article identified?'

Kitty stared at him in dismay. 'Flinders! Don't be so rude. Sergeant Barton has saved some pieces of my family's silver. He didn't have to come here today.'

'My point exactly.' Flinders walked slowly into the room and came to a halt beside Kitty. 'I imagine you need to return to London very soon, Sergeant.'

'Yes, I will indeed.' Barton turned to Kitty with an apologetic smile. 'I'm sorry if my visit has caused some upset in your family.'

'Not at all, Sergeant. Mr Flinders is my father's subordinate. Amethyst and I are guests here and very grateful for the sojourn, but I hope we will be able to return to London before too long.' Kitty shot a warning glance in Flinders' direction as she brushed past him to usher Barton from the room. 'I apologise for my friend, Sergeant. I'm sure he didn't mean to be so ill-mannered.'

Barton stopped to take his top hat from a chair near the front door. 'It simply demonstrates the fine line we tread with the general public, Miss Harte. Mine is not an easy profession, but it can be very rewarding.' He raised her hand to his lips. 'But for villains like Dagg and his son, I would never have met you or your family. I look forward to bringing you better news when we recover the rest of your property. Please thank Mrs Riley for her hospitality.' He put his hat on at a jaunty angle and left the house.

Kitty could see Flinders standing in the dining-room doorway. She ignored him and followed Barton outside.

'I'll walk to the stable with you, Sergeant. As I said before, I hope we will be able to return to London soon. My sister pines for city life.'

As they reached the stable, Barton came to a halt. 'When you do return to London, Miss Harte, I would consider it an honour if I might call on you at your new home, wherever it happens to be – if that is acceptable to you, of course.'

Kitty met his intense gaze, and she smiled. 'It is very acceptable, Sergeant Barton, but who knows when that will be?'

'I'm a patient man, Miss Harte.' Barton beckoned to Jem, who was in the process of saddling the hired horse. 'Goodbye for now, but we will meet again. That is a promise.'

Chapter Thirteen

Kitty stood outside the stable watching Barton ride away. His last words had caught her by surprise, although deep down she knew that the attraction she felt for him was mutual. However, as things were now, she realised that seeing him again might not be as easy as he had suggested. Everything depended upon her father's recovery and his eventual return, but that did not necessarily ensure a solution to their homelessness. Pa would not have an income until he was fit enough to take on another expedition, and Kitty could not imagine Grandmama Carstairs welcoming her son-in-law to Bridlebank. She had made plain her continuing disappointment in a man who spent his life chipping away at rocks to earn a living.

Kitty shielded her eyes as she watched Barton until

he was out of sight. She turned away and walked slowly back to the house.

Flinders met her in the doorway. 'That was an unnecessary journey for our valiant police officer,' he said crossly. 'The sergeant could have taken the silver to Bridlebank, and your mother or Ivory would have identified it. His coming here was just an excuse to see you, Kitty.'

'What if it was? Are you jealous, Flinders?' Kitty had not meant to snap at him, but she was stung by his remark and annoyed by his cavalier attitude.

'Your father begged me to look after you, and your sisters, Kitty,' Flinders said earnestly. 'It's what I have been trying to do, even if my natural concern seems a little unwelcome to you.'

She managed a smile. 'Not unwelcome exactly, but you do take it too far at times, Flinders. I am truly grateful for all your help.'

'I'm sorry if I care too much, Kitty. I owe such a lot to your papa, and I feel very responsible for you and your family.'

He looked so downcast that Kitty laid her hand on his arm. 'Let us be friends. Tell me about your trip to Manningtree. Did you get everything that your mama wanted?'

'Yes, I think so, but I'm sure to have forgotten something,' Flinders said ruefully. 'I'm not very good at shopping.'

'Next time you go perhaps I ought to accompany

you,' Kitty smiled. 'I am very good at remembering lists. We've had to be very careful with money recently, as you know.'

'If I have left anything off Mama's list it's too late to get back to town now. And tomorrow is Sunday, so if she wishes me to go again it will have to be Monday. You said you would go with me.'

'And I will, with pleasure. In the meantime, perhaps we could walk down to the village. I don't think I want to spend the afternoon picking up shells with Amy. Besides which, I think she has designs on Jem. She has a way of getting gentlemen and boys to do as she bids, and it's all done with a sweet smile and a few soft words.'

'She had better watch out for Gertie, who has already set her claim on young Jem,' Flinders said, laughing.

To Kitty's surprise Amethyst opted to accompany them to town on Monday morning. Her sudden desire to get away from Mill House might have had something to do with an altercation with Gertie on Sunday. The argument had happened after morning service, which Edith had insisted they must all attend, except Flinders, who was excused on account of a report he had to finish urgently. Kitty was tempted to ask why he had gone on a shopping trip to the nearest town when he should have been working, but she took pity on him and held her tongue.

When they arrived at the village church their appearance caused a ripple of interest to run though the congregation. Kitty followed Edith and Adeline into a back pew. However, Amethyst managed to sit next to Jem Jobson during the service. They left the church together, coming face to face with an irate Gertie, who lost no time in condemning Amethyst for being a harlot from wicked London, who had come to the country with the intention of flirting with any man who took her fancy. Warming to her theme, Gertie accused Jem of paying undue attention to another woman, thus breaking the promises he made during the handfasting ceremony. Jem protested angrily, but fortunately for everyone concerned, Edith stepped in, backed up by her mother. They dispersed the curious onlookers before berating both Gertie and Jem. Amethyst burst into tears, claiming innocence of any wrongdoing, and was hustled into the trap to sit beside Adeline, while Edith took the reins. Kitty had no option other than to walk home alone, leaving Jem and Gertie to sort out their differences.

On Monday morning it was Flinders who brought the pony and trap from the stable. He leaped down from the driver's seat to help Kitty and Amethyst into the vehicle.

'Did you finish your report yesterday?' Kitty asked innocently, although privately she thought that Flinders had used his work as an excuse.

He shot her a speculative glance as he climbed back onto the trap and took the reins. 'Yes, I did, surprising as that might seem. I'm going to post it today, although, having done what I was asked, I think I will be sent back to Georgetown sooner than I had hoped.'

'Really?' Kitty gazed at him in surprise. 'I thought you would have longer at home.'

'If I'm honest, I have been procrastinating, but I need to get back to British Guiana where, assuming your father is still incapacitated, I'll take over running the expedition. It's not my choice, but I must obey orders.'

Amethyst yawned. 'Don't send the report in, Flinders. Let them wait a while and stay with us. It will be deadly dull if you go away now.'

'Thank you, Amy, but it's my profession. I can't do as I please.' Flinders clicked his tongue against his teeth. 'Trot on, Bobbin.'

'Will you visit Papa when you get back to British Guiana, Flinders?' Kitty asked eagerly. 'You will let us know how he is getting on, won't you?'

'Of course, and I hope I'll have good news for you.' Flinders concentrated on the road ahead and Kitty lapsed into silence, thinking about her father and wishing that she could do something to help bring him home. However, without an income of her own, other than what she could earn with her paintings, she knew she was helpless, and it was frustrating.

Amethyst was surprisingly quiet during the rest of the journey to Manningtree, but Kitty did not encourage her to speak. It was a pleasant day, although the wind was chilly. Kitty was glad of her warm petticoats and her woollen cape. She settled down to enjoy seeing a part of the countryside with which she was not accustomed

By the time they reached Manningtree, a small town on the banks of the River Stour, Kitty was feeling refreshed and at ease. She could sit beside Flinders on the driver's seat in companionable silence and not feel the need to strike up a conversation. A quick glance over her shoulder made Kitty smile to see Amethyst curled up, sound asleep as if lulled by the rhythmic swaying movement of the vehicle. She awakened, however, when Flinders drew Bobbin to a halt outside an inn on the edge of town. Flinders alighted and handed the reins to a boy who had emerged from the stables. Flinders handed the boy a threepenny bit.

'Look after Bobbin, please. He's an old boy and needs special attention.'

The boy tipped his cap. 'Consider it done, guv.' He led Bobbin and the trap to the stables.

'I suggest we have coffee before we do anything else,' Flinders said calmly. 'I have a few things that my mother wanted me to get for her.'

Kitty laughed. 'You mean the items you forgot last time.'

'That's right, but I'm relying on you this time, Kitty. If I miss anything off the list Mother gave you, it will be your fault.'

Amethyst rolled her eyes. 'You two sound like bickering children. I'm thirsty, Flinders.'

'Then coffee it is.' Flinders opened the door and ushered them into the taproom. He strolled up to the bar. 'Good morning, landlord. Have you a private parlour where we might have some refreshment?'

'Morning, sir. I have a parlour, but it's occupied at present.' The landlord glanced at Kitty and Amethyst. 'But the bar is no place for young ladies. The other customers might be amenable to sharing the parlour, providing you have no objections.'

'None at all,' Flinders said, smiling. 'We simply require coffee before we make our purchases in town.'

The landlord disappeared through a door at the back of the bar, returning minutes later with a beaming smile. 'Follow me, if you please, and I'll bring you your coffee.'

Kitty did not hesitate. She was uncomfortably aware that the men seated at tables in the bar were staring at them, and that Amethyst was basking in the attention. Kitty shooed her sister through the open door and followed her, with Flinders close behind.

Amethyst uttered a cry of delight as she entered the parlour.

'Frances and Charles! What a lovely surprise.' Amethyst clapped her hands. 'Look who's here, Kitty.'

Kitty came to a halt. 'I thought you were going to your estate in Suffolk, Frances. But here you are. This is such an amazing coincidence.'

'Our home in the country is just over the border in Suffolk,' Frances said, smiling. 'More to the point, what are you doing here?'

'Good morning, Frances, Charles,' Flinders said without giving Kitty a chance to respond to Frances's question. 'I had no idea it was you when the landlord said the parlour was occupied,' he added hastily.

Charles stood up, eyeing Flinders with a frown. 'Had I known it was you, Riley, I would not have been so welcoming.'

'I don't doubt it, but it seems that fate has thrown us together yet again.' Flinders extended his hand. 'It's time the family feud was put aside. It was our fathers who fell out, and what's past is in the past, as far as I am concerned, anyway.'

Charles hesitated and then shook hands. 'I agree, with one proviso.'

'Which is?' Flinders eyed him curiously.

'That you never attempt to contest Grandpapa's will.'

Flinders nodded. 'I have no interest in Westbrook House or the estate, and that will not change. It is yours to do with what you wish, regardless of the bitterness it caused.'

'I have the law on my side, but at least we now

understand each other,' Charles said grudgingly. He turned to Kitty and Amethyst with a reluctant smile. 'Please take a seat.'

'There! That wasn't so hard, was it, Charles?' Frances said, smiling. 'I've been trying to make you see sense for as long as I remember. What went on between our fathers should be consigned to history.' She sank back on a wooden settle, patting the empty space at her side. 'Do sit down, Kitty. Tell me everything.'

Amethyst pushed past Kitty and sat down beside Frances. 'We have had a simply frightful time, Frances. We were evicted from our home and forced to flee to the country.'

'That's a slight exaggeration, Amy.' Kitty perched on the edge of an upright chair, folding her hands in her lap. 'It's true we lost our home, but we are very comfortable now, thanks to Flinders and his mama. Anyway, Frances knows the details, Amy. There's no need to dwell on our misfortunes.'

'I'm sorry,' Frances said earnestly. 'I mean, I'm sorry that you lost your home. That must have been terrible. Don't you agree, Charles?' Frances sent a meaningful look to her brother.

'Yes, of course. But we must go now, Frances. Have you finished your coffee?' Charles picked up his hat and gloves. 'I have an appointment with my solicitor, and I don't want to be late. I should add that our departure has nothing to do with your sudden appearance, Flinders.'

'And I have a fitting at my dressmaker's home,' Frances added ruefully. 'You must come and visit us at Westbrook House, Kitty.' Frances turned Amethyst with an apologetic smile. 'You, too, Amethyst. I meant to say both of you.'

'I would love to see where you live,' Amethyst said eagerly. 'That would be lovely. We have no engagements therefore we are free to come whenever you say.'

'Come along, Frances.' Charles opened the door and held it, glaring at his sister. 'Time to go.'

Frances put her cup down and stood up, 'We are having a soirée at Westbrook House this coming Thursday evening. You are more than welcome to attend.' Frances pulled on her gloves. 'Perhaps your mama and grandmama might like to join us, Flinders.'

'That's very kind of you, Frances,' Flinders said, smiling. 'I'll put it to them when we get home.'

'Excellent.' Frances followed her brother to the doorway. 'It was a lovely surprise seeing you, Kitty. Perhaps we will get a chance to have a proper chat on Thursday.' She left the parlour just as the landlord reappeared carrying a tray of coffee.

'I note she didn't include me in that,' Amethyst said, pouting. 'It's not fair, Kitty. Just because I am a year or two younger than you, I am ignored.'

'That's nonsense, Amy. We are all invited to the soirée. You might meet some very interesting people there.' Kitty smiled at the landlord as he set the tray on the table. 'Thank you.' She reached for a cup and saucer and sipped the coffee.

'It's no trouble, miss.' The landlord nodded to Flinders as he left the parlour. 'Just ring the bell if you require anything else, sir.'

'I haven't anything to wear,' Amethyst said urgently.

'We brought our best gowns, Amy. They will have to do.' Kitty turned to Flinders. 'Is it likely to be a very elegant occasion?'

He shrugged. 'Possibly, but you need not worry. You will both outshine all the other ladies present.'

'You are a man, Flinders,' Amethyst said crossly. 'You simply don't understand.'

'When we've drunk our coffee, I suggest we go shopping for ribbon or pieces of lace, or even silk flowers.' Kitty took a sip of her coffee. 'I will help you to trim your gown so that you will outshine even the most fashionable ladies at the soirée, Amy.'

'It will still be an old gown,' Amethyst sighed.

'There is an excellent haberdashery in the town,' Flinders said eagerly. 'I'm sure you can find everything you need there.'

'You see, Amy.' Kitty replaced her cup on its saucer. 'There's always a solution. We can look for trimming while Flinders arranges to send his report to London.'

Amethyst jumped to her feet. 'The coffee is cold

now. Let's go to the shops, Kitty. I want to look beautiful on Thursday. Do you think they sell ostrich feathers in the haberdashery, Flinders?'

He pulled a face. 'I think that might be a little exotic for the shop in town, but you never know what you might find.'

Amethyst was already at the door. 'Come on, Kitty. Don't dawdle.'

Kitty exchanged weary glances with Flinders. 'It's going to be a long morning,' she said as she hurried after Amethyst, who was already on her way to the taproom.

Flinders escorted them to the small haberdashery shop, which proved to be a treasure trove. There were drawers filled with everything they might need to trim last year's gown and bring it up to the moment, apart from ostrich feathers. The flustered woman behind the counter assured them that there was little call for such fripperies in this part of the country, much to Amethyst's disappointment, although Kitty was somewhat relieved. She could not imagine how her petite sister would carry off such extravagant folderols. When they finally left the shop Kitty realised that she had spent much more of her hard-earned pennies than she had intended, but at least Amethyst was happy. She chattered all the way home and was still talking when they entered Mill House.

'I can't wait to lay all these pretty things out on my bed.' Amethyst started up the stairs, pausing to look around at her sister. 'Come to my room when you have a moment, Kitty. I will need your help to decide which of the trimmings might look best.' She ascended the stairs, clutching her bundle as if it were the most precious of all her belongings.

Kitty almost tripped over a pile of luggage in the entrance hall, which she realised might well belong to Edith's boarders. It was Monday, of course, and the new gentlemen must have arrived. Edith emerged from the parlour, red-faced and clearly agitated.

'Oh, it's you. I thought it must be Mr Nesbitt, the last of my gentlemen to arrive today. But as you're here, Flinders, will you take these bags up to the blue bedroom on the second floor? Mr Collins has gone to the village to do some business. I'm not sure what he is selling but he seems very respectable. Mr Hawkins is in the parlour with a tray of tea and cake, which I always greet my guests with, and he's in the windmill room.'

'We're going to a soirée at Westbrook House on Thursday,' Amethyst said excitedly. 'Flinders took us to a dear little shop in town where we bought all sorts of trimming for my best gown.'

Edith's expression hardened as she turned to Flinders, who was about to pick up a large valise. 'You're going to Westbrook House? How did this happen, Flinders?'

'It was pure coincidence, Mother,' Flinders said hastily. 'We stopped at the Crown and Anchor for coffee, and who were in the parlour but Charles and Frances.'

'And you spoke to them?' Edith glared at him. 'You actually spoke to that dreadful man?'

'Mother, it was hardly Charles's fault that Father was omitted from Grandpa's will.'

'Your father was the eldest son, and he should have inherited everything. Had Charles's father been a gentleman he could have refused to accept the inheritance, or he could have shared it with your father.' Edith's nostrils flared with anger. 'I'm surprised at you, Flinders.'

Kitty turned to Edith. 'I'm sorry if this is an inappropriate question,' she said warily. 'But if your husband was Charles Westbrook's elder brother, why isn't your name Westbrook?'

For a moment Kitty thought that Edith was not going to reply, but she made an obvious effort to control the anger that she was feeling.

'Riley was my maiden name,' Edith said irritably. 'I decided to revert to it after my husband died.'

Kitty frowned. 'But your mama is Mrs Saunders, or so I thought.'

'My mother was twice widowed. Unfortunately, her second husband frittered away the money that my father left to provide for her after his death.'

Kitty eyed Flinders curiously. 'You chose to use the name Riley as opposed to Westbrook?'

'I was much younger then, but I wanted to support my mother in any way I could.' Flinders placed his arm around his mother's shoulders and gave her a gentle hug.

'We were left with virtually nothing while Oscar Westbrook took everything,' Edith added with a heartfelt sigh. 'Charles and his sister were brought up in luxury and I scrimped and saved just to keep my son fed and clothed.'

'Father supported us to the best of his ability,' Flinders said gently. 'Things might have been different had he lived on.'

'If the mill and the mill house had not come up for sale at a knock-down price, I don't know how your grandmother and I would have survived.' Edith shook her head. 'The past seven years have not been easy, and I am still working hard to make ends meet.'

'I know, Mother, and I appreciate everything you have done and are still doing, but Westbrook House was in a near-derelict state when Grandpa passed away. Uncle Oscar spent a great deal of money restoring the building to its former glory, or so I've been told.'

'Yes, Flinders, but some of that money should have come to your father and then to you. I don't care for myself, but I do feel the injustice as far as you are concerned.' Edith turned away. 'I have work to do, as always. And if you doubt the fairness of it all just go to the mill and see how your grandmother works her fingers to the bone.' She marched off in the direction of the kitchen.

Flinders was about to follow her, but Kitty laid her hand on his arm. 'She's upset – leave her for a while. She'll calm down and then you can talk to her, but perhaps it would be better if we did not go to the soirée. I wouldn't want to make matters worse for your mama. She's been very kind in allowing us to stay here.'

'You're paying for the privilege,' Flinders said wearily. 'At least, I am paying for you and Amethyst. I know you have very little money and I'm sure that Mr Harte will reimburse me eventually, not that the money is important to me. My mother never used to be so mercenary, but she has had a difficult time since Pa died. Life is very hard for widows who are not provided for.'

'That is the whole reason that Mr Trotter started the Bazaar. Life is hard for widows and orphans. I understand why your mother is upset, but none of this is your fault, Flinders. We seem to have brought all this upon you and for that I am very sorry. Amy will be disappointed if we don't go to Westbrook House, but she'll understand.'

Flinders shook his head. 'No, Kitty. It's time the resentment and bitterness were set aside. We will go to the soirée, and from now on I will do my best to put all past disputes aside. Maybe, one day in the future, Charles might decide to be generous and give my mother a small annuity from the estate.'

Kitty laughed. 'In that case we will have to attend the function and be very nice to him. It seems to me that fate has given you and me the task of restoring our families' fortunes, but how we go about it is a bit of a mystery.'

'I am not a heroic type of man, Kitty,' Flinders said ruefully. 'But I will do what I can to make life easier for both Ma and Grandmama.'

Kitty patted him on the arm, 'And I am going to do all I can to earn my keep. I'll go now and help Nellie to prepare dinner.'

'I'll take the bags up to the gentlemen's rooms.' Flinders picked up the valises and carpet bags, tucking one under each arm before mounting the stairs.

Kitty took off her outer garments and hung them neatly on the pegs before rolling up her sleeves and heading for the kitchen. To her surprise, Mr Beadle was seated at the table, peeling potatoes, while Nellie put the last dab of egg wash on the pies she had made earlier.

'So, you've come back at last. I dare say you've had a nice outing, leaving us to do all the work, Kitty.' Nellie tempered her words with a smile. 'Me and Henry have been getting along very well, haven't we, dearie? He's helped by peeling the spuds and he hasn't cut himself either.'

Kitty took an apron from the rail in front of the range and tied it around her waist. 'I'm very impressed, Mr Beadle,' she said loudly. 'You are doing a fine job there.'

'Eh? What? Yes, to be sure.' Mr Beadle smiled vaguely and continued to cut the peeled potatoes into surprisingly regular pieces.

'He really has been a help,' Nellie said proudly. 'He just needs supervising and he's so eager to please. It makes a nice change from having to bully people into doing tedious tasks.'

'You have a magic touch, Nellie.' Kitty glanced around the neat and tidy kitchen. 'What can I do?'

'There's pots and pans to wash up in the scullery. Young Gertie is upstairs making beds or some such thing. Mrs Riley said she was tired of seeing the girl's sulky face. She's still upset because her Jem has taken a liking to Amethyst. Your sister ought to wear a label round her neck, warning other women to keep their menfolk out of her clutches.'

'She can't help being attractive, Nellie,' Kitty protested, trying not to laugh. It was true, but for the most part Amethyst managed to beguile men young and old without any apparent effort.

'We need to marry her off, if you ask my opinion, Kitty. Find her a wealthy husband and we will all be in clover.' Nellie opened the oven door and began putting in the pies.

'I like pie,' Mr Beadle said soulfully. 'Can I have pie for my supper, wife?'

'I ain't your missis, you silly old buffer.' Nellie slammed the oven door. 'Be careful with that knife. We don't want bits of your fingers in the mashed tatties.'

Kitty took the opportunity to escape to the relative peace of the scullery. The stone sink was already filled with pans in need of a good scrubbing with sand and soda. Kitty added warm water from the bucket that Gertie had left on the floor and began the onerous task. However, she was rewarded by a hug from Gertie when she returned to duty in the scullery, and as Nellie had everything under control Kitty left them to finish off preparations for dinner while she went to find out how Amethyst was getting on with sorting the trimmings for her gown. She was about to go upstairs when the sound of someone rapping the door knocker made her retrace her steps. Thinking it must be the tardy Mr Nesbitt, Kitty went to open the door. She stared at the newcomer in astonishment.

'Good heavens. You're the last person I expected to see today.'

Chapter Fourteen

Before either of them had a chance to say more, Amethyst came hurtling down the stairs at breakneck speed.

'Sebastian, I knew you would come for me.' She pushed past Kitty and flung herself into Marriner's arms. 'I saw you from the window. My knight in shining armour.'

'That's more of a welcome than I was expecting,' Marriner said, laughing. He lifted Amethyst over the threshold and set her down beside Kitty. 'I take it that I am forgiven for abandoning you so peremptorily, Amethyst, my love.'

'I didn't doubt you for a second.' Amethyst seized his hand and held it to her cheek. 'I told you he would come for me, Kitty. I knew he loved me.'

At a loss for words, Kitty was about to close

the door when another gentleman stepped into the hall.

'Mr Nesbitt,' he said, eyeing Amethyst and Marriner curiously. 'I am expected. Tell me, do all Mrs Riley's boarders get such a welcome these days?'

Kitty was relieved to see a twinkle in his grey eyes. The last thing she wanted to do was to upset any of Edith's gentlemen, especially a new arrival. She turned to Amethyst, frowning.

'Please take his lordship to the morning parlour, Amy. I'll look after Mr Nesbitt.'

Amethyst grabbed Marriner's hand and led him, unprotesting, to the parlour.

'No hug for me, then?' Nesbitt asked with a wry smile.

'You must forgive my sister, sir,' Kitty said hastily. 'Lord Marriner's arrival was unexpected.'

'I take it that he is not one of my colleagues. I mean there cannot be many titled gentlemen who are commercial travellers.' Nesbitt lifted his cases into the hall and closed the door. 'I am teasing you, miss – er – I didn't catch your name.'

'It's Kitty Harte, sir. My sister and I are also guests here. If you would care to leave your luggage, I will have it taken up to your room. Mrs Riley will be down shortly, so if you would like to take tea in the parlour, I'll tell her you have arrived.'

'I know the way, Miss Harte. Mill House is one of my favourite resting places during my travels around the country. Not all landladies provide such good service as I get here, including a cup of tea and a slice of cake on arrival.' Nesbitt strolled off in the direction of the parlour.

Kitty was still feeling shaken by the sudden appearance of Sebastian Marriner, but the fact that Mr Nesbitt was able to take care of himself was one less problem. She was eager to speak seriously to Marriner. However, she owed it to Edith to follow her example and make Nesbitt feel at home. Kitty hurried to the kitchen to make a pot of tea and cut a slice of seed cake, which she took to the parlour. Mr Nesbitt was busy chatting with Mr Collins and Mr Hawkins. It seemed that they all knew each other, making introductions unnecessary and leaving Kitty free to go to Edith's private parlour.

She was about to enter there when Flinders joined her.

'I've taken Mr Nesbitt's luggage to his room, Kitty.' Flinders gave her a searching look. 'What's the matter? You look upset.'

'We have another visitor,' Kitty said in a low voice. 'I could hardly believe my eyes when I opened the door and saw Sebastian Marriner standing there, large as life.'

Flinders stared at her in amazement. 'How on earth did he track you down to Mill House?'

'He's in the morning parlour with Amy. You can ask him that yourself. She, of course, is overjoyed and made no secret of it. You know what my sister is like when she gets her own way.'

'I'm beginning to understand her a little, Kitty. Do you want me to come in with you?'

'Yes, I do. I'm not sure how to handle this, Flinders. I know what Mama would do, but I am not in her position.'

'Let's wait until we know exactly what he proposes.' Flinders opened the door and ushered Kitty into the room.

She came to an abrupt halt at the sight of Amethyst and Marriner kissing passionately.

'Amy!' Kitty had not meant to sound so sharp, but despite being used to Amethyst's capricious behaviour, this was not how a respectable young lady ought to behave. Kitty was no prude, but she did not like to see her younger sister behaving in such an unseemly manner. She could only imagine what Mama would say in similar circumstances.

Marriner released Amethyst with a rueful smile.

'I beg your pardon, Kitty, but your sister and I have been separated for far too long. We were carried away in a romantic moment.'

Kitty frowned, refusing to be cajoled by Marriner's overt charm. 'You would not behave so if my parents were present, sir. Amy is under my care, and I have only her best interests at heart.'

Amethyst slumped down on the small sofa. 'Don't be so mean, Kitty. You know how much I've missed Sebastian, but I told you that he would come for me.' She smiled up at Marriner, her eyes alight with excitement.

'I think you'd better explain yourself, Marriner,' Flinders said coldly. 'For one thing, how did you know that Kitty and Amethyst were here?'

'I suppose I should say that I had planned this reunion, but to tell the truth it was pure chance that I happened to discover your whereabouts, my dear Amethyst.'

'I've managed very well without you,' Amethyst said, pouting. 'But you could not keep away. Admit it, Marriner.'

He laughed and sat down beside her, taking her hand in his. 'Guilty, as charged. I did make enquiries when you first disappeared from the Bazaar, but then I had business on my country estate, and I had to leave London.'

'How did you discover their whereabouts, Marriner?' Flinders asked suspiciously. 'Your estate is in Suffolk, I believe.'

'It is, but I had business in Manningtree this morning and who should I meet in the High Street but Charles Westbrook and Frances. It was she who told me where to find you, Amethyst.'

'It was fate,' Amethyst replied, clasping her hands together, eyes shining. 'I don't believe in coincidences, Sebastian. First of all, we happened to stop at the Crown and Anchor for coffee and we shared the private parlour with the Westbrooks, and then, to top it all, you happen to see them later on this morning.'

Kitty pulled up a chair and sat down, facing

Marriner. 'What do you want, Sebastian? Why have you made the journey here so late in the day when you could have waited for Thursday? I assume you are invited to the Westbrooks' soirée?'

Marriner smiled confidently. 'You are very astute, Kitty. Yes, I will attend the party at Westbrook House, but I could not wait any longer to see Amethyst. I have tried to put her out of my mind, but for some reason I cannot explain she is there when I go to sleep at night and when I wake up in the morning.'

'I feel the same,' Amethyst said dreamily. 'It must be true love, Sebastian.'

Flinders stood behind Kitty's chair. He laid a comforting hand on her shoulder. 'Isn't Amethyst a little young for you, Marriner?'

'What has it got to do with you, Riley?' Marriner demanded, rising to his feet.

'Mr Harte asked me to take care of his family in his absence,' Flinders said evenly.

Marriner met his gaze with an unflinching stare. 'You seem to have done your duty, and I can assure you that my intentions towards Amethyst are entirely honourable.'

'I'm glad to hear it,' Kitty said hastily as Amethyst jumped to her feet. 'In which case you won't mind if I ask you to leave now. You may call on Amethyst tomorrow at an appropriate hour, if you so choose.'

'Sebastian has come all this way to see me, Kitty,'

Amethyst protested tearfully. 'Can he not stay for dinner?'

'I think not, Amy,' Kitty said firmly. 'This is a boarding house, and we cannot invite people to dine without asking Mrs Riley's permission. Besides which, it is the first night for her new guests.'

'Thank you, Amethyst, my love.' Marriner kissed her lightly on the cheek. 'I will behave like a perfect gentleman and take my leave now, but I will return tomorrow afternoon, if that suits you and your sister.'

'Oh, yes. It is fine with me,' Amethyst said breathlessly. 'I can't wait to see you again.'

Flinders moved to the door and opened it. 'Have you far to go, Marriner?'

'Ten miles or so, but I have a good pair of horses. Your boy took them to the stable, so they've had a brief rest.' Marriner wrapped his arms around Amethyst and kissed her soundly on the lips before releasing her and leaving the room, to her obvious distress.

Kitty followed him to the front door. 'You are welcome here, but only if you are sincere in your regard for my sister. Don't toy with her affections, Sebastian, or you will have me to deal with.'

He looked down at her and laughed. 'What will you do, Kitty? I suppose you could paint a very ugly portrait of me and pin it to your stall in the Bazaar, but otherwise you can do me very little harm.'

'Don't be too sure of that,' Kitty said boldly. 'However, if you are sincere then I will be only too happy for Amethyst. She may be young and a trifle flighty, but she has a true heart, and I believe that she genuinely cares for you. I don't want to see her get hurt by you, or by anyone else, come to that.'

'Your loyal spirit does you well, Kitty.' Marriner stepped outside. 'I'll see you tomorrow.' Marriner strode off towards the stable.

Kitty closed the door and turned to Flinders who was standing behind her.

'Do you think we can trust him, Flinders?'

He shrugged. 'I hope so, if only for Amethyst's sake. But he has a bad reputation with women, Kitty.'

'I wonder if I ought to take Amy to Bridlebank,' Kitty said slowly. 'She should have the protection that Mama and Grandmama could give her. I doubt if Marriner would stand up to Grandmama Carstairs.'

'I thought she refused to have Amethyst stay with her?'

'She did, but this is different, Flinders. I really think I might have to return to London with Amy, although I'll give Marriner another chance to prove himself. I'll see how he behaves tomorrow.'

At that moment Edith emerged from the direction of the kitchen. 'Is that you, Flinders? Bang the dinner gong, please. You are nearer to it than I am.' She turned on her heel and headed back to the kitchen.

Flinders picked up the striker and tapped the brass gong so that its sound resonated throughout the house.

'I'd better go and help serve dinner,' Kitty said, covering her ears as she hurried towards the kitchen.

Dinner that evening was a very social affair. The newcomers' paths had crossed many times during their travels, and they swapped amusing stories of their experiences. Kitty helped to serve and to clear the table between courses, taking special care to ensure that Mr Beadle's food was cut up small enough for him to eat it, and that he was not left out when the suet pudding and custard were served.

When it came to the family's turn to dine, Amethyst toyed with her meal and ate very little, causing Edith to ask if she was feeling unwell.

'I am not hungry, Mrs Riley,' Amethyst said dreamily.

'Is she sickening for something?' Edith demanded, turning to Kitty for an answer.

'I don't think so,' Kitty said carefully. She did not want to give her sister's secret away, but neither did she want to raise Edith's suspicions.

'A good dose of castor oil is what she needs.' Edith eyed Amethyst curiously. 'Or maybe tar water would be more efficacious.'

Amethyst became suddenly alert. 'What? No, certainly not. I am quite well, thank you, Mrs Riley.'

'Then stop daydreaming and eat your supper,' Edith said crossly. 'I can't stand to see good food wasted.'

Kitty sent a meaningful look to Amethyst, who

dutifully shovelled meat pie into her mouth, swallowing convulsively. In the end she almost choked and had to leave the table to be revived with a glass of water. At this point Edith rose from the table.

'I don't know what is wrong with your sister, Kitty, but she needs to stop moping and do something useful, otherwise I'm afraid I will have to send her up to London to her mother. I cannot carry passengers here. You must understand that.'

'Of course,' Kitty said hastily. 'I will speak to her, Edith. She is very young and things have been difficult for her.'

'I had Flinders when I was her age, Kitty. I had to mature very quickly and take care of my child and my ailing father when my mother could no longer cope on her own. We women have to be strong. I can see you understand that, but Amethyst needs to stop being a pampered baby and grow up.' Edith whisked out of the kitchen, leaving Kitty to help Nellie and Gertie clear up.

'No good will come of this, Kitty,' Nellie said darkly. 'Miss Amethyst will end up a fallen woman if that man has his way.'

'Is he a bad 'un?' Gertie looked from one to the other.

'He's a lord, and we all know they don't marry common girls.' Nellie tossed a damp cloth at her. 'Get on with your work. It's none of your business, Gertie.'

'I'm sure it will turn out well in the end.' Kitty

sent a warning glance in Nellie's direction. 'We don't want rumours to spread around the village, do we?'

They proceeded in silence. When everything was neat and clean, Kitty went upstairs to Amethyst's room and knocked on the door.

'Come in.'

'Are you all right, Amy?' Kitty said as she entered the room. 'You were out of sorts at dinner.'

'I'm so excited, Kitty. I can't believe that Sebastian came for me. It's like a dream.'

'You need to take things slowly,' Kitty said as she perched on the edge of the bed. 'Don't do anything rash.'

'He loves me, Kitty. He loves me.'

'Yes, so I gather, but he has loved other women, too. Don't get your hopes up too high.'

Amethyst laughed. 'You sound like Nellie. I wonder she hasn't been after me with one of her tonics and a cold compress to soothe my fevered brain.'

'I wouldn't joke about it, if I were you. Nellie might yet follow me upstairs.' Kitty glanced at the trimmings scattered over the bedspread. 'Shall we get your gown out and see what we can do to make it prettier for Thursday?'

'Sebastian will buy me a new gown if I ask him. I will be the most elegant woman at the soirée. He said that he's been invited, and I will enter on his arm. Everyone will look at me, the future Lady Marriner. Is it exciting, Kitty?'

'Very,' Kitty said doubtfully. 'I just hope that you won't be disappointed. In fact, I'm thinking maybe we ought to go to Bridlebank and ask Grandmama to allow you to stay there for a while.'

'Heavens, no!' Amethyst's eyes widened in horror. 'That's out of the question.'

'But we don't know how long Marriner will be staying in the country, Amy,' Kitty said calmly. 'If Sebastian returns to London, he could escort you to balls and the theatre. You would be introduced as Lady Carstairs' granddaughter, Miss Amethyst Harte of Bridlebank. Everyone would know you are his intended.'

'Do you really think so?' Amethyst eyed her doubtfully. 'I don't want to go back to being one in a crowd of his friends. I mean, it was fun going out with Carnaby and the others, but it was not just Sebastian and me, if you know what I mean.'

Kitty laughed. 'Can you imagine Grandmama Carstairs allowing you to behave like a common dollymop? You would have to be chaperoned, and everything would be aimed at protecting your good name. If Sebastian has honourable intentions, he will want things to be done properly.'

Amethyst stared at her in awe. 'Do you really think so? I mean, I have always behaved well in public. Maybe I flirt a little too much, but I never allow it to go too far.'

'Reputation is everything if you want to become

the wife of a baron, Amy.' Kitty stood up and walked to the door, turning to give Amy an encouraging smile. 'You understand what I'm saying, don't you?'

Amy nodded wordlessly.

'Then I suggest we wait and see if Sebastian turns up tomorrow, as he promised. I will have a word with him then, and when I know what his plans are we can arrange to get you back to London as quickly as possible.' Kitty opened the door and hesitated, waiting for Amethyst's response.

'I don't want to go to Bridlebank, Kitty. But if Sebastian thinks it's the best course to take, I suppose there is no alternative.' Amethyst sighed and began to pack away the trimmings they had purchased that morning.

Lord Marriner was not only agreeable to the plan, but he provided his private coach to take Kitty and Amethyst to the railway station next day. He also insisted on sending a telegram to his London home to arrange for his carriage to pick them up at the station and take them in comfort and safety to Bridlebank. Amethyst was ecstatic and Kitty could not help but be impressed by his thoughtfulness.

Next day, Kitty was slightly apprehensive when they arrived at the elegant Georgian mansion surrounded by trees and protected from intruders by a high brick wall. She had been so keen to get her sister to safety that it was only now she realised that their grandmother might yet refuse to take Amethyst into her care. However, it was too late to turn back. A footman had opened the carriage door and put down the steps for them to alight.

Henley, Lady Carstairs' stern-faced butler, stood in the doorway to welcome them, or rather to question their arrival.

'Good morning, Henley,' Kitty said with a confident smile, although inwardly she was growing more nervous by the minute. 'Is my grandmother at home?'

Henley bowed and ushered them into the entrance hall. 'If you will wait here, Miss Kitty, I will see if her ladyship is available.'

'Or Mrs Harte,' Amethyst added impatiently. 'Mama will be available, as you put it, Henley.'

'Indeed, Miss Amethyst.' Henley walked away at such a slow pace that Amethyst dug Kitty in the ribs.

'It will be time for afternoon tea before he gets there, Kitty.' Amethyst's voice echoed off the high ceiling. If Henley had overheard her comment, he did not show it, apart from a slight twitch of his shoulders. Kitty had no idea how old he was, but Henley seemed to have been a fixture for ever at Bridlebank. He had never looked young, but on the other hand he did not seem to have aged. Kitty suspected that the rarefied atmosphere of Bridlebank acted like pickling vinegar and spices, keeping the inhabitants in a state of suspended animation.

'Mind your manners, Amy,' Kitty said vaguely.

'Well, anyone would think we were selling clothes pegs or lucky white heather.' Amethyst pursed her lips. 'When I am Lady Marriner, I will be welcome anywhere.'

Kitty was not sure this was entirely accurate, but she did not want to burst Amethyst's bubble of happiness. Instead, she merely smiled and waited for Henley to return. However, the first person she saw was Ivory, who came hurrying towards them, arms outstretched.

'Kitty, Amy, I'm so pleased to see you.' Ivory kissed Kitty on the cheek and then Amethyst.

'You don't normally kiss me,' Amethyst said, rubbing her face as if wiping away the gesture of endearment.

'Nor me, if it comes to that,' Kitty added, frowning. 'Are you all right, Ivory?'

'I am so bored that I could scream.' Ivory clutched her hands to her flushed cheeks. 'I shouldn't say so, but this house is so quiet and dull. I even miss Nellie and her scolding ways.'

Kitty laughed. 'I'll tell her that when I return to Mill House.'

Ivory grabbed her sister by the hand. 'Is there room for one more at Flinders' house, Kitty?'

'Just a minute.' Amethyst stared at her wide-eyed. 'I knew it would be deadly dull here, but for you to want to get away it must be truly awful.'

'I know I'm being very ungrateful,' Ivory said, wiping away tears. 'We want for nothing, and everyone is very kind, except for Grandmama's maid, Miss Waters. She is a tight-lipped old misery, and Grandmama has a very strict routine, which we all have to obey. I am up at six o'clock every morning and each day is mapped out to the second, but not in an interesting way.'

Kitty laid a hand on Ivory's arm. 'Don't say any more, please. I was hoping that Amy would be allowed to stay here for a while. Don't put her off before we've even had a chance to speak to Grandmama.'

'But why the change of heart, Amy? Why do you want to stay here? You've always hated Bridlebank.' Ivory gazed at her sister in astonishment.

'You obviously haven't noticed the smart equipage outside,' Amethyst said excitedly. 'Look at the coat of arms in the lozenge on the door. It belongs to my fiancé, Lord Marriner.'

'You are not engaged yet, Amy.' Kitty shook her head, frowning.

'What's going on?' Ivory demanded eagerly. 'What has been happening in my absence?'

'Sebastian discovered that we were staying at Flinders' family home in Essex,' Amethyst said excitedly. 'He came to find me, Ivory. He says he loves me.'

'And I thought she would be safer here with Mama

and Grandmama,' Kitty added before Amethyst could begin to extol Marriner's rather dubious virtues, apart from his title and personal fortune. 'If Marriner is serious he will have to run the gauntlet of Grandmama Carstairs' uncompromising code of honour. He will have to be very much in love with Amy to take the challenge and win.'

Ivory was about to answer when Henley reappeared to announce that Lady Carstairs would see Kitty and Amethyst in the drawing room.

'Come with us, Ivory,' Kitty said urgently. 'I may need your support.'

'Maybe Amy and I would swap places.' Ivory linked arms with Kitty. 'Do you think that Mrs Riley would allow me to stay as well as you?'

'Are you really having such a hard time here, Ivory?' Kitty lowered her voice although Amethyst had gone on ahead and was close on Henley's heels. 'Just look at her. Who would believe that Amethyst Harte, the flighty one, is willingly putting herself in the position that you obviously hate?'

Ivory shook her head. 'She will have a battle on her hands if Grandmama does agree to have her here.'

'I rather think it will be the other way round,' Kitty said, laughing. 'If I had any money to spare, I would put it all on Amy. Grandmama has not yet met her head on.'

Chapter Fifteen

Lady Carstairs looked Amethyst up and down, peering through her gold-rimmed lorgnette in a way that might, to a less confident person than Amethyst, seem intimidating.

'So, you think that Lord Marriner intends to do the honourable thing and marry you?' Lady Carstairs lowered the eyeglass, squinting shortsightedly at her granddaughter.

'It is a great honour, Mama,' Isabella said gently.

'It might be if the man is sincere, but Marriner's reputation even reaches as far as Bridlebank. She is very young, Isabella. Too young, in my opinion.' Lady Carstairs' bony fingers hovered over a compote filled with sugared almonds, and then with a swift movement she selected one and popped it into her mouth.

'I might be young, Grandmama,' Amethyst said boldly, 'but I know my own mind, and Sebastian loves me truly. He told me so.'

Lady Carstairs shifted the almond from one side of her mouth to the other as she turned to Kitty. 'I take it that it was your decision to bring Amethyst here. What exactly is it you want, Kitty?'

'Yes, Grandmama, it was my idea. I thought that Amy needed your protection and guidance in such a delicate situation. It seems that Lord Marriner is sincere, but as you say, he has a certain reputation with women, and he could ruin Amy's name and that of the whole family.'

'Oh dear. Don't say such things, Kitty.' Isabella clutched her hands to her bosom. 'Surely he would not wish to harm a sweet and innocent young girl like Amethyst.'

'Don't be a ninny, Isabella,' Lady Carstairs said abruptly. 'It wouldn't matter to a man like him. He inherited a fortune from his father, and he probably thinks he is invincible.' She paused to crunch the sugared almond. 'Pass me my glass of sherry wine, Isabella.' She took a sip from the glass and handed it back to her daughter. 'However, as I was saying, if the fellow is sincere, Amethyst will be made for life. He might even be persuaded to help the rest of you.'

'My husband supports us, Mama,' Isabella said hastily.

'And a fine job he has made of that.' Lady

Carstairs curled her lip. 'If Robert Harte was a good husband he would not be gallivanting around the world, chipping away at rocks until some of them fell on top of him.'

'That's not fair, Mama,' Isabella cried passionately. 'It was an accident.'

'He should have been more careful.' Lady Carstairs eyed Kitty with a sarcastic curl of her lips. 'You seem to be the only female in your family with any sense. What do you think?'

'I think Lord Marriner has not met you yet, Grandmama. I don't imagine he would play fast and loose with Amy's affections if he knew that he might have to answer to you.'

A slow smile lit Lady Carstairs' pale grey eyes and her lips twitched. 'Exactly the response I would expect from someone with intelligence.' She glanced at Ivory, who had been sitting quietly with her hands folded in her lap. 'What have you to say, my girl?'

Ivory jumped visibly, as if she had been far away and had suddenly realised she was being questioned. 'I – I agree with Kitty, ma'am.'

'You are a disappointment to me, Ivory. You are too much like your mother for your own good. Neither of you would say boo to a goose. I've no patience with mealy-mouthed women.' Lady Carstairs glared at Isabella. 'Yes, daughter. I meant you, too. If you had spoken up when your feckless husband decided to go off on another of his expeditions, you might not have found yourself homeless and penniless. Pass me my glass. All this talk is making me thirsty.'

Isabella bit her lip. 'I knew what he was when I married him, Mama. I love Robert and all I want is to have him home, fit and well.' She handed the glass to her mother. 'If Kitty thinks that Amethyst will be better off with us, then she should move in straight away.'

'So, you have a tongue in your head when it suits you.' Lady Carstairs drained the glass and handed it back to Isabella. 'That's settled then. You, Amethyst, will stay here and your whey-faced sister, Ivory, may stay or she can go with Kitty to the windmill, or wherever she is living at present.'

Ivory rose slowly to her feet. 'Thank you, Grandmama. I will go now and pack my things.'

'You will stay for the night, won't you?' Isabella said anxiously. 'You won't be able to get back to the Essex coast today.'

'Yes, if that's all right with you, Grandmama.'

Kitty shot her a sideways glance, not knowing quite what to expect, but to her surprise Lady Carstairs nodded, smiling.

'Yes, of course. You may regale us at dinner with stories of life in a windmill. Ring for Henley, if you please, Isabella. He will organise rooms for the girls, and now I am going to my room for my afternoon nap. I will see you all at dinner.' She rose to her feet and walked somewhat unsteadily to the door, which opened as if by magic to reveal Henley, standing to attention.

'We have two more for dinner, Henley,' Lady Carstairs said casually. 'And my granddaughters will be staying here for one night.'

'Of course, ma'am. However, there is a gentleman at the door who is asking to speak to Mrs Harte.' Henley lowered his voice. 'A police officer, ma'am. He came twice yesterday but you were unable to see him.'

Isabella was suddenly alert. 'What is this, Mama? I was perfectly well yesterday. It might have something to do with the missing silver items.'

'We don't want uniformed police officers knocking on the door, Isabella. It looks very lower class.' Lady Carstairs beckoned to Amethyst. 'Make yourself useful and see what the officer wants.'

Kitty was already on her feet. 'I'll go, Mama. It might be Sergeant Barton. He has done his best to help us.'

'And Kitty has a soft spot for him,' Amethyst said mischievously.

'I'll deal with this, Henley,' Kitty said, ignoring Amethyst's sly dig.

She left the room and hesitated for a moment, checking her appearance in one of the many gilt-framed wall mirrors. It had not occurred to her until this moment that Grandmama must be rather vain if she felt the need to gaze at her reflection so often. Kitty inhaled deeply and breathed out slowly as she attempted to calm a sudden onset of nerves. She felt the blood rush to her cheeks as she forced herself to walk to the front door at a measured pace. After all, it might not be Barton. She came to a sudden halt when she saw him standing in the entrance hall chatting amicably with James, the footman.

Barton seemed to sense her presence. He turned to look at her with a genuine smile.

'Miss Harte, this is an unexpected pleasure.'

'I wasn't expecting to see you here, Sergeant Barton.' Kitty eyed him warily. 'Is it good news or bad? I understand you came here twice yesterday.'

'I was told that Mrs Harte was unwell. I hope she has recovered now.'

'I think there was a misunderstanding. Mama is perfectly fine and apologises for not seeing you. Is there anything you want me to tell her?'

'I think we have discovered more of the silver that was stolen. I was going to ask her if she would come to the station to identify the missing items.'

'I can do that,' Kitty said hastily. 'I am not returning to Essex until tomorrow, so I could come with you now.'

'Excellent. That would be most helpful. I have a cab waiting.'

'I'll be ready in two shakes of a lamb's tail.' Kitty turned to James. 'If you will be kind enough to fetch my outdoor garments, and please tell my mother that I will be back very soon.' She accompanied her request with a smile, and he hurried off, returning moments later with her mantle, bonnet and gloves.

Barton took Kitty's mantle and held it while she put it on. The brief touch of his hands sent a thrill rippling down her spine, making her feel quite dizzy, but she steeled herself, exasperated by her own weakness. She was behaving like Amy and that would never do.

'I'm ready, Sergeant. Shall we go?'

Barton proffered his arm. 'I could wish we were off somewhere more exciting than the police station.'

'Oh, I don't know. It is a rare occasion for me, so I do find it quite intriguing.' Kitty laid her hand on his arm and again she experienced a physical sensation that was both exciting and alarming.

'Wait a moment, if you please.' The sharp command echoed off the high ceiling, repeating eerily as if taken up by the long-dead ancestors whose portraits hung on the walls.

Kitty turned to see her grandmother's maid hurrying towards them, her bonnet on awry and her black cape flying out behind her. 'What's the matter, Miss Waters?' Kitty dropped her hand to her side.

'You are not to accompany this person unchaperoned. Lady Carstairs has ordered me to go with you.' Miss Waters glared at Barton. 'You ought to know better, Sergeant.'

'This is strictly police business, ma'am,' Barton

said calmly. 'But of course you may come with us, if you so wish.'

'I do as I am asked, Sergeant. I hope the hackney carriage is in a reasonable state. I don't usually travel by public transport.' Miss Waters marched out of the house and went to stand by the cab, waiting for someone to open the door for her.

'I expect she has a broomstick tucked away in a cupboard,' Kitty said in a low voice.

Barton laughed. 'I wasn't going to say so, but she does seem to take her responsibilities seriously.'

He went to open the door and Miss Waters climbed into the cab first with a blatant disregard for protocol.

Barton winked at Kitty as he handed her into the vehicle and climbed in after her.

Conversation was sporadic and stilted during the carriage ride, and Miss Waters maintained a frosty silence throughout. On arrival at the police station in Tottenham Court Road she entered the building with an air of martyrdom. She glowered suspiciously at the desk sergeant as well as any unwary constable who happened to walk past. Having sent a silent warning to anyone who might approach her, Miss Waters took a seat and stared straight ahead; her lips closed in a thin line.

After a word with the duty sergeant, Barton ushered Kitty into a room where the silver had been laid out on a trestle table. Miss Waters had made a half-hearted attempt to follow them, but Barton assured her it was unnecessary, adding in a conciliatory tone that Kitty could not have more protection if she were the Queen herself. He glanced up and down the passageway before closing the door.

'I was just checking to make sure that Miss Waters had not decided to follow us. That woman has the tenacity of a bulldog, although,' Barton added hastily, 'I'm sure she has your best interests at heart.'

'I doubt it, Sergeant,' Kitty said, smiling ruefully. 'I think she models herself on my grandmother, who is a stickler for propriety. Grandmama disapproves of me because I have a mind of my own, although today she complimented me on my intelligence. I think that was the first time she has ever said anything nice to me.'

'I've never met Lady Carstairs, but if her maidservant is anything to go by, I think her ladyship must be quite terrifying. I say that as someone who has dealt with the worst gangs in the East End.'

Kitty laughed. 'You are not wrong. I would pit Grandmama against the most nefarious bully in your cells. They would quake beneath her icy gaze.' Kitty walked over to the table and reached out to pick up a candlestick. 'This is one of the items.' She put it down and selected a serving dish. 'And this one, too. In fact, all the items here belong to us, Sergeant Barton. Mama will be so pleased.'

'Excellent, but you do realise we have to keep them until all the formalities are completed?'

Kitty nodded. 'Yes, of course. Anyway, we have nowhere to put them at present. Mama will continue to live at Bridlebank, and I will return to Mill House tomorrow.'

'I'm sorry,' Barton said earnestly. 'That is, it would have been nice to see you again, preferably without Miss Waters breathing fire and brimstone.'

'I agree.' Kitty met his intense gaze with an attempt at a smile. She knew she ought not to encourage him, but she had never been good at hiding her feelings. 'I don't know when we will be able to return to London. It all depends upon how quickly my father recovers and can undertake the sea voyage home.'

Barton took her hand in his and seemed about to say something when someone rapped on the door. He released her with a guilty start just as the door opened and Miss Waters entered the room.

'I think it's time we were on our way home, Miss Harte.' Miss Waters eyed Barton suspiciously. 'You brought us here, Sergeant. I trust you will pay for a cab to take us back to Highgate.'

'Yes, of course, Miss Waters,' Barton said evenly. 'I will just ask Miss Harte to sign a statement and then I will arrange transport for you both.'

'We do not need you to accompany us, Sergeant.' Miss Waters faced him with a challenge in her eyes.

'Of course not.' Barton ushered her out of the

room, followed by Kitty. 'Our business here is almost completed. Thank you for your time and trouble, Miss Harte.'

'It was no trouble, sir. I am glad we will have our silver back, eventually. Mama will be delighted.' Kitty followed him back to the reception area and sat down to sign the necessary paperwork while Barton sent a constable to hail a cab. Miss Waters stood by the door, tapping her foot on the tiled floor as if impatient to be on her way.

With the formalities completed, Miss Waters was first into the cab, leaving Barton to hand Kitty into the vehicle.

'Thank you for your cooperation, Miss Harte.' Barton held onto her hand a little longer than was necessary.

'Thank you for everything, Sergeant,' Kitty said, curling her fingers around his with a sinking heart. This seemed to be a final farewell as there was little likelihood that they might meet again, even when officialdom had no need to hold on to the Carstairs family's silver. Barton released her and the cab started off on the return journey to Bridlebank.

'You can forget him,' Miss Waters said abruptly. 'I've met men like him before. You've had a lucky escape, if you ask me.'

Kitty settled into her corner of the cab. 'I didn't ask your opinion, Miss Waters.'

'You think because I'm an old maid that I don't

know what it's like to have feelings for a man. Well, you're wrong, my dear. I was young once and I fell in love with someone not unlike your police sergeant.'

'Please stop,' Kitty said in desperation. 'I am not in love with Sergeant Barton. I hardly know him.'

'But you want to know him better. Take my advice and be content with your lot. Find someone who is solid and reliable and won't leave you at the altar.'

Kitty stared at her in surprise. 'You were jilted, Miss Waters?'

'He was a soldier. Very dashing and handsome, and we were to be married in secret because my family did not approve. I waited at the church for two hours, but he didn't arrive. I discovered that his regiment had left that day on board a ship bound for India, and I never saw him again. My heart was broken.'

'I am so sorry,' Kitty said softly. 'But he was at fault, not you.'

'That didn't make any difference. I could never bring myself to trust a man again. As I said, Miss Harte, don't fall into the same trap as I did. Move on, before it's too late.'

'I'm unlikely to see Sergeant Barton again, Miss Waters,' Kitty said sadly. 'But I am truly sorry for what happened to you. Did you never meet anyone who might have made you happy?'

'I did not, and I prefer not to speak of it again, Miss Harte. I only told you my story to warn you what could happen if you become involved with someone totally unsuitable. You are, after all, Lady Carstairs' granddaughter. You and your sisters deserve to marry well.'

Kitty shot her a sideways glance. 'You mean you approve of my younger sister marrying Lord Marriner, even though he has a questionable reputation?'

'It is not my place to approve or disapprove, Miss Harte. I am merely an employee.' Miss Waters turned her head and stared out of the carriage window, making it obvious that she had no intention of carrying on the conversation. Kitty sat back against the worn leather squabs, attempting to put Sergeant Barton out of her mind and failing miserably. By the time they reached Bridlebank Kitty had decided that she must try to be like Miss Waters and get on with life in whatever way fate chose to lead her. It was not a comforting thought.

It was late afternoon when they arrived back at Bridlebank, and, like Lady Carstairs, Isabella had gone to her bedchamber to take a nap before dinner. Ivory and Amethyst were in the drawing room, poring over the latest fashion plates. However, Kitty was not in the mood for small talk, least of all Amethyst's constant babbling about Marriner and how he was going to appear one day and take her away from all this. It was still light, and Kitty decided to take a walk in the extensive grounds. She needed to be on her own for a while to recover her equilibrium, and the sight of lesser celandines carpeting the ground beneath the trees in the woodland lifted her spirits. Their sunny yellow colour reminded her of happier times when they had visited Bridlebank as children and dabbled their toes in the stream that divided the parkland from the more formal gardens. The evenings were just beginning to draw out, but the sun had plummeted below the horizon, creating deep shadows between the trees. Kitty gave way to a sudden urge to search for early primroses, and she ventured further into the wood than she had intended. She was intent on her task when a man emerged from behind a tree and grabbed her around the neck, making it hard for her to breathe.

Kitty struggled and kicked, but her assailant was far stronger than she. His grip tightened until she was close to fainting.

'Stop struggling, you fool. I won't hurt you if you do what I say.'

Kitty nodded wordlessly and he took his arm away, slipping it around her waist instead. His breath was rank against her cheek, but she recognised him instantly.

'I thought you were in prison, Dagg.' Kitty forced herself to sound confident, although that was far from the truth. 'Don't tell me you escaped and left your father to take your punishment?'

'He's an old man. I doubt if he's got much longer to live anyway, but I'm still young. I ain't going to spend my best years in no prison cell, and you're going to help me get away.'

'Don't be ridiculous.' Kitty drew away from him. 'How far do you think you're going to get dressed in prison uniform?'

'That's your part in this, Miss Harte, seeing as how it was you and your ma who put me in this garb.'

'You did it to yourself by thieving and cheating people. Why should I help you?' Kitty drew herself up to her full height, but he still towered above her. She was afraid, but she was also angry and that gave her courage.

'Shut your mouth or I'll shut it for you.' Dagg closed his hand on her shoulder, squeezing her flesh until she flinched. 'Don't imagine I'm playing games here, miss. If you hadn't come by, I would have taken someone from the servants' quarters. I want fresh clothes, food and money to get me as far from London as I can.'

'I could say I would do this and go into the house to fetch help.'

'I would slip away but I'd come back when it was safe. I know your ma is here and I wouldn't be so generous if I got my hands on her. Pa said she was the one who took the silver to him, and she informed the police. I got a score to settle with that woman.'

Dagg leaned over her, his face so close to hers that she could see every scar, mole and deep line that made him look hideous as well as frightening.

Kitty did not doubt that he would carry out his threats. She had no previous experience of a man so desperate he would do anything to prevent recapture, but it was obvious that Dagg was in such a parlous state.

'I will do as you ask, but I want your word that no harm will come to anyone in my family.'

He grinned, revealing a row of broken, yellow teeth. 'You want the word of a felon. All right, miss. You have my word, for what it's worth. I'll give you ten minutes to get me what I want or I'm coming in after you.' He released her so suddenly that she stumbled and only just managed to regain her balance.

'Ten minutes isn't enough. I'll be back within half an hour, but you must remain out here, well away from the house. If you come closer, you will find yourself facing the gamekeeper's dogs.'

'All right, but don't try nothing clever.' Dagg retreated into the deep shadows, leaving Kitty free to return to the house. She ran all the way, arriving breathless and undecided. She could send James for the constable, but by the time help arrived Dagg would have made himself scarce. She did not doubt that he would carry out his threats if he did not get his way, and the only sensible course would be to do as he asked. There would be plenty of time afterwards to alert the police.

Kitty's first and most difficult task was to find garments that would fit such a tall, brawny man, to replace his prison uniform. She went straight to the laundry room, which she remembered from childhood was in an outbuilding, where the sheets and white articles were boiled mercilessly in a huge copper with a fire beneath. The drying room was adjacent, and on wet Tuesdays it had been a warm place to go and watch the laundry maids wielding heavy flat irons as they smoothed away the creases. As luck would have it, there were garments hanging on the airers that obviously belonged to some of the groundsmen, and Kitty snatched a pair of trousers and a cotton shirt. A leather jerkin had been left with the pile of mending and she took that, bundling everything into a pillowcase.

Satisfied with her progress so far, Kitty opened the back door and tiptoed along the passageway that led past the kitchen. She could hear Cook giving orders to the maids, and the clatter of pots and pans as they prepared dinner. She managed to get past the open door without being seen and made her way to the main larder. Once again, her memories of time spent at Bridlebank served her well. She remembered the frugal meals that Grandmama Carstairs decided were suitable for children, leaving Kitty and her sisters constantly hungry. This had been alleviated by forays into the larder to supplement their meagre diet. It had been on these occasions that Kitty, although young, had realised that the servants were fed better than those above stairs, especially the children. She smiled as she placed a raised pork pie, half a truckle of cheese, and a loaf of bread in the pillowcase. She added a bottle of beer for good luck, in the hope of sweetening Dagg's temper. All that remained now was to get out of the house unseen and deliver the goods before Dagg grew impatient.

Dagg was waiting for her beneath the trees. He rushed towards her and snatched the bulging pillowcase.

'You took your time. I was about to come looking for you.'

'No, you weren't,' Kitty said angrily. 'You wouldn't have been stupid enough to come into the house. I've got you what you asked for. Now I want you to leave here. Don't return or I will set the police on you.'

Dagg emptied the pillowcase onto the grass. He snatched up the pie and bit into it, mumbling appreciatively and spewing pastry crumbs from his lips.

Kitty backed away. 'Don't come near the house again. You can't hurt me because I'll be gone tomorrow. I suggest you go as far away from here as possible if you don't want to be caught.' She put her hand in her pocket and took out a few coppers and a florin, which she threw onto the ground at his feet. 'That's all the money I have. Take it and go far away from here.'

Dagg swallowed convulsively. He picked up the beer bottle and smashed the neck on a nearby stone to dislodge the cork.

'Pity you didn't think to bring a corkscrew, miss.' Dagg held the bottle above his mouth and tilted it so that a stream of beer trickled into his throat. 'And don't think you can get away from me so easily. I know where you've been living. I made it my business to find out. If you peach on me, I promise that you will be the first one to get what's coming to you, followed by your sisters. I'll get to them, one by one. Do you understand what I'm saying?'

Chapter Sixteen

Kitty barely slept that night, and when she did manage to doze off, she was plagued by nightmarish dreams with Dagg carrying out his threat to harm her mother and sisters. She knew she should alert the police, but she wanted to be sure that Dagg was far away, and that her family were safe, before she did so. When at last it was time to get up, she washed in cold water, dressed and put up her hair before going downstairs to the drawing room. She went to her grandmother's escritoire and penned an urgent note to Barton, which she folded, addressed and sealed. With it tucked in her pocket she went to the dining room and joined Ivory at the breakfast table.

'You look awful, Kitty,' Ivory said, frowning. 'Are you sickening for something?'

Kitty stifled a yawn. 'I didn't sleep very well. The bed was lumpy.'

'I don't suppose it had anything to do with Sergeant Barton, did it?' Ivory smiled sympathetically. 'I know you like him, Kitty.'

'I do, but I doubt if I will ever see him again.' Kitty's hand went automatically to pat the pocket that concealed the note to Barton. 'I'm not lovesick like Amy, if that's what you're thinking.'

Ivory filled a bowl with thick, sticky porridge and gazed down at it, sighing. 'I hope never to see this dreadful concoction again. Grandmama insists that it is the best way to start the day, but I disagree.' She reached for the sugar bowl. 'It's just about palatable if you are generous with the sugar, but not too generous. I suspect that Cook weighs the sugar bowl before it is put on the table and again when it goes back to the kitchen.'

'Surely Grandmama cannot be so parsimonious?'

'You haven't lived here recently, Kitty. I don't recommend it.' Ivory sprinkled sugar onto the gluey grey mixture in her bowl. 'Did you say that Nellie is doing the cooking at Mill House?'

'Yes, she took over from Mrs Potter, who went off in a huff because Mrs Riley praised Nellie's cooking. Anyway, we are all required to do our bit, Ivory. You will have to help in some way as well.' Kitty helped herself to a small amount of porridge and covered it with sugar. She tasted it cautiously. 'It's not very nice. It reminds me of that flour and hot-water paste that we used to concoct when we made paperchains at Christmas.'

Ivory pulled a face. 'I never tasted that, but I imagine there would be little difference.' She glanced at the brass clock on the mantelshelf. 'What time are we going to leave, Kitty? I'm packed and ready. All I need to do is to put on my outdoor things and say my goodbyes.'

Kitty pushed her plate away. 'I'm afraid I cannot eat that horrid stuff.' She rose from her seat. 'I'll go and find James and ask him to have the carriage sent round to take us to the railway station.' Kitty hurried from the room before Ivory had a chance to respond.

She found James in the entrance hall, polishing the brass door knocker.

'Good morning, James,' Kitty said with a bright smile. 'Would you please send for the carriage to take me and my sister to the railway station?'

'Of course, Miss Harte.'

'And, James, I have a special mission for you, which must be kept secret.'

He stared at her open-mouthed. 'Miss Harte?'

'I have a note for Sergeant Barton of the Metropolitan Police. I want this to go to him today. It's very important. Can you arrange that for me, James?' Kitty took the note from her pocket and handed it to him.

'Yes, I will make sure it goes straight to him, Miss Harte.'

'Thank you, James. I know I can trust you.' Kitty could only hope that James would carry out her instructions and that Barton would receive the note before the end of the day. She had done all she could and now it was time to return to Mill House. She went upstairs to say goodbye to her mother and Amethyst.

The journey back to Mill House was uneventful, but tedious, and it was mid-afternoon when they arrived. Flinders and Edith greeted them warmly, as did Nellie, who brought them tea and a cake she had made specially for Ivory, knowing it was her favourite.

'Of course I won't expect you to do anything today, Ivory,' Edith said firmly. 'But tomorrow I will give you a list of things you can do to help around the house. Kitty will show you what to do. My gentlemen this week are very pleasant and easy-going, and they get along well together, which is a bonus. Anyway, now I need to go to the kitchen and help Nellie prepare the evening meal.' Edith left the room without waiting to see if Ivory had any questions.

'Don't worry,' Kitty said, smiling. 'It sounds daunting, but you won't be asked to do anything difficult. If Amy could manage to help that must tell you something.'

'Who would have thought it would come to this, Kitty? I mean we had a nice life in London, even when we had to work in the Bazaar, but I never imagined I might one day have to wait on table or make beds like a common servant.' Ivory shook her head. 'What would Papa say if he knew?'

'He would thank Mrs Riley for taking us in and he would be proud of Flinders for taking care of us. It's not for ever, Ivory. Pa will come home eventually and then life will become normal again.'

'I hope you're right.' Ivory rose from the sofa. 'Am I to have Amethyst's old room? I would like to unpack now.'

'Of course.' Kitty jumped to her feet. 'I'll show you where it is. This is a very odd house and it's easy to get lost with all the different levels and narrow passages, but you'll get used to it.' Kitty opened the door and led the way upstairs. 'We've been invited to a soirée at the Westbrooks' home on Thursday. I didn't want to say too much in front of Amy, because she wanted to go, but it should be interesting, to say the very least.'

'I'm not sure I'm ready to socialise,' Ivory said anxiously. 'I don't know what Charles will say when he knows I am doing the work of a servant. It will be embarrassing.'

'Nonsense, Ivory.' Kitty ushered her into Amy's pleasant room. 'This is where you will sleep. As to the Westbrooks, they know our situation and they were very nice about it. I don't think we would have been invited to meet their friends and acquaintances had they found us an embarrassment.'

Ivory sank down on the bed. 'I hope you're right.' She yawned. 'I'm a bit tired, Kitty. Do you think I have time for a nap before dinner? I find all this really exhausting.'

'Yes, of course. Take off your shoes and lie down. I'll wake you up when it's time to go downstairs. I'm sure you'll feel better about everything when you've had time to settle in.'

Kitty left her sister to rest while she went downstairs. She met Flinders in the entrance hall, and she beckoned to him.

'I need to speak to you, Flinders. Come into the parlour because I don't want everybody to hear.'

He followed her into the room and closed the door. 'As a matter of fact, I have something to tell you, too. But you go first.'

'Sergeant Barton has found the rest of our silver.'

'That's splendid news,' Flinders said enthusiastically.

'Yes, it is. I saw it myself and it's all there, but there's something else. Something much more urgent. Dagg has escaped from prison.'

'The old pawnbroker?'

'No, his son, which is worse. I went for a walk in the grounds at Bridlebank yesterday evening, and he was lying in wait. He would have accosted anyone who ventured near him, but it just happened to be me.'

'Good God, you weren't hurt, were you, Kitty?'

'I was more scared than anything, but he made

me get him a change of clothes and some food. I had a little money, and he took that, too.'

'Why didn't you get help and have him arrested?'

'It wasn't that easy, Flinders. He threatened to harm my family if I so much as breathed a word of it. I did send a message to Barton this morning, and I only hope he's received it, but there was nothing else I could have done. At least not without putting everyone in danger at Bridlebank. I don't doubt that he's a desperate man.'

'So Dagg is on the run from the police. Did he tell you where he planned to go?'

'No, he didn't, but he does know that we are staying here with you and your mama. Not that I think he would try to follow us, but he has limited funds. Who knows what a desperate man might do?'

'He's a Londoner, Kitty,' Flinders said thoughtfully. 'He'll have connections in the East End. I doubt if he'll stray far from everything he knows.'

'I hope you're right, and the police will be aware of his contacts, I'm sure.' Kitty managed a smile. 'Don't look so worried, Flinders. I'm sure we will be safe here.'

'This news has come at a bad time.' Flinders put his hand in his pocket and drew out a letter. 'I've had my instructions to return to British Guiana. I want to go, of course, and most importantly I want to find out how your father is progressing, but I really don't want to leave you unprotected with that villain wandering free.'

'You mustn't worry about us, Flinders.' Kitty laid her hand on his arm. 'As you said, Dagg will probably remain in London. We will be fine.'

Flinders did not look convinced. 'I'll be here for the soirée at the Westbrooks'. I'll ask Charles to keep an eye on you. He's a decent enough fellow, even if we haven't been on the best terms in the past.'

'I'm sure he will be happy to oblige. I had the feeling that he was rather taken with Ivory when he first met her, and he did purchase her portrait.'

'I didn't think you were a matchmaker, Kitty,' Flinders said, laughing.

'Neither did I, but Amy started this off by assuming that Marriner is going to propose, when it's quite possible that he was just flirting with her. I hope that isn't the case, but I won't believe he has honourable intentions until I see a ring on her finger. Anyway, she is very young. Perhaps too young to be married, especially to a man with such a questionable reputation.'

'I agree, but from what I know of your sister, she will do what she pleases, no matter what anyone says.' Flinders stood up at the sound of the dinner gong. 'Did you warn Ivory to come down on time for meals?'

Kitty was already at the door, and she opened it. 'Don't worry about that, Flinders. My sister has been living with Grandmama for long enough to know the rules, and life at Bridlebank is governed by the gong. Anyway, I should be in the kitchen, helping. I'd better go and see what's left for me to do.' She hurried from the room and met Ivory at the foot of the stairs.

'I heard the gong, Kitty. Is that dinner for us, or do we have to wait on Mrs Riley's lodgers?'

'A bit of both really,' Kitty said calmly. 'Come to the kitchen with me and we'll see how far Mrs Riley and Nellie have got with service. We've been dining with the gentlemen so far, and I look after Mr Beadle and make sure he gets his food.' Kitty walked on in the direction of the kitchen.

'What's wrong with Mr Beadle?' Ivory asked anxiously. 'Is the poor man ill?'

'No, he's just old and deaf. He's almost blind, which makes it difficult for him to feed himself at times.'

'Why is he here, then, Kitty? If he's in such a state, he can't be a commercial traveller?'

'He never was,' Kitty said hurriedly. 'He used to own the mill and Mill House, but he took to drink. Mrs Riley keeps him here out of charity, but I get the feeling she considers him a burden and I feel sorry for the poor old fellow. Anyway, smile and offer your services. Mrs Riley is strict but very fair.' Kitty opened the kitchen door and a waft of hot air redolent with the delicious aroma of roast beef made Kitty feel suddenly hungry. She forgot all about Dagg and his threats.

'What would you like us to do, Mrs Riley?' Kitty asked dutifully.

Edith looked Ivory up and down. 'I hope you are not too much of a lady to get those dainty hands dirty occasionally, Miss Harte.'

'Please call me Ivory, Mrs Riley. I will do whatever you ask of me. I'm truly grateful to you for taking us in. I don't expect special treatment.'

Nellie laughed as she ladled gravy into a large jug. 'That's good, Miss Ivory, because you won't get it here. We all pitch in to help.'

'We eat the same meal as the gentlemen,' Edith added, watching Ivory carefully as if expecting her to protest.

'I understand, ma'am,' Ivory said graciously. 'You won't get any complaints from me, and the food looks delicious, Nellie. I've really missed your cooking.'

Nellie pulled a face. 'I've eaten in the servants' quarters at Bridlebank. No wonder you look thin and pale, Miss Ivory. They keep the best for themselves but that's not saying much.' She sniffed and took a roasting pan out of the oven filled with crisp golden potatoes.

Edith finished carving the joint and laid the meat on a serving dish. 'I feed my gentlemen well and that's why they return time and time again. They know they are going to get value for money, good food and a nice comfortable bed with spotless sheets and pillowcases. Now, Kitty, you and Ivory take the dishes to the dining room. I serve at table, Ivory. It makes the meal more personal. It's a system that seems to work to everyone's satisfaction.'

As usual, Kitty sat beside Mr Beadle. He turned his head and gave her a lop-sided smile.

'I missed you. I thought you weren't coming back, miss.'

Kitty patted his hand. 'Someone has to make sure you eat your dinner, Mr Beadle.' She cut his food into small pieces, put a spoon in his hand, and watched him carefully during the meal, helping him only when necessary.

The gentlemen were quiet at first as they tucked into their food, but when the apple pie and custard was served, they seemed to relax, and they began to chat freely. Mr Nesbitt managed to turn everyday events into amusing anecdotes, and soon everyone was laughing. Kitty kept an eye on her sister, but Ivory seemed quite at ease, and she listened politely when Edith spoke to her. Kitty was not listening, but she could not help overhearing snatches of conversation. Edith had obviously taken a liking to Ivory and that boded well for the sisters' future at Mill House. Kitty had realised early on that Edith could be harsh if she took a dislike to anyone, although Ivory's pleasant manner had always made her popular. Kitty was able to relax a little although, glancing at Flinders across the table, she knew that she would miss him more than she would have thought possible when he left for South America. He was, she told herself, the brother that she had never had.

The last crumb had been scraped off the plates and a murmur of appreciation rippled around the table. Edith rose to her feet.

'We will clear away so that you gentlemen may enjoy your coffee.' Edith signalled to Kitty and Ivory, and they stood up obediently, and began to pile up the dishes.

'I don't like coffee, Kitty,' Mr Beadle said plaintively. 'I like tea.'

'Don't worry, Mr Beadle.' Kitty leaned closer. 'I'll make sure you have a pot of tea all to yourself. Perhaps Mr Collins would pour it for you.' She gave Mr Collins an encouraging smile and he nodded.

'Happy to oblige, miss.'

Edith went to the doorway, then stopped, turning to her son. 'Flinders, I want you to take a tray to the windmill. Ma had a fall earlier and hurt her arm. I know she won't bother to feed herself.'

Flinders was on his feet immediately. 'I didn't know she had injured herself, Ma.' He followed her as she headed for the kitchen with Kitty and Ivory close behind.

'Did she break any bones?' Kitty asked anxiously.

'The doctor said it's just a sprain, but she won't be able to work for a week or two. Jem is helping. He has found a labourer to do the heavy work.' Edith placed the apple pie on the kitchen table. 'I want you to persuade her to come back with you, Flinders. She refused when I suggested it, but she thinks the world of you, and she might just agree, having been on her own for several hours.'

'Of course I'll go, but I won't take food. Grandmama must come here, if only to eat,' Flinders said firmly. 'You should have told me earlier, Ma. I would have insisted that she joined us here for dinner. I never liked the fact that she lives there on her own.'

'Would you like me to come with you, Flinders?' Kitty put the pile of dirty crockery on the table. 'I could pack some things for her if she agrees to stay here.'

'An excellent idea,' Edith said, smiling. 'I think this might be our chance to persuade Ma to give up the mill at last, but she is a very stubborn woman.'

Flinders laughed. 'I believe that's the pot calling the kettle black, Ma.' He held up his hands. 'I'm going, but I suggest we leave the food here to keep warm. Kitty and I will persuade Grannie to accompany us, even if we have to kidnap her. Are you coming, Kitty?'

Kitty was already at the door. 'I most certainly am. I met your grandmother, Flinders. She's an amazing person.'

'What can I do?' Ivory asked anxiously.

Nellie thrust a coffee pot into her hands. 'Go and charm the gentlemen in the dining room, Miss Ivory. I'll wager they have never been waited on by such a lovely young lady.'

'Mr Beadle wants tea,' Kitty called over her shoulder as she followed Flinders from the kitchen.

Adeline Saunders was seated on a small sofa in her living room. Kitty could see by her pallor and the way she protected the injured arm that she was in a great deal of pain.

'I'm sorry, Grandmama, but we all think it best that you spend a day or two at Mill House,' Flinders said gently. 'I would have come sooner had I known you were hurt.'

'I don't want a fuss, Flinders.' Adeline glared at him. 'I can't leave the mill unattended.'

'Mrs Riley said that Jem had found someone to do the heavy work, Mrs Saunders.' Kitty gave her an encouraging smile. 'You will get better much more quickly if you can rest and be looked after.'

'I'm perfectly capable to looking after myself, young lady.' Adeline winced as she tried to move.

'Grandmama, you will accompany us even if I have to carry you.' Flinders went down on one knee beside her. 'Mama has a tasty meal waiting for you and a nice warm bed. Don't worry about the mill. We will make sure everything runs as smoothly as possible in your absence.'

Adeline's set expression softened. 'You always were a charmer, Flinders. You take after your grandfather in that respect.'

Kitty could see that she was weakening. 'If you

will tell me what you need for tonight, I will pack a bag for you, Mrs Saunders.'

'I haven't said I will go with you.' Adeline frowned. 'Flinders, I warn you . . .' she broke off as Flinders rose to his feet and in a swift movement lifted her bodily from the sofa.

'No, Grandmama, you are in no position to argue. I'm sorry, but I can't leave you here on your own. You are coming with us for the night. Kitty will bring whatever you need, but I am taking you home. Ma would bar me from the house if I went home without you.'

Adeline leaned her head against his shoulder. 'It doesn't look as if I have much choice, but one night only. Tomorrow morning you can bring me back here. The new man didn't seem very bright, but it was an emergency.'

'Do you know him, Grandmama? Is he a local fellow?'

'I only saw him in the distance. I didn't recognise him, Flinders, but Jem said he seems eager to work.'

'What can I get for you, ma'am?' Kitty asked patiently. 'A nightgown and a wrap, perhaps?'

'Yes,' Adeline said wearily. 'There's a chest of drawers in the room above – that's where I sleep. There is not much space for luxuries in a mill.'

'Consider it done.' Kitty picked up an oil lamp. 'I'll lock the door on my way out, Flinders.'

'Come on then, Grandmama,' Flinders said,

smiling. 'It's fortunate that you are so light. I'm going to carry you all the way home.'

'I can walk. Put me down, you cheeky boy.'

'I don't trust you not to run away, Grandmama.' Flinders carried her from the room, leaving Kitty to go upstairs to find the things that Adeline might need for a short stay at Mill House.

It took a while for Kitty to select what Adeline might need, but eventually she was satisfied, and she made her way downstairs. She stepped outside, holding the lantern so that she could see to put the huge iron key into the lock, when a footstep on the gravel made her turn so quickly that she almost lost her balance. Everything went dark as a flour sack was dragged over her head. She dropped the oil lamp and found herself flung over a burly shoulder as her assailant descended the steps. Kitty struggled but he was far stronger than she, and he tossed her onto the hard boards of a cart, before binding her hands and then her feet. All the while he maintained a stony silence, which Kitty found almost more frightening than the violence of the assault. She lay gasping on the floor as the vehicle lurched forward. Her cries for help were muffled by the sacking and carried away on a sharp east wind.

Chapter Seventeen

Kitty huddled on the wooden floor for what seemed like hours and was thrown from side to side as the cart jolted over uneven tracks and rutted roads. She was cold, cramped and her wrists were sore from being rubbed by the coarse rope that bound them. She wondered vaguely if Flinders had gone in search of her, and she could only imagine the anxiety felt by Ivory and Nellie when she did not return to the house. But all this was fruitless, and she put her efforts into keeping positive. This was just a temporary setback. Whoever had kidnapped her must have mistaken her for someone else. There could be no other explanation.

She was suddenly aware that the horse had slowed down, and the cart came to a rumbling halt. Kitty braced herself, waiting for the inevitable confrontation with her captor. She stiffened as the back of the vehicle was let down and she was hauled into a sitting position. The sack was dragged off her head and shoulders, leaving her blinking as her eyes grew accustomed to the bright moonlight.

'Dagg! I might have known it was you.' Kitty stared at him with a mixture of disgust and anger. 'What do you think you're doing?'

'You thought you were free of me, but not yet, miss. You are my insurance when that nosy copper comes after me.'

'If you're referring to Sergeant Barton, I should imagine he has better things to do than to chase a nobody like you round the country, Dagg.' Kitty spoke more boldly than she was feeling. He was too close for comfort, and she could smell alcohol on his breath.

'That's where you're wrong. It's personal for Barton and has been from the start. I could tell by the way he spoke of you that there was more in it. A man, even a johndarm, loses all sense when a pretty woman is involved.' Dagg took a knife from his belt and held it close to Kitty's face.

She stiffened, glaring at him, but he laughed and bent down to cut the rope that bound her ankles. 'I ain't carrying you again. You're not a featherweight, even if you look as if a puff of wind could blow you away. Stand up.' Dagg's tone sharpened, and Kitty obeyed. She could tell that he was on the verge of violence, and she did not want to anger him further.

'Where are we?' Kitty looked around and was startled to see what appeared to be a derelict priory. A shaft of moonlight revealed arched windows and there were religious symbols on the ancient oak door. Part of the building was in ruins, with creeper growing over the piles of stone, and the crumbling archways seemed eerie rather than romantic against the star-studded sky.

'Where are we?' Kitty demanded when Dagg refused to answer.

'Never you mind,' he said sharply. 'This is a place of sanctuary for me and somewhere the law won't find you.' Dagg gave her a push so that she stumbled in the direction of the doorway. He was close behind her and he struck the solid oak several times with a wooden baton he drew from his belt. 'Brother Benedictus takes his time,' Dagg said, grinning.

'But surely this isn't a working priory.' Kitty turned to look at him. 'It's a ruin, and even if it were still a home for monks, they wouldn't be too keen on giving the likes of yourself sanctuary.'

'Harsh words, my dear. However, Brother Ben got left behind when the order moved elsewhere, or perhaps they abandoned him due to his addiction to the strong ale they brewed here.'

Kitty was even more alarmed now, but she could hear footsteps on the flagstone floor, and even if she could run, this place seemed to be in the heart of the countryside with no friendly lights flickering in the darkness. It was a chilling thought, but she had nowhere to go.

The heavy door creaked open, and a small, chubby man wearing a monk's habit held up a lantern, peering at them in its flickering light.

'All are welcome here,' he said thickly. 'Oh, it's you, Brother Silas.'

Kitty glanced at Dagg. 'You are called Silas?'

'Mind your own business,' Dagg said angrily. He turned to Brother Benedictus. 'I have brought a penitent to sit in the cell and pray for forgiveness.'

'She's a woman. We don't allow females into the priory, Brother Silas. You know that.'

'But you save souls, Brother Ben. This person needs saving, believe me.' Dagg nudged Kitty over the threshold.

'I should be sent back to my family, Brother Benedictus,' Kitty said earnestly. 'You don't want me here. It's not right.'

Dagg stepped in behind her and closed the door. 'It's the Devil speaking through her, Brother Ben. I'll put her in the cell where she can repent her sins.' He grabbed Kitty by the shoulders, despite her protests, and hurried her through a narrow passageway and out again into the cold night air. Amidst the shattered masonry Kitty could see a much smaller building with slits for windows and a large cross over the door.

'Not in there, Dagg. I don't deserve this. After all, where can I go? I don't even know where we are.'

'Shut up or I'll leave you in there to rot. I don't care what happens to you, Miss Harte, but Brother Ben might be more accommodating.'

Dagg opened the door and gave Kitty a push that sent her sprawling onto the hard stone floor. The door slammed behind her, and she heard the key turn in the latch.

It was very dark, and the smell of damp and mustiness was overpowering. Kitty got to her feet and felt her way along the wall. A narrow chink of light from one of the slits gave just enough illumination to see a low wooden bed covered with a hessian palliasse, and a small table on which was a stub of a candle stuck in a bottle and a single match. Kitty struck the match on the wall, and it burst into flame. She lit the candle and cried out with sheer relief, but on looking around the small prison-like cell, her spirits sank. The walls were thick, and even if she shouted there was no one to hear her. She shivered as she sat down on the bed. The palliasse was rough to the touch, but there was nothing she could do other than lie down and try to sleep. It was deathly quiet, but when Kitty closed her eyes, she could hear whispering, as if long-dead monks were trying to communicate. She told herself that it was all in her imagination, but even so, chills went down her spine and her skin was raised in goose pimples.

* * *

Kitty was awakened suddenly by the thud of the door hitting the stone wall and the sound of footsteps. A welcome shaft of sunlight flooded the cell and Brother Benedictus padded across the floor to place a mug of tea and a plate of bread drizzled with honey on the table.

'I reckon you're the first woman to sleep in this cell, miss,' he said grinning. 'The prior won't be too happy about this.'

Kitty picked up the mug and sipped the hot, sweet tea. It seemed that Brother Benedictus was generous with the honey, and she felt better almost immediately.

'Why am I here if the prior wouldn't approve, Brother Benedictus?'

He tapped the side of his bulbous red nose. 'Ask no questions and you'll be told no lies, miss.'

Kitty could have argued that a holy man must not tell untruths, but she was very hungry, and she merely swapped the mug of tea for the slice of bread and honey.

'My honey,' Brother Benedictus said proudly. 'I keep bees, miss. I talk to them, and they respond with golden blessings.'

Kitty managed a vague smile as she chewed and swallowed. 'Delicious, Brother Benedictus. Thank you for the breakfast, but I really should leave now. My family will be very worried about me.'

'Don't worry, miss. Brother Silas has put their

minds at rest. You are to stay at the priory for a while, even though women are not allowed here.'

Kitty was growing tired of the repetition. 'If women are not allowed, then why am I here, Brother Benedictus? What would the prior say, if he knew?'

'Well, there's a conundrum, miss. The prior has gone away, but he will return when he is ready. I will confess and beg forgiveness, and you will be gone by then.'

'Are you saying that Dagg – I mean Brother Silas – is going to take me home?' Kitty glanced past Brother Ben's portly figure, wondering if she could make a dash for the doorway. If she could climb over the fallen masonry, she might be able to reach the road and get away.

'I cannot say, exactly, miss. Brother Silas has gone about his business today, but he will return later. In the meantime, you are to come with me, and I will find some work for you to do. We all have to earn our daily crust in the priory.'

'But the other monks have left, have they not?' Kitty could not resist pressing him on this point.

'They will return one day,' Brother Benedictus said calmly. 'I am the guardian of the priory in their absence. You will ask no further questions. Come with me.' He walked towards the door, but then stopped and turned to stare at Kitty. 'If you are to stay here you must have a name.'

'I'm Kitty Harte.' Kitty rose somewhat stiffly to her feet.

'Come with me, Sister Kitty.'

Brother Benedictus waddled on ahead, leaving Kitty to hurry after him. She glanced around, memorising the layout of what remained of the original building to plan for her escape. She could only guess that Dagg was off somewhere attempting to steal items he could sell on to boost his income. It was too much to hope that he might be caught by the local police, but Flinders would have reported her missing, and they would be making enquiries as to her whereabouts. She wondered if Flinders would guess that the man taken on to help his grandmother was Silas Dagg. If he did make that connection, he would almost certainly have contacted Sergeant Barton by now. Perhaps that was too much to hope for, but Kitty was determined to stay positive.

She followed Brother Benedictus into the only part of the priory left standing. The beamed ceilings were low, and the flagstone floors worn down by the monks' feet over several centuries. Brother Benedictus locked the door behind them, adding the key to the bunch hanging from a chain around his thickened waist.

'You cannot escape, Sister Kitty,' he said pleasantly. 'I have a task for you.' He led the way to the back of the building where a large copper was bubbling with hot water. A pile of sheets, towels and soiled garments lay on the stone floor. He indicated them with a wave of his hand. 'That should keep you busy. I have work to do in the brewery. I sell the ale on market days as well as jars of honey. You do know how to launder?'

'I think so,' Kitty said doubtfully. She had watched the maid at Bridlebank, and occasionally helped Nellie, but this was both different and daunting. The large number of items that needed washing suggested that this was a whole year's laundry. Kitty rolled up her sleeves and began by sorting items into neat piles. If she could gain Brother Benedictus's trust, escape would be a possibility.

It was back-breaking work, and everything had to be wrung out and rinsed in clean water before being taken outside to the walled kitchen garden. The wet items were then hung on a washing line stretched between wooden stakes set into the ground. Kitty worked until there was no more drying space. The sun was high in the sky, and she was hot, thirsty and very hungry after her morning's exertions. She abandoned what remained of the laundry and went in search of Brother Benedictus. She found him in a large kitchen, and the smell of boiling hops, malt and yeast hit her forcibly. It was not unpleasant, but it was overpowering and made her gasp.

'What do you want, Sister Kitty? I thought I told you to stay in the laundry room.'

'I'm hungry, Brother Benedictus, and thirsty.'

He shot her a sideways glance. 'Help yourself to

bread and honey. You can make a pot of tea for both of us, but I can't stop. I must finish what I'm doing.'

'I don't know why,' Kitty said impatiently. 'There's no one here to reprimand you if you take a break to eat.'

Brother Benedictus rolled his eyes. 'The Lord sees all, Sister Kitty.' He reached for a flagon and took a swig of what Kitty could only assume was the strong ale that he had brewed.

She could see that she was not going to get any help, and she set about making the tea. She cut slices from the loaf that had been left on the table, and she spread them with honey. Brother Benedictus seemed to be in a world of his own as he worked, sipped the ale and hummed under his breath. Kitty filled two mugs with tea and set one down close to him, together with a slice of bread and honey.

'Is this all you have to eat, Brother Benedictus?' Kitty nudged him gently and pointed to the food. 'You should take better care of yourself.'

He blinked and stared at her as if she had spoken to him in a foreign tongue.

'I'm doing the Lord's work, Sister Kitty.'

'You might do it better if you looked after yourself, Brother Benedictus. And drinking all that ale cannot be good for you.'

'You have work to do, Sister Kitty. Take your food to the laundry room and finish what you started, or Brother Silas will be angry with you.'

Kitty shook her head. There seemed to be little point in talking to someone who was clearly under the influence of strong drink. Brother Benedictus seemed to live in a dream world, ignoring the fact that he had been abandoned by his order and left to survive on his own in a derelict and partially ruined priory.

She left him in the hot steamy kitchen and took her meagre meal outside to the kitchen garden. The washing that she had hung out to dry moved gently in a current of air. She looked around, hoping to find a gap in the high brick walls. Making a break for it was virtually impossible, and it was frustrating to know that freedom lay on the other side of the wall, so near and yet so far away. Dagg must have thought all this through before he incarcerated her in this holy prison.

Kitty sat down on a rusty iron bench and ate her food. She shivered as the shadows deepened and the sheets took on a ghostly sheen. This was not the sort of place she would wish to be after dark. If she closed her eyes, she could imagine the chanting of long-dead monks and hear the shuffle of their sandalled feet on the glassy surface of the flagstones. Perhaps it was better to have spent the night in the confines of the tiny cell. She wondered how long Dagg would keep her in this creepy place with a drunken monk, and she was not hopeful. Dagg was a desperate man, and he blamed Barton for his capture and incarceration. But Barton was in London, and she was here without anyone to help her to escape. However, there must be a way out, and if there was, she would find it.

Having satisfied her hunger and thirst, Kitty decided to take advantage of Brother Benedictus's devotion to duty. She put the last lot of sheets and drying cloths in the copper and left it bubbling away while she went to explore what was left of the ground floor. She went from room to room, most of which were dusty, disused and empty of any furnishings. She had thought she might be able to climb out of a window, but they were all boarded up, ruling out yet another means of escape. Kitty was frustrated but she was not going to give in to despair. The last room she found must have been the office of the prior himself, as it was furnished with a large mahogany desk and a chair. She sat down and began opening the drawers, but they were empty, for the most part. However, she did find several quill pens and a sheaf of bills from tradesmen. Kitty smiled to herself, wondering if all the debts had been paid before the monks abandoned the building.

There was nothing else to do, and Kitty was not about to return to the laundry room until it was necessary. She felt the sudden urge to draw something, and she dipped a pen into the ink. The only paper she had were the bills, and she selected one that had very little printing on it, turned it over and began to draw. The outline of the priory as she had seen it the previous evening suddenly appeared on the paper as if sketched by an unseen hand. It was then that an idea occurred to her, and she finished the drawing. Satisfied with the result, she wrote her name in the corner together with the word 'HELP'. She was warming to the subject and drew several more, folding each one neatly and tucking them into her pocket.

The sound of Brother Benedictus calling her name made Kitty jump to her feet. She stowed the ink, pens and bills back in the drawer and closed it firmly before leaving the office. She met Brother Benedictus in the narrow passageway outside the kitchen. He was very red in the face, and she could swear that the tip of his nose was glowing. He took a step towards her, tottered and leaned against the wall.

'It's time for my nap,' he said, grinning stupidly. 'You can tidy up the kitchen, Sister Kitty. And don't forget to take the washing off the line before dark. It gets very damp at this time of year.' He staggered off and Kitty heard the door of his cell open and close again.

This might be her only opportunity to carry out her plan. Kitty hurried through the maze of corridors to let herself out into the kitchen garden. She took one of the drawings and wrapped it around a stone. She hurled it over the wall and heard it fall on the dry soil with a satisfying thud. She repeated the process until all the sketches had been set free, wishing that she could have leaped after them. It was a slim chance, but someone might pick one of them up and would be curious enough to investigate. It was too much to hope that anyone would pass the message on to the local constable. However, she felt she had done something that might just have some effect.

Kitty took the washing from the line, folded it and laid it neatly in the large wicker laundry basket. Being a prisoner in a priory was hard work, and there were still sheets in the copper. However, she wanted to keep on the right side of Brother Benedictus, and she finished the task he had set before returning to the kitchen and tidying up the mess that he had made. She had just finished and was wiping the pine table when she heard footsteps. Dagg strode into the kitchen.

He came to a halt, staring at her. 'What? He's got you cleaning for him. The old dog.'

'I don't think Brother Ben would thank you for calling him names,' Kitty said primly. Her heart was pounding. She could only hope that Dagg had not found any of her messages on the ground outside, but he seemed calm enough and even slightly amused. He must have had a good day.

'Why have you brought me here, Dagg?' Kitty demanded angrily. He had no right to be smiling when she was suffering.

'I told you, love. You are a pawn in my game. The old man and I used to play chess when people popped their precious sets. I always won.'

'But surely you want to keep away from the police. You don't really want Barton to come looking for you.'

'Do I not?' Dagg grinned. 'I want him to see you one last time before I spirit you out of the country.'

'You can't do that,' Kitty protested hotly. 'I won't go with you.'

'You won't have no choice, my dear. Brother Benedictus has his uses, apart from brewing very good ale and making honey. He is also an expert in making medicines from wild plants. I believe that one of the monks he treated previously is still sleeping like a baby, and no one can wake him up.'

'That's ridiculous,' Kitty said angrily. 'And even if it's true, you can't force me to take any such potion. Besides which, you underestimate Barton. He's too clever for you.'

'And you underestimate me, Kitty. You think because my pa is a pawnbroker and I follow in his footsteps that I am a lesser being, but you are wrong.' Dagg opened his jacket and produced a hunk of red meat, which he tossed onto the table. 'You think you're so clever, then cook that for our dinner.'

Kitty stared at it in horror. 'I don't know how.'

'Then we eat it raw. You'd better learn quickly, or

you'll feel the back of my hand.' Dagg snatched up a flagon of ale. 'I'm going to my room – or cell, if you prefer to use the correct term. When I come back, I expect to find a meal on the table, or I will stand over you and force you to eat that raw sirloin bit by bloody bit.' He sauntered out of the room, slamming the door behind him.

Kitty stared at the uncooked joint with a feeling of disgust. She did not doubt that Dagg would carry out his threat. She racked her brains, trying to remember how Nellie roasted a large joint. Surely it could not be too difficult. Brother Benedictus had lit the fire in the range and there was a selection of rather battered pots and pans that the monks had obviously discarded. Kitty found a roasting pan, which was dented, but still useable. She put the meat in it and placed it in the oven. That was not too difficult, but they needed vegetables. She went once again to the kitchen garden, but, of course, this early in the year there was nothing showing above the soil. Then, at the far end of the garden, she spotted something that brought back a memory from childhood and her visits to Bridlebank. Grandpapa Carstairs had been a formidable old gentleman, but he had had a soft spot for her and had taken her for walks in the garden, instructing her in the names of the plants and flowers as well as the vegetables in the kitchen garden. She remembered a long narrow pile of earth that Grandpapa had called a clamp, beneath which the year's crop of root vegetables was stored for use during the winter months. Kitty found a broken garden spade propped against the wall, which she used to dig into the clamp, and sure enough, she found some potatoes, carrots and a few parsnips. With a feeling of triumph, she carried them back to the kitchen, where she washed off the mud, peeled them and placed them around the meat. No matter what Dagg said, they would eat royally tonight. Even so, now she had time to think about it, she was worried about Dagg's plan to keep her hostage, even when he intended to go abroad. That was not something she had anticipated, and it was to be avoided at all costs. Previously, she had not given him credit for anything other than deep cunning, but now she suspected that there was an ulterior motive behind his machinations. He wanted to get the better of Barton and it was more than petty revenge, but what exactly motivated him to behave in such a way was inexplicable. Kitty calmed her nerves by searching out enough crockery and cutlery so that she could lay the table. At least they would have one civilised meal before everything came crashing down around her.

It was over an hour later when Dagg wandered into the kitchen, and the look of surprise on his face made all Kitty's hard work seem worthwhile. Brother Benedictus followed him into the room, but he took his seat at the table and said grace before he would allow them to eat. Kitty served the meal and Dagg produced a bottle of wine, which he shared with Brother Benedictus, but refused to allow Kitty even a sip. She was not surprised, nor did she want to drink anything that might dull her senses. She ate little, keeping an eye on both her captors, but Dagg seemed to be in a good mood, and he opened a second bottle of wine. He chatted with Brother Benedictus, totally ignoring Kitty, which suited her very well. He became very loud, telling jokes that were unsuitable for either a lady's ears or those of a man of God, but suddenly he slumped over the table and began snoring loudly. Kitty assumed it was the wine, although Brother Benedictus had drunk an equal amount and he seemed a little merry, but not overly so.

Kitty was startled when Brother Benedictus rose to his feet and began to search Dagg's pockets. He took out a large iron key, a length of string and a handful of coppers. Then with a cry of triumph he pulled out a bulging leather pouch, which he untied and tipped the contents on the table. Gold sovereigns gleamed in the lamplight.

'I knew it. Brother Silas found the silver chalices and altar pieces that belonged to my order. They were left in my care when the brothers departed, to be collected when they had established themselves elsewhere. Brother Silas found out about them, – I don't know how – but I knew what he was going to do.'

Kitty stared at him in disbelief. 'And yet you didn't stop him. Why did you betray the trust placed in you?'

'Brother Silas offered to give me a share, but I've decided I've earned all of it. I couldn't sell it myself, but he did it for me.' Brother Benedictus stowed the coins back into the pouch and slipped it back into Dagg's pocket.

Kitty was even more confused. 'But you've just given it back to him.'

'The police will find the money on him, and I will claim it as belonging to the order. I will tell the prior that I can no longer remain a man of God, having allowed a felon to steal the silver. So far as the prior is concerned, the money will have disappeared, and Brother Silas will be in police custody.'

'But how will you let the police know he is here?' Kitty eyed him warily. 'Will you let me go free?'

'I've already told the local constable. I imagine the officers of the law will arrive at any moment, knowing that Brother Silas is a wanted man.'

'But what if he wakes up before they arrive? He will kill you if he discovers what you have done.'

Brother Benedictus tapped the side of his red nose. 'I slipped a sleeping draught in his wine when neither of you were looking. Brother Silas will sleep until morning if left undisturbed.'

'Then let me go now, Brother Benedictus. I will find the constable and confirm your story.'

'It's a good few miles to the village, Sister Kitty. You are safer here than out alone in the dark. Brother Silas told me about his desire to have revenge on Sergeant Barton for his part in sending both him and his father to prison. He guessed that the policeman had fallen for your charms and that's why he's holding you hostage. He'll use you to bargain for his freedom and enjoy watching the copper suffer. I don't think we will have long to wait for the law to arrive. Do you?'

Chapter Eighteen

Kitty was beginning to realise that she had underestimated Brother Benedictus. Until this moment she had thought of him as being rather slow and addicted to drink, but now she was seeing him with new eyes. He was both scheming and devious. He had planned all along to steal what belonged to his order, and he had managed to convince Dagg that they would share the proceeds of the crime. However, realising that Brother Benedictus would stop at nothing to get what he wanted, Kitty was careful not to say anything that might annoy or upset him. It was unnerving to have Dagg comatose at the kitchen table, and Brother Benedictus sitting opposite him, calmly drinking more ale.

Kitty set about clearing away the remnants of the meal, and began washing the dishes in the stone sink. She had almost given up hope of the police arriving when someone hammered on the front door, rousing Brother Benedictus from his inebriated state. He stood up, swaying on his feet and staggered from the room, returning moments later with a constable.

'Arrest that man, Constable,' Brother Benedictus said, pointing to Dagg's inert body. 'He stole the silver belonging to my order.'

The constable glanced at Dagg, but turned his attention to Kitty, staring at her in disbelief. 'What is a young lady doing here, Brother Benedictus? You never mentioned her.'

'That criminal brought her with him, Constable. She is nothing to do with me.' Brother Benedictus shrugged and turned away.

'I was kidnapped by that man, Silas Dagg,' Kitty said hastily. 'He is an escaped prisoner and Sergeant Barton of the Metropolitan Police will be looking for him.'

The constable inclined his head. 'Constable Fairweather, miss. Might I know your name and address?' He took a notepad and a stub of a pencil from his pocket. 'You must forgive me, but I am at a loss to see how a young lady like you became involved with a man like Dagg.'

'My name is Kitty Harte and at present I am staying at Mill House, Little Foxbury. I was taken by force and that man, Silas Dagg, is responsible. He is an escaped prisoner, and he intended to hold me hostage.'

'Well, he's not going to harm you now, miss.' Constable Fairweather wrote something in the notebook before turning back to glare at Dagg. 'Is he drunk?' He prodded Dagg in the back. 'He looks half dead.'

'A mild sleeping draught in his wine, Constable.' Brother Benedictus winked and tapped the side of his bulbous nose. 'Can't have him breaking loose and wandering around the countryside. Will there be a reward?'

'I can't say, but you reported he had stolen the church silver.' Constable Fairweather turned the page of his notebook.

'Of course, Constable.' Brother Benedictus swooped on Dagg and withdrew the pouch of money from his pocket with the air of a conjuror performing to an audience. 'This is what is left of the church property.' He set it down on the table. 'I will return it to the prior.'

Constable Fairweather snatched it up. 'I think not, Brother. This is evidence and will be needed in court. You will have a chance to claim it on behalf of your superior when it is no longer needed.'

'What happens now, Constable Fairweather?' Kitty asked eagerly. 'I need to go home. My family will be worried sick.'

He nodded. 'Of course, miss. Brother Benedictus

will help me to get this person into the wagon I have waiting outside. You must come with me, and once you've made a statement, we'll see about getting you safely home.'

Kitty could not wait to put the priory behind her and, having seen the darker side of Brother Benedictus, she was relieved when Constable Fairweather decided that there was no need for him to accompany them.

Half an hour later Kitty was seated in the warm kitchen at the constable's house, drinking tea and relating her experience to Constable Fairweather and his sympathetic wife. Dagg had been taken to the village lock-up to sleep off the potion administered by Brother Benedictus and would no doubt be up before the magistrate in the morning.

'I would really like to go back to Mill House tonight,' Kitty said, having finished her explanation.

'It's too late tonight, dear,' Mrs Fairweather said gently. 'I'll make up the bed in the spare room. John will make the necessary arrangements to take you home in the morning. Would you like some more tea, or another biscuit?'

'No, thank you, ma'am. You're very kind but I am rather tired. It's been a trying couple of days.' Kitty put her empty cup back on its saucer. 'Is there anything I can do to help?'

Mrs Fairweather was already on her feet. 'No,

dear. It will only take a few minutes to make the room ready. Our daughter used to sleep there but now she's a married woman with two little children. I keep the room as it was when she was at home. It's silly, I know, but it makes me feel she's still my little girl.' She opened the door and allowed it to swing shut behind her.

Constable Fairweather handed the written statement to Kitty. 'If you would like to read this and sign it, please, miss . . . That will be all for tonight.' He gave her a shrewd glance. 'I've sent a telegram to Sergeant Barton to let him know that we have recaptured the prisoner and that you are safe and well. The postmaster was not too pleased at being taken away from his supper to send it, but I told him it was an emergency.'

Kitty glanced over the document, but all she could think about was how Barton would receive the news. Perhaps she had made too much of the way he had been with her, and hers was just another case to be solved. She signed the statement and handed it back to Constable Fairweather. 'Thank you for everything. I don't think I could have faced another night in that awful priory.'

'It's reckoned to be haunted, miss. I wouldn't care to sleep there myself,' Constable Fairweather said, grinning.

'Don't you think it rather odd that the prior left the church silver in Brother Benedictus's care, Constable Fairweather?' Kitty eyed him curiously.

'I do, miss. As a matter of fact, I intend to have a word with the prior. I have a feeling that the silver mentioned was reported stolen some four or five years ago, before I came here. I think Brother Benedictus might end up in a prison cell rather than an ecclesiastical one.' Constable Fairweather laughed at his own joke. 'But you've no need to worry about anything, miss. Just get a good night's sleep and tomorrow you'll be back with the people who love you.'

Next morning Kitty was up and dressed very early. She had slept fitfully, awakened by bad dreams, all of which featured Dagg in some form or another, as well as the creepy ruins of the priory. Mrs Fairweather greeted her warmly and made her sit down at the table while she made her a breakfast of tea and toast.

'What will happen to Dagg, Mrs Fairweather?' Kitty spread butter thinly on a piece of toast.

'I don't know, dear. He might be kept in the lock-up until the next assizes, or maybe he will be sent back to London. John doesn't tell me everything and I don't ask. I have enough to do without worrying about police business.'

Kitty nodded and sipped her tea. 'I really do need to get back to Little Foxbury, but I haven't any money on me.'

'I'm sure that my husband will see you home safely.

He's probably arranging some sort of transport for you as we speak.' Mrs Fairweather stuck a slice of bread on the prongs of the toasting fork and held it close to the fire. 'Eat up, dear.'

Kitty finished her toast and was about to drink the last drop of tea when the door opened and Constable Fairweather walked into the kitchen, smiling broadly.

'We have another guest, Martha. Put the kettle on, love.' He stood aside to allow Sergeant Barton to enter the room.

'Good morning, ma'am,' Barton said, bowing over Mrs Fairweather's hand as she moved forward to greet him. 'Thank you for taking care of Miss Harte.'

Kitty rose slowly to her feet. 'Mrs Fairweather has been most kind,' she said. Her first instinct had been to jump up and grasp Barton's hand, but his formal attitude chilled her to the bone, and she eyed him warily. 'I take it you've come to re-arrest Dagg, Sergeant Barton.'

'A mere formality, Miss Harte. Constable Fairweather is going to have him taken to the county jail, where he will be tried at the assizes later this month. You will be required to attend as witness for the prosecution.' Barton met her gaze briefly and then looked away.

'Yes, I understand.' Kitty was distressed by his casual manner. She had expected a much warmer welcome, but they might as well be strangers.

'Sit down and have a cup of tea, Sergeant,' Mrs Fairweather said hastily. 'You've come a long way.'

'Thank you, ma'am, but we should be leaving now. Your husband has apprised me of the case against Dagg and Brother Benedictus, and these will be followed up in due course.'

'Sergeant Barton has put me in charge of the case,' Constable Fairweather said, puffing out his chest.

'That is correct.' Barton nodded. 'I came down from London on the milk train, and I hired a carriage to bring me from the station. It's waiting outside so that I can take Miss Harte back to Little Foxbury.' Barton turned to Kitty. 'Are you ready?'

'Yes, Sergeant.' Kitty turned away to give Mrs Fairweather a hug. 'Thank you again, ma'am.'

'My pleasure, dear.' Mrs Fairweather held her close for a moment, whispering in her ear. 'Gentlemen don't always show their emotions. Be patient, dear.'

Before Kitty had a chance to respond she found her hand clasped by Constable Fairweather. 'Safe journey home, miss. You've been very brave throughout your ordeal. I told Sergeant Barton how I found you at the priory. I can't say I would have been so calm under the circumstances.'

Kitty smiled and squeezed his fingers. 'Thank you for saving me from Brother Benedictus, Constable Fairweather. I don't think he is as harmless as he pretends to be.'

'I'll commend your actions to the Chief Constable,

Fairweather,' Barton said, beckoning to Kitty. 'We really must go now, Miss Harte. The horse will be growing restless.'

With a last heartfelt thank you to her hosts, Kitty followed Barton outside into the winter sunshine. He handed her into the chaise and climbed up beside her, taking the reins in his hands.

'Walk on.' Barton flicked the carriage whip above the horse's head, and the animal ambled off at a steady pace. 'You don't seem to have come to any actual harm from your undoubtedly trying experiences,' Barton said after a brief silence.

'You should be grateful to me for catching Dagg for you,' Kitty said sharply. 'You would still be searching for him, but for me.'

He shot her a sideways glance. 'You put yourself in jeopardy. That was not very clever, Miss Harte. The outcome might have been much more serious.'

'Did you come all the way from London merely to lecture me, Sergeant Barton?' Kitty gazed angrily at his set profile as he turned away to concentrate on the road ahead.

'I thought you would be safe living in the countryside, but it seems I was wrong. It might have been better had you remained in London where I and my colleagues could keep an eye on you.'

Kitty took a deep breath. 'I am so sorry to have put you to such an inconvenience, Sergeant. I will try to do better. Anyway, Dagg is locked up safely and the case is closed. You will not have to be bothered with me or my family again.'

'That is not what I said. You are putting words into my mouth now,' Barton said stiffly.

Kitty did not dignify this with an answer. She had a sudden urge to cry, which she told herself was ridiculous. Neither she nor Barton had made any promises to each other. As far as he was concerned, she and her family were just another case, and now that Dagg was safely under lock and key there would be no further need for them to see each other. She lapsed into silence, but then she became angry.

'Why are you treating me as if I were in the wrong, Sergeant Barton? I have had a truly horrible experience at the hands of Dagg and the wretched monk.'

Barton turned his head to give her a straight look. 'You put yourself in danger. I did everything I could to protect you and your family, but you would not listen. You might have suffered even more if Constable Fairweather had not been so astute.'

Kitty swivelled around on her seat to face him. 'How can you say it was my fault? Dagg was lying in wait for me. I didn't know he was hiding in the windmill.'

'Constable Fairweather told me what had happened. You were left on your own while your geologist friend took his grandmother to the safety of Mill House. What sort of man leaves a young woman to make her way home in the dark?'

'It wasn't Flinders' fault,' Kitty said angrily. 'He had to carry his grandmother. I was close behind, or at least I left just a few minutes after they did. He wasn't to know that Dagg was lying in wait.'

'But he did know that his grandmother had taken on a stranger to help in the mill. Why did he not interview the man personally to find out if he was a suitable person to leave alone with an aged grandparent?'

'I don't know.' Kitty shook her head. 'Why are you cross-examining me as if I were in court? I've done nothing wrong. In fact, I've helped you to catch an escaped convict, and Brother Benedictus is going to be investigated for stealing the church silver.'

'Yes, agreed, but all this could have turned out so differently. You might not have got off so easily, Miss Harte. You don't seem to realise how dangerous Dagg is. He's part of a larger gang.'

'I didn't know that. How could I?'

Barton gave her a sideways glance. 'How, indeed? Would you have behaved any differently had I told you the full extent of the Daggs' involvement in one of the worst and most vicious gangs in London?'

'This is nonsense,' Kitty said angrily. 'I don't know why you are saying these things since you've washed your hands of the case, and Dagg is safe in the county prison. I don't have to listen to you ranting on about things being my fault, Will Barton. As far as I'm concerned, the matter is closed.' She folded her arms and turned away from him. She knew if she said another word she would burst into tears of anger and frustration and that would never do. Barton himself seemed in no mood to compromise or to apologise for his dismissive attitude, and they drove on in frosty silence until they reached Mill House.

Kitty was saved from speaking to him when the door opened, and Ivory rushed out with an uncharacteristic show of emotion and wrapped her arms around her sister. Flinders was close behind, followed by Nellie and finally Edith, who invited Barton into the house. He politely refused, however, and he drove off without a backwards glance. Kitty dashed tears from her eyes. She was angry with him but furious with herself for allowing him to have such a hold over her emotions. That was over now. She would go on from here and forget that Sergeant Will Barton ever existed.

Later, after a light luncheon, Kitty sat in the parlour with Ivory and Flinders.

'Are you sure you are all right, Kitty?' Flinders asked anxiously. 'From what you told us at table you've had a terrible ordeal.'

'Yes,' Ivory agreed earnestly. 'Anyone else would have been in such a state, but you were always the brave one, Kitty.'

'I'm not brave. I was scared all the time I was

there, but I couldn't give way. I had to keep going if I were to survive, and survive I did.'

'I still think you are very plucky.' Flinders reached out to lay his hand on Kitty's arm. 'If I hadn't gone on ahead with Grandmama, I could have saved you from all that.'

'We didn't know that Dagg was the person Jem brought in to help Mrs Saunders,' Kitty said seriously. 'Anyway, it all ended well enough. Dagg is in prison and will no doubt get a much longer sentence. Brother Benedictus is suspected of stealing the church silver and he will be arrested, unless the prior intervenes. And I wasn't hurt, thanks to Constable Fairweather.' She looked from one to the other. 'But what about you? Did you go to the soirée at Westbrook House?'

Ivory shook her head. 'No, but Charles and Frances came here to visit us when they heard that you had been abducted. Charles was so kind and considerate.' Ivory's cheeks reddened and she turned away. 'And so was Frances.'

Kitty smiled. She had always suspected that Ivory had a soft spot for Charles Westbrook. 'Well, Frances has always been our friend and Charles was very generous when purchasing my paintings.'

'I'm sure they will be delighted to learn that you have come home unharmed,' Ivory added hastily. 'We were all so worried about you, Kitty.'

'Well, you're home now,' Flinders said, smiling.

'I was about to go in search of you when Sergeant Barton arrived on the doorstep. He was obviously very concerned about you, Kitty.'

'He lectured me the whole way home.' Kitty sighed, shaking her head. 'You would think that I wanted to be abducted and held in a haunted priory.'

'You saw a ghost?' Ivory's dark eyes widened in horror.

Kitty laughed. 'Not exactly, but I can tell you that it was very creepy. It was easy to imagine ghostly spirits in every corner of the near-derelict building, and the ruins were very eerie.'

Flinders cleared his throat nervously. 'I don't want to spoil your homecoming, Kitty, but I will be leaving tomorrow morning. I'm going back to British Guiana, although I don't like leaving you all without a man of the house.'

'But you'll be seeing Papa again,' Kitty said eagerly. 'That's wonderful, Flinders.' She was quick to see the hurt expression on his face and she seized his hand, giving it a squeeze. 'Of course we'll miss you terribly, but you might be able to do something to get Papa sent home soon.'

'At least you will be able to find out how he is progressing,' Ivory added, smiling. 'It won't be the same here without you, Flinders.'

'This is one of the times when I wish I had chosen a different profession,' Flinders said sadly. 'However, you are both right. I will make sure that everything is being done to make Mr Harte better so that he can return home.'

'What is happening about the mill, Flinders?' Kitty asked, changing the subject to something less painful than her father's injuries.

'I think it will have to be sold,' Flinders said regretfully. 'I know I am the man in the family, but I cannot give up my profession to become a miller, and it is too much for Grandmama. I don't know how she has managed to keep it going for the past seven years.'

'She is an amazing lady.' Ivory rose to her feet. 'I think I heard someone at the door. I'll see who it is.' She hurried from the room, leaving Kitty to give Flinders a questioning look.

'Why is my sister so keen to see who is calling? It might be a commercial traveller looking for a bed for the night.'

Flinders grinned. 'I think she is hoping it might be Charles. He's called a couple of times using the excuse that he and Frances were worried about you, but I think it's Ivory who is the real attraction.'

'I once thought that he was of the same ilk as Carnaby and the others, but I've changed my mind. Besides which, he's very wealthy and unmarried. I'm beginning to think like a real matchmaker, although the truth is that I would love to see Ivory settled with a good husband. She has spent too long in Amethyst's shadow. And speaking of my younger sister, heaven alone knows what she is getting up to at Bridlebank.'

Flinders reached out to grasp her hand, making Kitty turn to him with a start.

'Kitty, I know this is not the best time to say this, but we are never alone in this busy house.'

'What is it, Flinders? What are you trying to say?'

'I – I love you, Kitty. I did from the beginning. I knew that I would inevitably be sent back to British Guiana and there was no hope for me, but I can't leave without telling you how I feel.' Flinders gazed into her eyes, clutching her hand so tightly that it hurt.

Kitty was tempted to giggle from the sheer shock of his sudden pronouncement, but she could see that he was deadly serious.

'I'm very fond of you, too, Flinders,' she said, easing her hand from his grasp. 'You are the best friend anyone could wish for.'

'That's not what I want to be, Kitty. I really do love you and I want to marry you, if you will have me. I know I am not a senior geologist like your papa, but I do earn enough to support a wife, although not in the style that Charles could offer.'

Kitty shook her head. 'I'm truly honoured and touched by what you've just told me, Flinders. I'm very, very fond of you, but not in the way you want.'

He jumped to his feet. 'It's Barton, isn't it? I knew that something was going on between you.'

'No, it isn't Barton. I admit I was attracted to

him, but that is over and done with. There is no one else, Flinders. I'm truly sorry, but I can't marry you. It wouldn't be fair on either of us.'

'I would do anything to make you happy, Kitty.' Flinders wrenched the door open and hurried from the room, passing Ivory in the doorway.

'Look who has come to see if you are home safely, Kitty.' Ivory ushered Charles Westbrook into the parlour. He strode over to where Kitty had risen from her seat, and he embraced her fondly.

'We were all so worried about you, Kitty,' Charles said earnestly. 'Frances insisted that I should come again today and I'm very glad I did. Now I can give her the good news.'

'Thank you, Charles. It's good to be home safe and sound.' Kitty managed a smile although her emotions were once again in turmoil. She had not wanted to hurt Flinders' feelings, but she knew it would be cruel to give him false hopes. He was worth more than that.

'Why did Flinders rush out of the room, Kitty?' Ivory asked, frowning. 'He looked angry and upset.'

Charles laughed. 'I expect Kitty turned him down. He's always been obsessed with her.'

'Charles!' Ivory said angrily. 'Don't be so unkind.' She turned to Kitty, her pretty face a picture of concern. 'Is it true?'

'I think that's between me and Flinders. Don't either of you say anything to him. He's a good man and he deserves better than me.' Kitty was about to leave the room, but she hesitated. 'I think it might be difficult for us to remain here when Flinders leaves tomorrow, Ivory. Maybe we ought to think about asking Grandmama if we can stay at Bridlebank until we can find cheap lodgings in town.'

'Do you think Edith will ask us to leave?' Ivory asked anxiously. 'I don't think I could face going back to live with Grandmama.'

'We can't remain here for ever,' Kitty said gently. 'If Edith finds out that I turned Flinders down she might ask us to leave. After all, Mill House is getting rather crowded, and she does run the place as a business.'

'Frances wants to return to London,' Charles said thoughtfully. 'She's never liked living in the country, unlike me. However, we were thinking of returning to Duke Street soon. Why don't you both come with us?'

'To live with you in Duke Street?' Kitty stared at him in surprise.

'That is what I suggest. It's a large house and you will be company for Frances. You could even go back to your stall in the Bazaar, if you so wish, Kitty. You are wasting your talents waiting on table and helping in the house. What do you say?'

Chapter Nineteen

It had all happened so quickly. Flinders had left early next morning, Jem driving him to the station. It had been a tense farewell, leaving Kitty feeling guilty and ungrateful for all the kindness Flinders had shown. It hurt her to say goodbye, knowing that she had dashed his desire for a deeper relationship, but it would be cruel to give him false hope. He had accused her again of being in love with Barton, which she had refuted, but in truth she was not sure. Her own feelings were a maelstrom of contradicting emotions that she was unable to put into words.

Then, just two days later, Kitty, Ivory and Nellie had packed their bags and were on their way back to London. They had said their goodbyes to Edith and Adeline, and although Adeline seemed complacent, Edith was clearly resentful that Kitty had rejected her son's advances. She did not put her feelings into words but somehow that made it even more difficult. Kitty had given Mr Beadle a kiss on the cheek and a promise never to forget him, but she left Mill House with a feeling of guilt for seeming to have abandoned the people who had helped them in their time of crisis. Ivory, however, seemed to have no compunction about leaving so abruptly. She was already seated next to Jem on the driver's seat and Kitty climbed into the wagon to sit with Nellie and the luggage.

'Don't look so downcast, love,' Nellie said brusquely. 'You did the right thing when you rejected Mr Riley.'

'I can't expect his mother to agree with you.' Kitty made herself as comfortable as possible as the wagon lurched into motion. 'We're going to be covered in flour from sitting on the bare boards,' she added with a wry smile.

'If that's the most of our problems we don't have much to worry about.' Nellie clutched the side of the vehicle. 'Don't drive so fast, Jem.'

He turned his head and muttered something unintelligible beneath his breath.

'I'm going to start painting again when we are established in Duke Street,' Kitty said, wincing as the cart went over a rut in the road. 'If I can earn enough money in the Bazaar, we might find a small house or even a set of rooms to rent. I don't want to be beholden to Charles and Frances for any longer than necessary.'

'You'll have to paint a lot of portraits to make that sort of money.' Nellie pursed her lips. 'Let's hope that the master gets home sooner rather than later.'

'I agree, but we can't depend on it. We must look after ourselves, Nellie.' Kitty sat back and made herself as comfortable as possible.

When they arrived at the railway station Nellie marshalled porters with the authority of a sergeant major, and their luggage was stored in the guard's van, while they were escorted to a first-class compartment. Charles had insisted on purchasing their tickets and for that Kitty was very grateful. It was a comfortable, if rather slow journey due to the frequent stops at country stations, but eventually they arrived in London. The Westbrooks' carriage was waiting for them at Bishopsgate station, with a separate vehicle for their luggage, and once again they travelled in style, arriving in Duke Street in the early afternoon.

However, their reception was anything but what they might have expected. The front door was already open, and a police constable was stationed outside. Nellie alighted from the carriage and marched up to him.

'Let us in, Constable. We are guests of the owners.'

'I'm sorry, miss. No one is allowed in or out without the inspector's permission.' The constable stood to attention, staring straight ahead.

'Then fetch the inspector, my man.' Nellie faced him, although she only came up to his shoulder.

Apparently undecided, the constable shifted from one foot to the other. Kitty alighted from the carriage, followed by Ivory. They stood on the pavement for a few minutes while Nellie argued with the policeman, and finally Henderson, the Westbrooks' butler, emerged from the house.

'Allow the ladies to enter, Constable,' he said firmly. 'They are expected.'

'I have my orders.' The constable stood rigid, blocking their way.

'What has happened, Mr Henderson?' Kitty demanded anxiously.

'We've been burgled, miss. I am not allowed to say more.' Henderson attempted to edge past the constable, who elbowed him out of the way.

'Please ask whoever is in charge, Mr Henderson,' Kitty said urgently. 'It's started to rain.'

Henderson disappeared into the house, reappearing a minute or two later.

'The inspector says you are to allow the ladies to enter the house, Constable.'

'I should think so.' Nellie glared at the policeman, waiting impatiently for her turn.

Kitty was first to rush into the entrance hall. 'Is everyone all right, Mr Henderson? No one was hurt during the robbery?'

'No, miss. But we are all a little shaken. The

thieves must have broken in during the early hours of the morning. The police are questioning everyone who was in the house. I'm to show you into the morning parlour, miss.' Henderson did not wait for an answer. He led them across the hall and ushered them into the room. 'I'll inform Sir Charles and Miss Frances of your arrival.' He bowed out of the parlour, leaving Kitty, Ivory and Nellie standing in silence.

'What do we do now?' Ivory paced the floor, wringing her hands. 'We can't impose on them in a time like this.'

Kitty shook her head. 'Maybe we can help in some way. We have nowhere else to go, apart from Bridlebank.'

'Spare us that,' Nellie said, rolling her eyes. 'We'll just wait for someone to come and tell us what to do. I suggest we sit down and be patient.'

The words had barely left her mouth when the door opened, and Frances rushed in. She flung her arms around Kitty's neck.

'All my jewellery has gone, Kitty. All Mama's precious pieces, too.'

'I am so sorry,' Kitty said earnestly. 'But at least no one was hurt.'

'That's what Charles said, but those things are irreplaceable. It's not so much their monetary value. It's the sentiment attached to each piece.'

'Is there anything we can do?' Ivory asked gently.

'Would you like us to find somewhere else to stay while you are dealing with this, Frances?'

'Heavens, no. Of course not. I wouldn't hear of such a thing. It will be lovely to have you around to make things appear normal.' Frances released Kitty and sank down onto the sofa. 'I feel a little faint.'

'Have you eaten anything today, Miss Westbrook?' Nellie leaned over her, frowning. 'I think you need sustenance. Shall I ring for a servant?'

'They are all in the servants' hall being interviewed one by one,' Frances said faintly. 'Perhaps you would go to the kitchen for me, Nellie?'

'Of course, miss. Delighted to be of use.' Nellie rushed to the door and opened it just as a man in uniform was about to enter. She stepped back, staring at him in surprise.

'Sergeant Barton!'

He smiled. 'It's Inspector Barton now, Nellie. Thanks to Dagg I've been promoted.' Barton turned to Kitty, his expression changing subtly. 'Good afternoon, Miss Harte.'

'Congratulations, Inspector,' Kitty said breathlessly. 'At least Dagg did something good in his life if his capture meant you attained your promotion.' She looked away, unable to maintain eye contact. His very presence had set her pulse racing, but she forced herself to remain calm. Once, what seemed like aeons ago, they had seemed to be getting close but then they were at odds. It was not a comfortable place to be.

Ivory stepped in between them. 'I'm sure the promotion was richly deserved, Inspector. But I'm sorry that we meet again under such sorry circumstances.'

'Yes, indeed, Miss Harte.' Barton gave her a genuine smile before turning away to address Frances. 'I will require a detailed list of everything that has been taken, Miss Westbrook.'

'Of course,' Frances said dazedly. 'The pieces were irreplaceable. It's so upsetting.'

'I'll help you, Frances,' Kitty said hurriedly. 'When you are feeling better, we'll sit down together and write a description of each item.'

'Yes, I will need your help. Thank you.' Frances managed a watery smile.

'Perhaps you could start with the servants, Miss Harte,' Barton suggested, addressing himself once again to Kitty. 'They should check the silverware and any other valuables that might have been taken.'

Kitty nodded. 'Of course, Inspector. I can do that right away.'

'That would be very helpful,' Barton said seriously. 'The sooner we can issue a list of what has been taken, the more likely we are to retrieve some of the items, as you are well aware.'

'I haven't forgotten.' Kitty willed him to give her a sign that he too remembered their former relationship, but he seemed to be hiding behind a professional façade.

'I think I need to lie down for a while,' Frances

said, fanning herself with her hand. 'I'm not one given to swooning, Inspector, but I do feel a little faint.'

'You've had a terrible shock,' Ivory said gently. 'Would you like me to take you to your room, Frances?'

'Yes, if you please. I'm sorry, Inspector. I will have to leave you with Kitty. She will be more help to you than I will at present.' Frances allowed Ivory to take her by the arm and lead her from the room, leaving Kitty and Barton facing each other.

'It seems that we are doomed to keep meeting in such a way, Miss Harte,' Barton said with a hint of a smile.

'We can't blame Dagg for this robbery.' Kitty felt herself weakening, but he had hurt her pride once and she was not going to give him a second chance. 'I seem to remember we were on friendly terms when you were dealing with our case.'

His smile faded and once again he became aloof. 'That was unprofessional behaviour on my part, Miss Harte, and I should apologise. It won't happen again.'

'That is a pity. I rather liked being treated like a human being instead of merely a number in the incident book.' Kitty walked to the doorway. 'I will have the information you need by tomorrow, if that is good enough for you, Inspector.'

'Wait, please.'

The sharp note in Barton's voice made Kitty stop and turn to look at him. 'What now, Inspector? I'm doing everything you asked.'

He took a step towards her, holding up his hand, which he quickly dropped to his side. 'I didn't mean to speak harshly, but you must understand that I cannot allow my personal feelings to get in the way of my work.'

'What feelings would that be, Inspector?' Kitty asked angrily. 'Every time we meet you seem to make a point of lecturing me to the point of rudeness.'

'I care what you think,' Barton said simply.

'Then perhaps you could let me help you, instead of putting me in the wrong all the time.' Kitty eyed him warily, unsure of how he might react to her words.

'It's a pity we don't have ladies in the police force,' Barton said with a twinkle in his eyes. 'What is your opinion on this case, Miss Harte?'

'If we are to be acting as colleagues, I think you could call me Kitty.'

'Very well, Kitty. Then perhaps you could call me Will. It's short for William, but only my mother ever calls me that when she is angry with me.'

'Agreed,' Kitty said, nodding. 'Then, Will, as you've asked me so nicely, I'll tell you what I think.'

Barton laughed. 'I had a feeling you would do that anyway, Kitty.'

'I think that this robbery might have something to do with Dagg and his father.' Kitty held up her hand as he opened his mouth as if to argue. 'Hear me out, Will. I think they might be part of a larger gang, mainly because I don't see either of the Daggs as having the brains to organise crimes, but this seems to follow a similar pattern to their way of working.'

'Why do you say that?' Barton frowned.

'Well,' Kitty said slowly, 'Phineas Dagg was very keen to accept our family silver, and equally fast in putting it up for sale elsewhere. Then his son allowed Brother Benedictus to take him in completely regarding the silverware that belonged to the priory. Dagg was greedy and he didn't realise that the naughty monk had stolen the holy items. Neither of the Daggs seems to be very clever, and although I'm no expert, but it seems to me that the Daggs answer to a higher authority in the criminal world.'

'You are doing very well for someone who is not an expert, Kitty. I have come to the same conclusion, but the Daggs are both safely locked away, and they are not going to talk.' Barton managed a faint smile. 'I value your opinion, but please don't try to take this any further. These are dangerous people, and I meant it when I said I didn't want you to put yourself in danger. Please promise that you will leave it to me and my associates to solve this crime.'

Kitty met his sincere gaze, and she nodded. 'I promise,' she said, crossing her fingers behind her back. She had her own personal vendetta against Dagg, and anyone associated with him, as well as a taste for excitement.

She was saved from any further questions by a

knock on the door and a constable asking Barton to go immediately to the servants' hall.

'Will you be staying here for a while?' Barton asked as he made his way out of the room.

'Yes, for the foreseeable future,' Kitty said, nodding. She closed the door after him with a sigh of relief. At least they were on speaking terms again and she knew that he cared at least a little for her. It was a start, and she felt happier than she had for a long time.

Barton was called away on an urgent matter, but the questioning of the servants went on until late afternoon. Frances had recovered by then, with the help of a tisane prepared by Nellie, who had taken over in the kitchen while the rest of the staff were helping with police enquiries. Charles had employed a locksmith to change the locks at the front and rear of the building. Frances said it was locking the stable door after the horse had bolted, which amused her, but the humour of her remark seemed to evade her brother. Kitty and Ivory laughed and a little of the tension eased, although Frances was clearly upset by the loss of her treasured and irreplaceable jewellery.

It was a strange welcome to life in Duke Street, but Kitty was feeling much better since her last conversation with Will Barton. However, she did not see him again for several days and she was growing restless. Ivory was happier than she had been for a long time, and she blossomed under the attention she received from Charles. It was soon obvious that the pair of them were falling deeper in love with each other every day. Kitty was not jealous, but she could not help being a little envious. However, after days of doing very little, she unpacked her easel and her paints and found a quiet corner where she could work uninterrupted.

She started with the usual watercolours of flowers, but then she went on to views of the beach and sea at Little Foxbury. These coloured sketches served to get her back into practice, and then she tried her hand at remembering the semi-derelict priory. These paintings were atmospheric, but memories of her time spent imprisoned there were still fresh in her mind. She found herself making drawings of Brother Benedictus, but she interpreted her experiences with humour, making him a comic drunken figure rather than a more sinister one. These paintings were more for herself, and she had no intention of selling them, but Charles happened to spot them one day and he was impressed.

'These are very amusing, Kitty,' he said, holding one up and examining it carefully. 'I think these would sell, especially if you did a series of them. Have you thought of taking up the stall in the Bazaar again?'

Kitty stared at him in surprise. 'It did occur to me, but I would need to have money to pay the rent on a stall. I was just doing the drawings of the priory and

Brother Benedictus for my own amusement: that by seeing the funny side of that time I might forget the fear I felt while I was imprisoned.'

'I understand, or I think I do. Might it not be better to put the whole episode out of your mind, Kitty?'

'Maybe, but I need to do this whether or not it is the right thing. But getting back to the Bazaar, do you still go there, Charles?'

He shook his head. 'No, I have more important things to do these days. I'm still in touch with Inspector Barton, but so far there's no sign of the items that were stolen.'

'I'm sorry,' Kitty said earnestly. 'I know what it feels like, and we didn't lose anything like the worth of your possessions.'

'It's the sentimental value that can never be replaced, especially as far as Frances is concerned. She treasured Mama's jewellery and we both appreciated the silverware. Grandmama's French ormolu clock was also taken. Thieves don't take the hurt they do into account, and they probably don't care anyway.'

'What does the inspector say, Charles?' Kitty asked casually.

'He asked me to be patient. He said he will let me know the moment he has any news.' Charles picked up one of the paintings depicting Brother Benedictus, red-cheeked and lolling on a wooden settle with a pint tankard in his hand. 'Do you know, Kitty, these are extremely clever and very saleable. If you wish to take a stall at the Bazaar, I will give you the money you need. You may pay me back later if you wish.'

'Would you really, Charles?' Kitty stared at him in surprise. 'It would give me a purpose, and Ivory could help me, if she wanted to.' She put her head on one side, studying his reaction. 'Unless you disapprove, of course.'

He smiled ruefully. 'You know that I care deeply for your sister, Kitty. I just want her to be happy.'

'I know that, Charles. I love the fact that you are prepared to give her the freedom to choose what she wants to do.'

'You and Ivory have been through a difficult time, and I admire your fortitude, but I blame your grandmother for putting you in such a position. I think families have a duty to protect their children and grandchildren, but it is not my place to criticise Lady Carstairs.' Charles replaced the painting carefully on the table. 'Think about my offer, Kitty. Discuss it with Ivory and let me know your decision.'

'Thank you, Charles. I will give it some serious thought,' Kitty said calmly, although she knew already what she was going to do.

To Kitty's surprise, Matron Hume seemed pleased to welcome her back to the Soho Bazaar and she gave her a stall in a prime position. Miss Pollitt at the pay desk was all smiles, and Aggie Brown flung her arms around Kitty and gave her a hug. Several of the other stall-holders came over to tell Kitty they were pleased to see her, and when she set out her paintings, they crowded around to get a better look. The only person who kept to herself was Mrs Tucker, the woman with the jewellery stall, but Kitty remembered her as being difficult to get along with and she left her alone. Bella Tucker was more welcoming, and she admired Kitty's work before hurrying back to help her mother on the stall.

Ivory accompanied Kitty on the first day and helped her to set up the stall. However, she found it too noisy and complained of a headache. Kitty thanked her for her assistance and suggested that she leave early. Ivory did not argue, and Kitty was left alone to handle the prospective customers. It was certainly busier in the Bazaar now that the weather had improved, and there seemed to be more of the elegantly dressed ladies and gentlemen who came to amuse themselves by mixing with the hoi polloi. Carnaby and his friends were there, of course, although there was no sign of Lord Marriner. Kitty could not help wondering if he had ever called on Amethyst at Bridlebank. The robbery in Duke Street and her subsequent meeting with Barton had put all thoughts of visiting her mother and sister out of Kitty's head, but now things had quietened down Kitty decided she must make the time to visit them.

By mid-afternoon Kitty had sold all but two of her paintings: simple watercolours of the wild primroses and catkins she had seen growing in the hedgerows and on hazel trees in the Essex countryside. She decided to pack up and leave, but as she was about to close her portfolio, she turned to see Barton walking towards her.

'Will, this is a surprise. Did you come here just to see me?' Kitty uttered the question before she could stop herself. She had intended to keep a cool exterior when they met again, but she could not disguise her pleasure on seeing him.

'Sir Charles told me that I would find you here, Kitty.' Barton's smile enveloped Kitty in a warm glow. 'I called at the house in Duke Street because I needed to speak to you and your sister.'

'Is anything wrong?' Kitty asked, the blissful moment overshadowed by anxiety. 'You are looking serious. I can tell that it isn't good news.'

'Your grandmother has reported your younger sister as missing, Kitty. I'm sorry to have to be the bearer of such news, but she stated that Amethyst had run away with Lord Marriner, and she thinks they are headed for Gretna Green.'

Kitty clutched the edge of the stall as the news hit her with the force of a physical blow, and yet somehow she was not surprised. She had always known that one day Amy would do something silly, and it appeared that her intuition had been correct.

'When did this happen? Have they eloped or was she taken against her will?'

'I spoke to your mama, and she said that she suspected the former, but Amethyst is underage and Marriner is at fault. However, once they are married there is nothing I can do.'

'This is a blow to me and my family, although not altogether unexpected, but are you not too important now to handle such a relatively trivial matter?' Kitty eyed him curiously.

'Lady Carstairs sent for me personally,' Barton said with a wry smile. 'Who am I to refuse a command from your grandmother?'

'Grandmama expects everyone to obey her orders without question, but I imagine she is delighted to have been proved right about Amy.' Kitty sighed, shaking her head.

'Lady Carstairs thought this might happen?' Barton frowned. 'Then she should have done something to prevent it.'

'Grandmama refused to have Amethyst in the house when we lost our home. She knew exactly what rashness my sister was capable of, but we thought she was being unfair.'

'She certainly seems to have the measure of your sister. I'm sorry, Kitty.'

'Amy was certain that Marriner would come for her, and it seems that she was right. I should have seen this coming,' Kitty said ruefully. 'Is it too late to go after them, Will?'

'I'm afraid so. As far as I can gather, they left

in the early hours of the morning. I doubt if they travelled by road, and if they went by train they will probably be there by now. As I said, once they are legally married there is nothing to be done.'

'It seems that my younger sister is going to be a baroness after all.' Kitty laughed despite her worries for Amethyst. 'She will be insufferable when she comes home with a ring on her finger.'

'Sebastian Marriner may have a reputation as a ladies' man and a gambler, but he's risked a brush with the law by eloping with such a young girl. That makes me think he must be well and truly smitten with her, Kitty. They might do very well together.'

'I certainly hope so. Anyway, thank you for coming to tell me all this in person, Will.' Kitty reached for her shawl. 'I was about to go home as I've sold most of my work today. I've done well. Who knows, maybe I can support Mama and Ivory if I go on like this?' She glanced at Barton, whose attention seemed to have wandered. 'What are you looking at, Inspector?'

He turned to her with a serious expression. 'That stall over there with the jewellery. I could be quite wrong but one of those trinkets looks suspiciously like the description of one of the stolen pieces from Duke Street.'

'Which one is that? I am not acquainted with Frances's jewels.'

'I can't point at it without attracting the stall-holder's attention, Kitty. When I've gone perhaps you could wander over casually and have a closer look. It's a gold bracelet in the shape of a snake with ruby eyes. Don't arouse her curiosity, just take a good look at the rest of the items for sale. I'll go now, but I'll come to Duke Street this evening with the list of items that were taken.'

'Wouldn't it be easier if I asked Frances to come and look at it?'

'Easier, maybe, but we don't want the stall-holder to know we're suspicious. She might be totally innocent, or maybe she is acting as a fence for the thieves.'

'Surely she wouldn't put a stolen article up for sale in such a public manner?' Kitty turned to stare at Mrs Tucker, who was dealing with a prospective customer.

'You would think so, but you never know in a case like this. It might be a cheap imitation in pinchbeck and glass, but either way I don't want to alert that woman. She might have more of the jewellery stashed away somewhere.'

Kitty forgot Amethyst momentarily. 'How exciting. I really would like to be a detective, Will. Painting drunken monks is not nearly as interesting.'

He laughed and touched her cheek gently with his forefinger. 'But it probably pays more in the end, Kitty. You have a wonderful talent, and I'm delighted to see you using it. I must go now, but I'll see you later, unless I get any news about your sister and Marriner.' He strolled away without looking back.

Kitty picked up her portfolio and made as if she was going to leave the warehouse, but she stopped casually at the jewellery stand.

'Are you going to buy, Miss Harte? Or are you just looking?' Mrs Tucker glared at her.

'I always admire your stall, ma'am. I see you have some new pieces.' Kitty avoided the snake bracelet and picked up a garnet brooch. 'Very pretty. I will have to sell a few more paintings before I can treat myself to something like this.'

At that moment Bella arrived at the stall carrying two mugs of tea, which she put down carefully.

'I expect you're admiring our latest acquisition, Kitty,' she said, grinning. 'That brooch is pretty, but have you seen the snake bracelet? Look at his shiny ruby eyes.'

'Shut up, Bella,' her mother snapped angrily. 'Miss Harte don't have the dibs to pay for it. She said as much.'

'Me neither,' Bella said, giggling. 'Maybe one of them fancy gentlemen will come over and buy it for you, Kitty. A pretty girl like you must have plenty of admirers.'

'You talk too much, Bella.' Mrs Tucker took a sip of tea and pulled a face. 'You forgot the sugar again, you stupid girl. Go and get some from the tea stall, or do I have to do it meself?'

'Sorry, Ma.' Bella winked at Kitty. 'I'd forget me head if it weren't screwed on.' She ambled off in the direction of the tea stall.

Kitty took the opportunity to pick up the snake bracelet. 'Do you mind if I take a closer look, Mrs Tucker?'

'Look all you like but put it back. You're as bad as my Bella. She'd be wearing everything I have on the stall if I let her.' Mrs Tucker spotted a well-dressed woman approaching the stall and her lined face broke into a wide smile that did not reach her grey eyes. 'Can I help you, madame?' She snatched the bracelet from Kitty's hand. 'Might I interest you in this fine gold bracelet?'

Kitty was aghast. The last thing she wanted was for the piece to be sold before Barton had a chance to discover its provenance. She lowered her voice to a whisper as she walked past the woman. 'It's pinchbeck and glass. She's having you on, ma'am.' Kitty hurried towards the great double doors, hoping that Mrs Tucker had not heard her remark. She could not wait to get back to Duke Street and tell Frances that there was a hope, albeit a slim one, that a piece of her jewellery had been put up for sale in the Bazaar. But the overriding problem, as always, was Amethyst. Should she go to Bridlebank and comfort Mama, or should she wait for the newlyweds to come home?

Chapter Twenty

The first person that Kitty saw when she entered the house in Duke Street, other than stern-faced Henderson, was Nellie, who was clearly upset.

'I want a word with you, Kitty.' Nellie folded her arms and barred Kitty's way so that it was impossible to get past.

'What's wrong?' Kitty was in no mood to listen to gossip from below stairs, but she already knew that Nellie did not get along very well with the housekeeper – or with Cook, for that matter.

Nellie's frown deepened. 'Never mind me, what has upset you, Kitty? You have a face like thunder.'

'It's Amethyst, for a start. She's eloped with Marriner, or at least that's what Grandmama thinks.'

Nellie rolled her eyes. 'That was bound to happen. I knew she wouldn't stay long at Bridlebank, and I can't say I blame her. What else has caused you such upset?'

'We might have found a piece of Frances's jewellery on Mrs Tucker's stall. Inspector Barton spotted it first.'

'Hmm,' Nellie said, nodding. 'It seems that he takes a great deal of interest in what happens around you, Kitty.'

'He's just doing his job.' Kitty took off her bonnet and shawl and thrust them into Nellie's hands. 'I'm going to find Frances and tell her. If I describe the bracelet, she can tell me if it sounds like one of her pieces.'

'So, I'm lady's maid now, am I?' Nellie tossed her head. 'You'll be asking me to polish the brass door furniture next.'

Kitty held up her hands. 'Don't make things worse, Nellie. I know this isn't the best of situations, but we must deal with it, somehow.' Kitty could see that Nellie was genuinely upset and she relented. 'I'm sorry. I know you are having a hard time below stairs. Perhaps you would prefer to go to Bridlebank after all. I know Mama would love to have you with her, especially in the present circumstances.'

'Thank you, but I'll stay here for now. Maybe the new Lady Marriner will need a servant when she gets back from her honeymoon.' Nellie sniffed and was about to turn away when Kitty laid her hand on her arm.

'Do you think that's where they have gone? On honeymoon? I mean, I was thinking they would return to London straight away.'

'You know your sister better than anyone. Do you really think that Miss Amethyst would let an opportunity like this go by the wayside? I'll wager she's had his lordship going from fashion house to fashion house already. They are probably on their way to Paris as we speak, or somewhere more exotic. We'll never hear the last of it when she finally comes to earth.'

'I suppose you're right,' Kitty said, smiling. 'I'll have to ask Charles for his copy of *The Times* to see if they've announced their nuptials, but I can't help worrying about her. I hope Marriner proves to be a good husband and puts his bachelor days well and truly behind him.'

Nellie placed her hand on Kitty's shoulder. 'Your little sister is perfectly capable of looking after herself. You've all treated her like a precious baby doll, but she has a will of iron beneath that pretty face.'

'You're just saying that to comfort me,' Kitty said suspiciously. 'She's only seventeen, Nellie.'

'Wait and see, that's all I have to say.' Nellie gave her a searching look. 'You need to think about yourself, my girl. Never mind your sister, and don't bother your head about Miss Frances's jewels. She can afford to buy more gewgaws if she's so minded.'

Kitty smiled. She knew she could rely on Nellie to tell her exactly what she thought. 'What do you think I should do then?'

'Find a quiet spot and get your paints out. Those pictures you did of the drunken monk are clever and funny, but also a bit sad. I think you would do very well with those on your stall.'

'You're right, Nellie. The couple I did were the first paintings I sold today, and I think I could have asked more for them.'

'There you are then. Tell Miss Frances about the bracelet on old Mother Tucker's stall, but after that you should leave the detective work to the inspector. He'll be round again soon, no doubt. Any excuse, however flimsy, and he's here.'

'Nellie, there's really nothing going on between us. He's just doing his job.' Kitty shook her head. 'Don't give me that look. I'm not ten years old now, so you can't put me in the corner and tell me to mend my ways. I like Will, but that's the end of it.' Kitty marched off towards the staircase without waiting for Nellie to respond.

She went straight to the drawing room and found Frances sitting by the window, gazing down at the street. She looked up and smiled.

'I saw you coming towards the house. You looked very determined, Kitty. Have you any news?'

Kitty perched on the edge of a chair close to the window seat. 'It's true that Amethyst and Marriner have eloped. Did Ivory tell you that Inspector Barton had called with the news?'

'Yes, she did, and she was naturally upset. Charles has taken her to Bridlebank to see your mama.'

'She went with Charles on his own. No chaperone? What will Grandmama say?' Kitty giggled at the thought. 'But seriously, Frances, it does seem that they set off for Gretna Green in the early hours and that's all we know.'

'Who would have thought that a slip of a girl like Amethyst could tame Sebastian Marriner, the notorious ladies' man who spends most of his time at the gaming tables?' Frances rolled her eyes. 'Your sister must have hidden depths, Kitty. That's all I can say.'

'We don't know for certain that they are legally wed,' Kitty said worriedly. 'I mean, Marriner might have told her that they were going to Gretna Green and then taken her elsewhere.'

'I don't think he's necessarily a bad man, Kitty. He would have to be a complete rogue to do something like that.' Frances sighed. 'All this on top of the robbery is too much to bear.'

'I know,' Kitty said hastily. 'And I'm sorry to burden you with my problems when you have enough to worry about. But there might be a chance that one of your items has been found. Inspector Barton spotted a gold snake bracelet with ruby eyes on Mrs Tucker's stall. Did you have such an article?'

Frances jumped to her feet. 'Yes, definitely. It was

one of my favourite pieces. Are you sure about this, Kitty?'

'I saw it myself, although I didn't look too closely because I didn't want to make Mrs Tucker suspicious. It could be a cheap copy, I suppose.'

'I must see it, Kitty. I'll go to the Bazaar now and demand to know how she came by it.'

'That is not a good idea. If you alert her, and she has more of your jewels hidden away somewhere, you would never see them again.'

'I can't just sit here and wait for your policeman to make an arrest. The bracelet might be sold before anything can be done.' Frances paced the floor, wringing her hands. 'I really want to go to the Bazaar now, Kitty. I could buy it back without the woman suspecting that it is really mine.'

'Barton knows what he is doing, Frances,' Kitty said gently. 'We must leave it to him.'

'That bracelet belonged to my mama. It was made for her, and she loved it, although it wouldn't have been my choice. I am not keen on real live snakes, but this one was solid gold.' Frances took a hanky from her pocket and dabbed her eyes.

'I expect Mrs Tucker has packed up her stall now,' Kitty said carefully. 'The inspector is coming here to speak to you about it, so why not wait to hear what he has to say?'

'I wish Charles were here. He would know what to do, but all he can think about is Ivory.

I've never seen him so enamoured of a woman until now.'

'Ivory is a good person, Frances. She won't do anything to harm Charles. You mustn't worry about him,' Kitty said with a reassuring smile.

'I hope you're right. I wouldn't like to see my brother hurt. Anyway, it's too bad of Amethyst to run away at a time like this. I imagine she always knows how to draw attention to herself.'

Kitty rose to her feet and moved swiftly to Frances's side. 'Come and sit down. Try to keep calm. I don't think Amy did this on purpose to spite you, Frances. It's just a coincidence.' She guided Frances back to the window seat. 'Just be patient for a while longer and wait for Barton to arrive.'

Kitty had barely finished speaking when a knock on the door made them both turn with a start.

'Enter,' Frances said shakily.

Henderson opened the door. 'Inspector Barton, ma'am.'

Kitty crossed the floor, holding out both hands. 'Thank goodness you've come, Will. I've been trying to dissuade Frances from going to the Bazaar to confront Mrs Tucker. She thinks the bracelet might well be one of her most treasured possessions.'

'It's true,' Frances said tearfully. 'It is not the most valuable in monetary terms, but it is priceless to me.'

Barton nodded. 'I understand, Miss Westbrook.' He walked over to where she was sitting and put his hand in his pocket. 'Is this part of your jewellery collection?' He took out the snake bracelet and laid it in Frances's hand.

'Did you buy it, Will?' Kitty asked eagerly.

He grinned, looking suddenly boyish and uncharacteristically mischievous. 'I was working on the ethos that the end justifies the means, and so I persuaded a professional dip to purloin it off the stall just as Mrs Tucker was packing everything away.'

'You bribed someone to steal it for you?' Kitty said incredulously. 'You could lose your job for less, Will.'

He laughed. 'I had to do something radical before the woman realised what she had and sold it privately or put it with the rest of the collection, wherever that might be. Anyway, Miss Westbrook, does this piece of jewellery belong to you?'

Frances held it to her cheek, closing her eyes. 'Yes, Inspector. It has great sentimental value. I can't thank you enough for returning it to me.'

'I'm afraid it isn't quite as easy as that.' Barton held out his hand. 'I will have to take it as evidence, but it will be returned to you eventually. In the meantime, it will be safe, and Mrs Tucker is now under investigation.' Barton gave Frances a sympathetic smile. 'I can't promise anything at this stage, Miss Westbrook, but I hope to retrieve the rest of your property and arrest the felons.'

'Thank you, Inspector.' Frances laid the gold

snake on his open palm. 'You will take care of my mother's bracelet, won't you?'

'Of course I will.' Barton slipped the piece of jewellery into his pocket. 'I must leave you now, but I will keep you up to date on our progress.'

'I'll see you out.' Kitty followed him from the room. 'Thank you, Will. It was good of you to take so much trouble, especially to come and see Frances in person.'

He was suddenly serious. 'Have you heard anything from your younger sister?'

'No, I am hoping she will come home.'

'If you don't hear anything in the next few days you must let me know. I know that Lord Marriner has a dubious reputation and we must hope that his intentions are honourable, but until you see Amethyst again, we cannot be sure.'

'Do you think he has duped her into believing that he intended to marry her?' Kitty met his candid gaze with a tremulous smile. 'I can take the truth, Will.'

'To be perfectly honest, I don't know, Kitty.'

She nodded. 'Then all I can do is hope that Marriner is a gentleman at heart and that he truly cares for Amethyst. She is too young and innocent to have her life ruined by an unprincipled lothario.'

'I agree.' Barton stopped at the top of the stairs. 'You won't do anything rash, will you, Kitty?'

'Who, me?' Kitty said innocently. 'As if I would. I'm the sensible sister, am I not?'

He eyed her seriously. 'You are until one of those close to you is in danger, and then common sense flies out of the window. You were the one who was incarcerated in the old priory, if you remember.'

'I'm not likely to forget, but I'm trying to erase that memory by painting Brother Benedictus in his true light. It was Dagg who was the real villain, and you have him behind bars.'

'We do,' Barton said thoughtfully. 'But if the gang was larger than just Phineas and his son, the robbery here might be some sort of revenge for your part in the capture and arrest of the Daggs.'

'Surely not!' Kitty shook her head. 'How would they know that I and my sister are living here, and why take their spite out on the Westbrooks?'

'That is what I hope to find out.' Barton leaned over and kissed her briefly on the cheek. 'Remember what I said, Kitty. Let me know if you don't hear anything from Amethyst within a day or two and leave Mrs Tucker to me.'

He descended the stairs, leaving Kitty staring after him. She was finding his presence increasingly disturbing emotionally, and yet he always seemed to be so calm and even slightly detached. It was as if he kept a tight control on his own emotions and that he concealed his real feelings by reverting to his official capacity.

Kitty retraced her footsteps to join Frances in the

drawing room, where she was greeted with a bright smile.

'No wonder you like your policeman, Kitty. He really is wonderful. I can't thank him enough for retrieving my bracelet. I only hope he'll manage to find the rest of my belongings.'

'I'm sure he will,' Kitty said slowly. 'He's very good at his job.'

'And he has a soft spot for you.' Frances beamed at her. 'It's so obvious, only I don't think you can see it.'

'Why do you say that?' Kitty was suddenly wary.

'Because you hide your feelings when you are not sure of yourself. I know we haven't known each other for very long, but I've seen how you are with Will Barton, and it's quite different from the way you are with other people.'

'One has to be nice to a senior police office for fear they might arrest you,' Kitty said lightly.

'There you are, my point proved exactly. You're making a joke to cover your real feelings for him. Don't be ashamed of them. He's a good man.'

'You only like him because he stole back your snake bracelet,' Kitty said firmly. 'My main worry now is Amy, and what has really happened to her. I've a good mind to go to Marriner's home and demand to see him.'

'But they won't be there if they have gone on their honeymoon, Kitty.' Frances patted the empty space beside her on the window seat. 'Come and sit down.

Wait until Charles and Ivory return from Bridlebank and perhaps they will have some news.'

Charles and Ivory returned in time for dinner that evening, but they had no further information about Amethyst and Lord Marriner. However, Ivory was concerned for their mother, who had taken the news badly, and Grandmama Carstairs was apparently gloating and saying repeatedly that she had been right all along. There was little conversation at dinner, with everyone seemingly absorbed by his or her own thoughts. Ivory retired to her room early, on account of a headache, and Charles went to his study. Their departure left Frances and Kitty alone in the drawing room to enjoy their coffee. In the end it was Frances who went to bed first, apparently worn out by the events of the day.

Kitty sat by the window, gazing down at the street below where pools of yellow gaslight were interspersed with deep shadows. There were few people out and about at this time of the evening, although hansom cabs and private carriages tooled up and down Duke Street. However, after a while even these grew fewer. Kitty found that inactivity was harder to bear than the worry about what might have happened to Amy. In the end she went to her room, undressed and made herself ready for bed, but sleep evaded her. Then, in the early hours of the morning, heralded by the sound of a distant church clock striking two, she came to a sudden decision. Barton was dealing with the robbery, but he did not seem to consider Amy's absence to be a police matter. Kitty, on the other hand, considered it imperative that she should discover what had happened to her younger sister. Marriage to a man like Sebastian Marriner would not have been Kitty's first choice for Amethyst, but the alternative was scandal and ruin. She closed her eyes and willed herself to sleep with a definite plan forming in her mind.

It was still dark when Kitty finally awakened. She leaped out of bed, washed with what Nellie would call 'a cat's lick', dressed and put up her mane of fair hair in a rather straggly bun. She could hear the servants moving about the house as they lit fires and made everything ready for the new day, but she put on her bonnet and cape, picked up her gloves and reticule, and crept downstairs to let herself out of the front door. Fortunately for her, Henderson had not yet come on duty and the footmen were nowhere to be seen. At a guess they would be enjoying their breakfasts in the servants' hall. Kitty thought longingly of the cup of hot chocolate that she would be missing as she stepped outside onto the pavement in the cool light of dawn.

She walked towards Oxford Street and hailed the first cab that came along.

'Where to, miss?' the cabby asked cheerfully. 'You're out and about early.'

'Lord Marriner's town house, if you please.' Kitty

had no clear idea where Marriner lived, but she was certain that the cabby would know.

'It'll cost you, miss. He's not at his house in Regent's Park. I know that for a fact because I took a gent there last evening, and then I had to take him on to his club in St James's. The last young lady I took to see Lord Marriner was at his blooming great mansion in Primrose Hill.'

'That's what I meant,' Kitty said confidently. 'Primrose Hill, please, cabby. I can afford the fare.'

'Suit yourself, miss.' The cabby waited while she climbed in and was seated before he urged his horse to a walk and then into a spanking trot.

Kitty sat back, suddenly assailed by doubts. At least she had learned from the garrulous cabby that Marriner was not in his town house. Although quite what she would do if he and Amethyst were not at the mansion in Primrose Hill was quite another matter. She had not thought that far ahead, and it would leave her with no further information and a much lighter purse. However, she had come this far, and it was too late to turn back.

The footman who answered her knock on the door of the imposing residence set in well-cared for parkland, would only say that his lordship was not at home. He was about to close the door when Kitty put her booted foot in the way, and he was forced to pay attention.

'Have you any sisters, sir?' Kitty demanded angrily.

His eyes widened. 'Beg pardon, miss?'

'I asked if you have any sisters. If you have and you learned that they had been taken advantage of by an older man with questionable intentions, what would you do?'

'I don't fully understand the question, miss.'

'I think you do. I am sure you've seen many decent young women come here and had their reputations ruined by your master.' Kitty met his startled gaze with a steady look. 'Think how you would feel, sir.'

'Please go away, miss. I can't help you.'

'Do you expect your master to come home today?' Kitty asked in desperation. 'Can you answer that, at least?'

'I am not permitted to say, miss.' The footman tried again to close the door, but Kitty prevented it by keeping her foot firmly over the threshold.

'I will sit on the doorstep all day if necessary.'

The footman responded by giving her a none-too-gentle shove, which sent her staggering down the steps. He slammed the door before she had a chance to stop him.

'Well, I know now that something is going on,' Kitty said out loud. 'I am not going away until you tell me what you know.' She sat down on the cold stone step, prepared to carry out her threat.

It was still early, but the sun had risen and the

parkland surrounding the house was in springlike glory. The massive oaks and the avenue of copper beeches were unfurling their tight buds and would soon be bursting into leaf. Kitty wished she had her sketch book and charcoal so that she could capture the scene, but she was determined to sit here until someone in the household told her what she wanted to know. She leaned back against one of the stone pillars and closed her eyes, but the sound of hushed voices and the crunching of feet on the gravel carriage sweep made her open them again. Three housemaids were standing together, eyeing her curiously and giggling. The moment they realised they had been seen they scurried off, although they were replaced moments later by a couple of stable boys, who were not so shy.

'What are you doing there, miss?' the older boy asked cheekily. 'You won't sit there long when Mr Christian finds out you're here.'

'Who is Mr Christian?' Kitty asked, frowning.

'The butler, miss.' The younger boy grinned, tipped his cap and ran off, followed by his companion.

Kitty watched them go with a rueful smile. At least she was giving the servants cause for amusement. Perhaps Mr Christian would come to her aid and give her the information she needed. On the other hand, Kitty realised that it was a long walk to the main road, and hansom cabs were few and far between this far from the town centre. She had come here in such a hurry that she had given little thought to how she might eventually get home.

She shifted her position on the hard stone step, trying to get comfortable, but she was hot, thirsty and very hungry. However, she steeled herself to bear the discomfort and was determined to carry out her threat. The lack of a good night's sleep and the warmth of the sun was making her drowsy. She closed her eyes and dozed off, to be awakened later by the sound of horses' hoofs on the drive and the rumble of carriage wheels.

Kitty opened her eyes and struggled to her feet as the vehicle drew to a halt and the front door opened. The footman who has been so unhelpful before now rushed out, almost treading on her feet in his haste to assist the passengers to alight. Kitty barely had time to get out of the way when the butler appeared in the doorway. He glared at her.

'Who are you? Why are you here?'

Kitty was about to reply when she heard her name being called. She turned her head to see Amethyst rushing towards her, arms outstretched.

'Amy, are you all right?' Kitty demanded anxiously.

Chapter Twenty-One

'What are you doing here, Kitty?' Amethyst enveloped her sister in a tight hug. 'How did you know that we were coming home today?' She released Kitty, waving her left hand under her nose. 'Look at me. I'm Lady Marriner. I'm the first one in the family to be married.' Amethyst turned to wave frantically at Marriner, who had alighted more slowly from the carriage. 'Come and give my sister a kiss on the cheek, Sebastian, darling.'

Marriner strolled towards them, smiling broadly. 'Good morning, Kitty. I trust I may call you that now we are related by marriage?'

'You are married?' Kitty stared at Amethyst, hardly able to grasp the fact.

'Of course we are,' Amethyst said, giggling. 'We've just come all the way from Gretna Green. It was so romantic, wasn't it, Sebastian?'

'Indeed, it was, my love.' Marriner took Kitty's hand and raised it to his lips. 'Welcome to our home, sister-in-law.' He turned to the butler, his smile replaced by a frown. 'Why is Miss Harte out here, Christian? She should have been treated like an honoured guest.'

'I beg your pardon, my lord,' Mr Christian said hastily. 'I was not informed of her presence, and we were not expecting you to return so soon.'

'That is patently obvious. I will speak to you later about this matter, but for now you will ensure that Miss Harte has everything she requests. We will have refreshments in the drawing room.' Marriner ushered Amethyst and Kitty into the entrance hall as Mr Christian stepped aside.

'I'll need a maid of my own, Sebastian,' Amethyst said firmly. 'Someone must unpack all those bandboxes and the garments you purchased for me in town.' Amethyst turned to Kitty with a triumphant smile. 'You will be green with envy when you see my new clothes. Sebastian spoils me.' She blew him a kiss as she set off across the wide, marble-tiled entrance hall. 'Come with me, Kitty.'

Kitty hurried after her. 'Amy, are you really married?'

'Of course, I am. What did you expect?'

'We didn't know what had happened. You didn't think to tell us what your plans were or, for that matter, what Marriner had in mind for you. It could have been something quite different.'

Amethyst paused briefly to hand her cloak, bonnet and gloves to a maid, who appeared as if from nowhere. 'You can take off your cape and bonnet, too, Kitty. Or are you going to race back to town to tell everyone the good news?' Amethyst walked on until she came to the drawing room. She opened the door and marched in as if she owned the place, which Kitty realised, with a shock, was the actual truth.

'I will stay for a while,' Kitty said slowly as she gazed around the elegantly furnished room. She could see that no expense had been spared, and the Chinese hand-painted wallpaper was so beautiful that she could have spent ages just gazing at it in sheer admiration. The gilt-framed paintings that adorned the wall were also worth more than a mere glance, and the tall windows overlooking the parkland allowed light to flood in, illuminating every detail from the ormolu garniture on the mantelshelf to the silver candelabra and delicate porcelain ornaments.

'I own all of this now,' Amethyst crowed, executing a twirl with her arms outstretched. 'This is my home, or at least one of my homes.' She ran to Marriner as he entered the room and flung her arms around his neck. 'We are going to be gloriously happy.'

'Undoubtedly, my love,' Marriner said, smiling. 'Now you sit down and entertain your sister for a while. I have some arrangements to make before we leave tomorrow for Paris.' He blew a kiss to

Amethyst and acknowledged Kitty with a bow as he left the room.

'I knew you would choose Paris,' Kitty said tiredly. 'I'm glad it's working out so well for you, Amy. But we were terribly worried, you must realise that.'

'Why would you worry? I told you that Sebastian wanted to marry me, and now he has. We will have a wonderful honeymoon and when we return to London, I will make sure that you and Ivory are looked after properly. I will find rich husbands for both of you.' Amethyst collapsed onto a Louis Quinze sofa. 'Isn't it all wonderful?'

Kitty sat down on the nearest chair. 'I'm sure it is, but you ought to go and see Mama before you rush off on your honeymoon, Amy. She has been so worried.'

'She can come and live here,' Amethyst said carelessly. 'We have another house in Regent's Park, and I believe there's a family estate in Hampshire. I can't wait to see Grandmama's face when she sees my wedding ring. Sebastian is having an engagement ring made especially for me. He did offer me an ancient family diamond ring, but I wanted something new that was mine alone. He does treat me so well, Kitty.'

Kitty was saved from answering by the arrival of two housemaids bearing trays of tea and coffee as well as tiny sandwiches and cakes.

'Thank you. That will be all, for now,' Amethyst said grandly. She dismissed them with a wave of her hand and dissolved in giggles as the door closed on them. 'Isn't this fun, Kitty?'

Kitty reached for the teapot. 'Which do you want, Amy? Tea or coffee?'

'I should be doing that.' Amethyst picked up the coffee pot. 'You are a guest in my house, Kitty. But you may have tea, if you wish. I think coffee is much more sophisticated, and champagne is even better. We can have champagne whenever we want to, although I must admit I had to add a little lump of sugar to my glass.'

'Isn't that rather *de trop*?' Kitty said as she filled a cup with tea, adding a splash of milk.

'Sebastian thinks everything I do is rather sweet and extremely charming. I am going to have such a lovely time in Paris. Now tell me, what has been happening while I've been away getting married?'

In between sips of tea, Kitty told her about the robbery, but she could see that Amethyst was still in her dream world and barely listening. In the end Kitty finished her tea, ate a sandwich and then rose to her feet.

'I really should go now, Amy. I must walk to the main road to see if I can find a cab.'

Amethyst was suddenly alert. 'Nonsense, Kitty. Ring the bell, if you please. I will order the carriage to be brought round. You will go home in style. We are not paupers now, you know.'

'Thank you, Amy. It would certainly make things easier, but will Sebastian mind?'

'I am mistress here now. The servants have to obey me, and Sebastian will allow me to do as I please. Ring the bell, Kitty.'

'Well, that's a relief,' Ivory said when Kitty came to the end of her unexpected meeting with the newlyweds. 'Mama will be so happy, and Grandmama can hardly criticise Amy for marrying into the aristocracy.'

Kitty laughed. 'Grandmama will find something to complain about, especially considering Marriner's reputation. But Amy has undoubtedly done well for herself. What I saw of the mansion in Primrose Hill was very impressive.'

'She always said she would marry a wealthy man and now she has.' Ivory shook her head. 'I hope there is at least some love in the arrangement, or she might start looking elsewhere.'

'Don't be so gloomy.' Kitty patted her sister's hand. 'You at least have found the love of your life.'

Ivory's pale cheeks flushed prettily. 'Charles has never spoken about a permanent relationship, Kitty. You are getting ahead of yourself, as Nellie would say. I am fond of Charles, but that is all.'

'I don't believe you, but I won't say any more. One of us needs to go to Bridlebank and give Mama the good news. I did tell Amy she ought to do it herself, but she can only think of the wonderful time she'll have in Paris on her honeymoon.'

'I suppose that means I will have to do it,' Ivory said, rolling her eyes. 'You have your stall in the Bazaar to think about.'

'I need to earn some money, Ivory. We can't keep living off the Westbrooks' charity. It's not fair, and it puts you in a difficult position with Charles. He is such a gentleman that he would think it improper to make any advances to you while we are living under his roof.'

'Do you think that is so, Kitty?' Ivory's eyes widened in surprise. 'I hadn't thought about it like that.'

'I don't suppose you did,' Kitty said sympathetically. 'But I need paintings to sell on my stall, so I must stop talking and start work. Miss Pollitt will expect my rent, even though I've taken the day off.'

'Then don't let me keep you.' Ivory rose to her feet. 'I will go to Bridlebank and leave you to make our fortune with your witty sketches of the drunken monk.'

Kitty smiled. 'It wasn't funny at the time but looking back I can see the humour in the situation. I wonder what has happened to Brother Benedictus.'

'Who knows? But I hope he is being severely punished for what he did to you, and for stealing from the priory.' Ivory left the room, followed by Kitty, who made her way to the small unused bedchamber at the back of the house that Frances had said she might use for her painting.

She settled herself down to spend the rest of the afternoon engrossed in her work, sketching the pictures first in pencil and finishing with bold washes of watercolour. When the light faded Kitty packed everything away, satisfied with her achievements. However, what she really longed to do was to follow a similar theme but on a larger scale, and in oils, although this would be time consuming and there was no guarantee she could sell such a painting. She must be ever practical if she were to raise enough money to rent a couple of rooms for herself and Ivory, whose happiness was now Kitty's main concern. She had one sister who had achieved her ambition and was married to a wealthy titled man – it did not seem to matter to Amethyst that Marriner had questionable morals – and then there was Ivory. She was in love with someone who was too much of a gentleman to court her while she was living under his protection. As for herself, Kitty had been fond of Flinders, but he had left them all to follow his career, and whatever feelings she might have for Will Barton, he seemed to be married to his profession. Kitty knew she had always been the odd one out and being different was a cross she had to bear.

She shrugged and made her way to her room to wash the paint from her hands and get ready to go down to dinner.

* * *

Next morning Kitty was setting up her stall when Aggie sidled up to her. 'Let's have a look at your paintings, ducks. I love them ones of the fat old monk with the red nose. He reminds me of my uncle Ted.'

Kitty handed her the sheaf of watercolours that she had ready for sale. 'They seem to be more popular than landscapes and wildflowers.' Kitty glanced at Mrs Tucker's stall. 'Did Mrs Tucker come in yesterday, Aggie? She's not here yet.'

Aggie sucked in her cheeks, shaking her head. 'The coppers were here yesterday morning. They marched her off somewhere with young Bella running after them demanding to know what on earth they was doing. Only not quite in such polite terms, if you get my meaning?'

'That's bad,' Kitty said tactfully. 'Did you find out anything more?'

'Who, me? I ain't one to poke me nose into other people's business, but Miss Clancy at the pottery stall overheard someone say that there was stolen property on Mother Tucker's stall. Not that I'm one to gossip.'

'Of course not,' Kitty said carefully. 'I wonder if Bella will be in today.'

'She can't open up if there's nothing to sell. Anyway, I'd best get back to my stand. I can see Matron Hume coming this way. I don't want to get on the wrong side of her.' Aggie bustled off, leaving Kitty to finish setting up her stall.

All that morning Kitty was aware of the whispers going from stall to stall as everyone speculated on the fate of Mrs Tucker and her daughter. Kitty wondered what had changed in such a short time. Barton had made it clear that he did not want to arouse Mrs Tucker's suspicions, yet things must have escalated very quickly if he had made an arrest in such a dramatic manner. Kitty kept hoping that Barton would come to the Bazaar, but in her heart she knew this would have raised eyebrows and might link her inexorably with the law. She would have to wait until such time as he decided to call on her. She could, of course, go to the police station and ask to speak to him, but that would also be inappropriate. She was trapped by social mores and the need to prevent speculation. Her part in the investigation seemed to be over and there was nothing she could do other than wait and hope that Barton might call on her in Duke Street. After all, he would need to see Frances and let her know if any progress had been made in recovering her jewels and the other stolen items.

It was not until later that day that Bella Tucker sidled into the Bazaar with her shawl wrapped around her head and shoulders, as if she did not wish to be recognised. She was immediately accosted by Miss Clancy, and then Aggie strode over to give her a hug. A murmur of consternation mixed with sympathy rippled from stall to stall. Kitty did not wish to draw attention to herself, and she hung back, but moments later Bella broke away from the curious crowd gathered around her. She strode purposefully to stand in front of Kitty, but her tightly controlled emotions seemed to break, and she flung her arms around Kitty, weeping loudly.

'There, there, Bella,' Kitty said, patting her on the back. 'It can't be all that bad, can it?'

'They've arrested Ma and put her in a cell,' Bella sobbed. 'I dunno what to do, Kitty.'

'How can I help?' Kitty asked vaguely. 'Do you need money for food or anything, Bella?'

'No, we got enough of that. I just don't know how to help Ma. I thought perhaps you could have a word with your policeman to go easy on her.'

'My policeman?' Kitty held her at arm's length. 'I don't know what you mean.'

'Yes, you do. We seen him talking to you. It's easy to tell when a fellow is interested in a woman, and he certainly likes you, Kitty. Please speak to him for me.'

Kitty stared at her in dismay. 'I – I hardly know him, Bella. You're mistaken.'

'No, I don't think I am, Kitty. You could put a good word in for Ma, couldn't you?'

'I could try.' Kitty pulled up a stool. 'Sit down and tell me more. Did the police take everything on your mother's stall?'

'No. At least, I dunno. They come to our house and searched everywhere, but they sent me next door to my auntie Sally's rooming house. The next thing I knew they was walking Ma away and they put her in a police van and off they went. They won't tell me nothing.'

Aggie hurried over to them. 'Don't cry, love. We got together and collected the money to keep Miss Pollitt happy, so your ma's stall is safe. Maybe you can open up tomorrow?'

'Ta ever so, Aggie.' A fresh bout of sobbing shook Bella's shoulders.

'Can you do, anything, miss?' Aggie asked Kitty anxiously. 'We all know you're friendly with the inspector. Maybe he'll tell you what they've got on poor old Ma Tucker.'

'I suppose I could approach Inspector Barton,' Kitty said slowly. 'But he's unlikely to tell me anything about the investigation.'

Bella wiped her nose on her sleeve. 'I left him and some of his men at my house, miss. They was ripping everything apart. Can you come home with me and tell them to stop?'

Aggie put her head on one side. 'You could do that, Kitty. I'll look after your stall.'

Kitty could see that she would get no peace until she offered to help Bella, who was clearly distraught.

'Where do you live, Bella?'

'Brewery Yard, miss. It's not far to walk. Please come with me and talk to the policemen.'

Kitty hesitated. She could not quite place Brewery

Yard and yet she knew she had heard about it recently. However, Aggie was already holding out Kitty's mantle and Bella was clutching at her sleeve.

Kitty held up her hands. 'All right. I'm coming, but I will need to be quick.' She turned to Aggie. 'You will keep an eye on my stall, won't you? I can't afford to lose another day's trading.'

'Of course, Kitty. We all stick together in the Bazaar.'

Kitty slipped on her mantle and followed Bella out of the building into Soho Square. It was a fine day and there was some heat in the sun as it shone down on the city streets. Bella loped off so quickly that Kitty had to run to keep up with her, and they threaded their way across busy streets, dodging horse-drawn vehicles and traders' handcarts as well as other pedestrians. It was only when they entered Brewery Yard that Kitty remembered Dagg's pawnshop, and there it was on the corner, boarded up. The three gold balls hanging above the door were battered and broken as if they had been pelted with stones, and someone had attempted to kick in the front door. However, Bella hurried past the depressing sight and made her way to one of the narrow town houses that had obviously seen better days. The whole area was run down, and slatternly women hung about in doorways with small barefoot children hanging on their skirts.

'Ignore them,' Bella said in a low voice as someone

called out an insult, and another started booing. 'They don't like us because we're respectable.'

Kitty could see the police constable standing guard outside the Tuckers' home and she wondered what the definition of respectable was in this seemingly forgotten part of the city. Bella ran up to the constable and was gesticulating wildly, but Kitty came to a sudden halt. It was too much of a coincidence to think that Mrs Tucker happened to have part of a jewellery collection stolen from Duke Street with the Daggs living just a short distance away. Kitty hurried to join Bella as she was becoming increasingly loud in her demands to be admitted into her home.

'Good morning, Constable,' Kitty said calmly. 'Is Inspector Barton here?'

'He is, miss. But I can't allow the young lady to enter, even if it is her home.'

'I understand, of course.' Kitty smiled and nodded in agreement. 'Would you be kind enough to tell the inspector that Miss Harte would like a word with him?'

The constable looked uncertain. 'I'm not supposed to leave my post, miss.'

'It won't take you a moment, and I promise we will stay here and not attempt to enter.'

'Very well, miss. I'll pass on the message, but please remain where you are.' The constable turned to open the door and stepped inside, closing it firmly after him.

'What is it you want with Inspector Barton?' Kitty asked urgently. 'What good will it do you to go into the house? Is there something you want to hide?'

Bella shuffled her feet. 'Not exactly, miss.'

'There's something you aren't telling me, Bella. I can't help you unless I know what it is.'

'I just want to ask what's happened to Ma,' Bella said lamely.

Kitty did not believe her for a moment, but before she could question her further the door opened and the constable ushered them into the narrow hallway. 'The inspector is in the kitchen at the back of the house, miss.'

'Thank you, Constable.' Kitty allowed Bella to go on ahead. Her heart was beating at twice its normal rate, which she told herself sternly was ridiculous. She forced herself to remain calm as she followed Bella into the kitchen, which, considering the dilapidated state of the house, was incredibly clean and tidy. Barton was standing by the back door that led into an enclosed rear yard.

'Good afternoon, Miss Harte. You are the last person I expected to see here.' Barton's cool welcome was tempered by his genuine smile.

'I came because Bella is upset, Inspector. You have her mother in the cells, and she wants to know what is happening.'

'I do, sir,' Bella added eagerly. 'Ma hasn't done nothing wrong.'

'If that's the case she will be released very soon, Miss Tucker,' Barton said firmly. 'But you must be aware that we found stolen goods for sale on her stall.'

'You won't find nothing here, sir. We ain't thieves.'

'I don't think that's what the inspector was saying, Bella. How did your mother come by the piece of jewellery concerned?'

'I dunno what you're talking about,' Bella said sulkily.

'Never mind that for now.' Kitty met Barton's gaze with an attempt at a smile. 'Have you found anything incriminating, Inspector?'

'My men are still searching. There are all sorts of nooks and crannies in an old building like this.' Barton turned his attention to Bella. 'We should be finished by the end of the day. We will know by then whether to charge your mother or not.'

'But what about me?' Bella said tearfully. 'What shall I do if I can't come home?'

'You could help me on my stall.' Kitty laid her hand on Bella's shoulder. 'You could go now and take over from Aggie. It won't be for long and I'll relieve you as soon as I can.'

'Do you trust me to do that, miss?'

'I wouldn't offer if I distrusted you, Bella. Even if your mother is guilty that doesn't necessarily incriminate you, providing you have been telling us the truth.'

'I have, miss. I dunno nothing about stolen goods.'

Barton stepped forward. 'I would do as Miss

Harte suggests, if I were you, Miss Tucker. She trusts you so don't let her down.'

Bella made for the doorway. 'I'll do me best, sir.' She left the room, and her footsteps echoed off the bare boards in the hall.

'We seem to be brought together by criminals,' Barton said, smiling. 'I wish things were different, Kitty.'

Kitty was not immune to the teasing look in his dark eyes, but she tried to appear more casual than she was feeling. 'It is a coincidence, but on the other hand I would have thought that petty crime was beneath your new rank as an inspector.'

'I like to see a case through from the start to when it comes to its conclusion in court. Meeting you so often is a bonus.' Barton gave her a searching look. 'Is this just another coincidence? You seem to turn up wherever I go.'

'I didn't know you would be here today,' Kitty said hastily. 'I came with Bella because she wanted me to accompany her, but I had no idea where she lived.'

'I am put neatly in my place,' Barton said with a wry smile.

'That was not my intention.' Kitty eyed him warily. 'I was merely stating a fact.'

'How well do you know the Tucker family, Kitty?'

'I only pass the time of day with them normally and I'd no idea they lived in Brewery Yard where

Dagg's pawnshop happens to be sited. I saw that it is boarded up.'

'I think it highly likely that they were working together, but I haven't anything more than suspicion to go on as yet. Although I've always thought that the Daggs were part of a larger gang.'

'Mrs Tucker is a difficult woman, but I never imagined that she might be selling stolen goods on her stall.'

Barton frowned. 'I think the snake bracelet was a mistake. I doubt if she meant to display anything so expensive amongst the cheap gewgaws she sells. But it's a costly mistake if it leads us to discover the rest of the cache.'

'Matron Hume will be mortified if Mrs Tucker is proved to be a criminal,' Kitty said with a giggle. 'I know it's not funny, but Matron Hume is so strict with her ladies and so proud of the Bazaar's reputation for giving honest service, that she would be incandescent with rage.'

'It's good to see you laugh, Kitty,' Barton said, smiling. 'But it's wrong that you are forced to sell your beautiful paintings on a cheap stall in a common bazaar. Your father would be mortified if he knew the lengths to which you have had to go in order to survive since his accident.'

Kitty stared at him in amazement. 'It's not Papa's fault. He suffered a terrible injury.'

'But he made no provision for his family in the

case of such a circumstance,' Barton said angrily. 'I'm sorry, Kitty. I know you love your papa but look at what you and your sisters have been through because he didn't plan ahead.'

'You are being unfair.' Kitty backed towards the doorway. 'You don't know what you are talking about, Will. Papa is the best of men.' She was about to walk out of the room when the door opened, and a constable rushed past her.

'Inspector, we've found something. You need to come and look for yourself.'

Chapter Twenty-Two

'Wait here, please, Kitty,' Barton said as he hurried after the constable. It was an order rather than a request, but Kitty was not in a mood to be compliant, and she followed them to the top of the tall, narrow house.

The hatch leading into the loft was open with a rather rickety-looking ladder propped precariously in place.

'What have you found, Constable?' Barton mounted the ladder, but paused as he waited for an answer.

'I think you'd best take a look for yourself, sir.'

Barton climbed into the loft and disappeared into the darkness.

Kitty turned to the constable. 'What is up there?' she asked eagerly. 'Have they found the missing jewels?'

'I can't say, miss. Perhaps it would be safest if you went downstairs. The rafters might be rotten, and the ceiling could come down. You'll be in danger if you stay here.'

'I'll take my chances,' Kitty said calmly.

'Beddoes, come up.' Barton's voice echoed around the building and Constable Beddoes obeyed instantly.

Sounds of movement above were followed, as the constable had predicted, by a shower of plaster falling from the ceiling. Kitty stepped aside, but she was determined to stay and find out what exactly they had discovered.

Barton reappeared, feet first, and he descended, shaking dust from his uniform.

'I thought I told you to remain downstairs, Kitty. This old building is crumbling.'

'Never mind that.' Kitty faced him, unabashed. 'What did you find?'

'Enough evidence to charge Mrs Tucker with being a fence for stolen property.' Barton wiped a flake of plaster from his forehead.

Kitty could see a large cobweb clinging to his dark hair, and she automatically raised her hand. 'You have a spider's web on your head. Hold still a moment.' Their eyes met as she brushed it away in an unintentionally intimate gesture. They were so close together on the narrow landing that she could feel the warmth of his breath on her cheek. 'I hope the spider has moved on.' Kitty made an attempt to lighten the moment as she edged away.

'Perhaps I should have kept my hat on,' Barton said, holding her gaze. 'You really should go downstairs, Kitty. This isn't the place for you.'

Shaken by the strength of her feelings, Kitty nodded. 'I will, but only if you tell me what you found, other than spiders, of course. Are the jewels stolen from the Westbrooks up there?'

He smiled. 'You never give up, do you, Kitty Harte?'

'No, Inspector, I don't. Are you going to give me a hint? Or do I have to climb the ladder and see for myself?'

'There are several boxes, partially concealed by a huge amount of rubbish. They seem to contain valuables that are undoubtedly stolen. I won't know if Miss Westbrook's possessions are amongst the pieces I saw just now until I've had a chance to examine them further, but I promise I will let you know as soon as possible.'

'All right, but that does sound hopeful.' Kitty backed towards the top of the stairs. 'By the way, you have another piece of cobweb close to your left ear, and I think I can see the spider, too.' She laughed as she saw Barton's instinctive reaction. 'Would you like me to help you, Inspector?'

Barton shook his head as he dislodged both the spider and its web. 'No, thank you, Kitty. I think I've given you enough amusement for today.' He took a step backwards as a booted foot crashed through the ceiling close to his head.

Kitty snatched his top hat off the newel post and tossed it to him. 'You might need this, Will.'

He caught it and put it on at a jaunty angle. 'I will let you know what we find, but it will take a while, Kitty. Perhaps I could call on you in Duke Street this evening?'

'Yes, please. I'll be waiting eagerly to find out if you've recovered some or all of Frances's possessions.'

Barton took off his hat and bowed with a flourish. 'Until we meet again, Kitty, my lady detective.'

The teasing note in his voice was almost her undoing. She did not trust herself to answer, and she turned away, descending the stairs, treading carefully to avoid the cracked and damaged treads. If she returned to Duke Street, she would feel obliged to tell Frances what Barton had discovered, but she did not want to give her false hope. She decided to go to the Bazaar and check on her stall.

Kitty was met with a proud smile from Bella when she arrived back at the Bazaar.

'I've sold two of your drunken monk paintings, miss.' Bella rattled the tin that Kitty kept as a cash box. 'There's only two left unsold. You'll have to do some more quickly.'

'Thank you, Bella. You are obviously very good at selling things. But you're right, I do need to work harder.'

Bella's smile faded. 'I didn't mean it like that, miss.'

'I know you didn't,' Kitty said hastily. 'I must say I'm surprised that my old monk is so popular.'

'He makes people laugh. That's why they love him. He's very funny.'

Aggie bustled over from her stall. 'I had a sudden rush of customers, but young Bella's been handling your stall very well without me. What happened at Moll Tucker's place, Kitty?'

'I didn't see anything,' Kitty said truthfully. 'The police were there but of course they were not about to disclose their reasons for searching Mrs Tucker's house.'

'They think Ma is a thief,' Bella said sulkily. 'All they will find is the stock she stores in the loft. It's for the stall, but it has to be hidden to keep it from the light-fingered mob round our way. They'd rob their own grandmas if they felt so inclined.'

'There you are then,' Kitty said, trying not to sound too relieved by Bella's naïve interpretation of events. 'I'm sure we'll find out in good time.'

'I'm happy to stay on the stall until closing time.' Bella eyed her hopefully. 'Seeing as how I can't go home.'

Kitty thought for a moment. 'All right, if you are happy to remain here, I'll go back to Duke Street and do some work.'

'But you must promise to let me know if the inspector tells you anything,' Bella said urgently. 'I don't want Ma locked up in a prison cell.'

'I will come back here before the Bazaar closes this evening, and if the inspector does contact me I'll let you know.' Kitty made a hasty retreat before Bella could ask any more questions.

She set off for Duke Street at a brisk walk. She tried not to think about her conversation with Will Barton, or the confusing effect he had on her when they were in close proximity. Their frequent meetings were always connected to some sort of criminal activity, which made it difficult to behave normally in his company, a sentiment that he appeared to share. Her own feelings were a jumble of emotions, but Will seemed to retreat into his official capacity whenever there was a danger that he might reveal his inner self. She wondered if she had imagined the brief glimpses she had seen of the real William Barton. She hurried on, trying to concentrate on what she might tell Frances.

However, Frances was not at home when Kitty arrived. It was only then she remembered that Frances and Charles were out all afternoon. She found Ivory seated in the drawing room, looking small and very lonely, but she brightened visibly when Kitty walked into the room.

'I'm so glad to see you. I hate being alone in this house. I've ordered some tea and cake, but I feel as if I'm imposing on the servants when their master and mistress are absent.'

'I'm certain the servants don't think any such thing.' Kitty took a seat at the table. 'I hope they bring enough for two because I'm starving. It's been quite a morning.'

'You must tell me all about it. I confess I am so bored here that I could scream.'

Kitty gave her a straight look. 'I thought you were happy here, Ivory.'

'I am usually very content, but I don't know where I stand with Charles. Sometimes I think he really cares for me, but then he appears to be putting a distance between us.' Ivory clasped and unclasped her hands. 'I think you were right when you said it was because we are living under the same roof, but I don't know what we can do about it.'

Kitty was about to answer when a maid arrived with a tray of tea and cake, which she placed on a low table in front of Ivory.

'I brought two cups, miss,' the maid said shyly. 'I saw that Miss Kitty had come home.'

'Thank you, Iris. We'll help ourselves,' Ivory said, smiling as she picked up the teapot and proceeded to pour.

Iris bobbed a curtsey and left the room, closing the door behind her.

'I suppose you could ask Grandmama if you can go back to Bridlebank,' Kitty said thoughtfully. 'I am quite happy here.' She took a sip of tea.

'Are you?' Ivory gave her a searching look. 'Something is wrong, I can tell, and I think I can guess who is causing you so much trouble.'

'I never could keep anything from you,' Kitty said with a rueful smile. 'But I'm probably making too much of the situation.'

'You have always been the practical one, Kitty. If Inspector Barton has been toying with your feelings, I will have something to say to him.'

Kitty laughed. 'That I would like to see. You have never raised your voice to anyone, Ivory. But thank you, anyway. I don't need a champion, and Will is an honourable man. Too honourable in some ways.'

'If he cares about you, he should tell you as much. He cannot hide behind his uniform, Kitty. It isn't fair.'

'We were talking about you just now, but suddenly it's all about me and Will Barton. I can look after myself, Ivory, but I'm not so sure about you. There is one solution to your problem.'

Ivory eyed her warily. 'What is that?'

'You must speak to Charles. Tell him how you feel.' Kitty replaced her cup on its saucer.

Ivory's eyes widened in horror. 'I can't do that. You know it's impossible.'

'Nothing is impossible if you want it enough.' Kitty stood up.

Ivory pursed her lips. 'Perhaps you should take your own advice, Kitty. You seem to need it even more than I do.'

Kitty knew when to walk away from a rare difference of opinion with her sister. She backed towards the door. 'I should go to my room and change out of these dusty clothes. You can't imagine the state of Ma Tucker's house. Anyway, the inspector will be calling soon to let me know if he's found any of Frances's jewels stashed away under the eaves.'

Ivory took a slice of cake and laid it on a plate. 'It would be wonderful if it were true.' She put her head on one side, giving Kitty a knowing smile. 'You could invite him to stay for dinner. If he has found anything that belongs to Frances or Charles, they will be delighted.'

Kitty realised that she had lost this argument before it had even started. She left the room and was about to mount the staircase when someone knocked on the front door. She hesitated, waiting for one of the servants to answer the summons, but when no one came, and the knocking became louder, she crossed the hall and opened the door.

'Flinders!' Kitty stared at him in disbelief. 'You are supposed to be on your way to British Guiana.'

'I wasn't sure if you would be here, Kitty. Or if you would want to see me, for that matter.' Flinders hesitated on the doorstep, eyeing her nervously. 'I mean, we didn't exactly part on the best of terms, and for that I am genuinely sorry.'

Kitty shook her head. 'The fault was mine, Flinders. I could have behaved better, but you caught me by surprise. The next thing I knew, you had left

Mill House and were on your way back to South America, or so we all thought.'

'I should have stayed a while longer and said my goodbyes. It's been worrying me ever since I left.'

'Never mind that now. Come inside, Flinders.' Kitty ushered him into the hallway. 'What happened in Essex is in the past, and I'm delighted to see you, but why have you returned to London?' She frowned worriedly. 'You are not ill, are you?'

Flinders shook his head. 'No, nothing of the sort. I was in Southampton, waiting for a passage to British Guiana, when I had a message to return immediately to London and report to the Geological Society. I didn't question it, of course, and I came back to town as quickly as I could.'

'What did they want?'

'It's good news, Kitty. I've come to tell you that your father was examined by his doctor and considered well enough to travel. He is on his way home.'

'Are you quite certain, Flinders?' Kitty clutched his hand. 'Papa is really coming home?'

'He left Georgetown on a ship bound for Southampton some time ago. I haven't any details about his condition, but he must be reasonably fit to undertake the voyage.'

'Did they know when Papa will arrive at Southampton, Flinders?' Kitty asked eagerly.

'It depends on the weather, but we'll get a better idea soon.'

Kitty wiped tears from her eyes on the back of her hand. 'I'm so happy. I can hardly believe it. We must tell Ivory, and then someone will have to go to Bridlebank and give Mama the good news.'

Flinders smiled. 'What about Amethyst? Doesn't she deserve to know?'

'Amy is a married woman, Flinders. She and Marriner eloped and now they are on their honeymoon in Paris.' Kitty took a deep breath. 'I'm sorry, the good news has made me forget my manners. Have you anywhere to stay tonight?'

'I only arrived this morning. My luggage is still in the cab outside because I wasn't sure if you were here. I'll find a hotel for tonight and tomorrow I will set off for Little Foxbury.'

'I'm sure the Westbrooks will invite you to stay here,' Kitty said firmly. 'I'll ring for Mr Henderson, and he'll have your things brought in from the cab. I can always share Ivory's room if there is nowhere else for you to sleep.' She looked around at the sound of footsteps and saw Henderson striding towards them.

'I am so sorry, Miss Harte,' Henderson said urgently. 'There was a slight altercation with one of the tradesmen at the servants' entrance. I apologise for there being no one to answer the doorbell.'

'It doesn't matter, Mr Henderson,' Kitty said politely. 'Mr Riley has just arrived in London. I'm sure that Sir Charles will invite him to stay, so would you please send someone to get his bags out of the cab?'

Flinders took a money pouch from his pocket and tipped some coins into his palm. He gave them to Henderson. 'This should cover the fare and the extra waiting time.'

Henderson nodded as he took the money from Flinders and was about to step outside onto the pavement when Kitty called him back.

'Mr Henderson, would you be so kind as to have some refreshment sent to the drawing room for Mr Riley?'

'Of course, Miss Harte.' Henderson cleared his throat. 'I hope the little lapse will not be reported to Sir Charles.'

'Certainly not. It's between you and me, Mr Henderson.' Kitty caught Flinders by the hand and started off towards the drawing room. She came to a halt outside the door.

'Tell me one thing, Flinders,' she said, turning to face him. 'If my papa is on his way home, why did the Society stop you from going to British Guiana? Aren't you needed there now?'

'They called me back to tell me that the expedition is being brought to its conclusion. Apparently, the fellow who took over when I came home on leave has proved to be very efficient. He reported that the seam of mineral we were investigating has not provided the expected results, and the operation has been cancelled.'

'So you are unemployed,' Kitty said softly. 'I am so sorry, Flinders. What will you do now?'

'It's time I did my bit to help my mother and my grandmother. I'm going back to Little Foxbury and maybe I'll take over the mill for a while or try to persuade Grandmama to put it on the market.'

'They will be overjoyed to have you with them, even for a short time. Papa had quite long stretches when he was at home, and then he would be sent on another expedition. I'm sure your career isn't finished yet.' Kitty patted him on the hand as she turned back to open the drawing-room door.

'Look who's here, Ivory. Flinders has brought us the most marvellous news . . .'

After dinner that evening Charles insisted on drinking a toast in champagne. He raised his glass. 'To Robert Harte's recovery and safe return to England.'

Kitty raised her glass. 'And to Flinders Riley for bringing us the good tidings.'

Flinders smiled modestly. 'I really did nothing, but I am truly delighted that Mr Harte, my superior and my mentor, is on his way home to his loved ones. He is a fine man and I'm proud to have been associated with him.' He drained his glass and sank back onto his seat.

'It's really wonderful news,' Frances said, smiling. 'But that means we'll be losing you, Ivory, and you, too, Kitty. You'll be moving out soon.'

Kitty glanced anxiously at her sister. 'We will have to find somewhere where we can all live, but we don't know what state Papa will be in when he gets home.'

'You will always be welcome at Mill House,' Flinders said firmly.

Kitty gave Flinders a warm smile, but she could imagine the dismay on Mrs Riley's face when faced with the prospect of the entire Harte family turning up on her doorstep.

'Maybe we could take over the windmill,' she said, forcing a smile. 'It's kind of you, Flinders, but I'm sure we'll find something in London.'

Frances turned to Charles with a persuasive smile. 'There might be an empty property on the Westbrook estate, Charles. I'm sure we could help until Mr Harte is fit enough to return to his profession.'

'Something could be arranged,' Charles said calmly. 'I'm going to Westbrook tomorrow. I'll have a word with our estate manager and see if there's anything that might be suitable.'

'It's too good of you, Charles, but I don't think my parents would accept such charity.' Ivory had resumed her seat, but she stood up again, obviously flustered. 'We can't impose on your good nature.'

'Nonsense,' Charles said sharply. 'It's not charity, Ivory. It's called helping good friends when they are in need. Perhaps you ought to come with me so that you could give me an opinion first-hand.'

'I – er – that wouldn't be proper.' Ivory sent a desperate look to Kitty, who was also on her feet.

'Ivory is right, Charles,' Kitty said hastily. 'It's incredibly kind of you and Frances to think of us in that way, but it isn't up to Ivory or me. Our parents should be the ones to decide.'

Frances waved her hands as if sweeping objections aside. 'There is no harm in looking. I haven't anything planned for the next few days. I will accompany Charles and that will make it quite proper for Ivory to accompany us, and you, too, Kitty if you so wish.'

'I don't know,' Kitty said doubtfully. 'I have my stall at the Bazaar, and then there's Inspector Barton,' she hesitated, aware that she had everyone's undivided attention. 'I mean, he will be coming to see me about the robbery.'

'Why you, Kitty?' Charles demanded, frowning. 'It was our property that was taken.'

'Barton seems to be taking an unusual amount of interest in a relatively minor crime,' Flinders added suspiciously.

Kitty looked from one curious face to another. 'It's just because one of Frances's jewels was found on a stall close to mine in the Bazaar. The inspector suspects that person is acting as a fence for the thieves who committed the crime.'

'Are you officially helping the police with their enquiries?' Flinders asked.

'No,' Kitty said stoutly. 'Of course not.'

Her response was lost as someone knocked on the door and Henderson entered at Charles's command.

'Excuse me, Sir Charles, but there's a gentleman asking to see Miss Kitty Harte.'

'Who is it, Henderson?'

'It's Constable Beddoes, Sir Charles. He asked specifically for Miss Harte.'

'Yes, thank you, Henderson.'

Kitty felt her cheeks burning with embarrassment. She knew they were all drawing their own conclusions. 'I was expecting a visit from the police with regard to the robbery,' she added hastily.

'Shall I show the constable into the morning parlour, Miss Harte?'

'Yes, please, Mr Henderson.' Kitty met their curious stares with her head held high. 'It's police business,' she added as she hurried from the dining room.

Constable Beddoes was waiting in the morning parlour, clutching his top hat in his hands as he gazed around the elegantly furnished room, obviously impressed with what he saw.

'The inspector sent me, miss,' Constable Beddoes said awkwardly. 'I mean, he asked me to apologise for not coming in person, but he had to leave London suddenly.'

Kitty stared at him in surprise. 'Why was that, Constable?'

'I believe he had news of a death in the family, miss. I don't know the details.'

'I'm sorry to hear that,' Kitty said earnestly. 'Was it a close relative?'

'I believe so, miss. But the message I have for you

is about the boxes we discovered in Mrs Tucker's house earlier today.'

'What did they contain?' Kitty asked patiently. 'I mean, were the Westbrook jewels included?'

'Yes, miss. At least some of them, anyway. There was quite a hoard, and the items are being sorted as we speak, but the inspector wanted you to know that he was hopeful of finding most or all of the stolen jewellery and silver.'

'That is good news indeed. Thank you, Constable.' Kitty was delighted, but she was also disturbed by the news that Barton had lost someone dear to him. She tried to sound casual. 'Has the inspector gone to his family home? I believe it is in Essex.'

'I think so, miss. Like I said, I don't know any more details, although between you and me I heard it was the inspector's father who had passed away. I lost my pa a year ago, so I know how it feels.'

'I'm sorry, Constable Beddoes. Thank you for giving me the news. I suppose we just have to wait now until Sir Charles is invited to identify the stolen objects.'

'Exactly so, miss.' Constable Beddoes shifted nervously from one foot to the other. 'You didn't hear about the inspector's bereavement from me.'

'Certainly not,' Kitty said, smiling. 'I'll see you out.' She opened the door, prepared to lead the way, but she could see the head footman on duty by the front door. 'There you are, Constable. James will show you out.' She stood for a moment, thinking of Will Barton and how he must have felt on hearing the sad news of his father's demise. It brought back memories of the shocking time when she and her mother and sisters had learned of Papa's near-fatal accident, and she felt a desperate need to be with Will, if only to express her condolences. It was then that an idea occurred to her, and she made her way upstairs to the drawing room on the first floor, where Frances and Ivory were having coffee with Charles and Flinders, who had forgone brandy and a cigar in order to join them.

'Well?' Charles said abruptly. 'Why did the constable want to speak to you, Kitty? I am the head of the household.'

'I'm sure he knew that, Charles.' Kitty managed a smile even though she was suddenly close to tears as emotion welled up inside her. 'There's good news and some sad news, also.'

'Don't keep us in suspense, Kitty,' Frances said urgently. 'Tell us the good news first.'

'The police seem to think they have recovered all or at least most of your jewels and stolen goods, Frances.'

'And the sad news?' Ivory asked gently.

'You look upset, Kitty.' Flinders stood up and offered her his chair. 'Sit down and tell us what's wrong.'

'It has nothing to do with me personally, of course, but Inspector Barton has suffered a family bereavement and has had to leave London.' Kitty managed to control her voice with difficulty. 'It must have been very sudden because I was with him at

Mrs Tucker's house this morning, and he seemed cheerful enough then.'

'Oh, well. These things happen,' Charles said casually. 'I'm sorry for the fellow, but we've been talking while you were out of the room, Kitty.'

'Yes,' Frances added without giving him a chance to explain. 'We're leaving for Suffolk tomorrow morning. Ivory is coming with us so that she can inspect any likely property on the estate.'

'I'm going to Little Foxbury,' Flinders added quickly. 'You could always come with me if you wanted a change of scenery, Kitty. You know how much I value your company,' he added in a low voice.

'I do, Flinders,' Kitty said quietly. 'I wish I felt differently, but your friendship means everything to me.'

'You will come with us, won't you, Kitty?' Frances said firmly. 'Surely you don't want to stay in London on your own. I mean, you will, of course, have the servants to look after you, but you might find it very lonely.'

Kitty looked from one to the other. If she were to be practical, she knew she should remain in Duke Street and work on her paintings so that she had something to sell at the Bazaar. But perhaps this was the time to put common sense aside and to follow her heart. Something, or perhaps someone, was calling to her in the wilds of Essex and she knew she must search for the answer.

Chapter Twenty-Three

The Westbrook estate was even larger than Kitty could have imagined. The house was in the Palladian style and had a symmetrical elegance that appealed to her. The cleverly landscaped grounds had been set out on a scale and with an eye to beauty that would not have disgraced William Kent or Capability Brown, according to Charles, whose pride in his home was apparent from the moment they arrived late next day.

Kitty and Ivory were allocated adjoining rooms, both with wonderful views across the deer park at the rear of the house and the parterre garden below the flagstone terrace and classical stone balustrade. The four-poster bed in Kitty's room had a matching chintz tester and curtains, and these were repeated in the overall colour scheme.

'I feel like a princess in this room,' Kitty said happily.

Ivory looked around approvingly. 'My room is identical except for the floral curtains and the toning rugs. It's so elegant, I feel quite ashamed of our old house in Soho Square, at least by comparison.'

'It was home,' Kitty said stoutly. 'We grew up there and we all loved it, even Nellie, and she usually finds fault with everything.'

'She's happy here, at least for the time being,' Ivory added, smiling. 'She's unpacking my things because she won't allow the chambermaid to touch anything of mine. According to Nellie, most country servants have no idea how to do things. I imagine she has already upset most of the staff below stairs.'

'I suggest you leave Nellie with Mama or me if you decide to marry Charles,' Kitty said, laughing.

'Don't say such things, Kitty. He has never spoken of love or anything like that.' Ivory turned her head away, but Kitty had already spotted the bright colour that flooded her sister's cheeks.

'Why do you think he wants to have us living on his estate?' Kitty asked mischievously. 'You don't have to answer, Ivory. It goes without saying.'

'I'll admit that I am very fond of him, and of Frances, too, but Charles is just being kind and chivalrous in offering to find us somewhere to live.' Ivory walked to the door. 'I'm going to see how Nellie is getting on. Do you want her to unpack your valise?'

'No, thank you. I can look after myself. I think I might go for a stroll in the gardens before it's time to change for dinner. Thank goodness I have one reasonably smart gown to wear.'

Ivory pulled a face. 'I've no doubt I will feel terribly shabby if Frances decides to entertain. We missed the last soirée they gave because you were abducted and imprisoned in a semi-ruined priory.'

'I'd rather forget that, apart of course from the money I've made from the paintings of Brother Benedictus. That reminds me, I can't stay here for long, Ivory. I must pay the rent on my stall each day, even if I don't work. And this for me is purely temporary.'

Ivory hesitated, clutching the door handle. 'But I can't live here without you, Kitty.'

'If we find a suitable house you will have Mama and Nellie to keep you company, and I will return to Duke Street, if Charles and Frances don't object.'

'I will miss you.'

'Nonsense. You will have to study how Frances runs the household for when you become Lady Westbrook.'

'Stop saying things like that, Kitty. I won't be able to face Charles at dinner if you make fun of me.' Ivory left the room without giving Kitty a chance to apologise for teasing her.

Charles was as good as his word, and next day he took Ivory and Kitty around the estate in a chaise drawn by a grey horse that took an instant liking to Ivory. Every time they alighted to inspect a cottage the animal would attempt to get close to Ivory and nuzzle her hand. Charles was obviously impressed.

'I've never seen Hardy behave like that with anyone, Ivory. He must have taken a great liking to you.'

Ivory laughed and stroked Hardy's nose. 'I've never had the opportunity to learn to ride, but I think I could if the horse was as friendly as this fellow.'

Kitty patted Hardy on the flank. 'He's very intelligent. He recognises someone who is kind and gentle.'

Charles proffered his arm to Ivory. 'We'll leave him while we go into this property, which I think is the most suitable for your needs. There is a large room on the ground floor that might be used by someone who perhaps cannot manage stairs, and I imagine you will be bringing your father here to recuperate.'

'That does sound ideal,' Ivory said enthusiastically.

Kitty followed them up the garden path, which was bordered by neat flowerbeds and roses beginning to come into leaf clambered over the covered porch.

'This is a nice house,' Kitty said as she stepped into the square entrance hall. 'Surely this is not an ordinary worker's cottage.'

'We had an estate manager for a while, but I discovered that he had been swindling me, so he was sent packing, and now I run everything myself.

I prefer to do it that way.' Charles opened a door to the right. 'This is a reasonably sized room and there is another similar one on the other side of the hall.' He led the way through the ground floor, and he left Kitty and Ivory to explore the first floor and the top floor with attic rooms, which were adequate accommodation for Nellie and perhaps a live-in maid of all work.

'What do you think, Kitty?' Ivory asked eagerly.

'It's ideal, at least as a temporary measure,' Kitty said calmly. 'It would be good for Papa in his convalescent stage, although he would probably want to move back to London when he is fit enough. He needs to earn a living and it's unlikely that he could find anything suitable here.'

Ivory frowned thoughtfully. 'Maybe he doesn't want to go back to his old job, Kitty. He might not be physically strong enough to go on expeditions after such a bad injury.'

'Let's meet that problem if it arises. For now, I think this is a splendid house. It's big enough for all of us, but not too large. The only problem is that Mama might not want to live in the country.'

Ivory gazed out of the bedroom window. 'There is a lovely garden, Kitty. It's rather overgrown, but I'm sure it would be wonderful with a little loving care.'

Kitty laughed. 'You already sound like a countrywoman, Ivory. Maybe that's your destiny. I've yet to find mine.'

'You have a talent for painting,' Ivory said solemnly. 'I have no particular skills, but perhaps tending plants and flowers might turn out to be an unexpected one.'

'Your particular gift is in dealing with people, Ivory,' Kitty laughed. 'And obviously you have a knack of getting on with horses, if Hardy is anything to go by. Perhaps Charles could teach you to ride.'

'Now you're teasing me again.' Ivory gave her a reproachful look. 'But aside from that, do you agree that this house would be ideal? If so, I'll try to persuade Mama to come and see it.'

'I don't think you'll have much of an argument from Mama,' Kitty said, nodding. 'I think after spending all this time at Bridlebank Mama would consider living in a cave if it meant getting away from Grandmama.'

'I think you're right. Let's go and find Charles.' Ivory tore herself away from the view and hurried downstairs with Kitty following on her heels.

At luncheon, and with a prompt from Charles, Ivory announced their intention of taking up the offer of the estate manager's house, subject to their mother's approval.

Frances beamed at her. 'I'm delighted. That is the very place I would have chosen for you. It's a nice house and with a few extra touches it will be very acceptable.'

Kitty eyed her warily. 'What have you in mind, Frances?'

'Maybe some new curtains and a few colourful rugs. Anyway, I seem to remember you have your furniture and belongings in storage. If I were your mama, I would jump at the chance of having all my things returned to me.'

'Yes, of course,' Kitty said, smiling. 'Why didn't I think of that, Ivory? With our furniture and ornaments, as well as the family silver that the inspector is going to return to us, it will be just like home.'

'We could send some of the outdoor staff to tidy up the garden, couldn't we, Charles?' Frances fixed him with a look that dared him to disagree at his peril.

'Of course,' Charles said amicably. 'I'll do anything that needs to be done to the property.'

'I suggest we go to Manningtree tomorrow.' Frances put her knife and fork down, looking from Ivory to Kitty with an excited smile. 'We could get some samples of material for the curtains so that you could show them to your mama.'

'I should get back to London soon,' Kitty said seriously. 'Maybe the day after tomorrow, and I could go and see Mama at Bridlebank. I need to take some of my work to the Bazaar, and I'll leave Bella in charge of my stall.'

'Do you really trust her not to cheat you?' Ivory

frowned. 'I mean, her mother is under arrest for acting as a fence. Supposing Bella sells your work and then disappears with the money?'

'I don't earn enough to make it worth her risking her good name. We can't blame her for what her mother has done. I believe Bella is innocent.'

Charles shook his head. 'I doubt it, but she seems to have inspired a certain amount of loyalty where you are concerned, Kitty. You must do what you consider best.'

Frances raised her glass. 'Here's to success in all things. We will have a nice day out tomorrow and I hope it's the first of many. I know I will enjoy living in the country much more if both of you are here to alleviate the boredom.'

Kitty, Ivory and Charles joined in the toast.

'I am sure we must have plenty of odds and ends stored in the loft if you need anything for the house,' Frances said eagerly. She glared at her brother. 'Why are you smirking, Charles?'

'I'm smiling, Frances. I'm happy to see you so involved and interested, for once. Normally you get bored within half an hour of being here.'

'I am happy because I have something to occupy my mind, as well as good company. We are going to be like sisters, aren't we, Ivory – and you, too, of course, Kitty.'

'Thank you, Frances,' Ivory said before Kitty had a chance to speak. 'You can't imagine how relieved I feel to have the prospect of a home again. Isn't that so, Kitty?'

Kitty nodded. 'Of course. It's a wonderful offer, Charles. I don't know how we could ever repay you.'

'I have an idea about that, Kitty. I would like a large oil painting of Ivory with Hardy. Can you do horses as well as people?'

'I can try, Charles.'

'I have faith in your abilities, Kitty,' Charles said firmly. 'I suggest you close your stall at the Bazaar and bring your painting equipment from Duke Street. I will pay you for a portrait in oils of Ivory posing with Hardy.'

'We need to go to London to give Mama the good news about the house, Kitty,' Ivory said eagerly. 'And we should leave a message at Lord Marriner's London home so that Amy knows where to find us when they return from Paris.'

Kitty looked from one eager face to another, and she smiled reluctantly. 'I think I am outnumbered. Perhaps a stay in the country would be beneficial.'

'That's settled then.' Frances clapped her hands. 'Excellent. Tomorrow we will go shopping and Charles will make the necessary arrangements for you to travel up to London next day, if that suits you both.'

Kitty nodded. She could see that Ivory was thrilled at the prospect of bringing their mother to Westbrook and the thought of having her portrait painted once again, only this time in oils. Charles had made his intentions as clear as possible without actually proposing marriage, and Kitty knew her sister well enough to realise that this was exactly what Ivory wanted. She was happy for them both, but she had a nagging feeling that something was not quite right as far as she herself was concerned. She put such thoughts from her mind and tried to concentrate on sharing Ivory's good fortune.

They had been shopping in Manningtree before, and being a small town, it did not take long to peruse the stock in the only shop selling curtain material. The shop owner was eager to please and offered to send to London for samples if they could not find anything suitable in her limited stock. Ivory seemed ready to choose there and then, but Frances insisted on having a wider selection. They left with nothing but promised to return when the fresh samples arrived.

It was a warm and sunny spring day but as they left the shop, they encountered a funeral procession and out of respect they came to a halt amongst a growing crowd of onlookers. The solemn funeral director walking in front of the horse-driven hearse, together with the large number of mourners, seemed to indicate that it was a person of some consequence who was about to be interred.

Kitty held her breath when she spotted Will Barton

walking behind the hearse, followed by male friends and relations, all of whom were dressed in funereal black from their top hats to the shiny toes of their shoes. Then came a carriage bringing two ladies, heavily veiled, followed by two more, presumably with close family members, all similarly clad.

Two women standing next to Kitty were talking in low voices. Kitty was not paying much attention to their conversation, but the mention of Will's name made her turn to stare at them.

'Excuse me,' Kitty said, tapping the older woman on the arm. 'Did I hear you say that Mrs Barton is in the first carriage? Would that be Inspector Barton's mother? I mean, I don't know the family well, but I would like to pay my respects.'

The women turned to give her a fierce look. 'Leave 'em be to mourn in peace, miss. Young Mrs Barton is in the family way again, and Mrs Barton senior has taken to her bed.'

The younger woman nodded. 'That's Will's aunt Agnes in the carriage with Rosina. Are you related, miss?'

Kitty swallowed hard. Suddenly the clip-clopping of the horses' hoofs and the slow rumble of the carriage wheels seemed to fill her head with a sound so deafening that she felt quite faint. 'I know the inspector in his professional capacity.'

The older woman pursed her lips. 'At least the funeral has brought him back to his family for a while.'

'Yes, miss. He's very important in the city.' The younger woman turned away, pointing to someone on the far side of the road. 'There's that girl Ivy Morris. She's got no shame, showing herself in front of the family at a time like this. They say that she is carrying yet another Barton love child.'

Kitty turned away. She had heard enough to make her feel sick, and she staggered, bumping into Ivory, who steadied her with both hands.

'What's the matter, Kitty? You look awful. Are you unwell?'

'No, I mean, yes. I feel a bit dizzy.' Kitty leaned heavily on her sister's arm. 'I need to sit down.'

Frances eyed her anxiously. 'The carriage is only a street away, Kitty. Can you walk that far?'

'Yes, I just need some air.' Kitty took a deep breath. 'Did you know that Inspector Barton was married, Frances?'

'The Bartons are an old farming family,' Frances said slowly. 'I didn't associate Inspector Barton with them, but now I recall that he joined the police force instead of working the land. It was the talk of the town for a while.'

Ivory slipped her arm around Kitty's shoulders. 'The procession has gone past. Let's get back to the carriage. Please don't faint, Kitty.'

Kitty drew herself upright, holding her head high. 'I was surprised, that's all. I feel much better now.'

'I'll walk on ahead and tell Broughton to bring the carriage closer.' Frances marched off purposefully, leaving Kitty and Ivory to follow more slowly.

'Did Will Barton make improper advances to you, Kitty?' Ivory demanded suspiciously. 'If he's behaved in an ungentlemanly manner, I'll tell Charles, and he will report Barton to the police chief.'

'No, not really. I must have been mistaken, but I really thought he liked me, Ivory.' Kitty quickened her pace as she set off to follow Frances.

'There's no crime in that. But if he has a family here it looks as though he's led you on, which is appalling. He should be brought to book for his behaviour.'

'I will deal with him myself,' Kitty said grimly. 'He kissed me once, and it was only on my cheek, but it's obvious now that he was just flirting with me. I won't allow him to get away with it, but I want you to leave it with me, Ivory. Do you promise?'

'Yes, I suppose I must, if you say so.'

'I don't want to talk about it any more.' Kitty managed a weak smile. 'I was naïve. However, I won't make that mistake again.'

'Do you still want to return to London tomorrow? I mean, do you want a few days to recover from the shock?'

'I'm more annoyed at my own stupidity rather than hurt,' Kitty said firmly, although in her heart she knew this was far from the truth. 'Anyway, we must tell Mama about the house on the Westbrook estate. I will inform Matron Hume that I don't need the stall now, and I'll take up Charles's offer to paint you and that horse of his.'

Ivory sighed. 'It's a pity you sent Flinders away, Kitty. He obviously adores you.'

'And I'm fond of him, but I don't think that's enough.'

'Perhaps you were blinded by Barton's good looks and charm.'

Kitty forced herself to smile. 'I am going to concentrate on art from now on.'

Ivory insisted on accompanying Kitty to London next day. By the time they arrived at the house in Duke Street it was too late to set off for Bridlebank, but Kitty walked to the Bazaar where she sought out Matron Hume.

'I will be sorry to see you leave permanently, Miss Harte,' Matron said earnestly. 'You have not given me any trouble, unlike some of my other ladies.'

Kitty nodded. 'I was shocked to learn that Mrs Tucker was involved with criminals, but I truly believe that Bella knew nothing of her mother's business.'

'Really? I was going to let the stall to someone else.' Matron frowned, shaking her head. 'It's my job to keep everything running smoothly and no hanky-panky allowed.'

'If Bella wants to run her mother's stall, I hope you

will allow it, Matron. I trust her and she's proved herself to be good at selling.'

'She isn't in today, but she left some money for you from the last of your paintings.' Matron opened her desk drawer and took out a cash box. She counted out some coins and handed them to Kitty. 'She has proved herself to be as honest as the next person. If she wants to come back, I'll give her a chance, Miss Harte.'

'You can do no more than that. Thank you, Matron. It's been a pleasure working here and I'm only sorry it's come to an end, but you never know, I might return to London in the future.'

'You are always welcome here.' Matron slammed the drawer and stood up. 'I must do my rounds, so I'll take goodbye for now.' She waddled off into the main concourse.

Kitty pocketed the money and set off for Duke Street. However, acting on an impulse, she decided to go to Brewery Yard and chance seeing Bella. It would be unkind to leave London without thanking her for looking after the stall, and she felt oddly responsible for Bella, who seemed helpless without her mother to guide her.

After the intense police activity in Brewery Yard when Barton had discovered the stash of stolen property in Moll Tucker's attic, it was relatively quiet when Kitty arrived. She knocked on the door with little hope of finding Bella at home, but as she was about to walk away, she heard footsteps on the bare boards inside the house.

Bella opened the door, and her face lit up at the sight of Kitty. 'Miss Harte, you've come back to London.'

'It's just a short visit, Bella. I'm returning to Suffolk in a day or two, but I couldn't go without thanking you for looking after my stall.'

Bella's cheeks flushed scarlet. 'It were nothing, miss. I love working on the stall, but I got nothing to sell now. I'll have to give up Ma's stand.'

'Did the police take all the items your mother had for sale?'

'No, miss. They said it was just a lot of cheap rubbish, not worth anything. I got it all in a big box.'

Kitty put her hand in her pocket and took out the money that Matron Hume had given her. 'Take this, Bella. Go back to the Bazaar and ask Matron Hume to let you keep your mother's stall. This money will help to pay for it until you start earning again.'

Bella gazed at the coins in Kitty's palm. 'I dunno, miss. I can't take your money.'

'Consider it as wages for the time you spent selling my work.' Kitty pressed the money into Bella's hand. 'Good luck, Bella. I promise I'll come and see you when next time I return to London.'

'Thank you, miss. I'm very grateful to you. I will go to the Bazaar now, before it closes, and make sure Matron doesn't let Ma's stall to anyone else.' She stepped outside and slammed the door and locked it. 'Ta-ta for now, miss.'

'I'll walk with you a little way,' Kitty said smiling. 'And then I must head for Duke Street.'

Henderson opened the door when Kitty arrived back at the house. As she entered, she was aware that something had changed. There were sounds of activity behind the green baize door that separated those below stairs from the family, and a pile of luggage had been left in the entrance hall.

'What's going on, Mr Henderson?'

'Sir Charles has arrived unexpectedly, Miss Harte,' Henderson said with an irritable twitch of his shoulders. 'We were in the process of closing up the house for a few weeks while the family are in the country.'

'Oh dear, that does sound a little unsettling,' Kitty said sympathetically. 'But I'm sure you will rise to the occasion, as always, Mr Henderson.'

'Yes, of course, Miss Harte. You will find your sister and Sir Charles in the drawing room.'

Kitty was suddenly anxious. She could not think why Charles had followed them to London, especially when they could have travelled together earlier in the day. She hurried upstairs and entered the drawing room without knocking, but she came to a halt when she saw Ivory and Charles in a passionate embrace. They stepped apart but Charles caught Ivory by the hand and held it so that she stayed at his side.

'I think Kitty has gathered that something has changed, my love.'

Ivory blushed rosily. 'I'm sorry I didn't tell you before, Kitty. But you were so upset when you discovered the truth about Will, that I hadn't the heart.'

Kitty took off her bonnet and shawl and tossed them onto a chair. She rushed forward and wrapped her arms around Ivory, giving her a hug.

'Don't be silly. I've known all along that you two were in love. I'm so happy for you.'

'We were going to keep it a secret for a while longer,' Charles said, smiling. 'But Ivory has just done me the honour of accepting my proposal of marriage.'

Kitty released Ivory to give Charles a hug. 'Congratulations. That is the best news I've had since Flinders told us that Papa is on his way home.' She turned to Ivory. 'Have you got a ring? May I see it?'

Ivory held out her left hand and a sapphire and diamond ring caught the last rays of sunlight as they flooded through the window.

'Isn't it splendid, Kitty?'

'I had it made especially for Ivory, the woman with whom I want to spend the rest of my life.' Charles slipped his arm around Ivory's shoulders. 'I came to London to collect it from Garrard. I intended to propose in a more romantic way, but I seized the moment.'

'It was very romantic,' Ivory said, gazing at the ring. 'I can't wait to tell everyone, especially Grandmama, who always said I would marry beneath me if I didn't make more of myself.'

'Well, my darling, tomorrow I will go with you to face the Gorgon, and I will let her know that I consider myself to be the most fortunate man in the world.' Charles twisted Ivory around to kiss her soundly on the lips.

Kitty turned away, not wanting to intrude. She was happy for them, of course, but it did not do anything to ease the pain in her heart, nor the sense of betrayal she felt when thinking of Will. She perched on the window seat, but as she glanced at the street below, she spotted a carriage drawing up outside. She recognised the footman as he leaped down to open the door, and she jumped to her feet, putting her own feelings firmly aside.

'I think we will have a celebration dinner tonight. You'll never guess who's just arrived.'

Ivory twisted free from Charles's embrace. 'Who is it, Kitty?'

'It's Amethyst and Sebastian, Lord and Lady Marriner. You will have stolen her thunder, Ivory. You are the star today and Amy is now an old married lady.' Kitty laughed, but there were tears in her eyes as she fought to keep her own heartache from spoiling her genuine pleasure for both her sisters.

'For heaven's sake, don't tell her that,' Ivory said urgently. 'You know how she can turn on the tears at the slightest provocation.'

Charles smiled. 'I rather think that is Marriner's problem now, my love.'

The door burst open even as he spoke and Amethyst, dressed in the latest Paris fashion, rushed into the room to fling her arms around Ivory. She was followed more slowly by Marriner.

'I suspect we have arrived at an opportune moment, Charles,' Marriner said slowly. 'Judging by your beatific smile I imagine congratulations are in order.'

Amethyst released Ivory. She backed away, gazing at her sister's left hand.

'No! You haven't got engaged without me being present? How could you, Ivory?'

'You're supposed to congratulate the gentleman, Amy,' Kitty said, laughing. 'You make it sound as if Ivory has committed a *faux pas* by accepting Charles's proposal.'

Amethyst tossed her head. 'Of course I'm delighted for my oldest sister. It was very embarrassing to have me married before her, so now we will be equals.'

Marriner put his arm around Amethyst's waist. 'I think we should change the subject, darling. You're only making matters worse.'

Amethyst shrugged. 'Oh, well. No one pays any attention to what I say, Sebastian, except you, of course.' She turned to Kitty. 'It's your turn next. Has the handsome policeman come up to scratch yet?'

Kitty bit her lip, unable to speak, but Charles spoke up quickly, as if sensing her distress.

'I think we should all go out to dinner to celebrate being a family. It's unfair to expect my servants to provide such a meal when they didn't even know I was coming home. What do you say, Marriner?'

'I say we go to a restaurant where they keep the best champagne on ice,' Marriner said firmly. 'And you don't need to change your gown again, my darling. Everyone will realise that you're dressed in the latest fashion.' He turned to Kitty with a genuine smile. 'I married into a family of beautiful women.'

Ivory shot a warning glance at Amethyst, whose ominous pout was likely to lead to tears or a tantrum. 'Just give Kitty and me a few minutes to change into something more suitable for dining out. Fortunately, I didn't take many clothes to Suffolk, so we have a choice. Come with me, Kitty.'

It was a command that Kitty was only too glad to obey without saying a word. She followed Ivory from the room. It was going to be a difficult evening, but she had her emotions under control, or so she hoped.

Chapter Twenty-Four

The evening passed without further incident, largely due to several bottles of excellent champagne. Amethyst was very tipsy at the end of the meal and Marriner had to carry her to their carriage, which he did with great good humour, promising to visit Duke Street before he took Amethyst to their country estate in two days' time.

'He obviously dotes on her,' Ivory said in a hushed voice when Charles was busy settling the bill.

'It's hard to believe, considering his former reputation as a lothario,' Kitty added. 'But I'm glad that Amy has found someone who will take good care of her. She doesn't mean half the things she says. It's all bravado.'

Ivory rolled her eyes. 'You always had more patience with her than I have. But how are you,

Kitty? You hide your feelings very well, but I know you are still upset.'

'I have put it all behind me, Ivory. I must face the facts and get on with day-to-day living. I'm thinking ahead now for when Papa returns, and we have a home again. Also,' Kitty said, smiling, 'we have a wedding to plan. There'll be no more elopements, I hope.'

'No, of course not. I haven't thought that far ahead, but it will be exciting, You, of course, will be my maid of honour.'

Kitty laughed. 'Amethyst won't like that. You know she will want to be matron of honour. I will have to take second place.'

'We will see about that,' Ivory said primly. 'Here comes Charles. I think it's time to go home.'

Charles had sent a waiter to hail a cab, and they returned to Duke Street. Kitty thanked him for a lovely evening, and she embraced Ivory before making a tactful retreat to her own room. However, sleep evaded her for a long time. Just being in London brought back memories that were too painful now that she knew the truth about Will Barton. She still found it hard to believe that he could have been so deceitful, allowing her to think that he had feelings for her, even though he did not express them directly, when all along he had a wife and children. In the end she fell into a fitful sleep, filled with dreams that caused her to toss and turn. It was a relief to awaken to a bright sunny morning and a maid bringing her a cup of hot chocolate to start the day.

Ivory was already in the dining room when Kitty went down to breakfast.

'Good morning, Kitty,' Ivory said, sipping her coffee.

Kitty helped herself from the silver dishes on the sideboard and sat down at the table.

'Aren't you hungry, Ivory?'

'My tummy is filled with butterflies,' Ivory said with a rueful smile. 'I suppose it's excitement, or maybe it's the thought of telling Grandmama that I am engaged to Charles.'

'She can't object. It's a match made in heaven. Mama will be overjoyed.'

'I thought we'd go as soon as we've had breakfast,' Ivory said seriously. 'I want to get it over and done with. You might make a joke of it, but you know what Grandmama is like.'

'You're making me nervous now.' Kitty pushed her plate away. 'I've lost my appetite. I'll go and fetch my bonnet and shawl.'

Isabella Harte stared at her eldest daughter in amazement and then a slow smile spread across her face. 'My darling girl, I am so happy for you. The Westbrooks are an old family, and Charles is very handsome. You will be Lady Westbrook, and you'll never want for anything.'

'I knew you would be delighted, Mama,' Ivory said, glancing nervously at her grandmother, who was seated in her favourite chair by the ornate marble fireplace. 'What do you think, Grandmama?'

'Amethyst has outdone you, Ivory. I always said you would never amount to much,' Lady Carstairs said grimly. 'Marriner has a much larger fortune.'

'Being wealthy isn't the most important thing in the world, Grandmama.' Kitty sent her a challenging look. She was not in a mood to allow her sister to be browbeaten by an ageing termagant, who always had her own way and bullied the family and servants alike.

'What did you say, Kitty?' Lady Carstairs clutched her ebony cane as if she were about to rise to her feet, but she remained sitting and merely raised her left hand. 'No, don't repeat it. I am not interested in your trite comments, and you can hardly boast. Where is your engagement ring? I doubt if any gentleman of breeding would want a wife who voiced her own opinions regardless of whether they were welcome.'

'Mama, please,' Isabella said faintly. 'This is Ivory's time. We should be happy for her.'

Lady Carstairs bristled with irritation. 'If you had married the man I chose for you, Isabella, you would have had sons instead of feeble females. They would have taken care of you, had you been made a widow so young.'

To Kitty's surprise, her mother rose to her feet.

'Do not speak about Robert in that derisory tone, Mama. He is a good man, and a clever one. He was simply unlucky that he was injured so badly, but he is coming home soon. I am not a widow.'

'Don't get in a huff with me, my girl. You made your bed, and you can lie on it.'

Kitty also rose to her feet, despite a warning glance from Ivory. 'That is enough, Grandmama. I won't allow you to speak to Mama like that.'

'It's all right, Kitty,' Isabella said hastily. She turned to her mother, frowning ominously. 'I have put up with being bullied by you, for long enough, Mama. I will go with my girls and set up home far away from you.'

Kitty and Ivory stared at their mother in disbelief.

'Well said, Mama.' Kitty wrapped her arms around her mother's slender body. 'We will look after you and Papa, when he comes home. The house in Suffolk is charming and we will be able to have all our furniture out of storage. We will have a home again.'

Lady Carstairs rose majestically to her feet and reached for the bell pull.

'This is all the thanks I get for taking you in, Isabella. I put up with you – and you, as well, Ivory – and never asked for anything in return, except a little civility, which is sadly lacking.' She sank back onto her chair. 'Go and pack your pathetic collection of belongings, Isabella. Your girls will help you and then Henley will show you out.'

Ivory placed her arm around her mother's shoulders and led her, sobbing, from the room, but Kitty stood her ground.

'You are a disgrace to motherhood, Grandmama. I feel ashamed to be related to you, and from now on you are nothing to any of us.' Kitty swept out of the room without giving her grandmother a chance to respond.

To Kitty's surprise they found Miss Waters in Isabella's room, where she was busy packing Isabella's valise. She looked up with a hint of a smile.

'I know her ladyship only too well, Mrs Harte. I'm afraid I could see this coming, so I took it upon myself to help.'

Kitty stared at her grandmother's maid in surprise. 'That's good of you, Miss Waters, but how did you know what would happen today?'

Miss Waters folded the last garment and laid it neatly in the valise. 'I've worked for Lady Carstairs since I was a girl. We all know her ladyship's little ways. I'm afraid this was bound to occur sooner or later. When I saw you and Miss Ivory arrive, I knew it would be today.'

Isabella wiped her eyes on a hanky. 'Thank you, Miss Waters. I really appreciate your kindness.'

'Kind?' Miss Waters laughed. 'No one in this house knows the meaning of the word, ma'am. We survive the best we can. I hope you're happy in your new home.' She patted a stray hair in place and marched out of the room, closing the door behind her.

'Well, who would have thought it,' Ivory said slowly. 'That's the first time I've seen that woman acting like a human being.'

'And the last, I hope.' Isabella picked up a bonnet that lay on the bed cover and put it on, tying the ribbons beneath her chin. 'Pass me my shawl, please, Kitty. We are going to walk out of Bridlebank with our heads held high. I hope I never see this old house again.'

The next couple of days passed in a flurry of packing. Charles made all the arrangements for them to travel to Suffolk, together with some of the servants, leaving a skeleton staff behind to look after the house in Duke Street to await the family's return in the autumn. However, despite the frantic activity around them, Kitty, Ivory and Isabella found time to visit Amethyst in her town house, where they were suitably impressed by everything they saw, much to Amethyst's delight. After that they went on to the Marriner mansion in Primrose Hill, and again were effusive in their comments. Amethyst grandly invited them all to visit the country estate in Hampshire, although she had yet to see it herself. Isabella kindly, but firmly, told her that she would have to wait until her papa had arrived back in England. He would need to recuperate and to recover from the long sea voyage before he could undertake another journey. Amethyst took it all in good part, saying that she and Sebastian intended to travel on the continent during the summer months, and they might call on the family in Suffolk on the way home. Kitty and Ivory listened patiently. They had heard all Amethysts fantastic ideas of a wonderful life before, and Kitty did not doubt her younger sister's ability to get exactly what she desired. They returned to Duke Street, duly impressed, and totally exhausted.

Charles hired a large furniture van to collect Isabella's furniture from the warehouse and take it to their new home on the Westbrook estate. The family, including the indomitable Nellie and the Westbrooks' servants travelled by train. To Kitty's surprise, they were met at the railway station by Flinders.

'I wasn't expecting to see you today,' Kitty said.

'I had a telegram from Charles, asking me to meet the train and provide transport to take you to Westbrook. Apparently, he has something to say to me, although I can't think what it might be.'

'Are you going away on another expedition, Flinders?' Kitty said cautiously. She had missed his company, but she did not want to give him false hope. She knew what it was like to have a heart, if not broken, severely bruised by a cruel blow of fate.

'I'll tell you later, but I do have some good news for you. Your father's vessel is due to arrive in ten days' time. I was thinking of travelling to

Southampton to meet him and help him with the rest of his journey.'

'That's wonderful, Flinders. And it gives us time to get the house in perfect order before he arrives. Mama and Ivory will be delighted.' Kitty eyed him curiously. 'Have you any idea what Charles might say to you?'

'Honestly, no. But we're getting along reasonably well now, and he seems to be able to put our fathers' disagreement in the past. What is done is done.'

'Do you think perhaps he feels a little guilty that your mama and grandmama are having to work in order to put food on the table?'

'He never bothered about them before, so why would he change his mind now?' Flinders stood aside as Charles called for everyone's attention. He directed the servants to load the wagonette before turning to Isabella, whom he handed into the landau, followed by Ivory. He beckoned to Kitty.

'Are you coming with us? Or are you going to stay and chat to my cousin?'

'That's the first time he's called me his cousin since we were boys,' Flinders said, grinning. 'I'll ride in the wagonette. You should travel in comfort.' He handed her into the landau.

Charles nodded. 'Thank you, Flinders. There's room for you if you would care to travel with us.'

'I'm happy to travel in the wagonette and chat with Nellie, who looks as if she's rather taken charge. It will give the ladies more room. I'll see you at Westbrook, Charles.' Flinders strolled off to help the servants pack the luggage into the other vehicle.

Charles climbed into the landau and sat beside Kitty. 'Drive on, Phipps.'

'What do you want with Flinders?' Kitty asked in a low voice. 'I know it's none of my business, but he is my friend, and I care about him.'

Charles glanced at Frances, Ivory and Isabella, but they were chatting animatedly about the preparations to move into the former estate manager's house. 'I think you know about the family feud?'

Kitty nodded. 'Yes, Flinders mentioned it.'

'It's taken me a long time – too long, in fact – but I do see that Flinders' father was unfairly treated. To make amends I am giving him part of the Westbrook estate, and enough money to build a house for himself, his mother and his grandmother. I feel it's the least I can do.'

'That sounds like a wonderful solution, Charles,' Kitty said, smiling. 'Flinders is a good man. He's done his best for his mother and grandmother, who are hardworking women. It's only fitting that they should have a comfortable retirement.'

Charles pulled a face. 'You're making me feel even worse, Kitty. I confess that I never gave them a thought until recently. I was too busy adding to the fortune that I inherited from my father to think about anything or anyone else.'

'What changed your mind, Charles?'

'It was something that Ivory said. She made me take a good look at myself and I didn't like what I saw.' Charles smiled as he gazed at his fiancée. 'Your sister is a wonderful woman, Kitty. I'm extremely fortunate that she is willing to take me on.'

'I think you are both well suited,' Kitty said, smiling. She settled down to enjoy the carriage ride on a sunny day with the hedgerows bursting with new life, and starry white flowers opening on the blackthorn bushes. The neatly ploughed fields were showing the first signs of green growth and the air was filled with birdsong. Kitty, a city girl born and bred, still found wonder in the beauty of the countryside. Everything looked new and perfect. Even the horses seemed to trot on in a livelier manner than usual.

When they arrived at Westbrook House Charles took Flinders aside and they walked off together, Charles seeming to do all the talking. Kitty would have loved to have eavesdropped, but there was too much to do. Isabella was eager to go to their new home, but she stood aside and left it to Nellie, who was busy organising the Westbrooks' servants as they began unloading the luggage.

'I'll leave all this to you and your maid,' Frances said wearily. 'Moving between residences always exhausts me. I will be glad for Ivory to take over that task when she and Charles are married.'

'Some people would find it difficult to hand over the reins.' Kitty eyed her curiously.

'Not I, Kitty. I enjoy parties and socialising, but as to managing a household, I will think it a blessing to have a capable sister-in-law. Ivory won't find me interfering in any way.'

'You are quite remarkable,' Kitty said, smiling. She turned to her mother, who was standing at her side. 'Are you all right, Mama? Would you like to sit down in the shade?'

'No, my love. I just want to get into my new home and have all my lovely belongings around me again. I'm so looking forward to the return of the family silver, too.' Isabella shielded her eyes against the sun, which by now was high in the sky. 'It is lovely here. I feel at home already.' She clasped Frances's arm. 'I'll never be able to thank you enough for all this, my dear.'

Frances patted Isabella's hand. 'It's nothing, really. To be honest, I will enjoy having women to talk to rather than my brother and his cronies. They speak about stocks and shares and market prices for things, about which I know absolutely nothing. Anyway, come inside while the girls get everything sorted. We'll have a glass of sherry wine while we wait.'

Reluctantly, Isabella agreed and allowed Frances to lead her into the main house, although she glanced anxiously over her shoulder as if she was worried that her daughters might forget her.

Kitty was the first to notice her mother's anxiety

and she waved. 'Don't worry, Mama. I'll come and get you when we're about to leave.' Satisfied that Mama was being looked after, Kitty turned back to the task in hand.

With Nellie's impressive organisational skills everything went smoothly and within the hour they were in their new home. The furniture had already arrived and once again Nellie took charge. Frances sent two of the estate workers to help them move the heavy items and then Isabella came into her own. She was very particular as to where each piece of furniture should go, and she uttered directions, sometimes changing her mind, and making them move a sofa a few inches to the left or the right until she was satisfied it was properly placed.

Kitty left Ivory to deal with the situation as Nellie had taken over the kitchen and had appropriated a young scullery maid from the big house to assist her. Kitty made her escape from the house and was about to start walking back to the main house when she saw Flinders striding towards her. She stopped by the gate in the picket fence and waited.

'Well?' she said eagerly when he was close enough to hear. 'What did Charles say?'

'He's given me a parcel of land and what I assume is a generous share of the money so that I can build a house for my mother and grandmother, and for myself, when I am not working.' Flinders took off his hat and ran his hand through his thick brown hair. 'I'm stunned, Kitty. I was not expecting such generosity.'

'It's overdue, if you ask me,' Kitty said, smiling. 'But I'm happy for you and for your mother and grandmother, too. But do you think they will agree to move? Mrs Riley seemed quite happy looking after her travelling gentlemen, and they're both very independent ladies.'

Flinders frowned. 'I don't know. I can only put it to them.'

'They would have a considerable income if they sold the Mill House and the mill as well,' Kitty said thoughtfully.

'You're right, of course, but I might have to call upon your help if they decide to be stubborn.'

'I doubt if they would take any notice of me, but I will do anything I can to help, Flinders. After all, you and your mother took us in when we were homeless.'

'It was my pleasure,' Flinders said earnestly. 'I was more than happy to come home to a house where you were, Kitty.'

Kitty met his gaze, and she felt a rush of sympathy for him. She laid her hand on his as it rested on the gate. 'I know that, and I wish I could return your feelings, Flinders. You know that I really care for you as a dear friend, and of course I'll do anything I can to help you to persuade your mother and grandmother to accept Charles's offer.'

Flinders nodded. 'I know you will. I promised

not to pursue my suit any further, Kitty. I wish things were different, but I don't want to lose your friendship.' He gently removed his hand. 'I'd better leave now. It's a long ride home.'

'Goodbye for now, Flinders. And thank you for being so understanding.' Kitty stood by the gate and watched him walk away. She wished that she could return his love, but her heart belonged to someone else, even if her love was unrequited. Deep down she suspected that Will Barton had feelings for her, which made his deception even harder to bear. She turned to go back into the house. She would unpack her easel and her paints and start work on the portrait of Ivory and Hardy, Charles's much-loved horse. There was a boxroom at the back of the house that Kitty had earmarked for use as a studio, although she would have to make sketches of Hardy either in the stables or out in the fields. It was an exciting project, and she could not wait to start.

Kitty walked down the path and entered the house as the men were bringing in the furniture from the removal van. Nancy, the maid on loan from the big house, was running to and fro, carrying baskets of crockery and piles of linen. Isabella was sipping tea in the front parlour. She was enthroned in her favourite armchair, which had been placed at a strategic angle so that she was able to watch the comings and goings through the open door. Ivory was doing her best to unpack ornaments and the familiar things they had

had around them in Soho Square. Kitty could see how much all this meant to her mother, and she realised that her help was needed urgently.

'What can I do, Ivory?' Kitty asked eagerly. 'The sooner we get this place shipshape, the better.'

Ivory pointed to a large tea chest. 'I think the dinner service is in there, Kitty. I'm sure that Mama would love to eat in style this evening. I heard Nellie say that she is roasting a chicken, which was sent down from the kitchens in the main house. We are being so spoiled. I can hardly believe it.'

Kitty laughed. 'Well, you are the next Lady Westbrook. They are looking after their own interests.' She held up her hands when Ivory gave her a reproachful look. 'I'm just teasing you.' Kitty turned away quickly and began unwrapping the individual pieces of the dinner set, which she took bit by bit to the kitchen where a large oak dresser dominated one entire wall. Nellie was up to her elbows in flour and dough as she made the pastry to cover the prepared apples in a pie dish.

'I hope you all realise that I'm performing miracles in this old-fashioned kitchen. It will need a few changes before I can work here properly.'

Kitty sniffed the air. 'It smells wonderful already. You are a genius, Nellie.'

'I have to be,' Nellie said grimly.

'And we'll make the kitchen just how you want it,' Kitty added enthusiastically. 'You can supervise the work, whatever needs to be done. I'm going back for the rest of the crockery. It will look splendid when it's displayed on the shelves.'

'Huh! Well, I preferred the house in Soho Square, but I suppose this will have to do.' Nellie thumped the rolling pin down on the pastry and Kitty made a speedy retreat. She knew when to leave Nellie alone and this was such a time.

The next few days were occupied with making the house into a comfortable home. Frances came every day. She brought things from the main house that were no longer wanted but would prove useful to the family. Charles was also a frequent visitor, but of course he came to see Ivory and they either sat in the garden under the oak tree, or they went for walks around the estate. Charles also took Ivory to visit their neighbours, driving her himself in the chaise, and to Nellie's disgust, without a chaperone. However, their engagement was now public knowledge, having been announced in *The Times*, and Ivory wore the sapphire ring with obvious pride. Everyone seemed happy and Kitty did her best to put the past behind her. When she had a spare moment or two, she set up her easel in the boxroom and started doing preliminary sketches for the portrait of Ivory with Hardy. She also spent time in the fields, studying the handsome animal and she often took him an apple or a carrot. This, of course, made her very popular with Hardy and he would trot across the field to meet her, neighing and prancing as if showing off to his new friend.

Charles was very interested in the progress of her work, and eager to possess the portrait as soon as it was finished. In the end Kitty promised it to him as a wedding present. She had just started work on the large canvas when Nancy knocked on the door to announce that Mr Riley was downstairs in the parlour, asking to see her.

'Thank you, Nancy. I'll be down directly. I'll clean the charcoal off my hands first.'

'Yes, miss.' Nancy bobbed a curtsey and hurried from the room.

Kitty wiped her hands on a damp cloth and took off her apron before going downstairs to the parlour.

'Good morning, Flinders,' she said, smiling. 'Is everything going well?'

'Everything is always better for seeing you, Kitty.' Flinders rose to his feet. 'I think I've persuaded Ma and Grandmama to accept Charles's offer. As far as I'm concerned, I am more than happy to share even a small part of the inheritance. The possibility of building a house for my family is too tempting to dismiss.'

'So, you'll go ahead?'

'Definitely. Ma can't keep waiting on her gentlemen indefinitely and Grandmama has had to give up the mill. Not before time, if you ask me. Jacob Turner is the miller now and doing a fine job of it, so I've been told.'

'That's good news. I'm happy for her. Your grandmama is a brave woman.'

'What I came to tell you is that your pa's ship will dock sooner than expected. I'm going to Southampton tomorrow, but I need to stop off in London to go to the Geological Society to collect my pay. I intend to resign my post. I've had enough of travelling the globe. I want to settle down and raise a family of my own.'

'I can understand that. I hope you meet someone worthy of you, Flinders.' Kitty met his intense gaze with a sympathetic smile. 'I wish I could come with you to Southampton, but it wouldn't be a good idea in the circumstances.'

'I was hoping you might consider it, Kitty,' Flinders said hopefully. 'Is there no way you could accompany me? Your father might need more care than I am able to give him on my own.'

'I think if he's undertaken a sea voyage all the way from British Guiana that he'll be able to cope with a couple of train journeys. I would have loved to meet him, but you must see that it's simply not possible.'

Flinders sighed. 'There really is no hope for me, is there, Kitty?'

'I'm so sorry. I wish things were different.'

'I know what you've been going through, Kitty,' Flinders said slowly. 'There's something I should have told you before, but I knew it would be the end of all hope for me.'

Chapter Twenty-Five

Kitty sank down onto the sofa, staring at Flinders in disbelief. 'Are you sure about this? Might you have been misinformed?'

'I don't think so, Kitty. I'm pretty sure that what I said is the truth.'

'How did you find out? The women I heard talking when the funeral procession went past seemed certain that Will was married. I saw his wife in one of the carriages and he was leading the cortège.'

'I only found out by accident when I had business in Manningtree, Kitty. It's Barton's elder brother who has inherited the farm, and he is married with two young children. It was his and William's father who was interred that day. The gossips were talking nonsense.'

Kitty frowned dazedly. 'But if what you say is

true, why was William leading the procession and not his brother?'

'Daniel was in one of the carriages. Apparently, he had been thrown by his horse a few days previously and had broken his leg. It was as simple as that.'

Kitty rose to her feet and paced the floor. Flinders' news had shaken her more than she would have thought possible.

'If I had been in London, he might have told me that he had lost his father,' she said slowly. 'But I was here in Suffolk, not too far from his family home. He must think I am a hard-hearted woman not to have offered my condolences.'

'But how would you have known about his father's death, Kitty? You're making too much of it.' Flinders paused for a moment, eyeing her thoughtfully. 'I have an idea. Why don't you come to London with me tomorrow? I will travel on to Southampton after I have completed my business with the Geological Society, and you could stay in Duke Street. It would give you a chance to see the inspector and put things right.'

Kitty came to a halt, and she turned slowly to face him. 'Do you really think so?'

'It hurts me to say it, but if he feels the same way about you, it will be the answer to his prayers. I don't know the fellow well enough to second-guess his reaction, but as I see it this is the only way to put your mind at rest.'

'I didn't tell Will that I was leaving London, and I

suppose we were working together, in a way. It would not look out of the way if I were to contact him.'

Flinders managed a weary smile. 'For heaven's sake, Kitty, go and pack a few things. I'm leaving from Manningtree station at ten o'clock tomorrow morning. If you don't turn up, I will know that you have had second thoughts.'

'I suppose I could take Nellie with me. They can do without her here for a day or so.' Kitty reached out to clutch his hand. 'I won't change my mind. I'll be there, and I will stay in London until you arrive with Papa. Nellie and I will be able to help him on the last leg of his long journey home. It's almost a year since I last saw him. I can't wait to give him a hug.'

Next morning Kitty and Nellie were waiting on the platform at Manningtree station when Flinders arrived.

'So, you made it then,' he said, grinning. 'Well done, Kitty.'

'It wasn't easy.' Kitty stood on tiptoe to kiss him on the cheek. 'Mama wanted to come instead of Nellie, but Ivory managed to persuade her that it would be far better for her to be at home to welcome Papa.'

'Yes, and they didn't want me to come as chaperone because no one else is as good in the kitchen as I am,' Nellie said proudly.

'But you are here.' Flinders patted her on the arm. 'And very glad I am to see you, Nellie.'

'Ta. I could say the same, sir.'

'Who is going to cook for those left behind?' Flinders turned to Kitty for an explanation.

'I went to Frances and explained the whole thing. She was wonderful, as always, and she sent a replacement for Nellie. Not that she is as good a cook,' Kitty added quickly. 'But it's only for a few days and then we'll be home again.'

A short blast on the steam whistle announced the arrival of the train as it roared into the station, cutting short any attempt at conversation. Flinders found an empty carriage and they made themselves comfortable.

'Did you accept Charles's offer?' Kitty asked as they sat back in their seats.

Flinders nodded. 'It's all in hand. Charles is going to instruct his solicitor to do what is necessary and I'm going to find an architect to design the perfect house for me and my family.'

'I'm so happy for you, Flinders,' Kitty said earnestly. 'It's nothing less than you deserve, and your ma and grandmama, too.'

Nellie snorted. 'I wish someone would give me a house of my own. I'm doomed to always be a servant.'

'You are not a servant,' Kitty said crossly. 'You are part of the family, and always will be. If I had the money, I would buy you a cottage to live in, but you would miss us all and you would want to return to us.'

'There's always Mr Beadle.' Flinders winked at

Kitty. 'He will need someone to look after him when Mama sells Mill House.'

'I'm in me prime, young man. I'm not about to tie myself to an old gent with one foot in the grave,' Nellie said indignantly.

'Quite right. You deserve a fine gentleman who will treat you like a lady.' Kitty sat back, leaning against the window. 'But let's get the business in hand sorted out first, shall we? I hope the servants in Duke Street can cope with the two of us, Nellie. You might have to use your influence in the kitchen if the cook is reluctant to feed us.'

'Just leave it to me,' Nellie said smugly. 'I'll see that we get the best of treatment. You make sure you find your policeman. I don't want you moping all the way home again.'

'I don't mope.' Kitty frowned. 'And Will Barton is an inspector now. He's very important.'

'Let's hope he's not too important to forgive the young lady who ran away without telling him where she was going and left him to mourn his pa on his own.'

Kitty opened her mouth to argue, but closed it again, knowing that Nellie would inevitably have the last word. She turned her head to stare out of the window at the fields and hedgerows as they flashed past. Soon they would be back in London, and she would see Will again. She could only hope that Nellie's pessimistic assessment of the situation was inaccurate.

The journey passed uneventfully, and Flinders hired a cab at the station. He left them in Duke Street and went on to complete his business at the Geological Society, after which he intended to travel on to Southampton. If Mrs Dodgson, the housekeeper, took their arrival in her stride Kitty suspected that she was used to members of the family turning up unexpectedly. Nellie marched off to take control of the kitchen and Kitty went to her room to change out of her dusty travelling costume. It was early afternoon, and she knew if she waited until next morning, she might have had second thoughts as to whether she should seek Will out at his place of work. She had no valid excuse other than the fact that she wanted to see him and put matters straight, although what that meant exactly was something she could not easily put into words. She changed into a silk afternoon gown in a flattering shade of bright blue, which Frances had assured her was the latest fashion. She put on her best straw bonnet trimmed with a matching ribbon and draped a lace shawl around her shoulders.

By the time she reached the police station in Tottenham Court Road Kitty was so nervous that her hands were shaking as she paid the cabby. She hesitated outside and was tempted to hail another cab and return to Duke Street, but she had come this far, she took a deep breath before walking boldly up to the door and entering.

'Good afternoon, miss. What can I do for you?' The sergeant behind the desk gave her a kindly smile.

'I need to see Inspector Barton,' Kitty said firmly.

'I'm afraid the inspector is not here at present, miss. Is there anyone else who might be able to assist you?'

Kitty had been so certain that he would be in his office, or at least somewhere in the vicinity, that she was completely thrown by the sergeant's answer.

'Will he be in later? I could come back.'

'I believe he has gone to the country, miss. A family matter, I understand, but I'm afraid I can't tell you anything more. I don't know when he will return.' The sergeant gave her a sympathetic smile. 'Is it a police matter, miss? Or would it be personal?'

'It doesn't matter. I shouldn't have come.' Kitty turned away and headed for the door, narrowly avoiding bumping into a constable who had just walked into the station. It was about a mile and a half from the police station to the house in Duke Street, but Kitty did not mind the long walk. It was a warm day, but the humidity suggested there might be a thunderstorm later. However, that was the least of her worries. She had missed her opportunity to see Will in London and it seemed that he had gone home. They might even have passed on the way. Fate was certainly not helping, and now all she could do was to return to Duke Street and await her father's arrival. That, of course, would be wonderful, but the nagging pain in her heart would not go away. She might have lost even the smallest chance of making things right with Will, and it hurt.

That evening Kitty dined alone. Nellie had managed to create a delicious meal from simple ingredients, and she was enjoying her rule in the kitchen, as Cook had gone to Suffolk with the family. There was little to do after she had finished her meal and Kitty went to her room and was tucked up in bed much earlier than usual. Sleep evaded her, however. She tried to convince herself that it was probably just as well that Will was not present when she went to find him. What would she have said when face to face with him? She fell asleep pondering the question, and it was still on her mind when she awakened next morning.

There was very little that Kitty could do while waiting for Flinders and her father to arrive. She left Nellie to organise rooms for them for an overnight stay before travelling on to Suffolk next morning. Kitty wrote a note to Amethyst, telling her that their father was on his way home, and she gave it to the boot boy to take to the Marriners' town house, although their whereabouts was anyone's guess. Kitty smiled when she thought of her younger sister having achieved all her aims in life so young. She could only hope that Marriner would prove to be a good husband, and that Amy would be happy.

* * *

It was late afternoon when a hackney carriage drew up outside the house in Duke Street. Kitty had been gazing absently out of the drawing-room window when she saw Flinders alight and help her father from the cab. She rushed downstairs.

Robert Harte leaned heavily on Flinders' arm as they walked slowly into the entrance hall. Kitty wanted to fling her arms around her father's neck, but he looked so frail and exhausted that she merely kissed him on the cheek.

'It's wonderful to have you back with us, Pa,' Kitty said tearfully. 'We've all missed you so much.'

Robert managed a weak smile. 'It's good to be with you again, my love. But Flinders has told me of the problems you have all faced. I can't bear to think what you girls and your dear mama have been through in my absence.'

'It's all over now, sir,' Flinders said firmly. 'You will be home with your family tomorrow.'

'I wish I could travel on now, but I must admit I could do with a rest.' Robert patted Kitty's hand as she laid it on his arm.

'Perhaps you would like to go to your room and have a nap before dinner, Papa.'

'Yes, I think that might be for the best. Perhaps I could have my meal brought to my room? I don't feel up to much at the moment.'

'Of course, Papa. Nellie has made a special supper for you. I'll bring it to you myself.' Kitty shot an anxious glance at Flinders, but he gave her a reassuring smile.

'I'll help Mr Harte to bed, Kitty. He'll be fine after a good night's sleep.'

Kitty nodded and watched them as Flinders helped Robert to ascend the stairs. It was a slow process, and Kitty could see that each step was painful. She could only be glad that a ground-floor room had been prepared for her father in the new house. His complete recovery was obviously going to take much longer than she had anticipated. She went to find Nellie and give her the good news that Pa had arrived.

Nellie was in the kitchen supervising the servants who had remained in the house. She looked up as Kitty rushed into the room.

'He's home, Nellie,' Kitty cried happily. 'But he looks exhausted. Flinders has taken him upstairs to rest. I said I'd take his supper to him when it's time.'

'You'll do no such thing,' Nellie said firmly. 'I'll make him something special and I'll take it to him myself. I haven't forgotten how the master took me on when I was near destitute. He's always been good to me.'

'But I said I would sit with him while he ate,' Kitty protested.

'I don't think that's a good idea.' Nellie shook her head. 'You're obviously upset, so it's better if you sit in the dining room with Flinders and enjoy your dinner like a civilised human being. I'll see that Mr Harte eats his meal, and I'll have a chat with him if he feels like talking. You'll only wear him out with your questions.'

Kitty knew when she was beaten. When Nellie had that stubborn look on her face there was nothing on earth that would make her change her mind. She made her way to the dining room where she saw Flinders already seated at the table. Flinders patted the empty space on the sofa beside him. 'Come and sit down. Tell me about your day, Kitty. Did you see the inspector?'

Kitty shook her head. 'No, he wasn't there. The desk sergeant said he had gone home to the country. He didn't know when Will would be returning to London.'

'I'm sorry, Kitty. You must be very disappointed.'

'Yes, I am. I don't know what to do next.'

Flinders slipped his arm around her shoulders as she sat down beside him.

'I suggest you visit him at his family home.'

'I would feel so foolish, Flinders. What would I say to him?'

'What were you going to say to him if he had been in his office?' Flinders gave her a brotherly hug. 'You must have had some idea what you were going to talk about.'

'Not really. I suppose I would have questioned him about the robberies. I could have asked him if he had proof that Mrs Tucker was involved in the thefts or merely the fence.'

Flinders laughed. 'You see, Kitty. You are beginning to think like a policeman.'

'That's nonsense,' Kitty said with a reluctant smile. 'I can't think about it now. Let's just get Papa home as quickly and painlessly as possible. I must admit I wasn't expecting to see him quite so incapacitated. It must have been a very bad accident.'

'It was, Kitty. He's lucky to be alive, but the sad fact is that he's unlikely to be able to work again.'

'Did they tell you that at the Geological Society?'

'More or less, but it's obvious that his recovery is going to be long and slow. He's not a young man, Kitty.'

'No, he isn't, but I can't imagine him staying at home and doing nothing. But what about you, Flinders? Are you going to go on any more expeditions?'

He shook his head. 'No, I think your father's accident made me realise that it's dangerous work. I can't afford to risk being injured and out of work. It's time I took responsibility for Ma and Grandmama.'

'I think I will take on the role of matchmaker, Flinders. I'll find you a nice, kind and loving wife, which is what you deserve.' Kitty smiled, but she meant what she said. Flinders deserved to have someone who loved him beyond anything and anyone else in the whole world.

'Whatever happens in the future, I will always be there if you need me, Kitty.'

Kitty knew that he was sincere and that she had a friend for life. She wished that she could feel more for him, but she had come to realise that Will Barton was the only man she would ever love, truly and deeply. She sighed and leaned against Flinders, safe and secure in his company.

The return journey to Suffolk was slow, due to Robert's infirmity, but at last they arrived at their new home. Isabella was first to hurry down the garden path and she flung her arms around her husband's neck, laughing and crying at the same time. She was followed by Ivory and, to Kitty's surprise, Amethyst emerged from the house, dressed to the nines, but obviously delighted to see her father. Their voices rose in a crescendo, at which point Nellie clapped her hands and called for order.

'Thank you,' she said in the ensuing silence. 'Mr Harte must be exhausted so let us get him to his room where he can rest and recover from the journey. Miss Amethyst, go to the kitchen and tell that simpleton to put the kettle on. Mr Harte could do with a nice cup of tea.'

Amethyst opened her mouth to argue, but one look at Nellie's determined expression and she obeyed without question. Nellie marched on ahead and Isabella clutched Robert's hand while Flinders helped him into the house. Kitty and Ivory followed them as far as their father's room, only to find their entry barred by Nellie.

'Leave your ma and pa in peace. You can have your time with him later.' Nellie tossed her head and marched off in the direction of the kitchen.

Kitty and Ivory exchanged rueful smiles.

'It's easy to see who is really in charge of this household,' Ivory said, laughing.

Kitty nodded. 'Yes, I agree, but Nellie was amazing during the journey home. She knows exactly how to handle an invalid like Pa. He was as meek as a small child in her care.' She glanced over her shoulder as Flinders emerged from the room, closing the door firmly behind him.

'Your father will be all right now he's at home. I'm sure his recovery will be much speedier now he's with his loved ones.'

'Thank you for everything, Flinders,' Kitty said earnestly. 'I don't know how we would have managed without you.'

'It was the least I could do, but now I have a great many things to do. I have an appointment with Charles and his solicitor regarding the transfer of land to me, and then I have a meeting with an architect to design the perfect dwelling. I might need your advice on that Kitty, since you know my mother well.'

'I'll do anything I can to help, but I'm not sure that my ideas would be welcomed by your mama. I don't think she altogether approves of me.'

Flinders laughed. 'I think she was being protective of me, her only son.'

'Protecting you from me?' Kitty stared at him in astonishment.

'Ma thought you had designs on me as a future husband.' Flinders held up his hands in surrender. 'But little did she know it was the other way round. I was the one who was smitten, and you were just being yourself.'

'I'm sorry she thought I was a threat,' Kitty said, smiling. 'But you deserve better than me, Flinders. You can tell your mama that I said so, and that my affections are elsewhere.'

'Really, Kitty?' Ivory eyed her expectantly. 'Don't keep me in suspense.'

Kitty slipped her hand through the crook of her sister's arm. 'I need to ask your advice anyway, Ivory. Let's go somewhere private.' She turned to Flinders with a smile. 'That's no reflection on you, Flinders. And I will take your advice about a certain person. That's a promise.'

Ivory cleared her throat. 'I know who you mean, Kitty. I haven't had a chance to tell you, but Inspector Barton called here the day after you had left for London.'

Kitty released Ivory's arm, and her hand flew to cover her mouth. 'No! Did he really?'

'He wanted to speak to you, Kitty. I told him that you had gone to London with Flinders.'

'That won't have gone down too well,' Flinders said gloomily.

Kitty ignored him. 'What did Will say to that?'

'I think he said he would speak to you in London. He did seem to be a little on edge and he left almost immediately.'

'Did he leave a message?' Kitty asked urgently.

'No, Kitty. He left before I had a chance to ask him if there was one.'

'Did you tell him that we had gone to meet Pa?' Kitty grasped Ivory's hand.

'No, Kitty. The inspector left before I could explain.'

Kitty released her sister with a sigh. 'He must think that I went with Flinders for romantic reasons, which is ridiculous.'

Flinders pulled a face. 'It's not that ridiculous,' he protested.

'I didn't mean it like that.' Kitty had a sudden need to be alone. 'I'll say goodbye for now, Flinders. I hope your meetings go well.' Kitty turned to Ivory. 'I'm going to my room. I need to unpack.'

Family dinner that evening was a joyful, if subdued, affair. Robert insisted on taking his seat at the head of the table with his family grouped around him. Amethyst had made a fuss of him before leaving with Marriner, but they promised to call again in a couple of days to see how he was getting on. Nellie had outdone herself in the kitchen and the meal of roast chicken with a delicious stuffing, the recipe for which was Nellie's fiercely guarded secret, roast potatoes and cabbage, was met with approval all round. Robert's favourite dessert of apple pie and custard met with his earnest approval, and Nellie was all smiles. However, Robert soon tired and Isabella insisted that he must go to bed with a hefty dose of laudanum to ease the inevitable pain.

Kitty went to her room. She had managed to keep cheerful, but secretly she was eaten up with curiosity as to the reason for Will's visit. She tried to convince herself that he had intended to tell her about the result of his investigations into Molly Tucker's criminal activities, but she failed dismally.

After a night of tossing and turning in her bed she awakened next morning determined to travel on her own to London. This was one journey where she had no intention of taking a chaperone. She dressed in her riding habit and left the house, taking great care not to disturb any of the sleeping family or the servants. Fortunately, the girl who had been taken on to help in the kitchen had turned out to be lazy and there was no sign of her. Kitty walked briskly to the stables at the rear of Westbrook House, and if the head groom was surprised to see her so early in the morning, he was too used to the eccentricities of his employers to make a remark. Neither did he object when Kitty asked to be driven to the railway station. One of the under-grooms was given the task of driving the chaise and Kitty took her seat as if it were the most natural thing in the world for a young lady to travel to London unaccompanied. She had just enough money in her reticule for the return fare but no luggage. All she could think of was what she might say to Will when she eventually tracked him down.

Kitty had never been in a position to purchase a rail ticket or to do anything very much for herself and it was an intimidating experience, although she felt quite proud of herself as she took her seat in the third-class compartment. There were not many travellers this early in the morning, but the seats began to fill quickly as the journey progressed. There was some delay at Ardleigh station, when the eastbound train from London arrived at the next platform. Kitty watched a few passengers alight and then the train started to move off slowly. She gazed out of the window and found herself staring at none other than Will Barton. He had obviously seen her, too. He rose to his feet, his hands on the window and his lips moving as if he were attempting to tell her something, but the London-bound train had also started off and they were travelling in opposite directions. Kitty felt a sense of panic as she wondered what to do next, but there was nothing she could do until the train stopped at Colchester station.

She practically fell onto the platform in her eagerness to alight from the train and she ran to a porter to enquire the time of the next train to Manningtree. She could only assume that Will had been on his way back to the farm, or perhaps he had discovered that she was no longer in London and had come looking for her. She paced up and down, glancing at the station clock every couple of minutes as she waited for the train that would take her home and closer to the man she loved. Eventually, after what seemed like an eternity, the station was filled with steam and shrill whistles as the London-bound train and the one that Kitty had been waiting for arrived within seconds of each other. They came to a rumbling halt and as the steam dissipated into the atmosphere Kitty could see Will striding towards her along the platform. Without stopping to think she broke into a run, and he caught her in his arms, swinging her off her feet and covering her face with passionate kisses.

The Manningtree-bound train started to move, and Will picked her up in his arms and tossed her into an empty compartment. He leaped in after her and the guard slammed the door.

'I was going to London to find you,' Kitty said breathlessly as she scrambled to a sitting position.

'And I was on my way to see you.' Will wrapped his arms around her. 'I love you, Kitty. I never want to be parted from you again.'

Their lips met in a deeply tender kiss, and he held her as if he would never let her go.

'I love you, too, Will,' Kitty murmured when at last she could speak. 'Why did you take so long to tell me?'

He stroked her hair back from her forehead, looking into her eyes with a smile that melted her heart. 'You come from a good family, Kitty. My father was a farmer, and my brother has followed in his footsteps. I never thought a mere police constable would have a chance with someone like you.'

Kitty silenced him temporarily with a kiss. 'You nearly broke my heart, Will Barton. I don't care what you do for a living. It's you I love and it's you I want to be with for ever.'

'Your sisters have wealthy titled husbands, or at least Amethyst has, and Ivory will soon marry Sir Charles. You would just be Mrs Barton.'

She stroked his cheek with the tips of her fingers. 'Mrs Chief Superintendent Barton sounds achievable. But I would marry you even if you were a costermonger or a street sweeper, Will.'

He laughed. 'I haven't proposed properly as yet.'

'I don't need moonlight and romantic music, Will. This is perfect, just you and me.'

He went down on one knee and took her left hand in his. 'Kitty Harte, I love you with all my heart and soul. Will you do me the honour of becoming my wife.'

'Yes, William, I will marry you, and I'll be proud to be your wife, but you have no ring.'

'That's where you're wrong.' Will rose to his feet and took a small box from his jacket pocket. He opened it and a small solitaire diamond sparkled in the sunlight. He slipped it on her ring finger. 'When I achieve the situation you mention, I will buy you a much larger diamond.'

Kitty gazed at the ring with a rapturous smile. 'No, you won't. I love this ring. It will never leave my finger. You and I will make a perfect team. I can help you with your most difficult cases.'

Will silenced her with a kiss that sent her senses spinning with delight. He released her, laying his finger on her lips.

'When we are married, I want you to promise never to put yourself in danger on my account. Allow me to deal with the criminals while you concentrate on becoming a famous artist.'

Kitty smiled demurely. 'Of course, Will. I wouldn't dream of trying to interfere with your professional business.' She slid her arms around his neck. 'Let's go home and give everyone the good news.'

A Note From Dilly

Dear Readers,

Christmas has always been a special time of the year for me. It's the season when the house starts to smell of spices and fruit cake, and you find yourself reaching for things like cinnamon, cloves, and mixed peel – ingredients that seem to sit quietly in the cupboard for most of the year, then suddenly come into their own.

When I was a child there were not nearly as many Christmas decorations on sale in the shops as there are now. We made paper chains to hang from the ceiling and wound sprigs of holly round wire coat hangers to hang on the front door. The tree would be heavy with tinsel and lametta with glass baubles in a myriad of colours. No designer chic there, but lots of fun and a feeling of achievement. The scent of pine needles and the tangy zest of oranges stuck with cloves and tied with ribbon still evokes happy memories.

I have always loved cooking, and I still do the traditional Christmas dinner for my family. Years ago, Christmas puddings were made weeks before the big day and everyone had a stir and a wish, but I must admit that I cheat nowadays and buy my Christmas puddings from the supermarket, and they are delicious. I've even grown to love Brussels sprouts, which I would not have believed had anyone told me that when I was seven. Christmas is all about family and getting together, but don't forget to have a little 'me time', too. Sitting in a quiet place with a good book is a way to escape briefly into a different world.

I hope you've enjoyed reading about Kitty. I loved writing it so much. As a thank-you for being such a loyal reader of mine, this special edition of *The Winter Belle* includes an exclusive festive gift for you. Read on for some ideas and activities for making this time of year just a little cosier and more creative. I hope you enjoy them and perhaps find a quiet afternoon to give something a go.

Wishing you warmth, happiness, and a bit of time for yourself this winter.

Love,
Dilly xx

A Winter Crossword

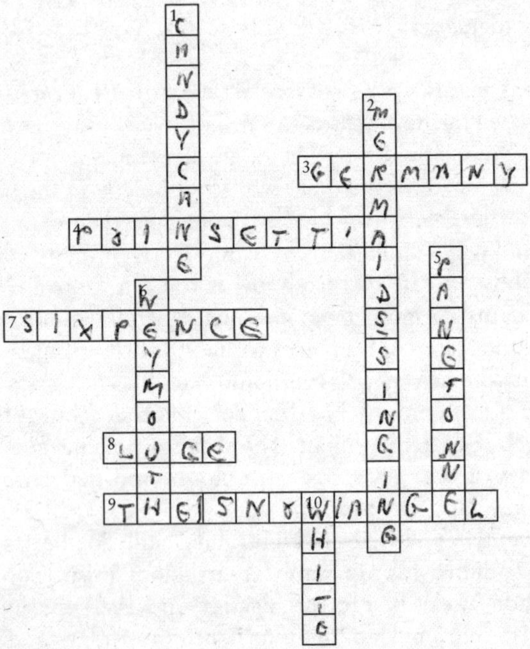

ACROSS

3. What country is credited with starting the tradition of the Christmas tree? (7)
4. What plant is known for its red and green leaves and is often associated with Christmas? (10)
7. What coin is traditionally hidden inside a British Christmas pudding? (8)
8. Which winter sport involves sliding down a track in a small one- or two-person sled? (4)
9. What is the title of Dilly's 50th novel? (3-4-5)

DOWN

1. What traditional Christmas decoration is shaped like a shepherd's staff? (5-4)
2. What is the title of Dilly's first novel? (8-7)
5. What is the name of the fruitcake traditionally eaten in Italy at Christmas? (9)
6. In which UK town does Dilly Court live? (8)
10. What colour are mistletoe berries? (5)

See final page for answers

A Christmas Recipe from Dilly

Spiced Apple & Ginger Loaf

Easy, warming, and best served thick-sliced with strong tea and good company.

Ingredients:

- 200g self-raising flour
- 100g light brown sugar
- 100g butter, softened
- 2 eggs
- 1 heaped tsp ground ginger
- 1 tsp cinnamon
- 2 cooking apples, peeled and grated
- Zest of 1 orange
- A handful of chopped stem ginger (from a jar), or crystallised ginger
- Optional: a tablespoon of black treacle or golden syrup, for richness

---

Method:

1. Preheat oven to 170°C (fan 160°C). Grease and line a 2lb loaf tin.
2. Beat the butter and sugar until pale and fluffy. Add the eggs, one at a time.
3. Stir in the flour, spices, grated apple, orange zest, and ginger. If using treacle or syrup, mix that in too.
4. Spoon into the tin and level the top. Bake for 45–50 minutes, or until a skewer comes out clean.
5. Cool in the tin for 10 minutes, then turn out onto a wire rack.

Now wrap in paper, tie with a string, and give to a friend or neighbour – or keep it for yourself!

A Christmas Table Craft

Kitty's Christmas Pomander

Clove-studded oranges to brighten up a Christmas table – and guaranteed to bring festive cheer!

What You'll Need:

- 2–3 fresh oranges (or clementines, if you prefer)
- Whole cloves (you'll need quite a few – roughly 50 per orange)
- A thin knitting needle or cocktail stick (for pre-poking holes)
- Ribbons (red, gold, or whatever matches your table)
- Optional: ground cinnamon, nutmeg, or orrisroot for extra fragrance

How to Make Your Pomander:

1. **Gently score** your orange skin with a knife if you want neat patterns – stripes, spirals, crosses, or stars. This makes it easier to guide your cloves.
2. Use a **cocktail stick** or blunt needle to poke small holes where you want each clove to sit. This saves your fingers and helps the cloves to go in cleanly.

3. **Push in the cloves,** following your design.
4. Optional: Roll your pomander in a bowl of mixed ground cinnamon, nutmeg, and orrisroot for a deeply spiced finish.
5. Tie a **ribbon around the orange,** looping it like a parcel, and secure with a bow. You can hang it, place it in a bowl, or pop one at each place setting for your Christmas table.

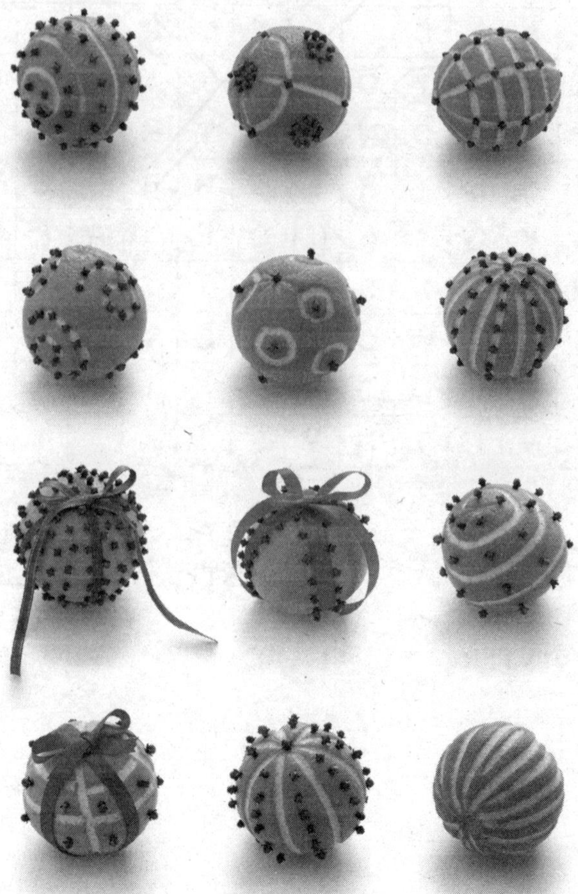

The Winter Belle Wordsearch

S	M	O	E	I	A	T	T	M	R	O	S
E	R	S	W	I	N	T	E	R	K	C	S
L	K	O	O	R	B	T	S	E	W	A	S
M	O	B	Y	L	B	A	Z	A	A	R	B
K	H	N	Y	T	O	E	Y	A	E	N	R
T	R	T	D	S	S	T	Y	D	V	A	F
H	A	M	Y	O	O	I	N	T	S	B	W
I	H	A	O	N	N	I	T	H	A	Y	A
D	S	S	T	R	L	O	R	R	S	E	R
A	Y	O	A	F	I	O	F	Y	A	R	B
M	B	L	H	R	V	F	T	T	T	W	A
B	A	E	W	O	O	S	O	T	O	L	M
S	R	K	O	O	R	B	A	I	T	A	N
A	M	E	T	H	Y	S	T	K	A	T	K

KITTY
SOHO
LONDON
WINTER

BAZAAR
AMETHYST
AMY
IVORY

ARTIST
CARNABY
WESTBROOK
FLINDERS

See final page for answers

Answers

A Winter Crossword

ACROSS

3. Germany
4. Poinsettia
7. Sixpence
8. Luge
9. *The Snow Angel*

DOWN

1. Candy cane
2. *Mermaids Singing*
5. Panettone
6. Weymouth
10. White

The Winter Belle Wordsearch

S	M	O	E	I	A	T	T	M	R	O	S
E	R	S	W	I	N	T	E	R	K	C	S
L	K	O	O	R	B	T	S	E	W	A	S
M	O	B	Y	L	B	A	Z	A	A	R	B
K	H	N	Y	T	O	E	Y	A	E	N	R
T	R	T	D	S	S	T	Y	D	V	A	F
H	A	M	Y	O	O	I	N	T	S	B	W
I	H	A	O	N	N	I	T	H	A	Y	A
D	S	S	T	R	L	O	R	R	S	E	R
A	Y	O	A	F	I	O	F	Y	A	R	B
M	B	L	H	R	V	F	T	T	T	W	A
B	A	E	W	O	O	S	O	T	O	L	M
S	R	K	O	O	R	B	A	I	T	A	N
A	M	E	T	H	Y	S	T	K	A	T	K